Kelly Elliott is a *New York Times* and *USA Today* bestselling contemporary romance author. Since finishing her bestselling Wanted series, Kelly continues to spread her wings while remaining true to her roots and giving readers stories rich with hot protective men, strong women and beautiful surroundings.

Kelly has been passionate about writing since she was fifteen. After years of filling journals with stories, she finally followed her dream and published her first novel, *Wanted*, in November of 2012.

Kelly lives in central Texas with her husband, daughter, and two pups. When she's not writing, Kelly enjoys reading and spending time with her family. She is down to earth and very in touch with her readers, both on social media and at signings.

Visit Kelly Elliott online:

www.kellyelliottauthor.com
@author_kelly
www.facebook.com/KellyElliottAuthor/

Also by Kelly Elliott (published by Piatkus)

COWBOYS & ANGELS
Book 6

NEW YORK TIMES & *USA TODAY* BESTSELLING AUTHOR

KELLY ELLIOTT

piatkus

PIATKUS

First published in Great Britain in 2018 by Piatkus

1 3 5 7 9 10 8 6 4 2

A CIP catalogue record for this book
is available from the British Library.

ISBN 978-0-349-41850-6

Printed and bound in Great Britain by
Clays Ltd, Elcograf S.p.A.

Cover photo and designer: Sara Eirew Photography
Editor: Cori McCarthy, Yellowbird Editing
Proofer: Amy Rose Capetta, Yellowbird Editing
Developmental/Proofer: Elaine York, Allusion Graphics
Interior Designer: JT Formatting

Papers used by Piatkus are from well-managed forests
and other responsible sources.

Piatkus
An imprint of
Little, Brown Book Group
Carmelite House
50 Victoria Embankment
London EC4Y 0DZ

An Hachette UK Company
www.hachette.co.uk

www.littlebrown.co.uk

This book is dedicated to Charlene.
"Tank you" for giving me Maebh.

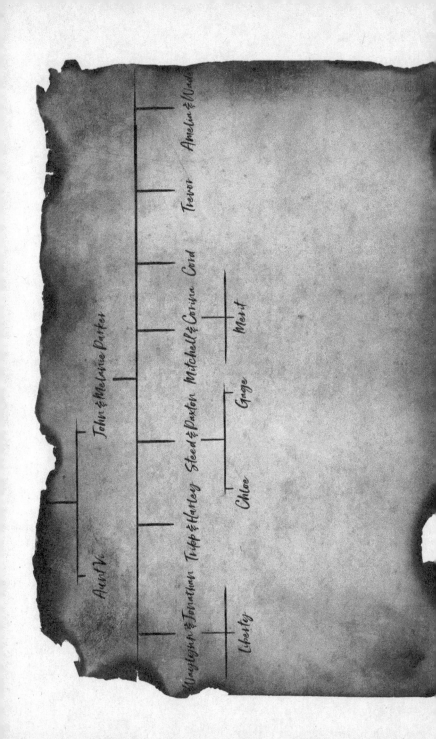

A Note to Readers

This Love is book six in the Cowboys and Angels series. The books in this series are not stand-alone books. Stories intertwine between books and continued to grow within each book. If you have picked up this book and have not read *Lost Love, Love Profound, Tempting Love, Love Again, and Blind Love* I strongly suggest that you read them in order.

For a list of characters in the series as well as other fun extras, please visit the series website: www.cowboysandangelsseries.com

A note about Maebh's dialect. Maebh is from Cork, Ireland. You'll see she says "me" in place of "my". I know it is written as "my" and pronounced as "me", but to make the flow easier for the reader, I have made it all "me". Even her internal thoughts.

Also, the pronunciation of Maebh is, "Maebh. It's like May with a V sound on the end."

I hope you enjoy Cord and Maebh's story

PROLOGUE

Cord

I'd had enough of everyone talking about this new Irish bar coming to town. I didn't want to think about a rival and what it would mean for my business. The pretty little thing on the other side of my bar was giving me a smile that screamed she wanted my attention, and I was happy to give it to her.

Time to end the family conversation I'd been having with my siblings on this subject.

"It's been real, but I see fun over there. I need something to take my mind off the competition, if you catch my drift."

Waylynn frowned. I knew she had seen the girl staring at me. I also knew my older sister thought I was a manwhore, which, if I was being honest with myself, I was. I couldn't deny it.

Giving my sister a wink, I turned around and ran right into someone.

"Shit!" I yelled out when her drink spilled all over me.

"I'm so sorry!" she said. Her voice sounded different, so I looked from my ruined shirt to her face.

My eyes caught on her green ones, and my breath stilled for a moment. Then she smiled and it felt like the fucking room tilted.

What. In. The. Living. Fuck.

"I didn't mean to run into you," she said. She had an accent, and I couldn't pick it up, but fuck if it didn't make her all the sexier, in a sweet, adorable sort of way.

Except, I wasn't into sweet and adorable. At least that was what I told myself to get rid of the weird feeling in my chest when I looked at this woman.

I smiled and watched her eyes light up. "No worries, sweetheart."

Her tongue ran over her lips so fast that if I hadn't been looking at her mouth, I'd have missed it. My cock instantly went hard. I needed to get away from this one, and fast.

I headed toward the woman who hadn't taken her eyes off of me since she walked into my bar. She grinned and told me her name, which I forgot in less than five seconds because I couldn't pull my eyes off the pretty little thing I'd just run into.

Nodding at Ms. No-Name, having no idea what she said, while my eyes were glued to Ms. Sweet & Adorable was not a good combo. What was it about her? She was a looker. Hell, even pretty. Pretty? Shit…she was gorgeous! I'd never seen a woman so beautiful. Her dark hair and green eyes made my chest tighten and that freaked me the hell out.

But I couldn't look away. I watched her as she walked to the bar and handed her glass to Jack, one of my part-time bartenders. She laughed at something he said, and I balled my fists, pissed at the idea that he was making her laugh.

Jesus, take the wheel cuz I'm about to lose my shit and fuck all if I know why.

I squeezed my eyes shut and quickly opened them just in time to watch my green-eyed beauty walk out of the door. The entire place felt cold…something was off now that she was gone.

Who was that? Where was she from? Was she walking over to talk to me and I blew her off? If so, I'm such a fucking prick! What in the hell made her eyes so green? I'd never in my life seen anyone with eyes like the color of an emerald. I couldn't get them out of my head. They reminded me of the meadows on the ranch in spring.

"So, want to take me back to your office, handsome?" the girl hanging on me purred into my ear. Her voice reminded me of my mission to get laid.

I cleared my throat and stepped away. With a forced a smile, I replied, "Sorry, darlin'. I need to go take care of something."

Her smile fell and for a moment, she looked more pissed than disappointed. "Enjoy your evening, ladies," I said to her and her three friends before I made my way through the crowd and back to my office.

Sitting in my chair, I pulled up the camera feed from the bar and went back a few minutes until I found her.

She was standing with her drink in hand as Jack pointed in my direction. My throat tightened as I watched her walk directly toward me. She looked like she might have said my name, but I never heard her. She went to talk to me again, taking a step closer when I turned and ran right into her.

"Fuck," I mumbled.

My emerald-eyed beauty had been looking for me, and I blew her off. Raking my fingers through my hair, I let out a sigh.

Zooming in on her face with the camera that caught people walking out of the bar, I stared at her. I scanned her face while I tried to memorize those eyes. I leaned back in my chair and slowly shook my head.

"Who are you? And why did you say my name? And why in the hell do you have my stomach twisted in knots?"

CHAPTER 1

Cord

"What the fuck does Aisling even mean?" I asked Trevor as we stood outside and watched Jonathon put up a sign for the new Irish pub, or restaurant, or whatever the hell that place was going to end up being.

"It means vision or dream."

I jumped at the sound of her voice.

"Christ almighty, Maebh! Don't be fucking sneaking up on people," I spat.

Maebh's smile faded, and I felt like a prick.

She glanced up at the dark sky. "Looks like it's going to be lashing down."

Trevor and I looked at each other in confusion. It was bad enough I could hardly understand Maebh with her thick Irish accent, but when she threw in her little Irish sayings, I was lost.

"Lashing down?" I asked.

She looked at Trevor like he had asked the question. She grinned and my legs shook a little.

"Raining hard," she replied.

Trevor glanced over to me. "Did you hear that, Cord? Lashing down means raining hard. Pay fucking attention, will ya?"

"Makes sense," I said, giving her a smile and praying like hell she would return one. She did, but it was nothing like the one she had given my brother.

"Jonathon said you'll be opening soon. Are you excited?" Trevor asked. I wanted to kick him in the balls. I hated that he was being so friendly. Not because I didn't want him to treat her nicely; I did. But the way she looked at him had me wanting to hurt my own flesh and blood. Maebh was Trevor's age, twenty-five. She stood at about five-feet-four inches, if that. We both towered over her with our six-two frames.

"Yeah, I'm excited. Me da has been langered most of this last week though trying to chase away the nerves."

Trevor laughed, and I looked at him. He had no fucking clue what in the hell *langered* meant, just like I didn't—yet that bastard laughed like he knew what she was talking about. What an ass. There was no way I was going to ask her. She probably would answer Trevor again and act like I wasn't even standing there.

Her eyes drifted up to mine, and we held each other's gaze for a few moments. It was like she could read my mind.

"Langered means drunk. It takes a lot for me da to get drunk so..." she shrugged. "It's sort of funny."

This time I smiled bigger. I liked hearing her call her father *da*. I liked hearing her talk, even though I couldn't understand her half the fucking time. Her voice was beautiful.

She was beautiful.

And all of that fucked with my head.

"You should teach a class on Irish lingo so we all know what you're saying," Trevor said, pulling a slight giggle from between Maebh's soft pink lips.

I balled my fists. My brother was flirting, and I didn't like it. Not. One. Fucking. Bit.

"Do y'all need any help with anything, Maebh?"

The offer was out of my mouth before I could take it back.

When Maebh worried her bottom lip, I moaned internally. My cock slowly started to harden as it pressed against my jeans. I couldn't pull my eyes from her mouth. Trevor cleared his throat, pulling my gaze from her mouth to him.

He smirked. The damn bastard must have known where my eyes were focused and where my thoughts were going.

"I hate to ask, but me da can't really help with this, and it's really got nothin' to do with Aisling."

With a shrug, I said, "That's okay. Just tell me what you need."

Her nose scrunched in the most adorable way, and I nearly had to reach for Trevor to hold myself up. My fucking legs were about to give out on me. I thought I was having a fucking heart attack; it was the only explanation.

"It's sort of a big undertakin', and I feel bad asking. It's just, I don't know a lot of people around here and…"

Her voice trailed off in sadness. It nearly brought me to my knees. Again. What was this, like the fourth time in the last ten minutes?

The idea of her not having many friends and feeling lonely made my chest ache.

"I can help," Trevor piped in.

Maebh's eyes sparkled with happiness.

"No, you can't." I quickly snipped. "You promised Mom you were going to get that fence taken care of at the front gate."

Trevor stared at me for a few seconds like he had no idea what in the hell I was talking about.

"*I'll* help, Maebh."

It hit him slowly. I was making up a story to get my own brother out of the picture. It wouldn't take him long to call everyone in the family and insist I had a thing for Maebh, when all I really wanted to do was get information on her new restaurant. That was all.

Wasn't it?

"*Riiight.* The fence. That needs repairing," Trevor said, a shit-eating grin on his face.

"Yep, the fence," I stated with a look that dared him to fuck with me.

Thunder cracked across the sky in the distance.

"Is it safe for you to be working outside in the rain?" Maebh asked Trevor. Why did she care? The fact that she harbored any concern for Trevor pissed me off.

"It's fine," I said before he could interject that it would be dangerous and that he should stay and help me with whatever project Maebh had in store.

"See ya later, Trevor." I motioned with my hands for him to move along.

His eyes widened in amusement. He looked between me and Maebh, and I could tell she was starting to wonder if she should have asked for help after all with the way we were glaring at each other.

My younger brother laughed and shook his head. "Maebh, it's been a pleasure, as always."

Trevor grabbed her hand and kissed the back of it. I saw red. Fucking red. I'd never wanted to hit my brother over a woman before. *Never*.

I grew even more angry when Maebh's cheeks turned slightly pink.

What in the hell?

"Bye, Trevor," I said, pulling him back and away before he moved his lips anywhere else. Lifting his hands in defeat, he laughed.

"I'm going! Jesus, Cord. See ya later, Maebh!"

She lifted her hand. "See ya!"

Trevor focused back on me as he took a few steps backwards, giving me a look that said he was going to tease the fuck out of me for this. At the moment, I didn't care. I had a chance to get to know the woman who was my direct competition. Shaking his head again, Trevor spun around and headed to his truck, but not before calling over his shoulder, "Talk to you later, *Greedy* Smurf."

My mouth dropped open. "I'm not a fucking Smurf, you asshole!" I shouted.

"What's a Greedy Smurf?" Maebh asked, her nose crinkled up again in the most adorable way.

Did the ground just move? Or was that my knees buckling?

My cock jumped, and my whole body trembled. I wanted to lean down and kiss her. This woman was driving me mad.

I took a step back and pushed my hand through my hair. "You don't know who the Smurfs are?" I asked, a smile on my face as I tried to ignore the weird feeling in my gut and the strain against my zipper.

She shook her head. "Nope."

"Then we're going to have to fix that problem and quickly."

She pressed her lips together, as a shy smile moved over her face. When she looked at me through her eyelashes, I saw her cheeks turn the most beautiful shade of red. I had made her blush just like Trevor had with the kiss on her hand, but this was different. The shade on her face screamed embarrassed *and* excited.

Clapping my hands to distract myself from those blushing cheeks and beautiful eyes, I said, "So, what did you need me to do?"

CHAPTER 2

maebh

Me hands shook as I unlocked the door to the apartment above Aisling and let Cord in.

"Where's your father?" he asked, looking around the room.

"Me da's in Ireland."

His head jerked back, and he stopped walking. Almost like he was afraid to be in here alone with me.

"Ireland?" Cord asked, his voice filled with something that sounded very much like fear.

I nodded. "Yep. He went to go pick up a few things from our house and some more whiskey."

"You couldn't just order the whiskey?" Cord asked, his brows pulled together. "That's how I get mine at the bar, no traveling for me."

"Not this kind," I replied, leaving it at that. He didn't need to know that da was only bringing one bottle back. The last bottle of whiskey me ma had drunk from. He'd been saving it for a special occasion and the opening of the Aisling was that occasion.

Cord stared into my eyes for the longest time. He seemed to do it a lot, and I loved it. It gave me a chance to stare back into his beautiful ocean-blue eyes. They reminded me of the clear blue waters of home. You'd stand on the hillside and cast your eyes out to the ocean and see the most amazing shades of blue.

I missed Ireland. Even though I loved it here, a part of me would always long for home.

Trevor had blue eyes as well, but they weren't as deep as Cord's. And they didn't hold as many secrets.

He finally pulled his gaze away from me and back to the apartment we were standing in.

"It's beautiful up here."

"Thank you," I said softly as Cord chuckled.

"What?" I asked.

"Your accent. It sounded like you said, *tank you*. And when you say what…you keep the H silent. It's hard to understand you half the time."

My heart dropped. I wasn't sure why Cord didn't like me. I'd done nothing to him. At least he was finally talking to me more. A few months ago he simply would give me the cold shoulder and barely speak two words.

"I'm sorry if you don't like it."

He jerked his head back around to me. "What?"

I felt my eyes burn with the threat of tears.

I will not cry. I will not.

Turning, I headed for the toilet. "I'll be right back." I barely got the words out as I walked down the small hallway. I shut the door and leaned against it. All of a sudden I felt wrecked. Me heart hammered in me chest and I wanted to cry so badly. I wished I hadn't asked Cord for help and just waited for me da to come back home. Why I wanted this man to like me so much was beyond me. I deserved a man who looked at me the way I'd seen the other Parker brothers look at their wives. I felt the first tear slip and cursed.

"It's stress from the opening," I told meself in a hushed whisper.

The knock on my bathroom door made me jump.

"Yes? Um, I'll be right out," I called, rushing to the sink to splash my face with water.

"Maebh, are you okay?"

After I got me voice under control, I opened the door. "Yes. I needed to splash me face with water. I felt faint. Let me show you what I need help with so you can get back to your day."

That was reasonable and very believable. It was summer in Texas and very hot.

Pushing past him, I walked back into the living room and up to the large painting.

"I just need this hung up." I pointed to the wall space above the fireplace.

His hands touched me shoulders, causing me to breathe in a big gasp.

"I really do like your accent. I'm sorry if you thought I didn't."

Me back faced Cord so I closed me eyes and counted to five. It was obvious Cord didn't have the slightest interest in me. I wish I could have said the same thing. His blue eyes visited me dreams nearly nightly. Me body trembled when he touched me. Hell, even with him being near I reacted. Not to mention the shot of heat that rushed through me veins and left me dizzy when he *did* touch me. Which was rare. Very rare.

"S'okay," I managed to get out.

I didn't dare move. If I turned to face him, his perfect, soft pink lips would be inches from mine and I'd only make a fool of meself when I stared at them.

"Maebh?"

His voice was soft and kind, and it made my stupid stomach flip. Every. Time.

"I'm sorry if I hurt your feelings, I didn't mean to. I swear to you. It's only that… I have a hell of a time understanding you."

He turned me body so I faced him. We were inches apart. It was the closest I'd ever been to him and I took the moment to study him. He was beautiful. The soft lines around his eyes hinted at what he looked like when he smiled. I couldn't see the dimples under his un-shaven face, but I knew they were there. His scruff looked handsome and me fingers itched to feel it. Me eyes lifted to his gaze.

"I would never intentionally hurt you," he said quietly. His stare was locked on me mouth, and I wanted him to kiss me more than I'd ever wanted anything in me entire life.

Me chest fluttered as his intense gaze moved across my face. It went from me lips to me eyes and back to me mouth. Cord exhaled loudly as he dropped his hold and took a step back, running his fingers through his gorgeous chestnut hair.

Lord Jesus above, give me strength with this man. He's a weakness I'm not sure I can afford to have in me life just now.

"Do you have the stuff to hang up the picture?"

I shook me head to clear it. His closeness had left me dizzy and his hands had left a burning sensation where they'd been touching me.

"Picture?" I asked, forgetting everything around me except for Cord.

Cord smiled and the dimples came out in full force. I swayed some. Help me, sweet Jesus, this lad is so good looking. Me pants were damp just from the small contact I'd had with him.

Me cheeks flushed with dirty thoughts, and I slapped me hands over me face, hoping to hide the blush that had crept up me neck to me cheeks.

"The picture you asked me up here to hang up. Are you sure you're feeling okay, Maebh?"

I spun around and rushed into the kitchen where I grabbed the hammer and the picture hanger I had gotten out earlier.

"Um…I attempted to put it up, but I'm afraid me balance is not so great."

He reached for the items and our fingers brushed. I swore I heard him hiss…like he'd gotten burned from a fire. At least that was how it felt for me.

Cord climbed up the ladder and motioned for me to hand him the frame.

"Tell me where you want it."

"I've already marked it on the wall…see the pencil smudge?"

He looked back at the wall and studied it. "Oh yeah, I see it."

After hammering in the picture hook, he handed me the hammer. "Trade you," he said with a chuckle that made me stupid knees weak.

The knock on the door startled me. Who in the world would be here right now?

"That must be Jonathon about the restaurant," I said.

When I opened the door and saw Jackson standing there, I smiled.

"What in the world are you doing here?" I asked, motioning for him to come in.

Jackson and I had gone out a few times, but we'd both decided we made better friends than anything else.

"Hey, Cord, fancy meeting you here." Jackson reached out and shook Cord's hand.

"Cord was helping me hang up a picture," I said.

Jackson looked above the fireplace. "You found one you liked for that space?"

If I hadn't known any better, I would have sworn I heard Cord growl from behind me.

"I did. Me da sent it from Ireland the day he got there. It used to hang in me Nana's house."

Jackson nodded. He wore a funny grin as he glanced at Cord. I turned to find Cord glaring at Jackson. They were having a silent pissing fight, and I had no idea why. Did they not like each other for some reason?

"You come here often, Jackson?" Cord asked, breaking the awkward silence that had filled the living room.

"Not often enough," he said, giving me a wink, then looking back to Cord.

What does the eejit mean by that?

Cord moved past me to the door. "Now that your boyfriend's here, he can help you with any other projects you have."

"Me boyfriend?" I asked in a shocked voice. "Jackson's not me boyfriend. We're just friends."

Cord's gaze bounced between us before he smirked and shook his head. "I'll see you around, Maebh."

Me mouth fell open. Did he think I was lying? Why would I lie with Jackson standing right there?

I rushed to the door and followed him into the hall. "Thank you for your help."

He looked over his shoulder and smiled. God, how I loved that smile. "Anytime."

And then he was gone. He practically ran down the steps. Me shoulders sagged, and I slowly moved back into the apartment. Jackson was looking at the painting as he said, "You know he likes you, right?"

I stopped in my tracks. "What?"

Jackson laughed. "Oh my gosh, Maebh, tell me you noticed how pissed off he was that I was here, and even more pissed off that I've been here a number of times?"

I stared at him like he was insane. "You're away with the fairies, Jackson."

He drew his brows together. "That doesn't sound good."

"It means you're crazy. Cord Parker doesn't like me. This is the most he's ever spoken to me, and he made fun of me accent."

Jackson laughed. "He for sure likes you then."

I waved him off with a flick of me wrist.

"Have you hit your head at work, Jackson?"

He placed his hands on my arms, gently squeezing them. "I've known Cord Parker for a long time, and I've never once seen him react like that about a woman. He's a player...or *was* a player. I'm not sure if he still his, but the way he was looking at you just now screamed the bastard was jealous that I was in your house. I do believe you have caught the eye of Cord Parker."

I frowned. "I think you're reading into something. Cord doesn't like me that way."

Jackson shrugged his shoulder. "If you say so."

"I do," I replied, me hands landing on me hips.

"Listen, I stopped by to see if you needed any help before opening day. I've got plenty of muscle I can bring down here if you've got some heavy lifting."

I chuckled. "Nah, Jonathon's crew is taking care of everything."

"Okay, well, I need to get going. I have a date later."

He wiggled his brows.

"Really? Is she a nice girl?" I asked.

"She is, but I hope she isn't *too* nice."

When he winked at me, I pushed him playfully on the chest. "You're bad, Jackson. Go on and get out of here, you bum!"

I walked him to the door and he kissed my cheek. "I'll talk to you closer to opening day. Check in again just in case you need anything."

With a nod, I replied, "Thank you."

When the door closed, I leaned against it and let his words replay in my head. I thought back to earlier today when it looked like Cord wanted to kiss me. Had I dreamed it? Maybe I wanted him to kiss me so badly that I made it up in me head that he felt the same way.

I headed to me bedroom and picked out a sexy dress. I got the courage to text Amelia and ask her if she and Wade wanted to go to dinner...and maybe to Cord's Place after. It didn't take her long to reply that they would love to go.

After spending entirely too much time getting ready, I stared at meself in the full-length mirror. The green dress popped against my dark hair, making me eyes stand out a little more. Me mother used to tell me I was special because I had emerald green eyes. Not many people had truly green eyes, even in Ireland.

I bit me cheek to keep my tears at bay when I thought of me ma. I missed her and could use her advice right about now. For the first time in my life I was attracted to the bad boy in town. I chuckled, because whether Cord was good for me or not, I wanted to find out *what* made him a bad boy.

"Cord Parker is certainly not a boy, Maebh O'Sullivan," I whispered to meself.

I gazed at me body. I didn't think I had a sexy body, but I was certainly not bad looking. I was barely five feet four and had curves. Me ma used to tell me I had good birthing hips, just like she did. I got her brown hair, but I had me father's eyes.

I'd pulled my brown locks up and let a few strands hang down around me face in curls. I didn't wear much make-up, and I was lucky to inherit me ma's darker skin tone, thanks to her Portuguese heritage. Growing up in Ireland, I stood out among the other girls with my year-round tanned skin up against the fair-skinned lassies who lived in our town.

After pulling in a deep breath, I slowly pushed it out. I had to know for sure if Jackson was right. I had to get Cord's attention. If I didn't, then I knew for sure I was barking up the wrong tree.

CHAPTER 3

Cord

The bar was packed, and I wasn't going to complain. I fucking loved summer. It meant a lot of business and a lot of tourists…female tourists…female tourists looking for a good time, no strings attached.

Trevor wasn't working for once. He sat with a group of young women who looked like they had all just turned twenty-one.

"Lori," I shouted to the waitress working the table. "Did you card them all?"

She nodded. "I did, and they're all twenty-one."

"Keep an eye on how much they drink. Limit it, okay?"

"Will do, boss."

Trevor was smiling at one of them, and I shook my head and chuckled. He pulled out his phone and read a text message. Standing, he tipped his cowboy hat to the women and made his way to the bar.

"I'm taking off, bro. You sure you don't need me tonight?"

My brows pulled tight. It was a Friday night, during the summer, and he was leaving solo? This didn't sound like Trevor.

"Who you going to meet?"

His mouth rose into a cocky smirk. "A friend."

"Uh-huh. Who?"

He shrugged and winked at a few girls who were staring at us…openly eye fucking the hell out of us, I should say.

"Scarlett."

"Are you fucking kidding me? What the hell are you doing, Trev?"

He looked back at me. "What do you mean?"

"Why are you leading her on?"

His head tossed back to laugh. "She sent me a text, bro. I didn't text her."

"Is she your fuck buddy now or something? You're still going to her regardless of who initiated it?"

Trevor's face grew angry. "Don't talk about her like that."

"Then don't fucking treat her like that. What's the matter with you? I've seen you go off with a number of girls since the benefit dinner, Trevor, and you're *still* hooking up with Scarlett? Does she know you're fucking around?"

He slammed his hands on the counter. "I don't belong to anyone. So what me and my cock do is no one's business. Especially not yours."

I shook my head and gave him a disappointed look. "Had she not texted you, would you have fucked one of them?" I asked, motioning with my head to the table he'd just left.

"Probably," he mumbled.

"Don't fuck up, Trev. You know she's mom's best friend's daughter and from the way she looks at you, she likes you…as more than a one-night screw."

"Listen, *Dad,* I don't need a lecture. Scarlett's sick, and she needed some medicine and couldn't get a hold of anyone else, so she texted me to see if I could pick something up for her. Her folks are out of town, so I told her I would get it. This ain't a booty call so back off."

My face softened. Trevor was actually going to do something without the reward of sex. Interesting.

"I'm sorry, Trev. What's wrong with her?"

He shrugged. "Not sure. She said she was on a prescription, but needed something for her chest. I guess she has a cough and isn't sleeping good."

"You better get going before everything closes," I said.

There was something in his eyes that looked like he wanted to tell me more. I knew my brother, and I knew he cared about Scarlett. There was no fucking way he'd be running out on a Friday night to play delivery boy—with no chance of sex—if he didn't like her. A lot.

His gaze fell to the floor and then back to me. His mouth opened, but he stopped himself. "I'm sure I'll be back later."

I nodded. "Okay, see you later. Tell Scarlett I said hello, and I hope she feels better."

The corners of his mouth rose. "I will. Later."

Trevor quickly walked through the crowd and out the door. Something was going on, and I wanted to dig deeper into it, but a pretty little redhead stepped up to the bar.

"Can I get something sweet?" she called out over the music.

"Sweet?" I asked.

She nodded.

"You mean like sangria or a daiquiri?"

"I guess. I don't know. This is my first ever drink, and they told me to order something sweet."

I grinned. "What's your favorite color?"

Now it was her turn to grin. "Blue."

"I'll make you a Blue Hawaiian. You'll like it." I looked over at the table where Trevor had been sitting and motioned with my chin. "Are you with all of them?"

She glanced over her shoulder and then back at me. Rolling her eyes, she huffed. "Yes. And they wouldn't let me order with the waitress. They said I had to come up and order with you. They all think you're cute and said I wouldn't have the nerve to talk to you."

I gave her a wink. "But you did."

She let out an exasperated sigh. "I had to! They wouldn't leave me alone. They think because we all turned twenty-one we have to come to a bar and get toasted. I don't want to get toasted, but they insisted I have one drink, at least. I don't want to hook-up with some random guy, so they said I had to at least kiss one guy. I sure don't want a shit kicker kissing me!"

I laughed. "A shit kicker? Where are shit kickers?"

She pointed over to a group of guys who were staring back at her friends. They were all local.

"You called it. Those are all shit kickers."

Her face beamed. "I'm good at reading people."

"I see that. Let me get your drink going."

After making her drink, I slid it to her.

"Oh! It's pretty. What does it taste like?"

I shrugged. "Sort of like a piña colada."

She slid me a twenty and told me to keep the change. I put the whole twenty into the tip jar shared between the waitresses and bartenders like I always did.

Her brows lifted. "Shit, that's good."

"So, you ordered your first fruity girly drink. Now you need the kiss."

The way her shoulders sagged told me she really didn't want to tackle that one.

"I guess I might as well make my way over to one of those guys and ask."

"Or…" I jumped over the bar and stood in front of her. "You let me kiss you."

Her eyes widened, and she took a step away from me.

"Y-you? You're so hot. Hotter even than your brother. I'm not…I don't know. The shit kickers seem like a more appropriate choice."

I shook my head. "You're a beautiful young lady, so stop putting yourself down. And for the love of God, stop letting your friends tell you what to do. Be yourself and don't be pressured to do anything you don't want to do. Do you want me to kiss you?"

She nodded and I took a step closer. I cupped her face and leaned down. I brushed my lips over hers, causing her to shake a little. Then I kissed her softly. She kept her mouth closed, so I didn't press her for more.

"Do that again," she whispered. "The shock faded, and now I really want a proper kiss."

I laughed and deepened the second kiss. Her free hand came up and landed on my chest and she groaned into my mouth.

Time to stop.

Stepping back, I smiled and she swayed a little.

"Holy crap. Best kiss of my life. You must have kissed a lot of women to get that damn good."

I winked. "You could say that, darlin'. Glad to hear you liked it."

Turning on her heels, she rushed back to the table where all her friends were laughing and whistling. I turned to see Amelia, Wade, and…fuck my life…Maebh. They stood at the opposite end of the bar, looking at me. At first, I couldn't pull my eyes off of Maebh. She looked beautiful, and my cock agreed. But she was also acting like she'd seen a ghost. When I flicked my eyes over to Amelia, she looked like she wanted to kick me in the balls. Wade shook his head and looked down at the floor. What was wrong with this sad group?

The music started up so I shouted, "Hey, y'all. What's going on? Want something to drink?"

Amelia huffed, and Maebh's eyes turned sad, like they had earlier when she thought I was making fun of her.

Talking over the music, Maebh said, "Amelia, I think I'm going to head on home."

My heart dropped; I didn't want Maebh to leave.

Before I had a chance to say anything, my sister whispered to Maebh. Maebh shook her head and seemed to be telling Amelia that it was a mistake to come here.

"Did y'all go out to eat or something?" I asked, moving closer to them. Wade nodded.

"Yeah, we had dinner and drinks and decided to come here."

I nodded and looked behind Maebh, making both her and Amelia glance over their shoulders.

"Looking for another slut to kiss?" Amelia hissed. I jerked back like I'd been slapped in the face.

"What?" My sisters had never had a problem with my flirting habits before, so why was my baby sister giving me a hard time?

She rolled her eyes. "Come on, Maebh. Let's go find a seat."

When the two of them walked off, I asked Wade, "What in the hell is wrong with Meli?"

He lifted his hands and laughed. "Dude, you're going to have to take it up with your sister."

"Is Jackson with y'all?"

His brows pulled together tight. "No, why would he be?"

"I figured y'all went on a double date."

Wade shook his head. "They're not dating. Maebh mentioned something about him going out on a date tonight with a different girl. I think they're just friends."

I couldn't hide my smile. "Is that so?"

Slapping me on the back, Wade said, "Yeah, dude, but as much as I love standing here talking to you, I want to dance with my wife. She's been feeling out of sorts lately. I think it's this book she's writing."

"Thanks, bud. Yeah, go dance with her. I'll bring y'all some drinks."

"Amelia's only drinking water," Wade said before he headed toward a small round table the girls had managed to snag.

I grabbed both Wade and Maebh a beer, as well as a bottle of water for my sister, and headed over to their table. I stopped and asked a few people if they were having a good time and smiled when they all said yes.

It made my fucking heart soar to be here. I'd dreamed of making this bar a success and worked my ass off. To see people enjoying themselves meant the world to me.

By the time I got to the table, though, some dickhead was trying to get Maebh to dance with him.

"I'm up next on her dance card, dude. You might want to move along," I said, loud enough that Maebh heard me while I handed her the beer. She politely smiled and thanked me.

The prick shot me a dirty look and walked off.

"Thank you. He wouldn't take no for an answer."

I held out my hand. "I wasn't only trying to get him to leave you alone. Will you dance with me?"

Her eyes lit up, and my damn knees knocked together. Fucking hell. What did this woman do to me?

Then she shrugged and took a drink of her beer. "I think I'll sit and enjoy me beer. Thanks, though."

My eyes widened, and I let out a laugh. "You don't want to dance with me?"

Her gaze shot over to the table where the young girls sat. "I'm sure…happy to dance with you. May want…her first."

Her accent was so fucking thick, and I couldn't hear over the music and got every other word.

"What did you say?" I asked, leaning in closer.

"The girl you were kissing…I'm sure she'll dance with you."

My eyes darted from Maebh to the table. None of them were even looking this way.

"It wasn't what it looked like, Maebh."

She shrugged. "I'm not your girlfriend. You don't owe me an explanation."

The waitress came up to the table. "Can I get y'all something?"

I was about to tell her Maebh's, Amelia, and Wade's drinks were on the house when Maebh pushed her beer away. "What minerals do you have?"

"Minerals?" we both asked.

"Uh, Maebh, you do realize where you are, right? We don't sell vitamins, it's a bar."

Her face turned red, and I knew in an instant I had embarrassed her.

She wrung her hands in her lap. "I meant soft drinks. Do you have a Diet Coke?"

"Yep! I'll bring you one."

Maebh nodded, and stared at the table.

I reached my hand out again. "Dance with me. Now."

Her head shot up and anger rushed over her face. It was about fucking time I saw something other than a polite smile on her pretty face.

"Excuse me?" she asked, her mouth gaping open.

"Get up, and get into my fucking arms, Maebh. Now."

She stood, and put her hands on her hips.

"No one tells me what to do. Especially you, stupid fecker."

"You just called me a stupid fecker. What the fuck is that?"

She shrugged. "I don't like taking the piss."

My eyes widened in shock. "Christ almighty, what are you even saying?"

"I'm saying I don't like being made fun of."

"I wasn't making fun of you!" I yelled back, over the music. My heart was pounding harder than the bass.

"I'm not an eejit!"

My brows pulled in tight. "Huh?"

"An eejit!"

My head was spinning and I rubbed my hands over my face. "What does that even mean, Maebh?"

She sighed. "Never mind. Me head is pounding."

"Yours? My head is throbbing," I mumbled. "All I wanted was a fucking dance."

Her eye filled with sadness. "What have I ever done to you? Why don't you like me, Cord?"

The wind was nearly knocked out of my lungs, and I took a few steps back. My stomach felt like a ten-pound weight was sitting in it.

"I need to, uh, get back to my bar."

I rushed from Maebh as fast as I could. Why did those six words nearly knock me on my ass?

She thought I didn't like her? Why the hell did she think that? I had just asked her to dance with me, for fuck's sake.

By the time I made it to my office, I was sure I was having a damn panic attack. I pulled out my phone and called Steed.

"Hey, what's going on?"

"Can't. Breathe. Panic. Attack."

He laughed. The fucker actually laughed.

"Seriously? You're having a panic attack. And you called my ass? Why?"

I dragged in a deep breath and heard Paxton saying something. Then her calm voice came on the line.

"Cord?"

"My chest hurts. I think…I'm dying. Heart attack."

I could practically hear Paxton rolling her eyes. "You're not dying. Take a deep breath through your nose and slowly let it out. Sit down if you're not already seated."

Walking over to the love seat in my office, I did what she said.

"Clear your mind of everything."

I shook my head. "I can't."

"Yes. You can. Do it."

My eyes were squeezed shut, and I tried to do what she said.

"I told you, you need to take a yoga classes with me. It calms you down."

Her voice wasn't harsh, more soft and caring. I kicked off my boots and crossed my legs the best I could on the sofa and tried to calm my racing heart. I was pretty sure they sat like this in those damn yoga classes.

"She's going to kill me, Paxton."

"Who?"

"The Irish vixen who is trying to steal my customers."

Paxton giggled. "Ahhh, so that's the reason for the panic attack. Maebh is as harmless as they come."

"She's not. She's trying to confuse me with her Irish words, and she talks so goddamn fast I can't understand anything she's saying."

"Did something happen with Maebh that started this panic attack?"

I huffed.

"I'll take that as a yes."

After a few seconds my breathing was back under control.

"It felt like someone was sitting on my damn chest."

"You need some time off, Cord. Time to relax and not think about work."

Dropping back against the cushions, I laughed. "Right. A new bar is opening in a week right down from me and you want me to take a vacation. Are you in on it with her, Paxton?"

"In on it?" she asked.

"Trying to take me down?"

She laughed. "Cord, listen to yourself. It's a totally different clientele at Aisling. It's more of a restaurant with a fancy bar upstairs."

"Whatever. It's still a bar."

Paxton sighed. "Your mom just had a great idea."

I jerked upright. "Mom's there?"

"Yep. She said you should go to the cabin up on LBJ Lake."

That sounded like heaven. I could do some fishing and get away for a bit.

"Are they not renting it out?"

Paxton covered the phone, and I heard muffled voices before she got back on.

"She said she'll look at the calendar and let you know what is open."

I stood, and a brown-haired beauty wearing a green dress caught my attention on the security screens.

"Cord? You still there?"

Walking closer to the TV screen, I watched as Maebh danced with one of the guys who had been standing in the shit kicker group.

"Cord? Are you…growling?"

"Everything's fine. Tell Mom to make it sooner rather than later."

"Oh, okay. I'll pass it along. Are you feeling better?"

My panic attack quickly morphed into full-on rage.

"I'm feeling something. Not sure it's better though. I gotta let you go, Pax. Got a situation to deal with on the dance floor that requires immediate attention."

CHAPTER 4

maebh

The young lad dancing with me was sweet, but touchy.

"Where you from, baby?"

"Baby?"

He wiggled his brows and pulled me closer. His body pressed against mine, and I wanted to gag.

"I think I'm ready to sit down. Thank you for the dance." Me hands went to his chest and I pushed him back with all me might. He didn't budge.

"Let me go," I said, anger building up inside of me.

"Come on, baby. Let's find a dark corner and I'll show you how good you can feel."

Me eyes widened, and I felt sick to me stomach.

"Get your fecking hands off of me now, you arse!" I shouted.

He laughed, but didn't let go.

I pushed him away with all me might and when he backed up, I kneed him in the bollocks. He doubled over and shouted a string of curses in me direction.

"Maebh!" Wade shouted, running over and looking between me and the guy on the floor.

"What happened?" Cord asked, appearing out of nowhere.

"He wouldn't let me go, so I kicked him in the bollocks."

Wade and Cord smiled as the bouncers grabbed the lad who was now moaning in pain. They practically threw him out the door.

"Are you okay?" Amelia asked.

I nodded. "It's not the first time I've had to teach a man for pawing me up."

My eyes darted over to Cord, and he looked pissed.

"In here?" he asked.

I shook me head. "Nah, back in Ireland. The lad's like to drink, especially during a lock-in. They get a little touchy feely."

"A lock-in?" Amelia asked.

All of a sudden I was wrecked and wanted to go home.

"I'll explain some other time. I'm knackered. Think I'm going to head on home."

"Wade and I will walk you back to your place."

Cord stepped between meself and Amelia. "No, it's okay, Meli. I can walk her down to her place. Y'all stay if you want."

Wade and Amelia smiled at each other, and you could see how much they were in love. I was happy for me new friend, but in some way, I also felt sad. Jealous of what they had.

"Are you sure?" Wade asked, taking Amelia's hand. "We're probably going to head on home."

"I'm sure," Cord announced.

"I don't mean to be a bother," I said. "It's just down the block."

Cord placed his hand on me back. "It's not a bother. Do you have a purse?"

Shaking me head, I replied, "No."

When his hand moved from me lower back to me hand, I nearly stumbled over me own damn feet. Butterflies had a fly off in the middle of me stomach.

Cord was holding me hand. Granted, his fingers weren't laced with mine, but it still felt good.

Of course, he was dragging me behind him, and I had a hard time keeping up, but he was still touching me. And he wanted to walk me home. That had to be a good sign.

"Christ, Cord!" I shouted over the music. "You're gonna pull me arm out if you keep tugging so!"

Once we cleared the crowd and got closer to the door, Cord whispered in one of the bouncer's ears. The guy nodded and looked at his watch.

I wonder what Cord had said. When I walked past him, he grinned, like he knew something I didn't.

The moment we stepped outside, I took a deep breath. The fresh air felt amazing, and I wanted to take a few moments to enjoy it. But his hand was back on me lower back, guiding us to the sidewalk that lead to the Aisling.

"What did you say to the bouncer?" I asked.

"That I'd be back in five minutes."

My heart sank. I was hoping he would want to walk me all the way to me place…and maybe stay for a few minutes, but that wasn't the case.

I don't know why that left me chest pained, but it did.

"You really gave it to that guy," Cord said, letting out a chuckle.

I shook my head. "Fecking shyster."

He laughed again, this time harder and louder.

"I'm going to have to carry a recorder with me so I can look up these words and phrases you're always using."

We rounded the corner, into the small breezeway that led to the stairs to me apartment.

I frowned and looked down at me hands.

Cord placed his finger on my chin and lifted me eyes to meet his.

"Hey, I already told you, I love your accent. I don't understand you most of the time, but I think it's sexy as hell."

I swallowed hard.

"You think me accent is sexy?"

He nodded. I wasn't sure where my bravery was coming from, but the next words out of me mouth stunned me more than they did Cord.

"What about me…do you think I'm sexy, too?"

His mouth parted and his eyes swept quickly over me body. I felt the heat hit my cheeks and cursed internally for being so forward. That wasn't really me at all.

"I'm sorry. That was not like me. You bring out the worst in me, Cord Parker." I moved to unlock my door and Cord put his hands on me arms.

The next thing I knew, Cord had me against the door, his body pressed into mine.

He opened his mouth to say something, but nothing came out. Me chest heaved as I fought to find breath. I loved feeling him against me. It was a scene from me dreams, and I didn't want to wake up and have it end, so I kept me mouth shut and stared into his eyes.

Cord pressed his hips into me, and I gasped as I felt his hard length pressing into me stomach.

Holy shite. He felt huge.

"Do you feel that?" he whispered, moving his mouth to within inches of mine.

I nodded. If I tried to speak, nothing would come out.

"That's how fucking sexy I think you are."

Swallowing hard, I searched his face. Did he do this with other women in the bar? Press himself against them and declare they were sexy? The question nagged, especially after seeing him kiss that girl when we walked in.

"Do you do this often?"

My question was like a slap to his face. He stepped back quickly, his hand pushing through his dark hair.

"I saw you kissing that girl, and I've seen you before bringing girls to a back room in your bar. I'm not like those women, Cord. I'm not going to spread me legs so you can shag me and then walk away. You don't even act like you like me half the time."

His face pained. "You keep saying that. Why do you think I don't like you?"

Shrugging, I replied, "You hardly talk to me, and when you do you're demanding, and often rude. Like you telling me to dance with you."

His gaze dropped to the ground. "I like you, Maebh. I *want* to be friends."

And like that, everything felt cold. Where he'd been pressed against me earlier cooled instantly. The warm, aching feeling between me legs was gone.

Friends.

I wouldn't sleep with him, so he wanted to be friends only.

"Okay."

He frowned. "Okay…what?"

"We can be friends, but you pushing your cock into me isn't what friends do."

Cord took another step back and shook his head. "I better get back."

I moved toward him, ready to ask him to come upstairs. I wanted to tell him I liked him as more than friends. That he made me entire body come to life. But I couldn't get the words out.

"Cord," I whispered. My voice sounded needy, and he noticed it, too. I dug me teeth into me lower lip and tried to figure out what I needed to say to make him understand I wanted him. In ways I'd never wanted a man before. I knew I should walk away. A guy like Cord Parker was bound to break me heart. He was a player, but damn it all to hell, the way he looked at me sometimes made me quiver with desire.

"Yes, Maebh?" he asked, moving closer.

I licked my lips slowly, a silent invitation for him to kiss me. When our eyes met, me unspoken words must have done the trick because he had me back against the door, his mouth covering mine. I moaned slightly and wrapped my arms around his neck. His hands went up my skirt and for a moment, I almost stopped him, until he gripped me thighs and lifted me. Me dress rose high, and I wrapped my legs around his body.

Christ almighty. I'd kissed men before, but never felt anything like this. He pressed his hard cock into my core and I groaned. I'd only ever had an orgasm at uni by me boyfriend's hand and me own. I longed to feel what it would be like to have a man drag one out of me while he made love to me. But not just any man.

Cord Parker.

My fingers laced into his hair, and I gave it a gentle tug, pulling his mouth even closer to mine.

Cord kissed me like his life depended on it. As if I was giving him air to breathe. It was magical. Intense. And so fecking sexy.

"Cord," I whispered when I pulled back for a much-needed air break.

He leaned his forehead to mine, his eyes squeezed closed. "I'm sorry. I lost control. You make me so damn crazy. I can't fucking think around you, Maebh."

He slowly put me down and slid me dress back where it was supposed to be. Then he took a few steps back and stared off into space.

What in the hell did he mean he couldn't think around me? *I* drove him crazy. *He* drove me insane.

Without looking at me, he stepped all the way out of the small porch area.

"Goodnight, Maebh. I'll see you around."

Me legs nearly buckled from under me as I watched him walk away.

Pressing me fingers to me lips, I held back the burning sting of tears that threatened to spill.

After a few minutes of trying to catch me breath, I unlocked the door and rushed upstairs. When I saw me da sitting on the sofa, I nearly screamed. I wasn't expecting him back from Ireland so soon. But seeing him here made me nearly break down into tears.

"You go out, half pint?"

I nodded. Afraid if I spoke he'd know something was wrong.

"You look pretty."

"Thank you," I managed to squeak out, making me way over to the bar and pouring meself a whiskey. "You're back early," I managed to say after I downed the hard liquor.

"The plane was available, so I used it."

I nodded. My father owned a distillery back in Ireland, a very successful one. He had his own private plane for the business. It was always available to him.

"I'm glad you're here."

He looked up at me again and frowned. "Are you okay, darlin'?"

The lump in me throat kept me from speaking, so I smiled and nodded.

"I'm knackered. Off to shower and bed."

"Good night, sweet girl."

"Night, Da."

After a long hot shower where I broke down into a fit of tears, I slipped on panties, long yoga pants, and a tank top. Pulling the covers back, I slipped under them, pulled them to me chin and let meself cry once more. Then I'd be done. I wasn't going to let a man make me feel this way...no matter how much his kiss burned.

CHAPTER 5

Maebh

A week had passed since the kiss. The kiss that had consumed me every thought. Last minute things had to be done with the Aisling to get it ready for opening night. I was a nervous wreck and it felt like me da and me had switched places. He was newly calm about everything.

"Calm yourself, Maebh. The place looks amazing. You've done a fine job."

"I need a shot of whiskey," I mumbled.

He chuckled and reached instead for a bottle of wine. "Sit down. Let's have a glass."

I looked around again. "Maybe I should check the kitchen again."

He rolled his eyes.

"Maebh, you've hired Eric to run the kitchen. The lad knows what he's doing."

I sighed and sank into a chair. We opened in a few hours, and I knew me da was right. Eric Riley was one of the best culinary chefs in Europe. When I approached him about opening an Irish restaurant in America, he was all for it. Then I told him it was near the small town me ma had grown up in. The country. He laughed for about an hour, then finally said it was an adventure he wouldn't turn down.

"Jonathon did a good job, didn't he?"

I smiled. "He did. Waylynn's very lucky to have him."

Me da grinned. "You've got some good friends, Maebh."

I'd become closer to Waylynn, Harley, Amelia, Paxton, and Corina. They were all amazing and so in love. A part of me was envious of them all. I wanted to find love. To have someone hold me when I drifted off to sleep and wish me a good morning when I woke up. Someone to share me dreams and fears.

"Corina and Mitchell won't be here tonight. They'll be home with baby Merit."

Me da smiled. He loved babies, and I knew he was counting down the days for me to pop out one or two.

"The poor thing. The last time I saw her she looked ready to pop."

I giggled. "The baby was a few weeks early, but they're all doing fine. Merit's a cute name."

He nodded.

Eric walked out from the kitchen area and into the main dining room.

"Are we good to go for tonight?" I asked, me fingers rubbing me temples.

"Stop worrying that pretty little head of yours, Maebh."

I forced a smile. Eric was older than me by ten years. He was still single and if I had a dollar for the number of times he'd asked me out I'd be opening another restaurant next to this one.

"You'll let me know if there are any problems?" I asked.

"Yes. Now stop worrying." He turned to me da. "Aedin, make your daughter relax, will you?"

"I've given her wine."

Eric shook his head. "Hell, give the lass a full bottle of whiskey. That's what she needs."

Me da shook his head. "She needs to have a clear mind. Maebh, go take a hot bath and get ready. Before you know it, it'll be time and you need to be relaxed and ready to go."

I wanted to argue, but instead I rolled me eyes and made me way up the stairs and through the door that led to me apartment. The third floor of the building held the main living, a bathroom, and a bedroom with a bath for me da. The fourth floor was me office, bedroom, and a beautiful spa-like bathroom that Jonathon had designed. Plus, I had a small staircase that led to the rooftop. There was also a staircase from the second story of Aisling that led to the roof that would someday host private parties, but for now it was all mine.

I went to the bathroom and ran the hot water for a bath. When I slipped into the tub, I let out a contented sigh. This felt lovely. I closed me eyes and let meself completely relax. When the dream of Cord kissing me jolted me awake, I groaned and scrubbed me hands over my face.

"Shite," I whispered.

I got out of the now-cold bath and quickly set about getting meself ready for the grand opening. Me hands would shake each time I thought about it. Everyone would be there. Melanie told me Cord closed his bar and was planning on being there as well. I smiled thinking back to a few weeks ago when she asked me what was the best Irish butter to buy. I hadn't thought much about it until this moment.

Why is Melanie buying Irish butter?

Shrugging, I pushed the silly question from me mind and made me way to the dress I had picked out for tonight. It was a Bien Savvy midi dress cut in embroidered lace. The pattern was a soft black and white floral and screamed romance which was the perfect attire for this evening with the ambience of Aisling. Aisling would soon be known as the romantic spot for dinner, as well a casual place for lunch.

I dropped the robe and picked up the fitted dress. There would be no bra. Me silk thong panties would be the only other piece of clothing I'd be wearing. After I slipped on the dress, I stared at meself in the mirror. Me teeth chewed me lip as I let me gaze follow the V-dip in the front of the dress that showed just a hint of cleavage through the see-through lace. Me fingers found the zipper on the side of the dress and I slowly zipped it up. The silk stopped just below mid-thigh, but the lace went down below me knees. I loved the peek-a-boo affect it had as it showed me skin, but still made the dress look elegant.

The knock on my bedroom door had me calling out for whomever it was to come in.

"Hey."

I glanced over me shoulder to find Amelia.

"Hi!" I made me way over to her. I took her hands and squeezed them. "How are you feeling?"

She shrugged. "I'm okay."

"Are you going to tell your family?"

She let out a sigh. "Wade thinks I should, but I'm nervous. I don't want to jinx it. You're the only other person who knows besides Wade."

"Amelia, your book is being made into a movie! You should be so damn happy."

"I am. Honest, I am. It's just, we didn't plan this and even though Wade is over the moon, I'm so worried he's going to resent me."

Frowning, I pulled her over to the bed and we sat. "Why would the lad resent you?"

She shrugged. "We talked about starting a family next year. I'm going to be so busy flying out to LA and getting ready for the release. A movie based on my book! How in the world will I even have time to start a family?"

I chuckled. "Stop this. Everything is going to be grand. Nothing says you can't have a baby when all this is going on. The worst part is over. They bought the book and now you can relax. I have one request though."

Amelia smiled. "If I can make it happen, I will."

"Scott Eastwood has to play the lead. That lad is some lash!"

Her brows pulled together. "Some lash?"

Rolling me eyes, I replied, "He's good looking!"

We fell into a giggle fit.

"Come on, let me fix your hair. How do you want to wear it?"

"I think half up, half down," I said with a smile. I loved having Amelia here. She was becoming the sister I never had.

She nodded. "I agree."

By the time Amelia had finished primping and spraying my hair, it was time to head down to Aisling.

I took the stairs with a deep breath. Amelia reached for me hand and squeezed it. "I'm here and if you feel like you need to throw up, I'll hold your hair back."

We stopped and turned to face each other. Me eyes filled with tears, and she held up her finger.

"No! That is not waterproof mascara!"

Me heart was full. Almost full. Something felt missing as I made me way around the Aisling. I welcomed everyone and made sure they had a drink in hand. We weren't serving meals this evening, this was more for people to walk around and see what Aisling would have to offer. Eric adored giving tours of *his* kitchen. I overhead him telling someone that he had followed me to America in hopes of winning me heart. The woman sighed and said, "How romantic."

I groaned and walked in the opposite direction.

"Maebh!" Bobby Hansen pulled his wife over to meet me. Bobby was on the city council and was the one person who had given me hell about renovating the historical building. I wanted to punch him square in the jaw, but instead, I plastered on a smile.

"Oh dear, look at you!" Melanie's voice echoed from behind me.

Amelia leaned over and said, "Be worried."

"Why?" I asked.

"My mother is meddling in your love life."

I scoffed. "I have no love life."

Amelia laughed. "Oh, that's what you think, my pretty Irish friend. My mother, on the other hand, has your love life all planned out and it includes my brother Cord."

I gasped. "W-what?"

"Don't worry, Waylynn and I have managed to hold her back from going full force."

My mouth gaped. "Full force with what?"

Me new best friend winked. I turned me back for one second, and Amelia had abandoned me, leaving me wide open for Melanie.

"Maebh, sweetheart. You look stunning!"

"Thank you, Melanie."

She smiled big. "I love that precious little accent of yours." She looked behind me. "Now, did you bring a date?"

"A date? No. I didn't bring a date. No time for that with all of the grand opening details."

An evil smile played across her face. And when I say evil, I mean a smile that made you know she was planning something. Something that would be giving me a headache no doubt.

The air in the restaurant changed, and I knew Cord was here. It would be the first time I'd seen him since the kiss.

The kiss.

Lord, I made it sound like it was a crime. In a way, it was. Cord Parker had gotten me so worked up, if he had asked to take me on that porch I would have let him. And that wasn't like me…at all.

My eyes traveled the room until I saw him…with another woman. The girl from his bar. I think her name was Tammy. She had been peeking in the window a few weeks back, and I had given her a tour. I had no idea she was dating Cord. I gasped and turned, quickly walking into the kitchen and making my way to Eric's office. I shut the door and leaned against it, taking in a long deep breath.

He was here with a woman. My eyes squeezed shut.

"You're so stupid, Maebh. Stupid to think a lad like him would ever like you."

"What are you going on about?"

Me eyes snapped open to see Jimmy, one of the waiters, sitting in a chair in the corner. He'd worked for me da before coming here to help start up the Aisling.

The heat in my cheeks inflamed. "Nothing."

He dropped his book and raised a brow. "Ms. O'Sullivan, pardon me for speaking out of turn but you're a beautiful woman. You shouldn't be hiding in here. If you want the lad, go out there and pretend like you don't care he's with the girl."

Nodding, I dabbed at the corner of me eye. I went to open the office door when he cleared his throat once more.

"And, miss?"

Glancing over my shoulder at him, I asked, "Yes?"

"When the bastard least expects it, give him a wink. It throws men off when a beautiful woman winks at them."

I frowned. "Why?"

He shrugged. "Beats the hell out of me, but it works every single time."

CHAPTER 6

Cord

Fifteen minutes earlier

"You're not going to the grand opening of Aisling?"

I shot Tammy a look. "Why do you think I'm not going?"

"Because you're sitting here reading the newspaper. Who reads a newspaper anymore? It's a beautiful place. Maebh gave me a sneak peek at it."

"First off, lots of people read actual newspapers, and are you friends with Maebh now?"

Tammy, who was third in command of my bar, smirked. "If I said *yes,* would that bother you?"

I shrugged. "Why would I care?"

Tammy sighed. "For fuck's sake, Cord. The bar is closed tonight. Don't act like you didn't do it because you knew it was her big opening. Which, by the way, was a nice thing to do."

"Don't know what you're talking about."

She let out a frustrated sigh. "Fine. Make yourself look like an asshole when you don't show up."

"I'm going! *Fuck*. Stop nagging."

A triumphant smile spread over her face. "Then come with me. I don't want to walk in alone."

I was already wearing dress pants and a button-down shirt. I'd claimed earlier that I'd been dressed for a meeting, but secretly I had planned on making a quick appearance at the grand opening of Maebh's new restaurant.

"Fine," I mumbled, grabbing my suit jacket and slipping it on.

Ten minutes later, Tammy and I were walking into Aisling. I'd been in here a few short days ago when Jonathon gave me a tour. Maebh had gone into Austin, to look for a dress her father said, so I knew I wouldn't run the risk of seeing her. I'd talked with her father some. Nice guy. Hard as fuck to understand, even harder than Maebh, but really nice.

My eyes scanned the place. It was packed, and I could hear people making comments about how elegant it was and how this was just what Oak Springs needed. The twitch in the corner of my mouth made Tammy elbow me in the ribs.

"You think it's pretty amazing, don't you? I see the smile tugging at your mouth."

I nodded. "I won't deny the place is beautiful. I think she's going to do really well."

Maebh was going to do better than really well. The place was packed.

"I love the books! Look at the books, Cord!" Tammy said, grabbing my hand and dragging me through the sea of people. It was more of a reception this evening. It wasn't a "sit down and enjoy the food" type of event but more of a get to know the staff, sample some of the menu, and drink. The rumors about the Irish were true; they certainly like to drink. I'd figured that out the other day when Aedin had asked me three times if I wanted more whiskey

Tammy pulled a book down and shoved it in my face.

"Look! Romance books!"

I rolled my eyes. "Oh, joy."

I glanced at the cover. It was one of the titles Amelia had bought for me to read last year. I wanted to chuckle but decided against letting Tammy in on the little secret of my reading habits.

A few people approached, and I made small talk. Everything from how the weather was and how good the fish were biting, right up to it was about time an elegant bar came to town. That was when I lost interest in the conversation. *Almost* became combative. My bar was nice, not fancy like the one upstairs, but it was nice.

Assholes.

My eyes scanned the room, and they locked on the most breathtaking green eyes I'd ever seen.

Maebh.

Holy shit. She looked beautiful. More than beautiful. She took my breath away in that dress. My mind instantly went back a few days ago when those legs were wrapped around me and my cock was pressed into her hot core.

Fucking hell.

Maebh's gaze jerked to Tammy next to me. She was going on and on about another book she'd found. Every now and then, she punched me in the arm.

Maebh looked back to the person she was talking to. She said something and headed up the steps to the reception area, otherwise known as: the bar with the whiskey. Just what I needed.

Tammy was buried elbows deep in books, allowing me to slip away.

The second I got up there, I found my family. Well, most of them. Mitchell and Corina were absent since Corina had just given birth to Merit a few weeks back.

Then I saw her.

My mother.

The huge smile she wore said she was on a mission.

Fucking great.

"Cord!" My mother exclaimed. "You made it."

Leaning down, I kissed her on the cheek. "Of course I did."

She pulled me close and put her mouth next to my ear. "Thank you for showing up."

"Why wouldn't I?"

Her brow lifted like she knew something I didn't.

What the hell is my mom up to now?

"Mom, can I ask you a question?"

She tilted her head and tried to look innocent. "Of course."

"Why did you put the Irish butter in my refrigerator?"

She wanted to laugh; I could see it all over her face. She did a damn good job holding it in. "Well, I read that it's much better for you. Just ask Maebh."

And there it was.

"Ma, don't be butting into my business."

"Cord Parker, I have no idea what you're talking about."

I balled my fists at my side. "I'm telling Dad!"

She glared at me before tossing her head back and laughing. She patted my chest and shook her head. "Good luck with that, son. Ask your siblings how well it's worked for them in the past. I need to go say hello to someone."

Groaning, I made a mental note to stop by my folks' place sooner rather than later. I needed my mother to keep her nose out of this.

I glanced around the room, searching for her. Maebh was standing behind the bar, laughing alongside some good-looking bastard whom I was hoping was just the bartender.

"Maebh!" Waylynn called out. "Show everyone the proper way to take a shot."

My dick strained against my pants when I saw her cheeks flush. The things I wanted to whisper in her ear to make those cheeks turn pink like that… I'd done it the other day when I kissed her and had my cock pressed against her body. I knew she wanted me as much as I wanted her.

I shook my head, clearing my wayward thoughts while I studied her.

Maebh poured a generous shot. Right before she brought the glass to her mouth, her eyes met mine. I smirked and shook my head slightly. No fucking way she was going to down all that.

She winked, tilted her head back, and took the shot in one fucking gulp. My knees actually trembled, and my stomach felt like I'd jumped a hill going a hundred miles-an-hour in my truck.

What in the fuck? I'd had plenty of women wink at me, but Maebh O'Sullivan winking and then downing a shot? Sexiest thing I'd ever seen. But what the hell did it mean? It made me both anxious and horny at the same time.

"A round for everyone!" she called out. Shots were poured and handed to everyone in the reception area. Maebh's father stood next to his daughter and lifted the glass.

"To Aisling!" he cried out, and everyone followed his lead.

I swallowed hard as Maebh took another shot with ease. She was soon walking around the room, mingling with everyone. I need-ed to find an escape before she got to me. I couldn't talk to her. Not after the dick move I'd pulled last week, but damn, I certainly couldn't control the way my body reacted to her.

"Where you going?" Tripp asked, pulling me to a stop with his hand on my shoulder.

"Need some fresh air."

"Why are you so afraid of her?"

I laughed. "I'm not afraid of her. I can't fucking understand a word she says."

He looked at me like I was full a shit.

"Maybe you should take your 'nothing to be afraid of self' and go hide out on the rooftop patio then," he said with a smirk.

"Yes!" Harley stated. "It's stunning."

My eyes narrowed as I glanced at Maebh. She was too busy talking to my parents to notice me leaving. I was pretty sure I had to go through a private entrance to get to the patio but didn't want to go snooping around looking for the doorway.

"How do you get to it?" I asked.

Tripp cleared his throat. "I don't think they're allowing anyone up there tonight. It's for future use, to rent out for special occasions. But you can just keep going up those stairs. You can also get to Maebh's apartment from that staircase." He pointed back to the set of stairs I had just come up on. Sure enough, the stairs went farther up.

"Well, I'm going to go check it out. I need some air."

They didn't even bother to stop me as I made my way to the bar, ordered a Murphy's Irish Stout, then took the steps two at a time. I wanted to hurry up and get out of sight before someone saw me heading to the rooftop.

The door was open, and I stepped out. A light breeze was blowing, making this July night feel more like a spring evening.

I made my way over to the edge and looked out over Oak Springs. It was pretty much the same view from my roof, but it felt more like a romantic scene out of one of Amelia's books. Twinkle lights made a faux roof above with tables and chairs placed in different spots. Candles that weren't lit sat on each table, and I was positive it would be a pretty romantic spot with them all lit. Not like mine that had oversized chairs, a Jacuzzi and an outside bar with a big screen TV. Mine was more like an outdoor man cave. This was a romantic hideaway made for lovers to enjoy a beautiful night, with low music and candlelight, while they ate a delicious meal under the stars.

I sat down and finished my beer as I studied the night sky. Leaning back, I put both hands behind my head and stared up at the distant stars, trying to recall the stories about the constellations I'd been taught in school…except my mind kept coming back to Maebh.

When I knew I couldn't hide out any longer, I stood—and realized that Maebh was watching me.

"Is everything alright?" she asked, a sweet smile on her beautiful face. Her thick Irish accent made my head spin, and my heart pound in my chest. Or maybe it was her smile. Or her eyes. Or the memory of that kiss. I wanted to kiss her again and then take her to bed and just hold her as I fell asleep.

Fucking hell. What's in this alcohol?

I wanted to hold her? No, I wanted to fuck her.

I cleared my throat. "Everything's fine. This is nice up here. The whole place is really nice. Beautiful." I swallowed hard.

"Thank you."

I grinned. I loved it when she said thank you because it sounded like she was saying, *tank you.* It was adorable as fuck, especially when she scrunched up her nose.

She took a step closer and all I wanted to do was run. Run to her. Run from her. Run and jump off the top of the fucking building. Scream for Tripp to get his ass up here. This woman both thrilled me and scared the piss out of me.

Get it together, Parker.

No woman had ever made me feel so messed up, yet Maebh O' Sullivan's smile turned me into a sixteen-year-old idiot.

"I'm glad you came." She looked out over the town square before she went on talking. "I didn't know you had a girlfriend."

My eyes widened. "What?"

"The woman you came with?"

"Tammy?" I said, laughing at the idea of Tammy being anything more than a pain in my ass. "She's the manager of the bar. We only walked down here together. That's it."

There went that goddamn smile again. Why wasn't she mad at me? I'd acted like such a dick the other day. I didn't deserve that smile. When my gaze moved to her lips, I groaned internally and my cock began to swell in my pants. A sure sign I needed to leave before I did something stupid again.

"What are you doing up here?" I finally managed to say.

"I needed a moment to meself and someone suggested I come up here for air. Why are *you* up here?" There was a playful edge to her voice, and I found myself liking it. I wanted to hear her talk more.

There was no way I could tell her the truth. That simply being in her presence made me stupid and I needed to stay *far* away from her.

"I, um, needed air. I also wanted to see if your view was better than mine."

"It's not the same as your view?" She smirked and my insides heated.

Fuck. Busted.

I let out a slight chuckle. Her mouth dropped open and her eyes seemed to light up. She liked it when I laughed. I needed to remember that.

"You got me on that one. Truth be told, I'm feeling a bit off. I think I'm going to call it a night."

She nodded. Was that disappointment? Maybe she was hoping I'd pull her into my arms and plant another kiss on her pretty little lips. I sure as fuck wanted to.

Dragging in a deep breath, I headed toward the door. Maebh reached out and lightly grabbed my arm, halting me in my tracks. My stomach dropped like a rock thrown into the river.

Our eyes met, and some weird feeling hit me in the center of my chest. My breath caught, and I swore to God it sounded like hers did too.

What in the hell is this woman doing to me?

"Thank you for coming this evening," she said softly. "It meant a lot."

My mouth opened but nothing came out. Clearing my throat, I got my shit back together and winked. "No problem. See ya around."

Her hand dropped to her side, and I quickly headed to the door. I loosened the tie that felt like it was cutting off my breath while I picked up my pace. When I got to the reception area, Steed took one look at me and asked what was wrong.

"Nothing. I'm going home. Tell everyone I said goodnight."

I headed down the steps, not giving him a chance to respond or even say goodnight.

The second I made it out of the restaurant I damn near ran to my place. Sprinting up the steps, I unlocked my door, stepped inside, and shut it like the apocalypse had started and a zombie was trying to get in.

I bent over, my hands resting on my knees, and I fought to pull in a few deep breaths. My arm still burned where she had touched it. Just like my lips did last week, a slow burn that lasted for days afterward.

I stood when I felt like I could breathe again. Leaning against my door, I dropped my head against it. What in the hell was happening to me? I couldn't bring myself to have sex with anyone, and I really needed to figure out a way to get my head clear. When I closed my eyes, I saw her smile. Her emerald green eyes staring back. This was not good. Not good at all. I wanted Maebh like I'd never wanted any other woman in my entire life. One kiss was never going to cut it.

I let out a laugh and jerked my fingers through my damp hair.

Am I sweating?

My phone buzzed in my pocket. Taking it out, I found a text from an unknown number.

Unknown: *You dropped your wallet when you were on the rooftop terrace. I'll bring it by the bar tomorrow. –Maebh.*

I swallowed. How did she get my number?

My mother!

It didn't matter; now I had her cell phone number. I quickly added a new contact and typed her name with shaking hands.

"Wait. She has my wallet? That means...I *have* to see her tomorrow," I said out loud like someone was there listening.

Walking to my couch, I dropped face down into the oversized pillows and groaned.

"I'm so totally fucked."

CHAPTER 7

Maebh

Glancing one more time at meself in the mirror, I took a deep breath while I chewed on the corner of me lip.

Rolling me eyes, I whispered, "For goodness sake, Maebh. Just go give him his wallet."

I headed down the steps and into the kitchen. "Da, I'm going to run an errand."

He glanced up from his newspaper. "Where are you going?"

"Cord's Place."

Me da's brow raised. "Cord Parker? You're going to his house, or his bar?"

I gave him a playful wink. "Does it matter? I am twenty-five, Da."

He grunted in response. "I don't like the way the boy looks at you."

Me heart jumped. "What do you mean? How does he look at me?"

Shaking his head, he replied, "Like he wants ya. I don't like it one bit."

Me cheeks flushed. "You're reading it all wrong, Da. Cord isn't interested in me. Sometimes I think he doesn't even like me, not since he found out I was opening a bar so close to his."

The newspaper dropped, and he started to laugh. "You're joking with me, right? I raised you to be smarter than that, Maebh." He shook his head. "Your mother was the same way. Never noticed the men staring at her. She was naïve, like you."

Me hands went to me hips. "Excuse me. I'm not naïve!"

"Uh-huh. You going to stand here and argue with me, or go see the boy?"

"It's not a visit, Da. It's simply to return the wallet he dropped last night. That's all."

His hands came up in a defensive position.

Reaching for Cord's wallet, I huffed and headed down the stairs.

"Don't let the blimey bastard put his hands on ya!"

Rushing down the steps, I tried to regain the confidence I'd had earlier. The plan was to march in and give him back his wallet and then leave. That was it.

Less than two minutes later, I was walking into the bar. It wouldn't open for a few hours, and I was surprised to find the door unlocked. A young girl about my age glanced up.

"What can I do for ya?" she asked. Her accent was thick, and I knew she had to be from this area.

"Is Cord around?" I asked.

Her eyes took me in.

"He expecting you?"

"Yes. My name is Maebh O'Sullivan."

Did she just snarl at me?

Picking up a phone, she glanced over her shoulder. "Boss, there's a Maebh O'Sullivan here to see you."

The smug look on her face fell, and she turned away. I took a few steps closer to hear what she was going to say.

"Send her back? To your office?"

I stepped away and tried to calm my racing heart.

His office? Oh hell, I'm in trouble.

She hung up and cleared her throat.

"He would like for you to go back to his office."

I swallowed hard. I was about to hand her the wallet and tell her to give it to him, but what if for some strange reason, she didn't? I didn't know this girl.

"Do you know where his office is?" she asked, clearly annoyed. She scoffed at my silence. "He won't bite, honey. Unless you ask him to. He seems like the type who'd be into that."

My eyes widened, and my cheeks flushed.

"Right," she said, laughing. "Follow me."

I followed her even though my head told me to run in the other direction, *away* from Cord Parker.

She pointed to the last door on the right. "That's his office. Just knock before you go in."

Why was I feeling like a little girl being sent to the principal's office? I was nervous as hell.

"Thank you," I replied with a smile.

She turned and headed back down the hall.

With a deep breath, I knocked on the door and held the air in me lungs.

"Come in."

Whoosh.

It all came out in one hitch as his voice filled me ears.

When the door opened, I found Cord behind a large, dark wooden desk. Me mind instantly went dark, and I pictured him on top of the desk, me underneath him.

Ugh. This is a bad idea. A very bad idea.

"Cord?" I whispered, my voice sounding weaker than I wanted it to.

When he looked up, my breath caught.

Why is this man so lush?

He smiled and stood while me insides did all sorts of weird things. Me stomach flopped around, while me heartbeat went crazy, me mouth went dry, and the room spun a bit.

"Come on in."

His voice practically purred.

Get in, give him his wallet, and retreat. I stepped into the office and held up his wallet.

"I went on a shopping spree this morning," I said, wiggling my eyebrows.

Cord laughed, and I nearly turned to Jell-O.

I forced me feet to walk over to his desk where I handed him his brown leather wallet.

"Thank you for bringing it back to me. It must have fallen out when I sat down."

"No worries. It gave me something to look forward to."

His eyes widened some.

"Not that I was looking forward to seeing you or anything. I meant it was keeping me mind off the grand-*grand* opening tonight. That's what I meant."

His eyes turned dark for a moment, making me stomach flip, but then the look was gone, and he gazed at me blankly.

I couldn't help it—I glanced at his desk. I felt a little sick thinking he'd had sex with other women on it. It turned me stomach and hurt me chest in a way that scared me. I shouldn't care what Cord Parker had done in this room, but I did. And I was jealous. Insanely jealous of all the women he'd had.

Me hand went to me stomach in an attempt to settle the sick feeling. When I took a step back, me eyes lifted to his. He frowned and that made me step back even more. It was like he knew what I was thinking because he narrowed his gaze.

"You're the first woman I've had in this office besides my sisters or an employee.

Was that his way of telling me he'd never shagged a woman in here? Why would he care what I thought?

I scoffed. "I find that hard to believe. I've seen you take women back here."

The venom in my voice shocked even me.

Holy hell, Maebh. Settle your tits.

His eyes filled with something like sadness, maybe even regret. "Storage room."

"Huh?" I asked, a confused expression coming over me face.

His hand pushed through his hair. "Nothing, it doesn't matter."

It dawned on me then. He had taken women to the storage room to have sex.

"You don't believe in having sex in your office?"

What is wrong with me? Why am I asking him this?

I waved my hands about. "I'm sorry. Don't answer that. I don't know what is the matter with me. You've left me all kinds of confused after th-that night."

The left side of his mouth rose slightly, and I knew he was fighting a full-blown smile.

"You think that's funny? Do you like kissing women and getting them all hot and bothered and then walking away? Does that get you off?"

Cord walked around his desk and headed toward the door of his office. Where in the hell did he think he was going?

He shut the door and turned back to face me. When he walked toward me, I stepped back until me legs hit his desk.

"You were hot and bothered by our kiss?"

The way his blue eyes searched me face had me panting. It was getting harder to breathe, especially with him nearly pressed against me body...again.

"No," I lied.

"That's not what you just said, Maebh."

I stood up straighter and squared me shoulders. "By your own admission, and on more than one occasion, Mr. Parker, you don't always understand what I say."

He laughed, and I moaned internally. God, I loved his laugh. And his smile. And the way he ran his fingers through his hair.

"Why are you so interested in if I've fucked someone in here?"

"I'm not," I stated, me hands going to me hips.

He leaned closer, a whisper away. "You're lying. I can tell because your cheeks are turning a beautiful shade of pink. I wonder how vibrant that pink gets when you come?"

Me mouth opened in utter shock, and I stared at him.

"I bet they turn vibrant."

Cord stepped closer.

"I've never found the right woman to bring into my private space and make love to, but there's always a first time..."

Me tongue bathed me dry lips. Cord's eyes followed, and he let out a soft growl from the back of his throat.

"You... You..."

Christ, what are you trying to say?

"May I ask you something, Maebh?"

The way he said my name made me knees knock together. The room was spinning.

"Y-yes."

"Did you like the kiss we shared? Did you like my hands under your dress? My cock pressed against you?"

I wanted to say yes, but I couldn't forget how he'd made me feel when he walked away and then pretended it had never happened.

"I might have enjoyed it more if you hadn't walked away from me like an arse."

His smile instantly disappeared.

"Maebh, I didn't mean to…"

My hands went to his chest to push him back, but I jerked them away when I felt the zap of energy rushing between us.

What in the world did this man do to me? He was dangerous. Very dangerous.

"I need to get back to Aisling. Have a nice one, Cord."

He stepped out of my way, and I was relieved I wouldn't have to argue with him.

Me eyes burned, and I couldn't figure out why I let this man get me so worked up. I headed for the door, but before I could open it, Cord took me arm and spun me around. He pushed me against the office door. I was having a déjà vu moment.

"You didn't enjoy any of that night, Maebh?"

A sexy smile moved over Cord's face. "Answer me."

Me eyes bounced all over his face as I fought to remember how in the hell to speak.

"What are you doing to me?" I whispered.

His forehead leaned against mine, and I noticed his chest heaving.

"I could say the same thing to you, agra."

Everything stopped, and I inhaled a sharp breath.

"Where did you hear that?" I asked.

Cord moved away and pushed his hands into his pockets.

"Answer me," I demanded. "Where did you hear that name?"

He shrugged. "You better get going, the restaurant opens in a few hours, and you'll need to be ready."

My mouth hung open. He was going to call me sweetheart and not even tell me how he knew that word.

"You confuse me, Cord Parker. One minute you make me think you want me, the next I'm like a bug you have to squash."

He stood there, not saying a word.

"Do you?"

His eyes jerked up to meet mine. "Do I what?"

"Want me?"

It was the boldest question I'd ever asked a man, and me neck and cheeks felt like they were on fire. But I had to know. I needed to know how he felt.

When he didn't reply and dropped his gaze, I had me answer.

"I didn't think so," I said, with a nervous laugh. "Stupid fool am I."

"Maebh—"

"It's okay. I see the women who throw themselves at you. I won't compete with the likes of that."

A look of horror moved over his face.

"I know I'm not as pretty or as...experienced..." I needed to leave before I kept spewing words.

"What are you talking about? Maebh, you're..."

Cutting him off, I tried to act peppy as I plastered on a fake smile. "Have a good one."

And like that, I was rushing down the hallway from Cord Parker. I'd just humiliated meself, and I would never forgive meself for being so damn weak.

It was a silly crush on a handsome boy who would never be happy with a girl like me.

CHAPTER 8

Maebh

A week had passed since Aisling's grand opening, and I was ready for a day off.

Amelia had invited me to go to the spa with her, Harley, and Paxton. Waylynn and Corina were home with the sweet wee ones. But the rest of us were staying the night at the spa, which was a good thing, because I ached to have some girl time.

I sank down into the hot water and sighed.

"Feels good, doesn't it?" Paxton said.

"The best! Me legs have been aching all week. I haven't stood this much since I was back in Ireland."

"Tripp said Aisling was packed the other day when he stopped in for lunch."

Harley's feet dipped into the hot tub, but that was all.

"Harley get your butt in here. It feels amazing," Amelia declared, her eyes closed.

"I'll pass."

Paxton stared at Harley. A smile grew on Paxton's face until she was full on beaming.

"Holy. Shit," Paxton said, making everyone look at her.

"Why are you staring, Paxton?" Harley asked.

"Yeah, why are you staring at her?" Amelia asked.

Slowly shaking her head, Paxton whispered, "You're pregnant."

Amelia and I gasped.

"It all makes sense. No drinking at the grand opening. The healthy eating. No getting into the hot tub. You're pregnant."

Harley didn't try to deny it. She smiled.

Amelia let out a scream then asked, "How far?"

"Not very. I'm due mid-March. We've been waiting until I'm a little further along before we tell everyone."

"You mean to tell me my mother hasn't sniffed it out yet?"

We all laughed, and I tried to ignore a twinge of jealousy.

"Look at you...the secret keeper," Amelia stated.

I looked at Amelia and raised an eyebrow.

Paxton and Harley exchanged looks—then turned to Amelia.

"You know, being in a hot tub isn't good for pregnant women," Harley stated.

Amelia nodded. "Yep, I know."

Paxton's eyes widened. "So...why are you in the hot tub?"

Looking confused, Amelia replied, "Because it feels good? Is this a trick question or something?"

Harley moved along the edge and got closer. "Is there something you want to tell us, Meli?"

Her eyes darted over to mine. "Maebh! Did you tell them?"

"What? No!"

"Maebh knew before me? How could you tell Maebh before me?" Paxton turned to face me. "No offense, Maebh."

I held up my hands. "None taken. In her defense, I walked in on it."

Paxton's eyes widened. "You walked in on it?"

Nodding me head, I replied, "I overheard Amelia on the phone talking to her agent about it."

"What!" Harley and Paxton shouted at once.

"Your agent knows?" Paxton said, pulling Amelia up and trying to push her out of the hot tub. "Get out of this hot tub! It's not good for the baby!"

I covered me mouth, realizing that the girls thought Amelia was pregnant.

"What in the fuck are you talking about, Paxton? Have you lost your damn mind? I'm not the one who's pregnant!" Amelia looked at me, her eyes pleading me not to tell her secret, mine pleading her not to make me keep it.

Paxton froze. "Wait. What?"

"Are you pregnant, Maebh?" Paxton asked, clearly confused.

I nearly choked. "Hardly! That would be hard to explain considering I'm a virgin."

Now all eyes were on me, and the heat was off Amelia.

"What!" they all yelled at once.

With an internal groan, I shook me head. *Why did I blurt that out?*

"How? What the… Like *how*?" Amelia asked, stunned.

My brows shot up. "If I have to explain that to you, Amelia…"

Paxton and Harley chuckled while Amelia rolled her eyes. "I mean, you're so beautiful, Maebh. You have a body to die for, so I guess I'm just surprised you've never had sex."

"Have you come close?" Harley asked.

"Come close?" I asked.

Paxton grinned. "How far have you gone with your old boyfriends?"

I felt me cheeks flush.

"I've only had one boyfriend and that was at uni. We kissed and messed around a bit. He wanted more, but I wasn't ready to give him more. I cared about him, but I didn't love him."

Harley shook her head in wonder. "Wow. Maebh, I think you have officially blown my mind. It's amazing that you've waited."

"You've had an orgasm though, right?" Amelia asked, moving closer to me. I nodded and shrugged.

"Just by his hand…or mine." Me face felt hot.

"That's it?" Harley asked. "Oh Maebh, you're in for a treat!"

The lasses laughed, and I covered me face with me hands and groaned.

Paxton pulled them down and looked in me eyes.

"You're saving yourself. I think that is beautiful. Don't let go of that. Stay true to your heart."

I glanced down at me hands, wringing them under the water in the hot tub.

"I've never met a man who made me want to give him that that until…well, you know who I'm talking about." I shrugged. "I mean, I think I'm getting impatient." I let out a soft chuckle.

The three of them looked at me like they could read me thoughts. I had almost said I hadn't met a man I wanted to give me-self to until Cord. But I knew that would never happen. He may have wanted one night, but I wanted the rest of me life.

"Men can be real assholes, Maebh. Half only want in your pant-ies, and the other half don't know what the hell they want. They're scared or afraid to make commitments. Two of my brothers fall into both of those categories."

Me heart ached thinking of Cord wanting in a girl's knickers for sex only. It actually made me stomach hurt.

I forced a smile. "It's a good thing I'm not looking to get into a relationship." I mused. "With Aisling opening and doing so well, my focus has to be on that dream. My other dreams will have to take a backseat until the right man comes along."

Their eyes grew sad.

"Maebh, for what it's worth, I know my brother likes you."

I scoffed. "He has a funny way of showing it. You know, he kissed me a few weeks ago."

They all gasped.

"Hold up!" Harley said, standing and motioning for us to get out of the hot tub.

"This conversation needs to be happening back in our room with orange juice for me and alcohol for y'all."

"I agree!" Paxton stated, grabbing me hand and pulling me out of the warm water.

Walking into the large sitting area, I stopped. Three sets of eyes were laser-focused on me.

"What are you all looking at?" I asked, dropping into the over-sized chair.

Amelia laughed. "The kiss story, Maebh! Tell us about the kiss!"

I shrugged. "It was the night he walked me home from his bar. It was confusing. He said he thought I was sexy and pressed into me. I felt his hard…you know."

Amelia snarled as Paxton and Harley said, "Dick?"

"Ugh… My brother and that word," Amelia said, shuddering.

The girls laughed at Meli's reaction.

"Then he told me he only wanted to be friends. I wanted to tell him I fancied him. A lot. He looks at me sometimes like he wants to swallow me whole, and I don't understand it. I can't tell if he likes me, or hates me, or both at any given time."

"He likes you…a lot," the three of them said at once.

I rolled me eyes. "But then he said he wanted to be friends, and I figured that was it. I started to leave and the next thing I knew, he had me against the door and lifted me up so me legs wrapped around him. He kissed me like no man ever has. I felt it down to me toes."

They smiled, and that made me smile, but the memory came back with the hurt.

"I needed air. I pulled back and whispered his name. He put me down and said something about me making him crazy, and how he couldn't think around me. Then he left."

"He *left*?" Harley asked, anger moving over her face.

"Then when I saw him again, he acted like it never happened. But then he did it again. He tried to kiss me in his office, too, then he went back to acting like he's me friend *only*. It's like a game of tennis and I'm the ball."

Amelia chuckled. "Oh Maebh, I can promise you have him a hell of a lot more confused than he has you. He likes you, and he doesn't know how to process that. Cord has prided himself on being one of the last family members to not get tied down, always saying the married life's not for him."

Me heart dropped. "I don't know, Amelia. I think I'm more of a challenge than anything."

"Don't say that!" Paxton said. "I can tell you from personal experience, the Parker men are a strange bunch."

"Amen." Harley giggled.

"I wish Corina was here. This is like déjà vu all over again!" Amelia chuckled.

"What do you mean?" I questioned.

"Corina and Mitchell shared an amazing night right after they first met. Mitchell got freaked by his feelings and walked away from her. Took months to get his ass out of his head and get his feelings sorted."

"She even dated Tripp for a bit, but they were more like best friends than boyfriend and girlfriend," Harley added.

"He walked away from her after they slept together?" My heart nearly broke at the thought of Cord taking me virginity and walking away.

"He did. It hurt Corina a lot, but I think Mitchell was even more tormented knowing what he'd done to her."

"What about Trevor and Scarlett? I'd like to slap that boy upside his head. Steed told me they've hooked up a few times, but I saw Trevor sneaking off at the bar with some bleach blonde," Paxton said.

It was then that I knew I had to fight me feelings for Cord. Men like him and Trevor didn't settle for one woman.

"Don't think whatever it is you're thinking, Maebh!" Amelia gasped. "I see the look on your face."

I forced a smile. Me heart was racing. "I like Cord. Honestly, I do, and I think I was attracted to him the first time I saw him, but I don't think I can give me heart—or me virginity—to someone who wouldn't cherish both."

Paxton, Amelia, and Harley reached for me hands. Guilt covered their faces, and I was sure they were regretting the stories they'd told me.

Amelia blew out a breath. "We didn't mean to scare you away. It's the opposite, Maebh. Please don't let his recent behavior stop your feelings."

Chewing on the inside of me mouth, I shrugged and tried to play it off. "It's a crush. I'm sure I'll move on. I'm knackered and ready for me head to hit the pillow."

The girls nodded. It was early, very early. We hadn't even gone to dinner yet, but a weariness rushed over me body.

"I think the opening of Aisling has finally caught up to me. You girls go and enjoy your dinner."

Standing, Paxton reached for me hand. "Do you want us to bring you any food back?"

"Sure!" I said, trying to sound like our conversation hadn't just planted an iron ball in me stomach.

"Have fun, ladies. I'm going to rest," I said, making me way up the steps and to me room. The spa had beautiful cabins, and Amelia and I had the two bedrooms upstairs while Harley and Paxton had the two down.

When I got into me room and shut the door, I pressed me lips together and willed meself not to cry. Maybe I was taken by Cord because he was so handsome. The first time he ever looked at me and smiled, me heart melted. I'd seen plenty of handsome men. Jackson was handsome, not like Cord, but he was pretty good looking, and I enjoyed being around him. And Sean, me old boyfriend, was a looker too. Everyone always said we'd make the prettiest babies.

Sighing, I kicked off me slippers and moved to the bed. Falling onto it, I closed me eyes and let me weary body give into the darkness.

CHAPTER 9

Cord

My parents' house was filled with laughter. It warmed my heart to see my whole family.

"Happy birthday, little bro!" Mitchell said, slapping the shit out of my back.

Forcing a smile, I nodded. "Thanks."

"How's it feel to be twenty-eight?" Steed asked.

"Better than almost thirty," I replied, giving him a wink.

"I'm not thirty yet, you little bastard."

Chloe came bouncing into the living room with Gage walking behind her, keeping up with his big sister the best he could.

"Uncle Cord!" she screamed, jumping into my arms.

"Hey, squirt! I haven't seen you in almost a whole week!"

She flashed me a smile that would guarantee her anything she wanted.

"Happy birthday! What do you want for a present?"

I lifted my eyes in thought and waited a few seconds, making Chloe think I was contemplating hard.

"I know what I want!"

Her smile grew. "What?"

Gage was pulling on my jeans, attempting to say my name. Reaching down, I scooped him up in my other arm.

"A kiss! From a pretty girl."

Chloe blushed.

"Good thing we have plenty of pretty girls around," Waylynn said.

As I looked up, my breath hitched at the sight of the prettiest girl of them all.

"Maebh?"

Chloe twisted in my arms to get a better look. "Wow! You're *super* pretty!"

I wanted to agree with Chloe. Maebh was beyond pretty. Every time I saw her I swore she looked more beautiful than the last.

Maebh's cheeks flushed, and she kept her eyes focused on Chloe and then dropped her gaze to Gage who quickly pushed to get down as he abandoned me and waddled over to Maebh.

"Typical Parker man," Paxton mused as Steed laughed.

"Hey, my son knows a pretty girl when he sees one."

Maebh bent down and reached for Gage, lifting him up with a squeal and holding him so close, I was envious. The smile on the kid's face said it all. The little lucky bastard was in Maebh's arms and I was jealous. Jealous of my nephew who could barely walk and had spit running down the side of his mouth.

"Hello, little lad. Aren't you the most handsome boy I've ever seen. Oh, his eyes melt me heart."

Chloe faced me, her eyes wide. "Who is she? Is she a princess? She looks and talks like Merida from the movie. Where is she from?"

"No, Chloe, Merida is Scottish. Why the hell do I know that?" I laughed and turned to Steed. "Typical Parker woman right here, always getting the Parker men wound up so tight they don't know which way is up."

He rolled his eyes. "Tell me about it."

"Uncle Cord!" Chloe demanded.

"Her name is Maebh. She's from Ireland, and I'm not a hundred percent sure, but I don't think she's a princess, at least not the kind you're thinking of."

Chloe looked back at her. "She sure looks like one."

Swallowing hard, I let my eyes drift over Maebh's body. She was wearing a sundress that hugged her curves perfectly. It fell to the floor and covered almost every inch of that creamy skin, but the way her shoulders were exposed had my heart racing. She looked fucking breathtaking.

"You might want to take a breath, little bro," Steed said with a chuckle.

Mitchell was on the other side of me. I turned away from Maebh and set Chloe down. "What, Mitchell?" I whispered. "Why the hell are you staring at me like that?"

"Do you remember that day in the bar with Tripp? That day you told me I looked like a goddamn Smurf?"

"Don't even fucking say it, Mitchell," I hissed in a low voice so Chloe or Gage didn't hear me. Steed's rumbling laugh came from behind me.

"Dude, that pretty little thing over there has you so flat on your ass you can't even get up. You know what this means? It means those blue balls are blue for more than one reason."

Steed clamped his hand on my shoulder and flashed a wide grin. "You've been Smurfed."

Pushing Steed away, I snapped, "Fuck off!"

"Cord Michael Parker!" my mother shouted from the other side of the room. "Watch that mouth of yours!"

"Sorry, Ma," I said.

I stared at Maebh for a moment before Amelia's death look nearly knocked me over. Maebh grabbed Amelia's arm and pulled her close. It was easy to read her lips as she laid into my baby sister.

"Why didn't you tell me your whole family was here?"

Amelia grinned devilishly and shrugged.

Wade walked up to us, wearing the same damn smile Amelia had plastered on her face.

"You knew she was coming?" I said, my voice low and directed only to him.

"Yep."

I rolled my eyes at how he popped his fucking *p* when he said that.

"Why didn't you warn me, you bastard?"

Wade shrugged. "Because this way was a helluva lot more fun. You can't pay enough money for a shit show like this."

"You're dead to me, Wade. No longer a part of this family!"

He punched me lightly on the arm. "Damn, I love this family."

I glared at my brother-in-law. "Did you tell Amelia anything I said?"

Wade ignored me.

My hands turned to fists, and I was about to knock him in the head when he turned to face me. "I didn't have to say anything because Amelia told me Maebh likes you…a lot."

My heart jumped into my throat.

"What?"

He shook his head. "She *did* like you a lot, but she mentioned you acting like a prick and that Maebh was no longer interested."

"What?"

Wade simply shrugged. "That's all I know, bro."

Wade had been privy to my drunken confession after poker two nights ago when I admitted I was attracted to Maebh and had no fucking clue what to do about it. The bastard's only advice was to talk to my father. I wasn't about to do that. My mother already was trying to push me and Maebh together. Talking to my father would only add fuel to the fire.

Maebh laughed at something Chloe said and my body jerked in response. *What in the hell is going on with me?* I wasn't the one-lady type of guy. I liked women. Lots of women. Seven days a week of women. I couldn't honestly see me settling down with just one.

Or could I? If it was Maebh, I could.

Maybe I no longer felt that way. Now it was only one woman who consumed my every waking *and* sleeping thoughts. Even thinking about getting laid by someone else made my stomach revolt. And I knew a lot of my problems were because I hadn't gotten laid in weeks. Hell, not since the first time I laid eyes on her.

Fuck. My. Life.

"Here. I got you something," Mitchell said, grinning from ear to ear.

"You know the rules, no presents," I replied, taking the box.

Mitchell shrugged. "I know the rule, but I had to get it."

"Uncle Cord's got a gift!" Chloe called out, and Mitchell's smile fell.

About that time, Corina walked into the room holding Merit and all the attention was diverted.

"Thank fuck," Mitchell whispered. "Do not..."

My mother cut Mitchell off when she announced, "Cord, who is the gift from?" She looked around the room, ready to reprimand one of my siblings.

Melanie Parker was a stickler when it came to following the rules. Or I should say, following *her* rules. Once we all hit eighteen there was no more gift exchanging. Christmas was the only time when gifts between siblings were allowed. Birthdays were meant to be celebrated with a family dinner and game night afterwards.

I pointed to Mitchell, and my mother frowned.

"You threw me under the bus! Dude!"

"Payback from the comment earlier about the Smurf," I whispered.

Mitchell's mouth opened. "That was Steed who said it! Not me!"

"You brought it up," I stated.

"Mitchell, please tell me you didn't?" Corina gasped.

Trying to hold back his laughter, he replied, "I did."

Our mother walked up and glared at Mitchell.

"If Mitchell thought this was such an important thing to get you, then you should open it. Now."

Mitchell, Corina, and Steed all shouted at once, "No!"

Of course, this piqued my mother's curiosity and made me want to throw the damn thing into the pool. Nothing good was going to come from this gift, I knew it.

My eyes darted to where Maebh was standing. Jonathon had walked into the room and at some point, she had taken Liberty from him and was holding her. My heart nearly stopped at the sight of her holding my niece. I had no fucking clue why it made my palms sweat and my legs feel like Jell-O.

"Open it, Cord," my mother insisted.

Snapping my gaze to my mother, I said, "Huh?"

Gesturing toward the gift, my mother said, "Open it so we can all see what it is."

I searched for my father frantically. When I found him sitting in a chair drinking scotch, I begged him with my eyes to make his wife come to her senses. All the bastard did was lift his glass and flash his dimples. The same ones I had inherited.

Turning casually to make it look like I was going to sit on the love seat, I asked Mitchell, "What the fuck is it? Some kind of Smurf?"

His hands scrubbed down his face. "I wish. It's a joke that was meant for you to open alone. Not in front of everyone and especially not in front of your girl."

"Oh hell." I shot him a dirty look. "She's not my girl!"

His eyes pleaded. "Dude, don't open it. You'll kick my ass after you open it in front of everyone."

We both turned and sat on the love seat. We barely fit on the damn thing. Each of us was over six feet tall and built about the same, so we were shoulder to shoulder.

"What do I do?" I whispered, the entire room staring at me.

"Are we late?" Tripp asked, walking into the living room holding Harley's hand.

"Nope!" Waylynn answered. "Cord was just about to open up a gift Mitchell snuck in."

Tripp's eyes widened, and he shook his head. I was beginning to think all my brothers were in on this little gag gift.

"What the fuck is everyone staring at Cord and Mitchell for?" Trevor said, and Amelia and Paxton slapped him upside his head.

"The kids!" Paxton said.

Chloe jumped up and was about to repeat it when Waylynn put her hand over Chloe's mouth and all we heard was Chloe's muffled voice singing a string of curse words.

Our mother walked closer. "Cord's about to open Mitchell's gift."

Trevor lost it laughing. "Um, Mom, I'm pretty sure you don't want him opening it with Chloe in the room."

Yep. All of my dirty rotten brothers were in on it. They would pay, and pay dearly, for this shit.

"I can take Chloe out of the room, if you like?" Maebh offered.

A chorus of male voices said, "Yes!"

This made my mother's eye twitch.

"No. Chloe stays and Maebh stays. Now open the damn gift, Cord."

Mitchell groaned. "Mom! Why are you making such a big deal out of this? It's just a gag gift. It was a joke. You weren't even supposed to see me give it to him." His eyes shot to Chloe who had busted us with the gift. When she grinned, I knew that kid had nine-ty-nine-point-nine percent Parker blood flowing through her.

"Do I open it?" I asked Mitchell in a barely-there voice.

"Yes, but just say it's a T-shirt and don't turn it around."

I groaned. Quickly ripping the wrapping paper off, I opened the box and widened my eyes as I read the T-shirt.

"What in the f—"

"Cord!" several voices shouted to stop me from swearing.

I stared down at the T-shirt that read…

My head jerked toward Mitchell.

"What's it say?" Chloe asked, a smirk on her face. The little shit knew it was something she wasn't supposed to see.

"Yes, let's see this gag gift," my mother stated.

"Mom, for the love of all things good, no," I said.

She grabbed the T-shirt and held it in front of her. She didn't read it out loud, thank God, but the way she was holding it, Maebh could see it. I was sure of it.

Balling it up, she shook her head. "Inside joke, I take it?"

I shrugged and acted like I didn't know, but I did. One of Mitchell's friends said he'd overheard some girl at the bar say I had a golden dick after I fucked her.

Sighing, my mother tossed the T-shirt at me and shook her head. I'd never seen her look so disappointed in me. Or maybe it was Mitchell she was upset with. Either way, my mother was not happy, and it was our fault. My birthday was always the hardest for her since I shared it with my grandfather, her dad. When she stormed out of the room, dad slowly stood.

"Keep the jokes outside the house, boys. I need to go calm your mother down."

We hung our heads. For the first time in my adult life, I hated that I'd slept with so many women, and worse yet, that I knew my mother knew. Trevor walked up and took the T-shirt. It took him a minute but then he started to laugh his ass off.

"Heck yeah!" He slipped it on and Mitchell jumped up and knocked him to the ground.

"What the fuck, dude!" Trevor cried out.

"Fight!" Chloe shouted before Paxton ushered her out of the room with Waylynn, Amelia, and Corina following.

"Get off me, you fucker!" Trevor shouted.

"Why would you put it on, you dickhead?" Mitchell shouted, trying to get the shirt off of Trevor and punching him in the stomach in the process; they weren't hard punches by any means.

"Knock it off!" Tripp yelled as he pulled Mitchell off of Trevor.

Trevor jumped up and turned, only to give Maebh, who was still watching the whole scene play out, a chance to read the shirt. She quickly read it before she took a few steps back and plastered on a fake smile. I walked up to her, and she stiffened as I got closer.

"It's a stupid joke, Maebh. That's all."

She shrugged. "I don't mind. Makes no difference to me."

And like that, she walked out of the room. I knew she'd heard rumors of my man-whoring ways. Hell, she'd even admitted to seeing me take women in the back of the bar, but for her to see that T-shirt did something to me. It was like we were bragging about all the women I'd fucked—and fucked—over the years. Maybe originally it was intended to be that way, but it was a joke only my brothers were supposed to know about. Certainly not my mother and Maebh.

This had officially become the worst fucking birthday of my life. Even worse than the one where Jenny Jonesman got her lip stuck on my braces when we kissed for the first time behind the school bleachers, and we had to walk to the nurse with our mouths locked together. Yeah, even worse than that.

"Why do you look so torn up, Cord?" Harley asked.

My hand pushed through my hair, and I was momentarily at a loss. Why was I so upset?

"Just upset my mother made us do that."

"It's a good thing you told Maebh you only wanted to be friends, huh? You might have scared her off, had you been trying to come on to her. You know. Kissing her and giving her the wrong idea and all that."

Turning to my sister-in-law, I wanted to push her into another room and demand she tell me everything Maebh had told her. Clearly she'd told Harley about the kiss.

"What are you getting at, Harley?" I asked, agitation lacing my words.

She shook her head as she dragged me into the game room. Shutting the door, she glared. "How could you do that to Maebh?"

"Do what?" I asked, drawing my brows in and staring like she'd lost her damn mind.

"Cord! You kissed her. You told her you thought she was sexy while you pressed your damn dick against her, and then you left! You just *left*!"

"What the fuck is she telling you that for?"

She rolled her eyes. "Because I'm her friend. We were all at a spa day, and it came out that I'm pregnant, and then we thought Amelia was pregnant, and she said she wasn't, and then Paxton got confused. She asked Maebh if she was pregnant, she laughed and said it was impossible for her to be pregnant. Then one thing led to another, and she said you kissed her."

Harley took a breath and went on. "We demanded she tell us everything, and she did. You're a complete ass, Cord."

"Wait a minute, hold up with the name calling. Why is it impossible for her to get pregnant?"

I tried to ignore the way my chest ached at the thought of Maebh not being able to have kids. I wanted kids...someday. When I was ready to settle down and do that whole bullshit family thing.

Her eyes looked as if they were about to pop out of her head.

"With all that I just said, *that* is what stood out?"

"Can she not have kids?"

Harley rolled her eyes. "That's her place to tell you, but I'm sure she can have kids."

"Then why did she say she can't."

My sister-in-law worried her lip. "She didn't say that."

"You said, that Maebh said, it was impossible for her to have kids. Why? If she told you we kissed, I highly doubt she left that part out."

"It's not my place to tell you, Cord. Just don't hurt her. If you're not interested, please leave her alone. She's...well...she's too special to be dicking around with." Putting her hands on her hips, she mean-mugged me.

My eyes narrowed at Harley.

"You dragged my ass in here and then dropped that on me. Spill it."

Harley's hands went up in the air and then dropped as she sighed.

"Did you even hear the part where I said I was pregnant?"

I nodded. "Congrats and 'bout damn time. So, why can't she have kids?"

"Ugh! Cord! Please, I'm asking you to not be a Parker!"

"What's that supposed to fucking mean?"

"Don't go after Maebh just because she's the latest flavor of your month. She's already turned off by your playboy ways, and she has…um…"

"You don't think I'm good enough for her?" I asked, my chest felt like it had been kicked. Is that what Harley thought of me? Did Paxton feel the same way?

"What! Of course I do. I think you're confused by your feelings, and she's so different from the girls you're used to. Her heart will be broken if you lead her on, and with her being a virgin and all, I don't want you to—"

Harley's face constricted with horror as she slapped her hand over her mouth. The silence was so loud, I couldn't even take a breath.

I stumbled and hit the pool table, grabbing it to keep my legs from going out from under me. My heart had never hammered in my chest like this before.

"W-what?"

"Oh, God! Oh, God! Cord, *please* don't tell her you know. She'll kill me for letting that slip. Stupid pregnancy brain!"

I pushed my hands through my hair and took in a few deep breaths. Maebh was a virgin? A *virgin*?

I looked at Harley. "That's not fucking possible. You must have misunderstood her. Have you seen her? How old is she?"

Her head tilted. "Does it matter how old she is? She's saving herself for the right guy. And the right guy isn't the guy who is going to lead her on and run."

My stomach knotted up, and I made my way to one of the stools.

"Cord, I mean it. You can't let her know that you know. That's for her to tell, if she even has a reason to tell you."

Snapping my head up, I met her gaze. "I... Wait, I need to process this."

Harley rolled her eyes and started going off in Spanish. "*Porqué hay hombres tan ignorantes!*"

I stood. "Okay, all I got was a word that sounded like ignorant!"

"Fine, how's this for ya? *Porqué los hombres son tan estupidos.* Better?"

"Why do I feel like you just called me stupid?"

She groaned. "You are stupid! I find it hard to believe you've never been with a virgin. Why are you freaking about this?"

"I have, but that's not the same thing. This is different!"

"It's not different. Maebh is an amazing twenty-five-year-old woman who is saving herself for someone who will love and respect her. I'm not sure you're the guy, and based on that T-shirt, I'm pretty sure Maebh knows you're not the guy."

My jaw nearly hit the ground. "I respect her! Why do you think I pulled away? I'm so fucking scared that if I get close I'll hurt her because I'm a prick who only likes to fuck women and move on. I'm scared of these weird feelings, and the last thing I would ever want is to hurt her. She's better off without me in her life. But I...can't... Ahh, fuck!"

I shouted the last two words, and Harley didn't even flinch. She was pushing my buttons, trying to make me realize what a dick I was, but she didn't need to remind me. I knew.

"You can't what?"

I dropped against the pool table. "I can't stop wanting to know her. Wanting to kiss her...touch her. Make her mine. Harley, I don't know what to do. I've always said I wasn't the settling down kind of guy, but tonight, seeing her holding Liberty..."

I slowly shook my head. "For a moment I let myself dream she was holding our baby. Then when you said she couldn't have kids, I panicked. I don't know what's wrong with me."

Harley took my hands in hers and looked up at me. "I'll tell you what's wrong. You, Cord Parker, have fallen for a girl. You've been Smurfed."

I closed my eyes while I groaned. "Not you, too."

CHAPTER 10

maebh

"Ignore the boys, Maebh," Melanie said with a sweet smile. "They like to give each other a hard time."

I smiled. "I'm not bothered by it."

It was a lie, but I didn't need to let Cord's mother know I was smitten with her manwhore of a son. Sighing internally, I tried to push me feelings away.

Melanie and I were in the kitchen finishing up Cord's birthday dinner. She had made lasagna, which was Cord's favorite meal, homemade bread, salad, and a chocolate cheesecake for dessert.

"Thank you for helping. I know the kids love to spend as much time together as they can. Especially with the two new little ones."

"It's my pleasure. I used to help me ma in the kitchen all the time. It's how I found me love of cooking, helping her with all her recipes. Me da loved it as well because she was always trying something new out since he was the tester."

Melanie gave me a warm smile.

"Well, you're welcome in my kitchen anytime you'd like."

I felt me face heat. "Thank you, I'd love that."

"Your accent is just precious. I love to hear you talk."

With a chuckle, I went back to mixing the lettuce up with the salad mixings I'd cut up earlier.

"Not everyone has a fondness for it."

She frowned. "Who doesn't like it?"

"Cord. He said it's hard for him to understand me."

She huffed. "That just means he likes you."

"What?" I asked, confused. "How does him not liking me accent mean he likes me?"

Melanie didn't bother to look up. "Trust me. A mother knows these things. You probably didn't notice how he perked up when he saw you standing in the doorway of the family room. The boy nearly lit up the entire room."

Hope bubbled in me chest. "I'm sure he was just surprised to see me here for your family dinner. Amelia didn't tell me the entire family would be here *or* that you'd be celebrating Cord's birthday."

Her gray eyes met mine and a wide grin moved over her face. "The apple doesn't fall far from the tree?"

I frowned and was about to ask her what she meant, but she laughed and waved off her comment.

While cutting up the cucumber, I yawned.

"You poor thing, you must be so tired with the restaurant opening and all."

"I am. I'm pretty wrecked and already longing for a holiday."

"That means a vacation, right?"

I nodded.

Melanie stared for a few moments before she set her spoon down and placed her hands on the island.

"Maebh, I've got a great idea."

"What is it?" I asked, matching her smile with one of my own.

"We have a house on LBJ Lake. It's a few hours away, and it's open next weekend. Four whole days of nothing but peace and quiet."

My teeth sank into my lip, and I wanted more than anything to tell her I'd take it.

"Oh, I'm not sure I can leave the restaurant. I mean, we just opened."

"Your father can watch it! I know he owns a successful business back in Ireland."

I was tempted to take her up. I knew my da and Eric would be able to handle the restaurant for a few days.

"Just think about it. We'll keep that weekend open for you."

"Thank you, Melanie."

Her face lit up. "Of course, my sweet girl! Now, go tell everyone to get into the dining room. Dinner is fixin' to be served."

I made my way through the kitchen and into the large family room. I loved hearing all the craziness coming from that room. Chloe was begging Mitchell to sing something from *Frozen*, while Gage was laughing. When I rounded the corner, me breath caught in my throat.

Cord was the one making Gage laugh hysterically. Me stomach dropped, and I instantly felt a throbbing heat between me legs.

Goodnight, nurse.

That man was so good looking. Hot didn't even begin to describe how handsome he was. I could see his ripped muscles through his shirt as he grabbed his little nephew, pulling him across the floor and back into his lap to tickle him. I didn't notice anyone else in the room, only him.

"He's good with Gage, isn't he?" Paxton asked, making me jump.

"Um, yes. Gage seems to really love his uncles and aunts."

Paxton's eyes were on me, but I didn't look at her. I'd told the girls I was going to move on and forget about my feelings for Cord, but Paxton had caught me staring. And when I say staring, I mean me tongue was practically on the floor.

Shite. I needed to be more careful with my ogling.

I faced Paxton. "Your ma said that dinner was about to be ready and for everyone to come sit down."

"Okay, I'll make the cattle call!"

We chuckled and I headed back to the kitchen to help Melanie. I felt so terrible for crashing their dinner, so much so that I was trying me best to help with whatever Melanie needed. I stopped in the hall, watching the Parker parents together.

"Oh man, sweetheart," John said, coming up behind Melanie and wrapping his arms around her. "It all smells so good."

Melanie lifted her head to look back at her husband. The way they held each other made me heart melt on the spot. It was beautiful how in love they were. For a few moments, they seemed lost in each other's eyes and me chest ached thinking about me own parents. I wanted a love like this someday. Not just wanted, *longed* for.

"They love each other very much."

His voice made the hairs on me neck stand and a tremble rushed through me entire body. I kept me eyes focused on Cord's parents while I answered. "You can see it with how they look at each other. It's beautiful."

"Do you need any help?"

Taking in a deep breath, I forced meself to look at him.

Ugh.

His deep blue eyes made me heart flutter, and when he smiled, me knees knocked together. They actually knocked together.

"*Hmm*, your eyes."

Squeezing mine shut tightly, I cursed myself for the slip-up and shook my head before looking at a smirking Cord.

"I mean, you can help getting ice for the drinks."

He lifted his chin and said, "Oh, *ice*."

I nodded. "Mm-hmm."

While Cord got a bucket of ice from the icemaker in the kitchen, I helped Melanie carry out the food. Harley and Amelia helped while everyone else got settled at the table. Waylynn had put Liberty down in a small portable playpen while Corina had Merit in a swing. Both babies were sleeping away.

A million and one conversations were going on at the table, and I loved it. It had always been just me, ma, and da for dinner. This was a nice change.

Cord had filled up everyone's glasses with ice and tea.

"Look at the birthday boy helping out!" Tripp teased as Cord walked the iced tea back into the kitchen.

"Oh, I just sat down. Maebh, will you grab the bread and butter, dear?" Melanie asked.

"Sure!" I said and headed into the kitchen. Cord came walking around the corner, and we ran right into each other. I let out an *oof* sound, the wind nearly knocked out of me.

"Sorry, Maebh. I was walking too fast."

"S'okay," I mumbled, trying to get me breath. How in the world did the man knock it right out of me? "It's like walking into a brick wall, though," I said, taking in a deep breath.

Cord lifted his arms and flexed, and I nearly dropped to my knees. He smirked a little. "Did you forget something?"

Me eyes raked over his body, and I didn't even care if he noticed. He was so nice to look at. It would give me a nice mental image for later when I was alone in me bed.

Cord stepped closer and brushed a piece of hair from me face.

"Why are you blushing, darling?"

I swallowed hard. Why was he calling me darling? It made me skin tingle from the tip of me toes to the top of me head. "It's warm in here and running back and forth from the kitchen and all."

He nodded and looked into me eyes like he knew I was handing him a line of bullshit.

I stepped away and his mouth dropped into a tight line.

"Your ma needs the bread and butter. I've got the bread, but not sure where she keeps your butter."

It took Cord a few seconds to acknowledge what I had said before he made his way across the kitchen to the refrigerator.

He held it up. "I've got it."

I laughed at the tub of Irish butter.

With a shake of his head, he smirked, "Grab the bread and let's eat."

CHAPTER 11

Cord

Her laugh made my chest squeeze. In a good way. A very fucking good way. I took a chance and glanced across the table at Maebh. Luck would have it, my mother made sure we were the last two to sit down and we were sitting directly across from one another.

"Maebh, spell your name!" Corina called out.

With a roll of her eyes, Maebh glared at Corina. "Why do you insist on having me spell me name all the time."

I couldn't help but smile. Damn that accent of hers. Because being beautiful wasn't enough, she had to add adorable on top of it. And innocent. Let's not forget the bomb Harley had dropped on me about Maebh being a virgin.

My eyes moved over her body, or what part of it I could see since she was sitting.

"M. A. E. B. Hache."

"No, it's H!" Waylynn chuckled.

Staring at Waylynn liked she'd lost her mind, Maebh teased her right back. "That's what I said, hache."

Jesus, I wanted her more than I'd ever wanted another woman in my entire life. The fact that she was a virgin and deserved someone who wasn't a whoring prick wasn't lost on me, but I didn't care. I was a greedy bastard.

Maebh smiled even bigger and turned her head. When our eyes met, her cheeks turned even pinker, and she glanced down to her plate.

"How's the restaurant doing, Maebh?" my father asked.

"It's amazing. We've had a steady crowd since opening night and have received some lovely reviews. The *Austin American Statesman* even gave us flying colors!"

The way she beamed made me sit up a little straighter. I was proud of her and amazed at the same time. I wanted to ask her why she'd picked America to open up an Irish restaurant and bar, and not Ireland.

"Your father owns a distillery in Ireland?" my father asked Maebh.

She nodded. "Yes, one of the biggest ones. He doesn't plan on staying in America full time. He loves Ireland too much."

"And you?" Mom asked, her brows hiked up almost to the middle of her forehead.

Maebh smiled gently. "I love it here. I love Ireland, too, but here I feel close to me ma, and I've fallen in love."

When she left her sentence dangling like that, the whole damn table leaned in and silently urged her to finish the sentence. Fallen in love with…

My heart was pounding as heat crept up my neck.

Who in the fuck had she fallen in love with? Jackson? The damn chef who was always hitting on her?

"You've fallen in love?" my mother asked, a tinge of hope in her voice.

"Oh! No, I mean, I've fallen in love…*with Texas*."

With a disappointed, "Oh," my mother dropped back in her chair.

"It's beautiful in the Texas hill country, isn't it?" Harley said.

Maebh nodded.

"Cord, you should take Maebh out on your motorcycle sometime and show her just how beautiful it is here." My mother stated.

My eyes snapped over to my mother. "Huh?"

"Wouldn't you love to do that, Maebh?"

"Mom," Steed said in a soft voice like he was gently trying to remind our mother to keep her nose out of everyone's business.

"Well, um, I've never been on a motorcycle before so I'm not sure I would enjoy it."

My mother grinned an evil smile. "Cord would make sure you were safe. Wouldn't you, sweetheart?"

Furrowing my brows, I glared at her. "What?"

"Sweet baby Jesus in heaven," Waylynn sighed. "Mom, not now."

"I think it would be fun. You should hurry and eat. Then take her for a ride."

I nearly choked on my own spit as Trevor lost it laughing, and Maebh glanced down at her hands that were now in her lap.

"What?" I cried out.

Looking at me like I was ruining her grand plan, my mother shook her head. "Why do you keep saying what?"

"Why do you keep talking?" I asked as my father let out a chuckle that earned him a dirty look from my mother.

"I'm just saying, I think you and Maebh should—"

I don't know why I did it, but I blurted out, "Harley's pregnant!"

That's a lie; I knew why I did it. I needed the heat off of me. It was better than shouting "Maebh's a virgin so stop pushing me on her." Harley and Tripp would forgive me. At least, I thought they would. Maebh would never forgive me.

"Cord!" Harley gasped as Tripp kicked me so hard I nearly screamed like a little girl.

"You asshole!" Tripp growled.

My mother looked at Harley and tears formed in her eyes. "Is this true?"

Harley looked over to Amelia and then Paxton. Fear was all over her face.

"Amelia's book is being turned into a movie!" Harley shouted.

"Hey!" Amelia cried out as everyone gasped.

"Oh. My. Gawd! What!" My mother screamed as she jumped up. She waved her hands all about and faced Harley. "You're pregnant?"

She smiled and nodded. "We wanted to wait a bit longer before we told anyone," Harley said, looking my way and throwing me a death stare before focusing on my parents with a huge smile. It wasn't long before my father and mother were hugging both Harley and Tripp and then Amelia.

The rest of the family followed, congratulating Harley and Tripp, as well as Amelia. Even Maebh congratulated them, although I got the distinct feeling she already knew about the baby *and* the movie deal. By the time the family was finished making the rounds, I glanced around for Maebh but she was nowhere to be found.

"Everyone, sit! I've got chocolate cheesecake for the birthday boy! What a beautiful day this has turned out to be!"

I was happy my mother was over the moon. I was even happier that her attention had been diverted from me and Maebh. Today had always been such a struggle for my mom. Fighting to celebrate my birthday and dealing with it being her father's birthday, as well.

I leaned over and asked Tripp, "Did you see where Maebh went?"

He glared.

"Come on, cut me some slack. Mom was killing me! Besides, your wife threw our sister under the bus just as fast."

The corner of Tripp's mouth twitched. "That was sort of fun seeing you nearly choke on your own tongue. Especially the comment about you riding her. You fucking wish."

I blew out a frustrated breath. "Tripp, where's Maebh?"

"She walked into the kitchen," Tripp answered with a sigh.

Pushing my chair back, I tried to stand, but Mom brought out the cheesecake and started to sing happy birthday. Everyone joined in, and I felt someone's eyes on me.

With a quick glance over my mother's shoulder, I saw Maebh standing there, singing along, a forced smile on her face.

When my mother set the cheesecake in front of me, it had one big candle in the middle. She was never one to put the exact number of candles on your birthday cake. It was always one and she insisted you had to make a wish.

"Make a wish!" she demanded.

Closing my eyes, I made a wish and blew out the candle.

When I looked back to where Maebh had been standing, my heart sank. She was gone.

My wish had just walked out the door, and I couldn't get up fast enough to go find her.

"Do you want to cut the cake, Cord?" my mother asked.

I shook my head. "You do it. I'll be right back."

I made my way into the kitchen and looked around. Out the window I saw Maebh walking toward the swings my father had put up last fall for Chloe and Gage.

When I reached for the door handle I had to laugh. So much for my wish of giving me strength to stay *away* from Maebh. I was drawn to her even more. A moth to a damn flame.

This birthday was really starting to suck ass.

I made my way over to her, trying to make noise since so I didn't scare her.

She pushed lightly off the ground and swung, not hearing me approach. When she dropped her head and body back and lifted her legs, I stopped. I watched as she swung on the swing, and I had no idea why I thought that freedom, that joy on her face in that moment was the sexiest thing I'd ever seen in my life. She looked so carefree and relaxed. Like she didn't have a worry in the world.

I knew that wasn't true. I'd seen how tired and stressed she was. Her restaurant hadn't been open long, and I overheard her telling my parents it was doing much better than she had anticipated. I was honest to God happy for her. And I hadn't seen a dip in my own sales the entire time Aisling was open. As a matter of fact, our sales had increased. My guess was Maebh's restaurant was bringing in new people for dinner and drinks, and they were ending the night at my bar.

"Maebh?" I said, making her sit up and stop swinging. She spun on the seat and looked at me.

"Cord? Is everything okay?" she asked.

With a nod, I made my way to the other swing and sat down. She was still sitting with the chains twisted.

"I never wished you a happy birthday," she said.

"Thank you. And thank you for coming. I enjoyed having you here with the family."

She gave me a sweet grin.

"Race to see who can get higher the fastest?"

She giggled. "I think you'll win. Your legs are bigger and stronger."

"Chicken?"

Her brow lifted. "Hardly, I simply know when I can't win."

My smile faltered at the double meaning behind her comment. I offered, "I'll give you a head start. Ten seconds."

"I guess that sounds fair."

Maebh walked back as far as she could, took a running start. She jumped on the swing and started pumping her legs and pulling with her arms. She got high pretty fast.

"Ten!" I shouted as I pretty much did the same thing. We were neck and neck, and for some reason I couldn't get any higher. Maybe I wasn't trying harder because I didn't want this to end. I hadn't laughed this much in a long time. The last time I was on a swing, Savannah Hughes was wrapped around me, fucking the shit out of me.

The memory tainted the moment, and I started to slow down. Guilt ripped through my body.

Maebh laughed harder. "Giving up, Parker?"

"I guess my legs aren't in the shape I thought they were."

She scoffed. "I think you gave up to let me win."

"Maybe," I replied, seeing the blush on her cheeks even in the moonlight.

Fuck, I loved seeing her face flushed. I wanted to see it like that when I fucked her.

I closed my eyes and cursed myself. Maebh was the type of girl who deserved more than a one-night fucking. A man should make love to her. I don't think I'd ever once made actual love to a woman. Hell, half the time I took them from behind just so I could fuck them as fast and as hard as I could.

Prick.

"What?" she asked.

My head jerked toward hers. *Shit, did I say that out loud?* "What?"

"Did you just call yourself a prick?"

I smiled big. "Maybe you thought it in your head."

She frowned. "No, you said it."

I shrugged, trying to blow off my blunder.

We sat for a few minutes in silence, barely swinging.

"So, you have a motorcycle?" Maebh asked.

"Yep," I replied, giving her a sexy grin.

"I've always wanted to have sex on a motorcycle."

My entire world stopped. My breathing stopped. My heartbeat stopped. My fucking brain stopped. The only goddamn thing that worked was my cock. And right about now it wanted to make that wish come true for her.

"W-what?"

She chuckled and shook her head. "Sorry. That wasn't a very ladylike thing to say. I've just never met anyone with a bike before. Have you…you know?"

My head tilted. I wanted to hear her say it again so damn bad. "Have I what?"

Her face looked so adorable as she scrunched her nose. "You know!"

"No. I don't know. You're going to have to spell it out for me, Maebh."

"Have you…*done it* on your bike?"

Jesus, why are you being so cruel.

"Done what on my bike?" I asked with the biggest shit-eating grin on my face, more turned on than I'd been when I kissed her.

She covered her face and issued a loud groan. "Have you had sex on your motorcycle before?"

"No. I've never fucked a girl on my bike." But my God, if she wanted that right now, I'd part the fucking seas to make her wish come true.

Her brows pulled together before she went back to barely swinging. "How come?"

Christ Almighty. Was I having this conversation with the only woman I'd ever had reoccurring dreams about? The only woman I wanted more than air? The one woman I couldn't allow myself to take because I wasn't worthy of her?

"I guess I've never found the girl I wanted to fuck on my bike."

"Are you always so crude when describing sex?"

"Yes. Because that's what I do, Maebh. I fuck."

Her mouth fell open a little before her tongue made an achingly slow swipe across her lips. My cock was painfully hard and jumped when her teeth sank into that pretty pink lip of hers.

"I'm sure your family is missing you in the house," she finally said, breaking our intense stare.

That was my signal that she no longer wanted to talk. Maybe I'd scared her off with my blunt words. I got the feeling Maebh wasn't the type to want a guy to whisper how much he wanted to sink his cock into her pussy. More like the type who wanted a man to whisper sweet nothings and make slow, passionate love to her.

I wish I could test my theory.

"Does it bother you when I use the word fuck?"

She shook her head, and what she did next shocked the living shit out of me.

Maebh stood in front of me. With a steady face, she replied, "Just the opposite, Cord. It turns me on."

My pulse shot off like a rocket as I watched Maebh give me a sexy little smile then head back toward the house.

Had I heard her right? Her accent was known to throw me off. Did she just say I turned her on? My dick pressed against my jeans even harder.

Scrubbing my hands down my face, I mumbled, "Fucking hell. It's going to be a long night."

My phone vibrated, and I glanced down to see it was Tammy. I picked up.

"Hey, I know it's your birthday and you're with family, but I need you to come to the bar."

"What's wrong?"

"One of the draft beers is stuck."

"Stuck?"

"Nothing is flowing out, and I've tried everything I could think of. It's the Belhaven."

"Shit," I grumbled as I headed back to the house. That was one of our best-selling beers, and I wanted it to be fixed before tonight. "I'm on my way."

"Sorry, Cord," Tammy said, her voice filled with regret for having to call me in.

I made my way back into the dining room where everyone was still going on about Harley and Tripp's good news, or asking Amelia a million questions about her book being made into a movie.

I walked up to Amelia first.

"Hey, sis. I'm so proud of you. I know I said it earlier, but I really am."

She leaned up to kiss me on the cheek. "Thanks, Cord. It's all still up in the air what I'm going to do, but I'll figure it out."

"I wish I could hang around and ask you about it, but Tammy has an emergency at the bar."

Amelia frowned, and I pulled back. "What's wrong?"

With a shake of her head, she smiled. "I just hope you don't end up working on your birthday."

I winked. "Aww, it's not so bad. I do need to talk to you later, though."

Her brow quirked. "Oh? Why?"

My eyes lifted, and I looked right at Maebh. "I'm a little curious about why you brought Maebh."

Her hands went to her hips. "I brought her because she's my friend. Not just mine, but Paxton's, Harley's, Corina's, and Waylynn's. We like her and want her to feel welcome here. Unlike you."

I pushed my fingers through my hair. "Knock it off. That's not true. I do want her here. I mean, I want y'all to be friends with her. I mean…shit. Listen, I can't argue with you about this. I've got to run. I love you."

Her face softened. "I love you more, Cord."

After making the rounds and thanking everyone for coming, I glanced in the direction of Maebh and said, "See ya around, Maebh."

She smiled and my stomach jumped.

Fuck me, was that another wink?

Leaning down to kiss my mother, I said, "Thank you so much. I'm so sorry I have to leave."

"It's okay! We love you and enjoy the rest of your birthday."

My father reached a hand out, shook mine, then pulled me in for a quick hug.

"Have a good night, son. Behave."

I laughed. "There's no fun in that, Dad."

When I turned around, Maebh was looking at me with pinched brows. I knew she'd taken my words the wrong way, but I didn't have time to explain. I needed to get to the bar.

CHAPTER 120

Maebh

"How was the birthday dinner?" me father asked as I made me way over to him. He was sitting in the lounge with a glass of whiskey in hand.

"Nice. The Parker family is incredible. Makes me wish you and ma had more kids."

Me da laughed. "Lord, we could hardly handle you!"

The heat in me cheeks made me press me hands to them.

"Get a drink and join me, Maebh. It's your day off. You shouldn't even be here."

I kissed his forehead before walking over to the bar and stepping behind it. Jeffery was working this evening, and he moved to the side and let me pour my own drink. I paused when I overheard a conversation between two patrons at the bar.

"Seriously, you think Cord and Tammy are hooking up?"

My eyes shot up, and I looked at the two women sitting at the bar. I'd recognized them right away and instantly knew they were waitresses at Cord's Place.

"I mean, she calls him back to the bar with some *lame* excuse that the draft beer is clogged up and when he gets there nothing is wrong. Then they went back to his office to do what? Talk about the bar? Don't be stupid."

The other girl frowned, and I tried to act busy as I listened to them.

"I don't know, June. Cord doesn't even flirt with any of us. None of his employees. I find it hard to believe he'd be screwing the manager of the place."

"Tell me you don't see the way Tammy stares at Cord. What about the night we all went out, and she got drunk, said her life's mission was to ride Cord Parker's..."

Her voice lowered and I leaned in enough to hear her say, "Cock."

I jerked back like I'd been slapped across the face.

Spinning on my heels, I headed over to my father. I sat down and drank the shot of whiskey.

"Well, okay. So much for taking a moment to enjoy it."

"I needed it more than I thought."

"Get out of here, half pint. Everything is fine. Enjoy your evening."

Forcing a smile, I nodded. "You're right. A nice hot bath will make me feel better."

He nodded. "Go, now."

"Night, da."

"Night, half pint."

I walked back to the bar. The two girls were still there, but now they were joined by two men. They were all dressed up, and I overheard one mention dinner reservations.

"Jeffery, do you need anything?"

He glanced at me and shook his head. "I've got it covered, Ms. O'Sullivan."

"Maebh. Please call me Maebh."

"Maebh," he replied, his smile grew bigger. He quickly swept his eyes over me body before turning back to what he was doing.

Ignoring it, I made me way to me place and started me bath. A long hot soak would do me wonders.

As I laid in the lavender-scented water, I couldn't shake what the two waitresses were talking about. Tammy had been with Cord at the dinner and then they came to the opening of the restaurant together.

I squeezed my eyes shut.

He kissed *me*, though. But maybe he also kissed her a time or two.

Laughing, I shook my head. Why in the world would it surprise me that a man like Cord would kiss me, but still have a causal relationship on the side?

I dropped into the bath and went underwater for a few seconds before coming back up.

When me head popped out of the water, me phone went off.

Reaching for it, I nearly dropped it when I saw his name.

Cord: *Amelia said you went home. Are you in for the night?*

Me heart raced. Why was he asking me if I was in for the night? Did he want me to come to the bar?

Trying not to shake too much, I decided I would tell him I was in for the night. After all, I'd just dunked me entire head under water and wasn't in the mood to primp myself up.

Me: *Why? Did you have something in mind?*

I groaned. Me reply had completely negated what I'd just told meself. This man was me weakness.

It didn't take him long to reply.

Cord: *I'm on my rooftop, and I've discovered a path directly to your rooftop.*

There was no way I could hide me smile. What in the world did he mean he found a path? I wasn't going to bite though. The conversation I had overheard earlier was still bothering me.

Me: *I'm at the bar, with me father... Sorry.*

I wasn't sure I could take anymore of Cord Parker tonight. He'd probably finished shagging his manager and thought he could get some action from me next.

Cord: *Really? Because you left the blinds up in your bathroom, and I'm looking at you soaking in a bath right now, your hair's all wet. I have to admit, I'm slightly jealous I'm not in there with you.*

Me heart dropped to me stomach as I stared at the text. I must have read it five times before me head popped up, and I looked out the window. Right into Cord's eyes.

Sitting on one of the small tables with his feet on a chair was Cord. He had on a cowboy hat and a smile that made me insides quiver.

"Oh, holy shite."

Cord lifted his hand and waved.

I snarled at him. "Little fecker!"

His head dropped back, and he laughed like he'd just seen the funniest thing ever. As if he'd just picked up the art of lip reading.

Fine, if he wanted to play this little game, I was going to give him something to look at.

I stood and when he looked back at me, his smile dropped as he stared at me naked body like it was the first time he'd ever seen a naked woman. It felt wonderful to see his eyes rake over me. I wasn't the least bit embarrassed. This was not something I would normally do, but when Cord Parker was involved all sense went out the door.

Taking me time, I stepped out of the bath. I wanted desperately to look back at him, but I didn't as I walked across the room and reached for the robe. I turned and nearly laughed me ass off when he leaned over to get a better look and missed the edge of the table with his hand. He fell right off with a thud.

"That's what you get, you arse!"

I dropped the robe onto my arms and wrapped it around me body as I made me way to the door that led out to the rooftop.

Cord stopped me before I could step out. I glared at him.

"You pervert!" I shouted.

"Pervert? You're the one taking a bath with your damn blinds open. What the fuck, Maebh? Anyone could look up here and see you. That shit needs to be shut when you're in there naked."

It was like his words reminded him of what he had seen only moments ago. A hungry look came over his eyes.

"I'm on the top floor. Who would be looking in?"

Cord snapped out of it and pointed to the buildings across the square. "Anyone can look with binoculars at you, Maebh. It's dangerous."

Me eyes darted past him to the buildings. Wrapping me arms around me body I suddenly felt like people were staring. It was the first time I'd thought about the other buildings and people living over there.

"Shite."

"Yeah, and I think that means shit."

Me gaze darted back to him. "How did you get over here?"

He shrugged. "I walked across all the roofs. The little barrier walls are short so you can climb over them."

I looked over and saw what he was talking about. "Why are you here and not with Tammy?"

Cord's brows pulled tightly. "Tammy? Why would I be with Tammy?"

Me head dropped to the floor, and I shrugged. I was feeling silly for being upset. It wasn't like Cord was mine.

I felt his body heat and looked up. Cord was standing directly in front of me.

"Why did you think I was with Tammy?" he softly asked.

"I overheard a couple girls who work for you. They said you went into your office with her to…you know."

A slow smile made the corner of his mouth rise up in a sexy way. Me insides warmed when I should have been angry.

"You can stand and show me your naked body, but you can't say something about sex. Why?"

There was no way I was going to tell Cord he made me a nervous wreck when it came to sex.

"They said she called you back to the bar for a nonexistent problem and that you both went into your office. Then they said she wanted to ride your cock and was making it her life's goal."

Cord's eyes widened, and he took a few steps back. "What the fuck? Who said that?"

I shrugged. "I don't know who they were, but they work for you."

"That's fucking bullshit. Tammy is a professional and nothing has or ever will happen between us."

I was hoping me body didn't let him know how happy I was with that statement.

Cord's anger disappeared, and he took a few steps closer, making me take a few back.

"My sweet little Maebh. Were you jealous?"

With a scoff, I said, "First off, Mr. Parker, I'm not your little *anything*, and I wasn't jealous. Hardly."

"Then why did you lie and say you were with your father when you were really soaking in a bath?"

His eyes swept over me again. And I realized I was standing in front of him with wet hair and probably smeared makeup.

For feck's sake. I groaned to meself for being so stupid.

His ocean blue eyes were looking into my green, and I felt like he was going to drown me with the intensity of his stare.

"I was...tired."

His brow quirked. "Tired?"

"Yes."

Cord took another step toward me. "Let me ask you something. If I told you the moment I saw your naked body I wanted to be inside you more than I've ever wanted anything in my entire life, would you believe me? Would it turn you on enough to do something about it?"

I swallowed hard and lifted my chin in defiance. I wasn't going to let him get to me. "I'd say you were lying."

"Why?" he asked, lifting his hand and brushing his fingers over the exposed area of me shoulder where me robe wasn't all the way on. I gasped at his touch and fought to breathe. It appeared Cord had a similar reaction to our touch.

"I'm a simple girl. I see the women you've been with. I can't compete with that level of your playing field when I'm not even at the same game as them."

Cord frowned, a pained look moving across his face. "What?"

I took a step back into the room, breaking his contact with me. "I think you should leave, Cord."

"Maebh, you're *nothing* like those women."

Tears filled my eyes as I looked back at him. "Please leave."

He shook his head. "Wait, what I mean is you're the most beautiful woman I've ever seen."

"You only want me because you think you can't have me. I'm a challenge."

A slow smile appeared on his face. I held my breath realizing the mistake I'd just made.

"Why can't I have you, Maebh? Do you not want me?"

Oh, shite. Why did he have to ask that?

"N-no."

He took a step closer.

"Liar."

Me chest heaved as Cord's hands cupped me face. "I think you want me as much as I want you."

I shook me head and was about to push him away when he slid his hands into me wet hair and pulled me head back slightly. I'd never had a man touch me in such an aggressive, yet sexy way. I liked it more than I wanted to admit.

"Knowing you're naked under this robe is driving me fucking nuts. And what I saw under that robe in all of its beauty just a few moments ago is making me hard as stone."

"Cord," I panted, trying to get me senses back. It felt like the air was changing around us. It was warm and crackling with energy I'd never experienced before.

"I want to slip my hand under your robe and make you come on my fingers. Will you let me do that to you, *agra*?"

Me head dropped back and me eyes closed. Cord had said *agra* again. Was he calling me sweetheart or did he realize it also meant love? Me world spun, and I was beginning to lose whatever control I had left.

"Baby, will you let me touch you? I'm fucking dying to touch you. I need to touch you."

When I felt his fingers on the top of my thigh, I jumped. He moved his fingers up, and I almost let him before I forced meself to wake up from the Cord-induced coma I was slipping into.

"No," I whispered, and Cord stopped.

"No?" he asked, his voice pained.

Using what energy I had left, I placed my hands on his massive chest. I wanted to dig me fingers into his body, but I pushed him away slightly.

Cord took a few steps back and stared. Pained disbelief marred his features.

"I'm not like those women who let you shag them and walk away."

"Maebh, I—"

Me eyes burned with tears. "I want a man who wants to court me. Who makes me feel like he wants me not only for me body, but for me heart as well."

Me words choked out. Cord made me so emotional.

His eyes widened.

Me chin trembled. "You're not that man. You want me because you can't have me the way you normally do with other women."

He took a step closer. "That's not true."

Cord looked panicked. I was telling him something he didn't want to hear.

Me eyes filled with tears as the truth of how I felt about Cord hit me right in me heart. "I do want you, Cord, more than you know. But I wish you'd told me you wanted to kiss me...not fuck me with your fingers while I stand here at your mercy. I have no idea what you'll do to me body, much less me heart, if I let you have your way with me."

His eyes closed while his head dropped. He took a few deep breaths before looking at me.

"Fuck, Maebh. I'm not used to feeling this way about a woman. I don't know how to *court* someone. I've never dated a girl before, and this is confusing as fuck."

I wiped me tears away, and he stood, probably as close as he thought I'd let him stand.

"Christ, please don't cry. I didn't mean to make you feel that way. I'd *never* want to make you cry. Ever. You drive me so fucking crazy with these feelings. I think I'm losing my mind."

A small laugh slipped from me lips as Cord rested his forehead against mine.

"I don't mean to drive you crazy," I whispered.

He barely smiled. "I know you don't, but you do and I don't think you even realize it."

Lifting me arms, I wrapped them around his neck, letting our bodies press together.

"You scare me, Cord Parker."

Cord drew in a deep breath and replied, "You scare me a helluva lot more, Maebh O' Sullivan."

CHAPTER 13

Cord

The moment she wrapped her arms around me, I nearly died. She was naked under her robe, and she had no idea how close I was to pulling that robe open and showing her exactly how insane I was for her. I'd never wanted a woman like this before. And it wasn't just wanting to fuck her and then stroll on back to my place. I wanted to make love to her. Slowly. Learn every single thing that made her body come to life. Make her come in more ways than she could count. Be the first man inside her, make her mine.

My dick was getting hard again, just thinking about it.

Christ. Stop thinking, Cord.

I wrapped my arms around her tighter, not wanting to let her go. Something about having her in my arms blew my damn mind. It felt…like home.

Perfect. Content. Happy. And horny as hell.

"Maebh?" I softly asked.

"*Mmm?*"

I smiled because I imagined she felt the same way I did. Content in my arms.

"Will you be patient with me? I've never done this before, but I know I could never walk away from you. Something happened when I first saw you. I haven't been myself since that first day you smiled at me."

She dropped her arms and drew her head back. Our eyes met, and she smiled.

"You mean…you want to date me?"

Why did she find that so hard to believe?

"I want to get to know you…all of you…but I promise to go slow and not do anything you don't want to do until you're ready."

Maebh worried her lip. I pulled it from between her teeth with my thumb. "Talk to me, baby."

She swallowed hard and cleared her throat. "I need to tell you something that might make you, um… It might make you change your mind about me."

Already knowing what she was going to say, I prepared myself for the answer she deserved.

"Tell me," I whispered.

Panic washed over her face before she dropped her gaze. "I'm a virgin. I know it's old-fashioned, but I was saving meself for a man who made me feel things I'd never felt before. A man who made me want to live in the moment and take me to places I never dared dream I would go. I wanted to be sure if I gave meself to someone, he would deserve every touch, every whisper, every part of me."

My heart felt like it was slamming against the wall of my chest. Placing my finger on her chin, I lifted her face so that her eyes were looking into mine.

"And you think I'm that man?"

Her lips pressed together before she softly replied, "Yes and no, but more yes. Me mind is all over the place about you."

My head was spinning. How in the hell did this amazingly beautiful woman think I was the one to get something she held so close? I'm the type of guy who's more comfortable dancing with the devil, and Maebh is an Irish angel so far out my league it was unreal.

"I don't deserve you," I mumbled, knowing that every word was true. I didn't deserve her, but hell if I wasn't going to do everything in my power to change that.

Her eyes widened.

"If you do decide to give yourself to me, I swear to God I'll treasure you and prove that I am worthy of you for as long as you'll have me."

The corners of her mouth rose into a beautiful smile. "What do we do from here?"

"First thing I have to do is kiss you."

She giggled, and it felt amazing. I felt like we'd just went through hell and came out the other side, a little battered, a lot bruised, but both victors.

"Alright. Kiss me, then."

When I smiled she leaned against me, like my smile made her legs weak.

Sliding my hands into her hair, I pulled back slightly, lifting her mouth so I could look at it.

"You're so beautiful, Maebh."

Her eyes fluttered closed and her mouth parted open, a silent gesture to claim it.

"So fucking beautiful."

As I brushed my lips over hers, she let out a slight moan and then whispered, "Cord."

I smiled when my name fell from her lips. I wanted to hear that every single day for the rest of my life and that revelation scared the piss out of me.

"My beautiful Irish cailin."

Maebh melted as I pressed my mouth to hers. I was instantly hit with the smell of lavender and it made me relax into the kiss even more. It started off tender, slow and meaningful as we explored each other. Maebh's soft lips had me letting out a moan of my own, which made her grip onto my arms tightly. I'd never in my life experienced such a sensuous kiss. My hand dropped from her hair to the middle of her back, and I pulled her closer. Our tongues moved faster, the moans grew louder, and the kissing got more intense. My pulse was racing, and we both pulled back at the same time, chests heaving in an attempt to pull in much-needed air.

Our eyes met, and Maebh pressed her fingers to her swollen lips.

"That was the most amazing shift of my life."

My brows pulled in tightly. "Shift?"

Her eyes closed. "Kiss. I've never…that was…wow. You make me live in the moment, Cord, and that both thrills and scares me."

Smiling, I kissed her again. This time wasn't so slow. Maebh's hands moved over my body while mine did the same to her. Slipping to her perfect ass, I squeezed it hard, making Maebh gasp into my mouth.

Her hand was under my T-shirt, running her fingers over my skin, leaving me aching for more. Lifting her leg with my hand, I felt her skin and nearly came undone when she wrapped her leg it around mine. If we didn't stop soon, I was going to be begging for more. Knowing she was naked under her robe was driving me insane and I only had so much willpower.

"Maebh, baby, we have to stop or I'm going to rip that robe off and lick your pussy," I whispered against her lips.

"Oh God," she whimpered.

"Has anyone ever done that to you?" I asked, looking into her eyes. They were glassy like she was drunk from our kisses. It made me feel so fucking good to know I made her feel this way.

She shook her head.

With a slow smile, I ran my nose along her jaw and kissed her neck.

"I can't wait to taste you and make you mine. To know that my tongue will be the only one that's tasted you is such a fucking turn on, Maebh."

Her head dropped back, and she moaned. I knew if I didn't stop things, we'd go too far, and I didn't want her to regret anything. Stepping back, I broke our connection. Maebh stood with her arms wrapped around her body, holding her robe shut as she took one deep breath after another.

"I better go."

Maebh didn't respond; she nodded. When her gaze fell to the large bulge in the front of my jeans, she went to say something but stopped before lifting her eyes to mine.

"What about… Will you…?"

She looked worried. Like if we left things like this, I'd run off and find someone else to take care of my hard-on. I hated that she thought of me that way.

"A shower and a handful of baby oil will be waiting for me at home."

Her cheeks flushed, and she smiled.

"Go in, and shut your damn blinds in your bathroom, then text me when you get into bed."

Nodding, she replied, "Alright."

When she looked at my cock again, I lifted her chin so we were staring at one another. "I'm leaving you exactly the way you're leaving me. Stop worrying, okay?"

"I'll try."

Kissing her quickly, I made it over the walls and across the roof until I was back at my place. First thing I did was strip down, get in the shower, and jack myself off while pulling up the memory of Maebh naked in her bathroom. I came so hard I cried out her name, then leaned against the wall, panting.

I had a feeling I was going to be taking a lot of showers until I made Maebh mine.

Standing behind the bar, I shook my head. "I don't know if I should leave."

Trevor groaned. "Not again. The bar will be fine! Tammy knows what in the hell she's doing, and I'll be here. I already told Wade to expect me to be away from the ranch the next few days."

I was getting ready to leave for my parents' lake house for four days. Four days I'd be away from the bar and Maebh. Two nights ago I'd held her in my arms and kissed her like she was the last woman I'd ever kiss. Then I'd promised her something I'd never promised another woman in my entire life.

Me. Exclusively.

"Did you tell Maebh you were heading out of town?" Trevor asked, pouring himself a Coke and then adding a bit of rum into it.

"Not yet. Dude, it's only seven in the morning. What the fuck are you doing adding rum to your Coke?"

He rolled his eyes. "Trust me, I need it."

I quirked a brow up in question. "What's going on?"

He shook his head. "Nothing. I made a mistake, and I'm not sure what to do about it."

"What kind of mistake? Not the 'oh God, I think I'm late' type of mistake I hope."

Trevor laughed. "Nothing to worry about. Listen, go get your head clear and figure this shit out. I see the way you look at her, Cord. You like this girl. A lot."

My hand pushed through my hair. "Yeah, I do. Scares the shit out of me."

Trevor looked like he knew *exactly* what I was talking about. I wanted to ask him more about Scarlett, but I knew he would shut me out. Like I'd done before when it came to Maebh.

"Have you seen her since the other night?"

I shook my head. "No. The last couple of days have been insane with me getting ready to leave town. Maebh's been busy as well. We've talked on the phone, and I ran over there for lunch yesterday."

Honestly, I was worried what might go through Maebh's mind when I told her I was heading out of town. Would she think I was running? Or worse, going with another woman? Maybe I should invite her to go with me?

Fuck. I had no clue what in the hell I was doing. I felt like I was damned if I did and damned if I didn't.

Trevor shot me a smirk. "You know when Steed, Mitchell, and Tripp find out, you're going to catch hell."

I rolled my eyes. "Believe me, I know."

He laughed hard. "Prepare for another shirt."

Groaning, I closed my eyes and tried not to think about it. I knew my brothers, and once they found out I'd been bitten by whatever the fuck this was, they would give me hell.

My phone buzzed in my pocket with a text message.

Maebh: *Are you free for a quick breakfast?*

The way my stomach dropped at the sight of her name shouldn't have surprised me. But it did.

"Damn."

"What's wrong?"

"Maebh asked if I was free for breakfast. I guess it's now or never that I tell her I've got plans this weekend."

Trevor grabbed my arm. "Dude! Do you want her to think you're spending it with another woman?"

"No."

"Then don't tell her you have plans. Shit, you'll make her think you're going with someone else."

I frowned. "Then what in the hell do I tell her?"

"The truth. You're going up to our folks' place to take a much-needed weekend away."

"Maybe I should ask her to go with me?"

Trevor gave me a horrified look. "What? Y'all are just getting started with the whole dating thing and you want to take her away over the weekend? What the hell is wrong with you?"

I shrugged. "What's wrong with that? I want to be with her. Get to know her better."

He shook his head. "Might as well put a ring on her finger."

My heart dropped. Maybe he was right. We needed to date before I started talking about taking her away for long weekends. Drawing in a deep breath, I hit her number and called her.

"Hello?"

I smiled when I heard her voice. "Hey, it's Cord."

"A phone call, huh? This must mean bad news."

I chuckled. "Not at all. Listen, I'd love to have breakfast with you, but I'm heading out of town for the weekend."

"Oh?"

That was all she said.

Oh.

What did that mean? Was that an '*Oh! I'm happy you're getting away*' or was it an '*Oh, who are you going out of town with*' comment?

"I'm sorry. I was about to call you and let you know I was heading out of town, but if you want me to stay, we can meet for breakfast."

"That's alright." I could practically hear the smile in her voice. "I don't want to interrupt your plans. I'm actually heading out of town meself and wasn't sure how to tell you. With everything that happened the other night, I didn't want you to think I was avoiding you if I didn't answer a call or text, but I had the holiday planned before the other night."

"Really? You're going out of town, too? Alone?"

She laughed. "Yes! Are you going alone?"

"Just me and some fishing poles. I've needed the time away. Where are you going?"

"It's funny you should ask because I'm heading to your…"

"Cord! Cord!"

Screaming came from the back supply closet.

"Is everything okay?" Maebh asked

"I've got to run, baby. I'll text you when I'm leaving and call you when I get to the lake house."

"Lake house?"

"Cord!" Tammy screamed again.

"I've got to go. Something just happened to Tammy. Please be careful and let me know when you get there."

"Um, yes. Of course."

"Talk soon, my beautiful Irish cailin."

"Bye, Cord."

Her voice was soft and sweet, and I hated hanging up. As I raced back to the storage room, on the heels of Trevor, I hit End and pushed my phone into my pocket.

We got to the storage room, and my heart about jumped out of my damn chest.

"What happened?"

Tammy was lying on the floor holding onto her ankle.

"I fell trying to reach that case of club soda."

Trevor rushed to Tammy and looked at her ankle.

"It's not swelling up, so you didn't break it."

"Thank goodness. It sure hurts though," Tammy stated.

"That's it. I'm not leaving," I said, letting out a frustrated breath. Hell, Tammy wasn't even supposed to be here this early and had only come in because I was leaving town.

"Bullshit, you're leaving," Trevor said. "Tammy's fine. I've seen plenty of broken and sprained ankles. Her ankle isn't even swelling. I'm sure she twisted it, and that's all."

Tammy looked at Trevor and then back to me. "He's right, Cord. It just scared me. I thought the case was going to fall and land on me. I panicked."

I moved around and grabbed the case before it could fall.

Trevor helped Tammy up. "Dude, it's fine. Even if she did hurt her ankle, I can run this bar. I did it when you went to Vegas."

Vegas.

I shuddered at the memory and the hook-up from that weekend. My past hook-ups were starting to bother me, and I knew it was because of Maebh. The last thing I'd ever really want was for her to know exactly how much of a manwhore I'd been my entire life.

A thought hit me. Was I ready…or even able…to make a commitment to Maebh? I knew I wanted like hell to try.

Maybe I should see where Maebh is going for the weekend and go with her?

Fuck. I'd never been so confused. I wanted to call Maebh and ask her where she was going. Would she even agree to go somewhere with me? Trevor must have seen the wheels spinning in my head. He walked over while Laney helped Tammy out of the storage room.

"You need the break from here, Cord. And what a better way to test this whole *you want to commit to one woman thing* out than to be around a bunch of hot women in bikinis."

I laughed as I rubbed the back of my neck. "You're right. You sure you got this?"

He slapped me on the side of my arm.

"I got this. Just go fish and don't worry about anything."

Placing my hand on his shoulder, I gave it a squeeze. "Thanks, man. You know I'm here if you need to talk."

He nodded. "I know, dude. I know."

Trevor headed out to the main bar while I went to my office and grabbed the bag I'd packed for this weekend. Only the bare essentials. I planned to either sit around and watch movies, or float on the lake and fish.

It was going to be heaven.

As I walked to my truck, it felt like a piece of my heaven was going to be missing, though.

My Irish angel isn't going to be there…

CHAPTER 14

maebh

"Stupid phone!" I shouted as I pulled into a store and parked in the supermarket lot.

The address was right, so why was my phone telling me to go a different way than the directions Melanie had sent?

With a sigh, I mumbled, "Might as well get some petrol and a snack."

After filling up the tank, I headed into the store and looked at the minerals. After deciding on Diet Pepsi, I grabbed a bag of crisps and headed to the check out.

"He was so dreamy!" the young girl gushed. I couldn't help but smile at how silly they were being. Oh, to be a teenager again.

"Dreamy wasn't the word. He was hot! Did you see him smile at me?"

"Sounds like you ladies found yourself a handsome lad."

They both grinned. "He was!"

I nodded me head and handed the girl the cash to pay for me goods.

"Did you get his number?" I asked with a smile.

"Nah. He was older than us and was trying to call his girl-friend."

"Or just a friend!" the other girl interjected with hope in her eyes.

"Nah, it was his girlfriend. You should have seen the way his eyes lit up when her voicemail came on. He's smitten!"

All three of us giggled.

As I walked to my car, me phone buzzed, and I had voicemail from Cord. Grinning just like those two girls, I pulled up the message the moment I got back in me car.

"Hey. I'm almost here. My signal...not so...these hills...call back...answer, keep trying. I should...asked you....here...talk..."

Me brows furrowed. The message had gone in and out, and I'd only gotten bits and pieces. I thought he said he was going to a lake? Now he's going to the hills? What hills?

I had to admit, a small part of me was hoping he was heading to his parents' house to surprise me. What were the odds we were both heading out of town this weekend and both going to a lake house?

Hitting his number, it went straight to voicemail. I left a message and pulled up the directions on my phone again. It appeared I was less than ten minutes away.

Soon I was pulling up to a driveway with a large iron gate.

"Holy shite," I whispered as I punched in the gate code Melanie had given me. The drive was long and winding, but when I finally reached the house, I couldn't help but smile. I was instantly taken back to Ireland, and the summer home we had on the coast.

Me heart ached at the thought of Ireland. I was going to have to go back and visit soon.

At the end of the drive, I found a three-car garage. I'd have to ask Melanie what the code was to open it so I could park inside. I was still trying to get used to this Texas heat and leaving me car out to bake was not ideal.

Reaching for my phone, I sent Melanie a text.

Me: *Just got here. Looks beautiful from the outside!*

Before I put my phone back in me purse, she replied,

Melanie: *You haven't gone in yet? What are you doing? Sitting in the car? Go in! Go in! Go in!*

I dropped the phone in me purse, grabbed me bag, and headed up the stairs to the grand entrance.

"Does everything have a code to get in?" I mumbled, pressing the numbers for the door code. It made a noise and the door unlocked.

Stepping inside, I felt giddy. The home was glorious. It wasn't like I didn't love me little apartment above Aisling, but growing up in a home that had twenty bedrooms and bathrooms, and then switching to one that had two of each, was an adjustment. This home had ten bedrooms Melanie said, and two of them were master suites. Making me way up the grand staircase, I decided to drop me luggage off first and change into me swimsuit. I'd try Cord again and let him know where I was and see where exactly he was. I was missing him already.

"Left or right?" Melanie had said the masters were at the very end of each hallway. I went left as I made me way down the hall. I had a strange feeling Melanie had something up her sleeve but couldn't pinpoint what it was.

It wasn't a coincidence that Cord was out of town the same weekend as me, or was it?

Lake house. Melanie's excitement for me to get here. It was all falling into place.

Me chest tightened as I peeked into the bedroom, and I stopped when I saw a bag thrown onto the bed. Me heart raced, and I quickly looked around the massive room. Cord's broken message made sense now. We had both been heading up here for the weekend.

Me gaze landed on the large picture window that overlooked a lake and I gasped. It was stunning.

And romantic.

The perfect place for someone to push two people together.

"Melanie!" I hissed. Grabbing me phone, I dialed her number.

A noise in the bathroom made me jump.

"Hello?"

"Melanie! What did you do?"

"What was that? Maebh, sweetheart, I can't hear you. Are you whispering?"

Taking a step toward the bathroom, me heart pounded in me chest. "You double booked the house!"

"I didn't double book, dear. I knew *exactly* what I was doing."

I froze.

Holy. Shite. She did. She set us up.

"What did you do?"

Melanie laughed. "Enjoy your weekend with my son!"

The line went dead, and I spun around to look at the bag on the bed. Moving closer, I saw a wallet. Me hands shook as I reached down and picked it up, instantly recognizing it as the same wallet that Cord had dropped a few weeks back.

"Cord."

I dropped the wallet like it was about to bite me and took a few steps backwards.

"Oh, she wouldn't!"

A hard object stopped me, and I held me breath as I felt a rush of electricity.

"She would, and she obviously did."

I spun around, and I jumped back when I saw him.

Cord Parker was standing in front of me with a towel wrapped around his waist. Very, very low on his waist. Me greedy eyes roamed over his perfect body. From the V that dipped below the white cotton towel, up to the perfect set of abs, to the chest that should have been registered as a danger to women's health, and finally up to his deep blue eyes.

By the time I remembered how to breathe, I was sucking in a breath and saying his name.

"C-Cord?"

It sounded strained and somewhat frightened.

"Maebh, are you stalking me?"

Me eyes widened, and I quickly started to back away from him.

"What! No! I…your ma…I wasn't…I'll leave."

I headed to the door, grabbing me bag and walking as fast as me feet would carry me.

"Maebh! Wait!"

His arms wrapped around me, bringing me to an immediate stop.

His warm breath on me neck made me legs tremble. Not to mention I was against his naked body. Now I knew how he felt a few nights back when I was naked under me robe.

Lord Jesus, please don't let me attack him and do something stupid.

"I was kidding, baby. I figured the second I saw you that my mother had arranged this whole little thing. Truth be told, a part of me was hoping you were heading up here when you said you were going out of town."

Shaking me head, I replied, "I didn't know you were on holiday this weekend until this morning. I swear. Do you really want me to stay?"

Cord moved his hands to me arms and turned me around.

"Are you fucking nuts? I was just thinking about how much I wanted to see you. Kiss you. I left you a voicemail saying how much I wished I'd asked you to come with me."

He waggled his brows, making me grin.

"Really?"

Leaning down, he rubbed his nose against mine. "Really, really."

I worried me lip. "It's your holiday though. I don't want to be a bother."

"Do you like to fish?"

Looking down at the floor, I replied, "I've never gone fishing."

"What!" Cord exclaimed. "You've never gone fishing?"

"Nope."

His smile nearly blew me over. "Then I get to be the first one to take you. I like this whole thing about me being the first to do things with you…and to you."

Me cheeks felt hot.

Cord pulled me into him, causing me body to light up with a heat so strong it made me lower stomach pull and the throb between me legs grow.

Me arms were down at me sides. If I lifted them, I'd be forced to touch him, and if I touched him, I wouldn't stop.

Every. Single. Inch.

The hug was over as fast as it started.

"Why don't you unpack your stuff, and we'll grab lunch if you haven't already eaten."

"I haven't. You're alright with this?"

He smiled and it took me breath away. "One hundred percent."

"Alright, I'll go to the other master bedroom."

"You sure you don't want to share this room with me?"

The sexy way he spoke made me want to tell him yes. Sometimes I felt like I would say yes to anything this man asked of me.

"I'm sure. Give me a couple of minutes to change?" I said.

He nodded and me eyes roamed over his body again. A slow smile moved across me face, and I felt like being a little daring.

"You know, it seems only fair that you drop your towel."

Cord looked at me with confusion. "You want me to drop my towel?"

Lifting my brow, I nodded. "You saw me naked. Tit for tat."

Never in my wildest dreams did I think he would drop his towel. But he did. And I nearly passed out at the sight in front of me. Half of a naked Cord played with me body, but the full thing nearly made me hit the floor.

It honestly would have been better if I had passed out because all I seemed to be able to do was stand there, mouth open, staring at the most impressive cock I'd ever seen. He was huge and circumcised.

Holy shite. So that's what a circumcised penis looks like?

I stared at it a little too long, studying the way the edge of it looked. It was smooth. Me fingers itched to trace a path along the rim.

For feck's sake. Did I just really think that to myself, that Cord's dick looks smooth?

I wanted to lick it and tell him how big he was, but I was positive the eejit would make some sort of sexual remark. So I closed me trap, shrugged me shoulders, and looked back into his eyes.

"Guess we're even then…I'll go change. Five minutes, tops."

The look on Cord's face was one I would never forget for as long as I lived. It took everything out of me not to smile.

With a quick turn on me heels, I rushed out of the room and down the long hall to the other bedroom.

"That's it? Not even one comment?" he called after me.

"Like?" I asked, gazing over me shoulder and seeing him walking down the hallway, wrapping the towel back around him.

"Oh, I don't know. Maybe like, *Wow, that's impressive*. Or, *Gosh, Cord, your dick is pretty big*!"

Stopping at the door, I turned, lifted a brow, and asked, "Is it? Impressive and big? I don't have much experience with this sort of thing…remember?"

Cord let out a gruff laugh. "You want me to tell you if my cock is big?"

Me teeth sank into my lip, and I had to force meself to stay strong.

He stepped closer and buried his face in me neck, taking in a deep breath. Me body trembled and he chuckled. He knew exactly what he was doing to me.

Bastard.

When his lips brushed over me skin, I held me breath. Cord's mouth was next to me ear as he whispered, "You'll have to decide that for yourself when I make love to you, agra."

Me legs trembled, and I reached for the doorjamb with both hands to hold me up.

Where is Cord learning all these words in Irish? The other day he'd called me his cailin, which meant "girl."

And just like that, Cord Parker's muscular, hot body was walking down the hallway while I stood in tatters, yearning for him to do things I'd only read about in romance books.

One last glance back and I saw that he had the nerve to pull his towel off again, giving me a great view of his arse.

Dead, I'm simply dead. And all I can think about are all the things I know he's capable of doing to me.

Very naughty things.

CHAPTER 15

Cord

After tugging on shorts, a T-shirt and baseball cap, I slipped my feet into flip flops and headed downstairs. It was nice forgoing the jeans, boots, and cowboy hat.

I grabbed my phone off the counter and looked to see who might be the mastermind behind this.

Paxton.

Hitting her cell phone number, I waited.

"Cord! How's the lake?

"You knew?"

She chuckled. "I might have planted the idea in your mother's ear."

"You little shit."

"Tell me you're upset Maebh is there, and I'll do anything you want me to do for a whole year."

My hand raked through my hair. "I wanted a few days to think, Paxton."

"About?"

"If I can do this?"

She scoffed. "Do what?"

"This whole one-woman thing. I've never had the desire to date one woman. What if I—"

"Stop right there. You never had the desire because the right situation never presented itself. Cord, you don't have to ask her to marry you. Take a deep breath and enjoy the next four days getting to know each other with no interference from anyone. Not your family, your jobs, nothing. It's just the two of y'all. Let your guard down and live in the moment. I can hear it in your voice. You're not upset she's there."

I grinned. "Maebh said I made her feel like she was living in the moment the other night."

Paxton chuckled. "See. Stop thinking too hard, and just *be*."

A voice cleared from behind me, and I turned to see Maebh coming down the steps.

Holy Christ. She was in a pair of cut-off jeans, a white tank top, and pink Converse. It was topped off with a baseball cap that said *I'm Irish, bitch. Back off.*

Swallowing hard, I whispered, "I think I just fell in love."

"Let me guess, the cut-off jean shorts I suggested she pack?" Paxton asked, laughing.

"Bye, Paxton."

"Wait! Cord!"

I hit End and let my eyes move over her body. "You look adorably sexy."

"Adorably sexy? Is that a Texas thing?"

"It's a Maebh thing."

Her gaze traveled over my body and then back up to the baseball cap I had on backwards.

Her teeth captured the corner of her mouth, and she chewed on it as she eye-fucked the shit out of me.

"You're in flip-flops and a baseball hat."

I nodded. "We're at the lake. The whole cowboy attire gets put up."

Her cheeks blushed. "It's just…I'm used to seeing you in jeans, boots, and a cowboy hat."

"And I'm used to seeing you covered…a bit more."

Maebh glanced down to what she was wearing. "Do you not like what I have on?"

"Fuck yes, I like it, but I'm not going to like all the guys staring at you."

Her face lit up. I found myself liking the way I could make her smile.

"Ready?"

She nodded and laced her fingers with mine. For someone who thought he needed a few days to think this shit over, I was eager as fuck to get our weekend started. I was going to have to do something special for my mother and Paxton when I got back.

We headed to the back door instead of the front.

"Um, where are we going?"

"To the boat."

"Boat?"

"Yep."

She looked confused, and it was cute as hell, especially when that round button nose scrunched up. "Are we eating on the boat?"

Laughing, I pulled her closer and wrapped my arm around her shoulders as we headed to the boat dock.

"I called on the way here and had Rick, our neighbor and a good friend of my father's, get the boat ready to be taken out. I thought I'd be grabbing a quick bite and heading out to fish, but with the appearance of my sweet Irish beauty, those plans changed. We're taking it out and going to a restaurant."

She giggled. "I feel stupid now."

After helping Maebh onto the boat, I got us ready to head out onto the lake. Maebh leaned her head back and let the sun hit her face as I drove us over the water. She held onto her hat as I made my way across the lake. A strange feeling hit me in the chest each time I looked her way. Maebh O'Sullivan was working her way into a part of my heart I never dreamed I'd open up. I found myself trying to think of ways to make her see that she was so much more to me than a hook-up. That I was serious about a relationship, even though at times it still freaked me out.

When a gust of wind hit her hat and blew it off, Maebh jumped up and screamed. She somehow managed to get it and plopped it back on her head. She was laughing the entire time, and I found myself laughing along with her. Laughing in a way I'd never done before. It felt fucking amazing.

If my brothers were here I knew they would be teasing me. If I could look at myself in a mirror I'd see I was wearing the same damn smile I'd given them all hell about. Maebh looked at me with a huge smile. Her emerald green eyes sparkled as she yelled, "That was close! I almost lost me hat!"

Christ. After only a few minutes alone with her, I knew.

I'd been freaking Smurfed.

"I'm stuffed!" Maebh said as we walked back toward the boat.

"Was it good?" I asked, wrapping my arm around her waist as an asshole walked toward us, checking her out. When his eyes caught mine, I smirked.

That's right, fucker. She's mine.

"It was really good."

I stared at the asshole as he walked by. He tipped his head as if letting me know he got the hint.

Dick.

"Now what!" Maebh asked, excitement laced in her voice.

"Well, what were you planning on doing when you got here?"

She shrugged. "Don't know. Relax. Read. Take long walks."

I took her hand in mine and helped her onto the boat. Then I grabbed the lines and tossed them to her as I pushed the boat from the dock and jumped in.

"How about we do some fishing next? You game to learn?"

She grinned. "If it means spending time with you. Yes."

"Then let's do this. I'll teach you how to fish."

"Will you be catching our dinner for tonight?"

I lifted a brow. "If I catch it, you have to prepare and cook it."

"What if I catch it?"

Laughing, I hit the throttle, causing her to stumble back and land on the chair.

"Let's not get ahead of ourselves, babe."

An hour later, I was watching Maebh reel in a fish. A big fish. The kind of fish that if I had caught it I'd most likely be getting my phone's camera ready to send a picture to my brothers and rub it in their faces.

"This thing weighs a ton!" she yelled as I helped her bring the fish in.

"Use your index finger like I showed you to control the release of the line."

"Got it!" she gleefully shouted. I loved working at reeling in what looked like a pretty big fish.

"Let me grab the net," I said. "This thing is huge. Looks like a bass."

The way she giggled made my heart soar. She was loving this and that made me happy. I loved to fish, so dating a woman who enjoyed it had to be a plus.

When I saw the damn fish jumping out of the water, my eyes nearly popped. I knew the little bastard was big, but holy shit.

"There it is!" Maebh screamed.

"Don't let go of the pole, babe! Let me get this under it."

Once I got the fish into the net, I got a good look at it and laughed.

"What's wrong? Is it the wrong kind of fish?"

"No! This is a largemouth bass. Shit, it has to be about ten pounds."

She grinned. "Is that good?"

I loved how damn innocent she was. Grabbing the back of her neck with my hand, I pulled her to me and kissed her quickly. Then I dumped him into the live tank and grabbed my phone.

"Let's get some pictures of you holding him, then we'll put him back."

Her smile dropped.

"What?"

"What?" I asked. Was she upset we were putting him back into the lake?

Her face turned white. "You want me to hold him?"

"Yes! You've got to get your picture with your first badass fish."

Maebh slowly shook her head. "I can't hold him."

I frowned. "Why not?"

Her eyes jerked down to look at the fish swimming in the live well.

"He…he looks slimy."

Trying my best to hold my laughter back, I glanced between Maebh and the bass before settling my stare on her. "Maebh, you cook fish all the time. You can't tell me you've never handled a whole fish before."

"I have. It was dead though. This one will be looking at me…and squirming."

"You're afraid the fish is going to look at you and wiggle?"

She nodded. "I don't want him to be mad at me for taking his life."

That's when I knew I was fucked. Because just when I thought I couldn't fall for this woman any more than I already had, she went off and said something like that. Her heart was the purest I'd ever known. That was sexy as hell.

"Baby, he's not going to be mad at you. You're going to take a picture with him and put him back into the water."

Her eyes widened. "We're not keeping him?"

I shook my head. "No."

Her smile actually made my knees weak, and I had to take a step to make sure I didn't tip over the edge of the boat.

Chewing on the corner of her mouth, Maebh finally said, "Alright. Let's take a picture with Bob."

"Bob?"

"He looks like a Bob."

Laughing, I drew her into my arms and looked into those beautiful eyes. They'd visited my dreams from the first moment she ran into me at my bar.

"I don't think I've ever met anyone like you before."

Her eyes lit up. "Is that a good thing?"

"A very good thing," I whispered, covering my mouth over hers. Maebh wrapped her arms around my neck and I lifted her off the ground, causing her to let out a little moan that shot straight to my dick.

My heart hammered in my chest as our tongues danced around each other. She tasted like mint, and I wanted more. So much more.

I slowly set her down, and we broke the connection. "I love kissing you," I said against her mouth.

"You leave me dizzy with your kisses, Cord Parker."

I smiled. "Good. That means you'll come back for more."

Our eyes met, and I saw the same hunger in hers that I knew were in mine.

Slow. Go slow, Cord. This is all new.

"Let's get that picture."

Maebh nodded, and I was stunned to see her lean into the well and ask how to take the fish out. After I told her how to hold it, I got my phone ready and quickly took a few pictures.

"He's so heavy!" Maebh said as she leaned over the boat and let *Bob* slide out of her hands and back into the lake. "There he goes!" she said, clapping while she jumped. My eyes landed on her breasts, and I had to fight the urge to push my hands under her tank top and cup them.

Spinning back to face me, Maebh declared that this had been one of the best experiences of her life. I wanted to tell her I felt the same way. But I didn't, I simply smiled at her.

"I think I love fishing!" she exclaimed, her accent thick and heavy in her excitement.

Laughing, I cast my line back out, then put my pole in the rod holder before sitting down on the chair and taking in the lake. I loved it out here. This boat was one of two my father owned. This one was used more for fishing and tooling around the lake. His other boat was stored at the coast, a yacht. Trevor and I both said we were going to take it around the world when we were in college. I'm pretty sure my father would have let me if it had meant not opening Cord's Place and coming to work on the ranch, but that bar was my dream and one I would never regret.

"You say that because you just caught an impressive fish. Sit here for hours with no bite at all and tell me if you feel the same way."

Maebh smiled, then looked at a boat passing us by.

"What type of boat is that?"

I turned to look. "A bass boat. See how they can stand on either side and fish. This is a fishing boat, but you can seat six people on it."

She looked back at me as I adjusted my ball cap on my head. Her eyes darkened, and I wanted to know what she was thinking. It didn't take me long to figure out when she sat down on me, straddling me so that her core was against my quickly hardening cock.

"Maebh," I groaned while she took my hat off and laced her fingers in my hair.

"Is this alright?" she asked, moving her lips over my neck and to my ear.

My hands grabbed her hips, and I pulled her into me, letting her feel just how alright it really was. I fucking loved her confidence and how she wasn't afraid to let me know what she wanted.

Maebh searched my face while digging her teeth into her lip and wrinkling up that cute nose.

Hottest fucking thing ever. She was so damn adorable it was turning me on even more.

"I want to kiss you, Cord."

Smiling, I cupped her face and replied, "Then kiss me, arga."

Her eyes closed, and she pressed her lips to mine. My hands slid under her tank top, and Maebh jumped. When I stopped, she pulled back and panted. "Don't stop touching me. Please."

I brought my hand around to her front, brushing my knuckles against her flat, toned stomach. When I rubbed my thumb over the lace of her bra and made her nipple pebble up, she grinded against my cock, making me moan while her hands tugged harder at my hair.

Christ, she responded to me like no woman had ever before. Or maybe I was only noticing how *this* particular woman responded to me...and how I responded to her.

"Maebh," I whispered, pushing into her.

"More," she groaned, kissing me. "Please."

I pushed her bra up and cupped her perfect tits in my hand. When I squeezed her nipple slightly, she gasped and pulled back from my mouth for some air.

"Yes," she hissed, rocking against my cock. "Oh, God."

I'd dry humped plenty of women, but Maebh grinding into my cock with us both fully clothed—and right the fuck in the middle of the lake—was hot as hell.

Using my other hand, I pulled her mouth back to mine, kissing her hard and fast. Maebh rocked faster and the friction of my cock against her pussy was causing a build-up. Jesus, it felt like high school, and I was actually worried I'd come in my pants if she let go.

"Cord," she gasped.

I pinched her other nipple as she pressed her hips into me more.

She pulled back and looked directly into my eyes. "I'm going to come," she whimpered. I felt her entire body tremble as she rocked faster against me.

"That's it, baby. Let me hear you come."

Her forehead dropped to mine, and she cried out my name softly along with a few moans as her orgasm hit her.

Holy Christ.

My heart was pounding. That was the hottest fucking moment of my life, and we weren't even naked. All I had done was touched her nipples and kissed her. What in the world was she going to be like lying on my bed with me touching, kissing, and licking every inch of her?

She'll be screaming my name all night if I have anything to say about it.

Maebh froze on me, her forehead pressed to mine. Her eyes closed as she let her body settle back down. My cock was aching in my shorts.

When she snapped her eyes open, she looked embarrassed. "I'm sorry. I don't know what came over me. You were sitting there looking all hot, and I wanted…I wanted…"

"To come?"

She nodded.

"I'll make you come whenever your pretty heart desires, baby."

A wide smile grew over her face. "I like it when you call me that."

"Baby?"

She nodded. "And your Irish cailín."

"You are my girl, Maebh."

Her eyes filled with tears before she quickly blinked them back. I wanted to know what she was thinking and was about to ask when I got my answer.

"I want to make *you* come now."

I swallowed hard. "Um, Maebh, I don't need to come. *Ahhh…*"

She moved off me, her hands quickly unbuttoning my shorts. I shut my mouth. I didn't have any boxers on, so she was fixin' to get a surprise.

My cock lifted out of my pants when Maebh unzipped them. She stared at me for the longest time. I was so damn hard it was throbbing. Her staring wasn't making things any easier.

"Unless you've got some sort of superpower that will make me come just by staring at it, I don't think this is going to work, darlin'."

She slapped my shoulder. "It's just. Well. You're so big."

I grinned. "So you *do* think I'm big."

Maebh's cheeks flushed.

When her hand landed around my cock, I nearly bucked her off.

"Shit!" I hissed. My whole body felt like a shock had bolted through it. Plenty of women had jerked me off, but Maebh touching me felt different. Like I knew I'd never want another woman touching me again…except for her.

When her eyes lifted and she looked around, I knew what she was about to do.

She kneeled before me and leaned forward, her mouth inches from my cock. "I've never given a blowjob before, so tell me if I do something wrong."

My eyes widened, and I couldn't even think to form words in my head.

Wait. Did she just say she's never blown a guy? Am I her first?

My head spun when she wrapped those pretty pink lips around me, and I nearly came right then and there. Grabbing the boat, I held on and gritted my teeth while Maebh worked me with her mouth and hands.

"*Fuck*," I groaned, her head bobbing up and down on my shaft.

This was too much. I was on overload and going to come any second, and she had just started. I'd never had a woman make me feel this way before. With any other woman I was cursing under my breath for this shit to be over with. With my Irish beauty, I didn't want this to end. I wanted to enjoy every second of Maebh's mouth on my dick.

"Fucking hell. Baby...oh, God. Maebh! Fuck. Fuck. Fuck." I was so close to the edge it was unreal.

When her eyes lifted to mine, I lost it.

"Maebh, I'm going to come! You might want to move away...fuck!"

She took me in deeper and sucked harder, and I couldn't hold back. A long groan slipped from my mouth as I dropped my head back. I came so hard I saw stars. She continued to move and swallowed my cum like a pro. I'd always pulled my cock from a woman's mouth before I came. There was something about coming in a woman's mouth that seemed...even more intimate than my dick shoved down her throat. I'd never done it before.

But with Maebh, I was physically unable to pull myself away from those gorgeous lips of hers. I didn't want to. I wanted her to swallow every ounce I poured into her mouth. I'd never had an orgasm feel so goddamn good, and I was positive I'd never let another woman have me like this...no one except for Maebh.

When I finally realized her mouth was no longer on me, I dragged my head up and looked at her. Her cheeks were flushed and she was worrying her lip, seemingly unsure if I'd enjoyed that.

I smiled. I needed a moment to get my thoughts together. Knowing I was the only man she'd ever done that to did weird things to me. The thought of her doing that to someone else nearly made me sick to my stomach.

I was ruined.

Maebh O'Sullivan had just ruined me for other women…she'd ruined me forever.

CHAPTER 16

maebh

I had no idea what came over me. One look at Cord sitting there, the cap backward, the smile on his face. The muscles teasing me. I lost control and acted like a horny teenager.

Chewing on the inside of me cheek, I watched his face. He looked happy…but pained at the same time.

Shite. I hope I didn't do anything wrong.

When Cord opened his eyes and caught mine, he smiled the most brilliant smile I'd ever seen. I felt me stomach flip and me chest squeeze. He tucked himself back into his shorts and the pull in my lower stomach had me wanting him desperately. Wanting him in ways I didn't even know how to want him.

"You've never done that before?" he asked softly.

"No." I cringed and asked, "Was it good?"

He shook his head in disbelief and then reached for me, pulling me onto his lap.

"I fucking came within two minutes. It was more than good."

Burying my face into his neck, I tried to hide from him. I knew I was blushing.

"I don't think I even came that fast with my very first blowjob."

Hearing him say that made an ache build in me chest. I knew other women had done that to Cord. Thinking it and hearing him say it were two different things.

Drawing back, I went to get off his lap, feeling me moment of happiness disperse.

"Shit, I'm sorry. I didn't mean to say that."

Cord pulled me tight against him. Even if I wanted to leave his lap, his hold wouldn't allow it.

His mouth was in me hair, pressing a kiss to me head. "Maebh, that was amazing, and I've never in my life had an orgasm hit me that hard, that fast, and that strong before. Thank you."

Happiness bubbled, and I snuggled deeper into his chest, letting his earlier comment slip away. This wasn't new to me, dating. Yet, it was new. I'd been in a serious relationship before, but this feeling with Cord was unlike anything I'd ever known. It felt passionate, thrilling, dangerous. Like I was freefalling and I had no control over how my heart was opening to him and what would happen if he broke it in two. One touch and I knew Cord was what I had always wanted, and more importantly, what I had always feared.

"Cord?"

"Mmm?" he said into my hair.

"I really need to get a drink. This taste in me mouth is vile."

His body shook with laughter. Not letting go, he reached into the back cooler and pulled out a bottle of water.

Taking it, I nearly downed the whole thing. I even leaned back and gargled the water, causing Cord to tickle me.

"It wasn't that bad!" he said, nearly causing me to pee me pants from laughing so hard.

"Mercy!" I cried out, pushing Cord away as hard as I could.

He stood and held his hand out for me to take. "Come on, let's get back and head to the store. We need food for dinner."

"We're eating in tonight?" I asked, handing back his baseball cap that I had dropped to the floor when I nearly attacked him.

"Yep. You're cooking me something amazing."

Rolling me eyes, I pushed his shoulder back. "Then you provide dessert."

He smirked and pulled me against his body. "Oh, I can handle dessert. Leave that one up to me."

Me stomach dropped, and I tried not to let out a moan. I was anxious to see what Cord Parker's idea of a dessert would be.

After changing, Cord and I loaded up into me car since it was still parked out front. A quick trip to HEB proved to be a challenge when it came to shopping with Cord.

"Oh, I love these!"

Glancing over to see what Cord was holding up, I frowned. "What are those?"

He looked at the bag and then back to me. "Deep fried pig skins."

I snarled. "Gross."

"Let's have some for dinner!"

"Piss off," I said as Cord laughed. "What are they even doing in this section?"

He stared at me, and I knew he hadn't understood what I had just said. I wanted to giggle. If I spoke too fast for him, he would give me that look.

I spoke again, this time slower. "Don't they belong with the crisps?"

He shrugged. "I have no clue what a crisps is. Looks like some-one left them here. Probably a mom who found them in her cart and tossed them out."

"Smart mom," I replied with a chuckle.

Cord set the bag down. "So, what's on the menu for dinner to-night, chef?"

I grabbed some garlic and lemons and headed over to the sea-food section.

"Honey garlic salmon."

"Shit, that's making my mouth water already."

Glancing over my shoulder, I smiled. I loved cooking and hav-ing someone who appreciated it was nice. My old boyfriend, Sean, thought it was strange that I wanted to cook for him, especially when my parents had a full-time cook on staff. His thought that because we were one of the wealthiest families in Ireland, we should have people cooking for us, not the other way around.

"What do you have in your basket?" I asked.

He held it behind his back. "None of your business. You stick with what you're making, and I'll stick with my little surprise. I've got to go to the frozen food section. I'll find you in a second."

Lifting me eyes, I replied, "I'm intrigued."

He winked. "You should be."

Cord checked out separately, not letting me see what he bought for dessert. I was curious as hell, but I was acting like I had no inter-est, which was driving him crazy.

"Is there a cast iron pan?" I asked, searching through the cabi-nets.

"Down to the left of the stove."

I bent down and found it. Placing it on the stove, I turned back to me ingredients and got to work.

"Want some music on?" Cord asked.

"Yes! I love to listen to music while I cook."

There was a small Bose speaker on the counter, and Cord synced his phone to it. I didn't recognize the song that started.

"What song is this?"

Cord dropped what looked like an ice cream sandwich onto the island.

"You don't know this song?"

I shook me head. "Who's the singer?"

Clutching his chest, Cord stumbled back. "What! You don't know who Foreigner is?"

"Must you be so dramatic, Cord?"

"It's Foreigner, Maebh!"

Wrinkling me nose, I added, "Is this an old band? It sounds like old music."

"You're kidding, right? I'm not sure I can date a woman who doesn't know classic rock."

I shrugged. "I honestly don't know him."

"Them! Them! It's a band."

I couldn't help but giggle. He looked so cute standing there with a shocked expression. The urge to kiss him was unbearable, but I glanced back to the food I was preparing while Cord went on mumbling about how I didn't know one of the most iconic bands in history.

"Boston? Do you know who they are?"

"As in the city?"

He rolled his eyes and hit something on his phone. Another older-sounding song played.

"I take it this is Boston?"

His face fell. "You're killing me."

Smiling, I went back to chopping the garlic and cutting the lemons.

After the cast iron was heated, I put the salmon in and poured me sauce on it. A catchy song was playing so I danced a little as I moved about the kitchen. It was a country song. I found meself liking country since I'd moved to Texas and had even taken a two-step dance class in San Antonio.

"You like this song, agra?"

Me heart skipped a beat at the endearment.

"I do. It's catchy."

He grinned. "You want to dance with me?"

Turning the salmon down, I faced him to say yes, but paused when I saw him. He was leaning against the counter looking handsome as ever. Before we'd started with dinner preparations, he'd changed into jeans and a black T-shirt, and the way his arms crossed his chest made it appear even bigger. I swallowed hard while me eyes explored his body.

"Yes," I finally managed to say.

Cord hit something on his phone and held his hand out for me. The moment the song started, I chuckled. Never mind that it was slow and sensual; it described our relationship perfectly.

"You trying to tell me something?" I asked as he pulled me into his arms.

"Maybe," he whispered against me lips, hovering there and not kissing me. Our eyes stayed locked as Cord started to move and me body mimicked his. Our bodies were like one, swaying and dipping in a slow salsa dance. I'd danced close to a man before, but never so sexual as this. It felt thrilling, and it turned me on. When the chorus started he pushed me out and spun me before drawing me back to him.

When he started to sing about his heart being in danger, I nearly melted. Our eyes never broke apart. He would smile during certain parts of the song and each time me breath would hitch, and I found meself struggling for air.

He sung softly about living in the moment while piercing me with his intense blue eyes and leaning me back some in a dip that made me giggle.

He spun me and pulled me against his front and sang the chorus to me once again. His mouth moved lightly across me neck while he sang. I couldn't help but wonder if he knew how beautiful his voice was.

Our hips moved together like we'd practiced this dance for weeks, and I couldn't imagine what it would be like to have this man make love to me.

The song ended and a fast country tune started. Cord stopped dancing, held me tighter in his arms, and kissed me along me neck. Tingles erupted over me skin, and I let out a slight moan.

"You're so beautiful. You take my breath away."

Me head dropped to his chest, and I let him move his hands under me shirt. I inhaled sharply when he pushed me bra up and cupped me breasts with both hands. I was positive all he would have to do was play with me nipples and I'd come. The man had magical fingers.

"I want to taste you, Maebh. Tit for tat."

Smiling, I felt like me feet were floating off the ground. I'd never let a man do that to me, not even Sean. He'd get so angry when he used his fingers to make me come and want to move down on me, and I'd say no. It hadn't felt right to let him get that intimate.

But with Cord, everything felt right.

Me hand lifted back to his neck, slipping me fingers into his dark hair. I wanted him desperately and would take him anyway I could get.

"Seems only fair," I finally replied.

Before I knew what was happening, I was in Cord's arms and he was walking out of the kitchen.

"The salmon!" I cried out, causing him to turn back and shut the stove off.

He nearly ran into the living room and set me down on the sofa. Me breathing was heavy, and I felt a slight panic attack coming on.

Cord's eyes looked dark with lust, but when he smiled, I was relaxed. "I can't wait to be the only man to have his mouth on your pussy."

I gasped, his crassness sending me libido into overdrive. Cord talking dirty was an instant turn on.

All I could do was nod.

He closed his eyes and groaned. His hands moved up me thighs, making me spread them instinctively. He planted soft kisses up and down me leg, driving me utterly insane.

Leaning back, Cord moved away a bit and rested on his heels. "Take your shorts off, baby."

Me mouth fell open slightly. He wanted me to undress meself in front of him?

Why was that so hot?

I stood and the moment I unbuttoned me jean shorts, the song in the kitchen changed. A wide grin moved over Cord's face as "Filthy" by Justin Timberlake started playing.

"Fuck yes," he hissed as I slipped me shorts down slowly. I tried to think back to all the movies I'd seen where the lady undressed in a sexual way. I swayed me hips some. By the look on his face, I had nailed it.

He sucked in a breath when he saw me light-blue panties then closed his eyes for a brief moment before focusing on me again. He used his hand to adjust himself in his pants. I couldn't help but feel so powerful in that moment. It was me that was turning him on, and I loved it.

I slipped me thumbs into my panties, but Cord lifted his hand to stop me.

"Keep them on."

Frowning, I glanced down to me panties.

Cord slowly moved closer, on his knees. He placed his hands on me arse, his forehead falling to me bare stomach as he whimpered almost incoherently, "Thong," before kissing me lower stomach.

"Cord," I panted, me hands sliding through his hair. "I…need …"

He squeezed me arse hard, and I pulled on his hair, making him let out a low growl.

When his fingers pulled at the fabric string on the sides of me hips, I knew he was about to see me completely. He'd seen me naked in me bathroom, but now he was up close and personal. Tugging slowly, he stared and licked his lips like he was ready to devour me.

"Christ," I mumbled and dropped me head back. His intense stare was enough to push me over the ledge.

I stepped out of me panties and felt his breath at my core.

I stared down at him. He was placing kisses all along me lower stomach, inches from me sensitive clit.

"Sit down, Maebh."

Holding me breath, I did what he said. Cord pushed me legs open and then brought me to the edge of the sofa. Me breathing was hard and fast as he stared. I was positive he'd be able to hear me heart hammering, and he'd barely even touched me.

"Cord," I whispered. Even I could hear the fear in me voice.

"Tell me if you don't want to do this."

"I want this," I whispered. I'd never heard me voice filled with such need. I knew if I touched meself I would be soaked.

Cord slipped his finger inside me and closed his eyes. "You're so fucking wet. Are you turned on, baby?"

All I could do was nod. His eyes were still closed, so when he opened them again, I repeated the nod.

The song changed to Justin Bieber's "The Feeling" and as the words started, a strange feeling came over me. I knew I was falling in love with Cord Parker. It wasn't because I was about to let him do something I'd never let another man do; it was because me heart. I had never felt like this before.

Swallowing hard, I pleaded, "I want this, Cord."

"Don't close your eyes. I want you to watch me. I want you to watch yourself come on my mouth."

Oh, shite.

I watched as he moved lower, never taking his gaze from mine. I jerked when I felt him lick through me folds. Me heart pounded as I watched him lick through me wetness. He moaned.

"Fucking hell, Maebh, you taste amazing. You're mine for always."

He licked again but this time he flicked the bundle of nerves that was ready to send me over the ledge of pure pleasure.

"Oh!" I closed me eyes. He sucked me clit and groaned, making me open me eyes to look at him. He flicked again and smiled.

"I want you looking at me when you come. I want you to see it's me making you feel so good."

Nodding like a crazed person, I pulled his head toward me, desperately wanting more. He smiled and gave me exactly what I wanted.

Me entire body warmed, trembled, shook... I didn't even have the words to describe what was happening to me. All I knew was it felt fecking amazing. Like nothing I'd ever experienced. I had always thought a man going down on me was going to be more embarrassing. But with Cord, it felt so natural. Me friends used to talk about how good oral sex was, but how they didn't like tasting themselves when their man kissed them after. I wouldn't care. If Cord kept doing what he was doing he could kiss the living shite out of me after this and I wouldn't care one bit.

Cord slipped his fingers inside and hit a spot that nearly had me jumping off the sofa and trying to climb away from him. It felt so good, too good. He held me down with his hand on me stomach and licked me clit faster while rubbing his fingers inside of me at the same pace.

"Oh God, Cord!" I didn't care that I was screaming his name. I was falling apart, and I loved every single second of it. I was sinking faster as I let Cord take me to a place I could only describe as heaven.

I trembled as the feeling moved throughout me whole body. Warmth burst through, causing me to shake. Cord's eyes met mine and I lost it completely.

"Cord…I'm coming! Oh God!"

I dropped back, no longer able to focus on him, only on the orgasm that was ripping through me, wave after wave. I swore me mind left me as I tried to breathe. I'd never in me life had such a powerful orgasm. I was rocking with such pleasure I thought for sure I'd pass out.

"I can't…take it. Cord."

I wasn't even aware he was kissing me stomach until I was coming down from the euphoria.

Lifting me head, I looked at him staring at me.

Panting, I managed to speak. "You've ruined me…for all other men."

The corner of his mouth rose into a sexy-as-sin smile. "Good. Wait until I make love to you."

Me head dropped back down, and I let out a groan.

When his lips touched mine and his tongue slipped into me mouth, I tasted myself. The only reason I didn't pull away was because the man kissing me made me drunk with that kiss. I never wanted this moment to end.

Ever.

It all became so clear as Cord kissed me. I was completely and utterly falling in love with him.

CHAPTER 17

Cord

Maebh moaned into my mouth when I kissed her. I thought for sure she would have pushed me away. Most women didn't want to be kissed afterwards. Not that I gave a lot of women oral sex. I could count on my hand the women I'd gone down on.

Kylie Burks, my fuck buddy in high school and college, was the one I'd done it to the most. She'd taught me how to lick, when to suck, how many fingers to put inside. She would have slapped the shit out of me had I tried to kiss her after oral sex. Neither one of us was interested in a relationship, but we liked to fuck each other. A lot. Kissing was something we didn't really do. Not sure why, we just didn't. But I certainly kissed her pussy a lot.

Thank you, Kylie, for letting me learn on you.

"How do you feel?" I asked Maebh, noticing that her breathing still hadn't settled down. It could have been because I just kissed the hell out of her.

"Like I'm floating."

I kissed her lightly. "You're okay?"

With a sleepy voice, she replied, "Ah, sure, I'm grand."

With a laugh, I asked, "Does grand mean good?"

She giggled. "More than good."

Her fingers twirled in my hair, and it was relaxing as fuck. I bet she could put me to sleep each night doing that alone.

"Good. I'm still hungry though."

Her eyes widened, and I laughed. "For food, Maebh."

She smiled big, and warmth radiated through my body. An ache grew in the back of my throat, not to mention my chest.

"If you'll let me get dressed, I'll get back to dinner," she said.

I peeled myself away from her and reached for her panties, helping her slip them back on just as slowly as I'd taken them off, leaving kisses in my wake.

With a wink, I said, "It's sort of a shame I had dessert before dinner."

She blushed and goddamn it if my heartbeat didn't quicken.

Gripping my hair with her hands, she leaned down and kissed me, then buttoned her shorts and made her way back into the kitchen while I sat on the floor staring after her.

I'd never in my life met a woman like Maebh.

Never.

I rubbed the back of my neck, then moved my hand to my chest and touched the strange ache. Standing, I saw my reflection in a mirror. I was smiling. Exactly like my three older brothers had been when they realized they had fallen for a woman.

Taking a step back, I slowly shook my head. There was no denying what I saw.

Holy. Fuck. I'm falling in love with Maebh.

We ate out on the back deck since it was such a beautiful evening. It was cool for this time of year, thanks to the breeze blowing off the lake. Maebh's dinner was fantastic, and I devoured it faster than I should have.

"Do you want something else to eat?" Maebh asked, glancing at my empty plate. It was so good I damn near licked the plate.

"I'm stuffed. Thank you, babe. It was delicious. Do you cook like that every day?"

She shook her head. "No, I rarely get to cook these days outside of the restaurant, and even then I don't do a lot of the cooking. The most cooking I've ever done was in culinary school, and after I moved into me first house."

"You didn't help your mom cook when you grew up?"

Her eyes darted away for a quick moment and then back. She simply shook her head.

Was her mother a sore subject? I thought she had moved to Oak Springs because of her mother.

"Do you not like talking about your mom?"

Maebh's eyes widened. "What? I love talking about me ma. It's just, she didn't cook much when I was growing up. I wish she had. She was the one who first taught me to cook, but me da's ma, me grandmother, well, she didn't think it was Ma's place to be in the kitchen."

I frowned. "Why?"

She squirmed in her chair, and I knew this was a conversation she didn't want to have. As curious as I was, I was going to let it go. For now.

"Tell me what life is like back in Ireland? Where exactly are you from?"

Her eyes lit up, and I knew this was something she was interested in talking about.

"I'm from Cork. It's beautiful there." A smile spread over her face. "Lots of water and boats. Beautiful old buildings and small markets. There's so many things to do and places to visit."

"I'd like to go sometime."

"That would be amazing. I can show you around."

Reaching for her hand, I brushed my thumb over the top of it and grinned. "It's a date."

Maebh dug her teeth into her lip before softly saying, "It's a date."

"How about I clean up these plates, then take you somewhere fun?"

"What kind of fun?" she asked, her brow quirked up.

"We could head over to the Buchanan Dam Beach Club. Live music and cold beer."

She smiled. "Sounds like fun. Are you sure you don't want help?"

"I'm positive," I said as I grabbed the plates and walked back into the house, motioning for Maebh to go in first.

"Alright! Let me go change."

Standing, I watched her until she was out of sight. A strange twinge happened in my chest, and I pushed it aside as I quickly cleaned up the kitchen and ran upstairs to change as well.

"Cord?" Maebh called out.

When I poked my head around the corner, I nearly tripped over my own feet.

"Holy shit."

My eyes moved over her perfect body. There was no fucking way she was wearing that out.

Daisy Duke shorts, cowboy boots, and an off-the-shoulder, off-white shirt. She was the most beautiful woman I'd ever laid eyes on, and I nearly choked on my own tongue as I stared at her.

"Is this alright?"

I shook my head.

"Should I change? I didn't bring a lot of clothes. I figured I'd be staying in all weekend. If I look bad I can…"

I crossed the room and pulled her into my arms. Lifting her, Maebh wrapped her legs around my body and her arms around my neck. I pressed my mouth to hers. She returned the kiss with as much passion as I was dishing out.

Turning, I laid her on the bed and crawled over her body. Slipping my hands under her shirt, I groaned when I found she wasn't even wearing a fucking bra. My hips pushed into her, making her moan and dig her nails into my bare back.

Shit, I wanted to strip her bare and bury my cock into her so bad I could hardly stand it.

"You look so fucking hot, Maebh. I'm going to kill any man who looks at you the wrong way."

She smiled, her cheeks flushing slightly. Then her smile faded, and she opened her mouth to say something, but closed it.

Resting my arms on either side of her, I studied her face, locked my eyes with hers. "Talk to me."

Her lips pressed together, and she rubbed them quickly. "I want you, Cord. I'm scared of how badly I want you."

My eyes closed, and I dropped my mouth to hers, kissing her ever-so-lightly.

"Baby, I want you so much, too. So fucking much."

We laid there for a few more minutes before I spoke.

"But I want you to be sure, Maebh. The first time with you has to be perfect."

"If it's with you, it will be perfect."

Swallowing hard, I trembled from the way she looked at me.

"I don't want to hurt you."

A slow smile moved across her face. "Physically or emotionally?"

"Both."

She touched my cheek while her green eyes searched my face. "I'm ready for you whenever you're ready. I'm not as fragile as you think I am. I know the risk I'm taking."

My head pulled back. "Risk?"

"I'm not naïve, Cord. I know the moment we make love you might run for the hills."

"I won't," I promised, pressing a kiss to her lips. "I swear to you I won't."

Her eyes filled with tears, and I knew a part of her didn't believe me. "I believe you," she whispered.

I pushed up to look down at her. She was so beautiful with her dark hair spread out over my pillow. Taking her hands, I pulled her into a sitting position. I lifted her shirt over her head, taking in her beautiful tits. They were mine now. All mine.

And I'd do whatever I had to do to prove that I was also hers.

"Lie back, Maebh."

She did as I asked. Leaning over, I took one of her nipples into my mouth and sucked on it hard, drawing out a low groan from my Irish beauty.

"Yes," she hissed, gripping the sheets and arching into me. "Oh, Cord."

My phone started to ring, and I ignored it as I kissed all over her breasts. She was so worked up that I knew if I reached between her legs she'd come on the spot.

The voicemail on my phone went off, then a text message. I continued to ignore it. Then my phone rang again, and I groaned.

"Don't stop," she whimpered, wrapping her legs around me to keep me where I was.

Fuck whoever was trying to call. I didn't care if it was Trevor saying the bar was burning down. I was about to make love to Maebh and nothing else mattered.

Her hands went to my jeans, quickly unbuttoning them and pushed them down.

My girl had a greedy side, and I loved it. I wasn't going to last a minute inside of her, I knew it.

When I heard my phone ring again, I cursed and moved away. Maebh sighed when I drew back.

"I need to get it."

Her eyes filled with disappointment, but she nodded in understanding.

Rolling off, I grabbed my phone from the side table. I nearly threw it when I saw Tammy's name. What in the fuck did she want?

"Hold on, baby. It's the bar."

She forced a smile, and I knew she knew it was Tammy.

Tapping the phone, I tried to push the anger down, especially when I saw Maebh slipping her shirt back over her head. Clearly the moment was gone.

"Cord, I hate to bug you," Tammy said.

"What's up?"

"You didn't pay the invoice for one of the IPA distributors, and they won't deliver until it's paid."

Frowning, I pushed my hand through my hair. "Get Trevor to pay it. He knows what to do."

"Trevor's writing checks now?"

I could hear the hurt in her voice. Tammy managed the bar and did a hell of a job keeping all the employees in line, but I was not ready to give her control of my books.

"Just have him take care of it. I left him in charge for a reason, Tammy."

Maebh walked out of the bedroom, and I sighed.

Fuck. Why did I answer the phone?

"You're sure?"

"What? Why are you questioning me? Yes, I'm fucking sure."

I instantly felt terrible for lashing out at her.

"Shit, I'm sorry, Tammy. I didn't mean to jump all over you. It's just, I took this weekend off to get away from the bar, and I haven't even been gone a full day. Trevor's staying upstairs at my place, I thought I told you that. If you need something, give him a call."

"You did tell me," she stated.

Anger raced through my veins. If she fucking knew, why the hell did she call me? "Just call him and he'll take care of it, not me."

"Fine, I won't bother you again." Her voice was short and filled with hurt.

"Wait, Tammy."

She sighed. "What, Cord?"

"I'm sorry. You just caught me at, um, a bad time."

Her silence nearly killed me. The last thing I wanted was to lose Tammy. She was the best manager I'd had since I'd opened the bar and she was damn good at her job.

"It's okay. I'm not really much of a manager if I can't handle these kinds of things while you're gone, and like you said, it hasn't even been a day. I'll call Trevor and get him to pay them ASAP."

"Thanks, Tammy. Everything else okay?"

"Yeah, it's picked up some for a Thursday night, but nothing too bad."

Nodding, I grabbed a shirt. "Good. Listen, I'm going out with Maebh for the evening. If you need anything, get Trevor to handle it."

"Maebh?" I could hear the shock in her voice. "She's with you? At the lake house?"

"Yeah, it's a long story, but we're fixin' to head out for the evening to catch a live band so I doubt I'll be able to hear my phone anyway."

"Well. Well. Well. When did you get with her? I thought you didn't like her."

"What?" I choked out. "I never said that."

"Are you...together?" Tammy asked, a hint of something I didn't recognize in her voice. The last thing I was going to do was talk to her about my personal life.

"Listen, I need to go. Only call if it's an emergency. Okay?"

"Of course, boss."

I hit End without saying goodbye. I had no idea why I was trying to get off the phone with Tammy so fast. Maybe it was because of what Maebh had overheard, that Tammy was after me. Shaking my head, I brushed the thought away. Slipping on my boots, I grabbed my wallet and headed downstairs.

"Maebh?" I called out. "Maebh?"

Shit, where in the hell did she run off to?

Walking into the kitchen, I looked out the back window. She was down at the dock, laughing at a guy who had pulled up next to my father's boat in similar boat to ours.

It didn't take me long to head down the trail made of crushed granite and wood.

"If you're interested, I can show you around the lake," he said.

My mouth dropped. *What in the hell?*

"She has *me* to show her, but thanks for the offer," I said loudly.

Maebh turned to look at me, and so did the guy. He held up his hands as if saying, *Sorry, dude, I didn't know she was yours.*

"You finished with your call?"

My eyes bounced to Maebh. She was smiling, but it didn't reach her eyes. I wanted to take her in my arms and tell her how sorry I was that I answered the damn thing, but I couldn't worry about that right now. What I had to worry about was some fucker moving in on my girl and me trying not to beat his ass.

I stopped walking. It hit me so fucking hard, I stumbled a few steps, nearly falling on my ass.

Am I...jealous?

I was fucking jealous that this asshole was talking to Maebh. Making her laugh and offering to show her around. I'd never been jealous of another man in my entire life.

"Cord?" Maebh asked, rushing over to me. "Are you okay?"

Dragging in a deep breath, I fought to find air for my burning lungs.

"Is he okay?" I heard the bastard say, snapping me out of my moment of insanity.

"I'm fine. Sorry about that. I guess I moved too fast and got a little dizzy."

Maebh looked at me with concern in her eyes. "What are you doing out here?" I asked, looking at her and then directly at the dick in the boat.

"I wasn't sure how long you would be on your call. It's a beautiful evening, so I came outside."

"I'm going to go ahead and dock the boat. If y'all would like to come over later, we're having a small party."

Staring at the guy, I asked, "You live next door?"

He grinned. "My grandparents own the property." His smiled dropped some, and he looked at me hard. "Holy shit, Cord Parker, is that you?"

Fucking hell. Trent Winston.

I nodded, trying not to act like I knew who he was.

"It's me! Trent! Dude, tell me you haven't forgotten all those crazy nights! The booze, the girls, the good times."

I could almost feel Maebh stiffen. It wasn't a secret that I had slept with a lot of women, and I knew Maebh knew that. She didn't have to hear about it, though.

"Sorry, it's not ringing a bell. If you'll excuse us, my girlfriend and I are heading out for the night."

Maebh sucked in a sharp breath as Trent's eyes widened in shock.

Before he could make some shit comment about "the Cord Parker he knew wouldn't have a girlfriend," I laced my arm around Maebh's waist and started back toward the house.

"Hey, if you feel like joining us when you get home, just come on over!"

Maebh glanced over her shoulder and was about to respond when I beat her to it. "Thanks, but we'll be fine."

I could feel her eyes on me, and I was positive she was wondering why I had acted like a complete asshole. Not to mention my little freak-out moment when I could barely move another step without losing my shit.

"Are you alright?" she asked, looking at me as I opened the door to let her into my truck.

"Yes." I was short with her and I instantly regretted it.

She didn't move except to cross her arms over her chest and glare.

"Something's wrong, and I'm not moving until you tell me what it is."

Dragging my hands down my face, I sighed. "I'm pissed, okay?"

"I see that. Want to tell me why?"

Did I tell her the truth or play it off? I wasn't good at this relationship shit. In the end, I went with truth.

"I'm pissed we got interrupted. I'm pissed you walked away when I was on the phone. I'm pissed Trent was flirting with you, and I'm pissed that I'm fucking pissed about all of that."

Her brows lifted and she stared for the longest time before turning away from me and climbing into my truck.

"And they say the Irish are short-tempered," she mumbled.

Shit, this woman made my damn chest flutter. "I'm sorry. I wanted to make love to you, Maebh, and you left."

Stone-faced, she said, "Then don't answer the fecking phone next time and don't be a jealous eejit."

She stared straight out the truck window. My mouth twitched with the threat of a smile and a part of me was curious as hell what pissing off Maebh O'Sullivan would be like. I had a feeling it would be interesting. Very interesting.

I got in and shut the door.

She was right. It was my own damn fault for not putting her first, especially with where we had been heading. I was a fucking idiot, and I knew it.

Maebh didn't speak the entire time we drove to the club, and I was starting to think it had been a mistake to even come out. If she was going to give me the silent treatment, this wasn't going to be a very fun date.

Parking, I turned the truck off and took her hand in mine. "I don't know why I answered the phone. Maybe I was nervous. Or scared."

She turned and let her gaze go straight to my eyes. "Of what?"

I brought her hand up to my lips and gently kissed it. "I've never felt these feelings before, Maebh. It's not that I'm afraid of committing. The first time I kissed you, I knew I never wanted to kiss another woman again. Yes, it threw me for a loop, and I honestly wasn't sure if I was going to be good at...at...well, this thing with us."

She smiled that smile that I would walk to the moon for, the one she saved only for me. The way it made her green eyes sparkle made my heart flip.

"I feel like once we make love, you will own my heart a hundred percent, and I'll be honest, that scares the living hell out of me. And worst of all, what if you say something or ask me to do something while we're making love and I don't understand with that damn accent of yours?"

Her lips opened slightly, and a tear slipped from her eyes and rolled down her cheek. At the same time, she busted out laughing.

She unbuckled, crawled over, and straddled me. I was quickly learning that this was something she liked to do, and I wanted her to do it as often as she liked.

Her mouth crashed to mine while my hands went to her hips, pulling her pussy into my hardening dick. We kissed like two horny teenagers parked at the local make-out spot. Our teeth hit, we nipped each other's lips, and when I sucked her tongue into my mouth, she let out a moan that went straight to my cock. I was positive I was about to come in my pants. No one had ever made me feel like this before. It was a high I was sure I'd never come down from, and I loved every minute of it.

"Maebh, if we don't stop I'm going to have you fuck me right here in the truck."

"Alright…if we have to," she gasped between kisses.

She started to grind into me, and I was about to lose control. Grabbing her ass, I squeezed it, and bucked my hips into her.

"I want you," she whispered.

"I know, baby. I want you, too."

Both of our hands went to the other's pants. All rational sense left me, and I was actually going to fuck her in my truck.

No. We need to stop. Now.

My hands froze. "I'm not fucking you for the first time…for *your* first time…in my truck, Maebh."

She stopped. It was as if my words got through to her. Her chest was heaving like mine.

"Jesus Christ," I whispered, leaning my forehead to hers. "You're like a curse that's also the cure. How did I ever live without you before?"

"I feel the same way," she said softly, her eyes looking into mine.

I wasn't sure if what I was about to say would scare her away, because this shit was all happening so fast, but I didn't care.

"I think I'm falling in love with you, Maebh."

Tears filled her eyes and she looked at me like I was the greatest thing on Earth.

She spoke so softly I barely heard her. "I've already fallen."

CHAPTER 18

Maebh

Today felt like a dream come true. Cord was holding my hand as we made our way across the dance floor to the bar.

"Hey, baby," a guy said, giving me a creepy-looking wink. I glanced away, making sure not to look him in the eye.

A few women shot me dirty looks after saying hi to Cord. He completely ignored them as he focused on the bar.

It was childish of me, but I wanted to stick me tongue out and declare he was mine.

We got to the bar, and Cord looked to me for what I wanted to drink.

"Whiskey. Irish if they have it."

He smiled, which made me knees weak. Would I always react this way to him? I was positive I would.

"My girl isn't afraid to drink."

I winked and watched his eyes turn dark with lust. Me panties were soaked in an instant.

Damn that Tammy for calling Cord. It hadn't even been one day, and she was calling him for help. Truth be told, I was more hurt that he'd taken her call than I was angry. Especially after hearing what those two waitresses had said about her. Cord insisted it wasn't true, but I was still going to keep me eye on her.

Cord handed me a beer and frowned. "No Irish whiskey."

With a giggle, I took the beer and pressed it to me lips as Cord pulled me against his body while we looked out at the dance floor. The live band had taken a break and the dancers had cleared from the floor.

A song started to play, and Cord leaned down, his mouth moving lightly across me neck before he whispered into me ear, "Dance with me."

Me body trembled and I lifted me beer for him to take and set on the table next to us.

Leading me to the dance floor, Cord faced me way and smiled. Me chest fluttered when he pulled me into his arms and held me close. Melting into his body, I closed me eyes and listened to the song. It was by one of me new favorite singers, Blake Shelton. Cord sang softly, and I was lost to him completely. I wanted to pinch me arm to make sure this was all real.

"Is this really happening, or am I dreaming?" I asked.

"I keep asking myself the same thing," Cord replied, pulling me chin up to his.

"That night you ran into me. Do you remember that night?"

I nodded. "Yes."

"You smiled, and I was nearly knocked onto my ass. My brothers always told me when I met the right woman, it was going to do just that. You drove me so crazy after that first night I saw you. I pretended to not like you because you scared the shit out of me. You were this Irish vixen I couldn't stay away from."

"Do I still scare you?"

He shook his head while he ran his tongue over his soft lips. "The only thing that scares me now is you not being in my arms."

We danced slowly and gazed at one another. This was what falling in love felt like. Was it too soon? Could I honestly be in love with him?

Yes. I'd been drawn to Cord for months, and even though we hadn't dated, he had taken hold of me heart like no other man had before.

"I want to leave," I whispered.

Cord flashed me a knowing grin and laced his hand in mine. We headed back through the crowd and out into the mild summer night. When we got to his truck, I went to say something when he pressed me against the door, covering his mouth with mine.

Me hands instantly moved up his chest and around his neck. If I could crawl inside of this man, I would.

"Maebh," Cord whispered against me lips while he slipped his hands under me shirt. He groaned while running them over me bare skin. I wanted him to move them to me breasts. "I don't deserve you."

His words rattled in me head before I pushed them away. There was no other man I could ever imagine I'd want to be with. This man owned me heart already…he just needed to believe it.

"Yes, you do. Take me home, Cord," I spoke against his ear.

Cord withdrew his hands and opened the door, helping me up inside. When he smiled, me heart felt like it was about to burst from me chest.

The ride back to his family's lake house was silent as we listened to the radio, and Cord rubbed his thumb over me hand. The sensation made me tummy tumble with each stroke. I was beginning to wonder if I was imagining it after a while. How could he make me feel this way with the same touch he'd repeated for the last fifteen minutes?

We pulled into the garage, and Cord rushed around the side. Instead of reaching his hand out, he lifted me out of the cab, causing me to laugh. When he bumped me head walking into the house, I let out a yell, making him laugh so hard he almost dropped me.

"I thought you were a stronger lad than this!" I proclaimed as he stumbled up the stairs, nearly losing his balance.

He snorted and then got his balance back. Giving me a wink, he replied, "Be quiet, I'm about to make love to you, and I'm nervous as fuck. I feel like it's my first damn time."

Me smile fell. "You're nervous? Really?"

Cord glanced down to me and went to speak, but tripped over the last step, causing us both to tumble to the ground. Except he tossed me forward, and I made it to the landing, while he fell down the steps. I cried out his name as well as, "Please, God. No! Please!"

"No, you don't need to come here, Mom. I'm fine."

Standing off to the side, I tried to hold back me smile as Cord tried to talk his mother out of driving up to the lake house.

"Mom, Maebh is here with me. I don't have a concussion, and nothing is broken. I don't see why you would want to come."

I chewed on me lip. If Cord's parents came we would for sure not be making love this weekend. That was twice in one day something had stopped us. I was hoping these weren't warning signs.

He rolled his eyes. "Mom, I'm gonna have to be blunt. I can't make any moves on Maebh if you're in the house. I don't care that you and Dad would be on the other side of the house. She's a screamer, and this is our first time."

Me jaw dropped and I stared with a shocked look while I stumbled back into the chair. "Cord!" I gasped.

He laughed and then stopped. "Yes. I'm positive I'm okay, and you don't need to drive here. We're enjoying ourselves and getting to know each other—just like you planned, right? Yes, mother, I'll use extra caution."

I groaned and dropped into the chair in the hospital room. Never would I be able to show me face to Melanie again.

"I love you, too. Bye."

Then the bastard started to laugh.

"Shit, it hurts to laugh. You sure I didn't break any ribs?" the eejit asked as he looked me way.

"How could you say that to your mother?" I asked, a horrified look on me face.

He snorted. "Calm down. She had answered the other line to let Waylynn know I was okay. She wasn't even on the phone when I said that about you being a screamer. I just wanted to see those cheeks flush."

Me hand covered me pounding heart. "Oh, thank God!"

He chuckled. "I love it when you say thank. It sounds like *tank*."

I rolled me eyes. "So you've said before. You may not have anything broken now, but wait till I batter ya! You scared the piss out of me."

Cord flashed a brilliant smile, then let it falter some. "I'm sorry, baby. Seems like we can't catch a break."

I walked up to him and pushed me fingers through his hair. "It will happen when it's supposed to. How do you feel?"

"Sore all over."

"The doctor said you should take a hot bath when you get home."

He wiggled his brows. "Will you take one with me? I know how much you like baths."

Pulling me lip into me mouth, I felt me cheeks blush. "We'll see."

It was all I could say. I knew if we took a bath, things would turn naughty, and Cord had just fallen down a flight of stairs.

"Okay, Mr. Parker. You're all set to go. Just need you to sign these discharge papers and then you and Mrs. Parker can head on out."

Me breath hitched in me throat, and I was about to correct the nurse, when Cord replied, "Thank goodness. I'm ready to get my Irish cailin home."

The nurse flashed me a sweet smile.

"Must be newlyweds. I can always tell."

Me eyes widened, and I wasn't sure what to say. The idea of being married to Cord sent a strange thrill through me body.

As if her last comment wasn't enough to jolt Cord, she went on. "Your wife certainly loves you. It's obvious when she looks at you, the same when you look at her."

Me stomach dropped to the floor, and I stood speechless. Cord had been signing his discharge papers when he looked directly at me. I'd thought for sure he'd be running away at the nurse's words. But he wasn't, and what he had said next made me entire body warm.

"I'm a hell of a lucky man, that's for sure."

He winked, and I grinned like those two silly teenagers I'd met at the store earlier today.

After pulling up me car, I jumped out and ran to the passenger door to help Cord get in.

The nurse was trying her best to help Cord, but he refused. "I'm fine, honestly," Cord said to the nurse. I had a sneaky feeling she wanted to put her arms around him.

"You kids have fun this weekend. No rushing! You'll have plenty of time with your wife!" the nurse called out. I groaned and walked back to me side of the car as I heard Cord thank her.

"Thanks, Betty! You know young love! Hopefully she'll keep her naughty down for a few days."

The nurse giggled and covered her flushed cheeks.

Cord had informed the older nurse that while we were, in fact, on our honeymoon, I had asked to try something new in the bedroom, and it had caught him off guard when he was carrying me up the stairs. That's when he tossed me to safety and fell. He had the poor woman eating out of his hand with our made-up honeymoon story. Before that, I swore every nurse who came into his room checked his ribs "just once more" to make sure they hadn't been broken…as if the X-ray wasn't good enough.

Once I got into the car and pulled away, I slapped him on the chest.

"Ouch! I'm sore, Maebh! I just fell down a flight of stairs."

"And you'll fall down another one if you tell one more person I'm doing naughty things to you!"

He leaned his chair back and closed his eyes. "Well, you did blow me on the lake. I get the feeling you like public sex."

Rolling me eyes, I drove back to the lake house. It was two in the morning, and I was exhausted. They had given Cord something for the pain at the hospital, along with a prescription if he felt like he needed it.

We had been five minutes away from the hospital when he fell asleep. It took another ten minutes to get him into the house and up the stairs to his room.

Cord reached out his hand and took mine. With a pouting lip, he whispered, "Don't leave me. Please stay."

Oh, sweet baby Jesus. How do I say no to that face?

Keeping me shirt and panties on, I crawled into bed and let Cord pull me against his body. I had envisioned this night being totally different, but something about him holding me in his arms felt perfectly right.

Me eyes drifted closed and snapped back open when Cord spoke.

"I've never slept with a woman in my bed."

"Never?" I asked, me heart racing.

"Mmm…never."

And just like that, he fell asleep, and I laid there another hour letting his words replay over and over in me head.

CHAPTER 19

Cord

My eyes opened, and I smiled. Then panicked.

My heart beat twice the normal beats per minute, and I was positive I was sweating.

Maebh was in my bed.

In my arms.

Sleeping.

And we both had clothes on.

And I fucking loved it.

Jesus H. Christ. What in the hell is wrong with me?

I had never in my life slept next to a woman. Never had a woman in my bed. Not even for a quick fuck. I fucked in their beds, got up and left. I'd rolled around in a few hotel beds—but never stayed the night. I *never* spooned or cuddled. And I sure as fuck never had my hard-as-a-rock cock pressed into a woman's panty-covered ass.

I groaned internally. Not because I didn't love every single second of this. I did. I groaned because I wasn't the type of guy who liked this shit…until Maebh O'Sullivan entered my world and turned it upside down and inside out.

Nothing about my life had been normal since this Irish beauty ran into me at my bar. I wanted her like I'd never wanted another woman. Hell, I didn't even want any other woman. The idea of flirting with one of the nurses last night was the last thing on my mind, even if the two young pretty ones kept coming in. Maebh rolled her eyes a time or two, and I found myself wondering if she was jealous. If the roles had been reversed, and it had been male nurses falling all over Maebh, I'd have beaten their asses. Maebh was mine, and I had no problem letting any douchebag who tried to get her attention know that fact.

Fucking hell, I've turned into my brothers. I've been bitten by the bug.

Maebh wiggled next to me, and I froze. That perfect ass pushed against me some, and I had to fight with all my strength to keep from stripping her down and burying myself into her. We'd tried twice yesterday to make love and each time we were stopped. I was tired of waiting for the right moment.

But first I had to piss. Slowly moving from her, I got out of bed and made my way to the bathroom.

Motherfucker. My entire body was sore from my tumble down the stairs.

After doing my business, I brushed my teeth. When I glanced at myself in the mirror, I took a good look at myself. "So, this is what being happy looks like?"

As much as all of this freaked me out, I knew it was what I wanted for the rest of my life.

I walked into the bedroom and stopped. The sight before me was the most beautiful thing I'd ever seen. Maebh lying in my bed sleeping. She stole the air from my lungs by simply existing in the same room as me. The sun was peeking through the window, casting a light straight from heaven down on her.

It hit me so damn hard I stumbled a few steps. "Holy shit," I whispered. "*This* is what I want to wake up to every…single…day."

Maebh moved slightly and let out the sweetest little moan as she rolled over and tucked her hand under her chin.

I looked for my phone. Maebh must have put it on the end table. Grabbing it, I quietly made my way out of the room and down the stairs to the kitchen, every step unleashing a new level of pain.

Hitting Tripp's number, I took in a deep breath.

"Hey, how's the fishing?"

"Christ Almighty, I need your help! Mom set me and Maebh up. Maebh is here with me, and yesterday was the best fucking day of my life. No, wait, I take that back. Today is the best day because I woke up with her in my bed, but we didn't have sex. She's driving me crazy with everything she does. I keep thinking how sexy she looks or how sweet her face is when she wrinkles her nose. Shit, don't get me started on the large mouth she caught and how fucking adorable it was that she named the damn thing Bob. I want to make her breakfast, but what do I make? Should I make love to her now, when I really want to, or should I wait? Did I mention she's a virgin? I don't even know the last time I was with a virgin. Wait, yes I do. Fucking high school!"

I stopped and waited for Tripp to answer as I pulled the refrigerator door open and scanned the food we'd bought at the grocery store yesterday.

"Tripp?" I asked when he didn't say anything.

"Cord?"

"Yeah, it's Cord. Can you hear me?"

"I can hear you, but I can't believe my damn ears. I'm trying to process all of that shit you just threw at me. Please tell me you have us on a three-way call with at least Steed."

Frowning, I replied, "It's just you, asshole."

"Holy. Shit. I need a moment. Honest to God, I never in my life thought this day would happen. Steed had hope for you, but me? I was doubtful."

"Thanks for that, bro."

"So let me get this straight. You're at the lake house?"

"Yes."

He cleared his throat. "And Maebh is there, and Mom somehow set all that up?"

"Yep."

"And so yesterday was a good day?"

"Something weird is happening to me, Tripp. It's like I'm a user, and she's my drug. She makes me crazy."

"Crazy how?"

My hand threaded through my hair. "Crazy like not myself. I keep having these thoughts. About punching a guy who flirts with her. Or…like this morning, she laid down next to me last night in bed and I woke up spooning her. With our clothes on! Then…then I got out of bed and the fucking damnedest thing happened."

"What? What happened!" Harley shouted.

"Seriously? You put me on speaker, you prick?"

"Cord!" they both yelled at once.

"Fine! I may have thought it would be nice to wake up with her in my bed every day…forever."

"Oh my God!" Harley squealed as Tripp laughed. The fucker actually laughed. Some brother he was. I was going to remember this, and he was going to pay for it.

"Cord Parker, if you hurt her I will rip your balls off your body and feed them to an animal."

I swallowed hard and covered my junk. "What the fuck, Harley?"

Tripp snorted.

"Can we get back to my problem here? This obsession, or need, or desire, or whatever this is."

Harley cleared her throat as if she was fixin' to make an earth-shattering proclamation...and Jesus, what she said next shattered something, although I'm sure it wasn't even remotely close to earth. "It's called being in love, Cord."

"Now, now. Let's not get carried away, Lee. This is new for Cord. I don't want him running out and jumping into the lake to try and get away."

I scoffed. "Harley's right. I think I am falling in love with Maebh."

Silence.

Waiting for them to let that soak in, I sat down at the bar and sighed.

"Are y'all done screwing around yet?" I asked.

"Did you...did I hear...oh my gawd! I have to go call the girls!"

Groaning, I heard Tripp say something to his wife before coming back on the line. "Cord, listen, I think it's freaking amazing that you're feeling this way. I always knew when you found the right woman, it was going to put you on your ass."

"That's for sure. It's weird. I mean, I'm freaked out, yet at the same time I'm so damn happy it doesn't bother me that I'm freaked out. I'm more afraid that the bubble will break, and I'll go back to being a dick."

"You won't. Now, let's go through some of those issues. First things first. Make her breakfast and bring it up to her. Women like that romantic shit."

"Okay, what should I make?"

"Pancakes. Fruit if y'all have any."

"I can do that, Mom always leaves stuff for pancakes up here."

"Now, the next thing on the list. Making love to her. Is she ready?"

I laughed. "Considering we almost got there twice yesterday, I'm going to say yes. She's also told me she wants me on more than one occasion."

"Okay. Don't get crazy. You have to go slow and remember that this is her first time, let her tell you how fast or slow to go."

Nodding, I took everything out for the pancakes and got to work on them. "Right, I got that."

"Use protection," Tripp said sternly.

"What the hell, bro. I've never forgotten a condom."

Tripp laughed. "Trust me, you'll almost forget. Trust me."

"No way. I've always housed the hose before I curl the toes."

"What?"

"I cover my stump before I hump."

"Jesus."

Smiling, I kept going. "When they go into heat, I package my meat. I wrap it in foil before I check the oil."

"Please stop."

"No glove, no love."

"Cord, I'm going to drive up there and punch you."

I laughed as I poured four small pancakes onto the griddle. "Sorry, I got carried away. Anyway, I always wear a condom."

"Good. Do you think it will be today?"

My stomach dropped. "If I have anything to say about it, it will happen in the next hour."

He chuckled. "You know I have to say it."

I closed my eyes and groaned. "You really don't."

"Payback is a bitch, bro."

Sighing, I flipped the pancakes. "Fine, I'm a little blue fucking person. Are you happy?"

"Say it. Wait, where is my recorder? I need to document this."

Why I even bothered to call my brother was beyond me. The only thing he'd managed to do was calm my ass down, and now he was going to harass me.

"Okay, let's hear it."

Groaning, I pulled the phone away and motioned like I was slamming it on the counter.

"Cord?"

"I've been Smurfed."

"I get to pick which Smurf."

"Hell no! Trevor already tried to pin me with Greedy Smurf. The name-giving is my job!"

"Ha! You can't give yourself a Smurf name."

"Who says I can't?"

"The rules!"

I pulled my phone back out and stared at it for a good thirty seconds. "There are no rules, you motherfucker!"

"There are now, and you can't Smurf yourself. Now, I think you have to be Gutsy Smurf. The whole accent thing and all."

I rolled my eyes. "He's Scottish, dude, not Irish!"

"Close enough."

"Why can't I be Jokey Smurf? Everyone knows I'm the funniest."

"Who is everyone?"

"Everyone! Like all of Oak Springs. Our family, our friends. It's perfect for me. I declare I'm Jokey Smurf, and you can't do anything about it because I started this tradition."

"This is the most ridiculous conversation I've ever had," Tripp mumbled.

I couldn't help grinning. "Then it's settled."

"You wait until you get back home, dude. Payback is a bitch."

"I believe you already said that, bro."

"Go make your girl breakfast. Enjoy your day, asswipe."

Flipping the pancakes onto a plate, I replied, "I intend to. Thanks, Tripp. Later."

My finger hit End, and I dropped my phone onto the counter. I turned to get out the strawberries, then washed and cut them up. My phone buzzed and I looked down to see I had a text from Tripp. When I opened it, I lost it laughing.

A picture of Gutsy appeared on my screen.

"Eejit," I said in my best Irish accent. I placed everything on a tray and headed back upstairs to the woman who was either going to drive me insane or kill me when I finally made love to her. I was honestly fine with either of those outcomes as long as she was involved.

Walking back into the room, I cleared my throat, hoping to wake her up.

Maebh stretched and let out a long moan that went straight to my cock. I was still in my jeans from last night, but Maebh had managed to get my shirt off.

"Good morning," I said, waiting for her to sit so I could put the tray down.

"What is this?" she asked, a stunning smile on her beautiful face. Shit. Her hair was going every which way, her make-up smeared under her eye and…was that a drool spot on the right side of her mouth?

Good God. I'd never seen a creature so perfectly beautiful.

"Breakfast in bed."

"Cord! You shouldn't have! How are you feeling?"

I placed the tray in front of her and shrugged. "Slightly sore, nothing too bad."

She looked my body over from head to toe. She lingered a little on the trail of hair leading into my jeans. Her cheeks flushed and her gaze dropped to the tray of food.

She picked up a strawberry and pressed it to her lips but didn't eat it. Instead she stared at me as I pulled my jeans off and slipped a pair of old sweats on. At least now my poor dick wouldn't be suffocating.

"You see something you want?" I asked, giving her a wink when her eyes met mine. She returned my wink with one of her own.

"As a matter of fact, I do."

Pointing to her breakfast, I demanded, "Eat first, you're going to need your energy for what I have planned for the rest of the day."

Maebh swallowed and then looked down at her food. I reached over and took the plate that had a few pancakes on it.

"Hope you like pancakes. Mom always keeps batter here."

With a grin, she replied, "I love pancakes."

After settling in next to her, I bumped her with my knee. "Thank you for staying with me last night."

Her cheeks turned pink. "It was such a hardship, me body pressed to yours all night."

I laughed.

Tucking a piece of hair behind her ear, Maebh cleared her throat. "May I ask you something?"

"Always," I said, taking a bite of pancakes.

Our eyes met, and she pressed her lips tightly together before speaking. "Last night you said you'd never had a woman sleep in your bed. Explain to me what you meant."

Lifting the corner of my mouth, I gave her a sexy smirk.

"I meant, I've never spent an evening, hell an hour, snuggling up next to a woman in my bed. Unless you count my mom when I was sick."

"Why?" she asked, her nose wrinkled in the cutest way.

I placed my hand on the side of her cheek and brushed the pad of my thumb over her soft skin.

"Because I've never wanted anyone in my bed. Until you."

CHAPTER 20

Maebh

Those two words sent me heart into a massive explosion of beats.

Cord Parker felt like a free fall, and it was the best fall of me life.

"Maebh," Cord said in a soft voice.

"Yes?"

"I'm going to make love to you now, so are you finished with those pancakes?"

I swallowed hard.

Oh, holy shite. This is it. Me virginity is about to be taken and by the most amazing man I'd ever met in me life.

"W-what pancakes?" I asked.

His chuckle vibrated through me entire body and went straight between me legs.

He took the tray over to the sitting area and set it on the table.

When he turned back to face me, his eyes were filled with desire.

Lifting his hand, he motioned for me to come to him. I did, scampering out of the bed like a child who had been summoned to go out and play with all the other kids. Stopping short of him, I watched as he lifted me blouse and pulled it over me head, dropping it to the floor.

His tongue ran over his lips and I let out a soft moan. When his hands came up and cupped me breasts, I closed me eyes.

"Do you have any idea how perfect your body is? Your breasts fit in my hands like they were made for them."

When his thumb ran over me nipple, I struggled to breathe. I sounded desperate for air, but when it came to Cord, I was beyond desperate. For everything.

Me hands shook as I placed them on his massive chest. The feel of his hard muscles under them made me shudder. Shite, he was so built. His abs had abs. His arms were massive, and I loved the idea of them pulling me to him as he slipped inside of me for the first time.

Then it hit me. I was about to have sex. A man was about to put his penis inside of me. What if it hurt? What if I sucked? What if I just laid there, too afraid to move?

"Stop thinking so hard," Cord said, pulling me against his body.

Cupping me face within his hands, he kissed me. The sweetest, most gentle kiss. Our tongues danced together while me fingertips ran down his body to his sweatpants. Dipping me hand in, I found him hard and ready. When I squeezed slightly, Cord moaned into me mouth, his hand wrapping around me neck, deepening the kiss. *Lord, this man can kiss.* Then he was on his knees and I was panting, needing him to keep kissing me. He left me so dizzy I hadn't realized he was stripping me of me panties until the heat from his touch jolted me out of me daze.

I stepped free of me panties and proceeded to remove his sweatpants. Me mouth watered when I looked at Cord's dick. It was big, thick, and jumping against his perfectly toned stomach.

"Don't even think of it, Maebh. If your mouth touches me I'm going to blow, and I want to come inside of you."

Me heart slammed against me chest with Cord's admission. To know he was as turned on as I was had me core throbbing.

Cord lifted me up, and I instinctively wrapped me legs around him. I held me breath as I felt his dick close to me entrance. For a moment I panicked, feeling the need to remind him about a condom, but he was soon lying me down on the bed.

He dropped to his knees and grabbed me ankles, pulling me until me arse was at the edge of the bed. Cord placed me legs over his shoulders, and I felt the heat building not only between me legs, but on me cheeks as well. He was going down on me, and I anticipated it more than I'd ever realized I would. This was so intimate, so sexy. Memories of yesterday hit me hard. I was spread open for him and the way he stared at me pussy had me all sorts of embarrassed, yet it also turned me on something fierce.

"Cord, you're staring."

His eyes flitted up to mine. "It's so beautiful. And it's all mine. No other man will ever have what's mine."

Me mouth opened in shock at his possessive tone. It both thrilled and scared me. I liked him being possessive…and I wasn't sure why it scared me.

Pushing me legs farther apart, Cord moaned before he licked through me folds and up to me clit. I jerked me hips and let out a muffled groan, all thoughts of why I had been scared only moments ago gone.

"Baby, you can be as loud as you want. It's just us."

His soft tongue on me pussy was my new favorite thing. It felt amazing, mind-blowing. The most intimate thing I'd ever experienced, and he'd done it to me twice now, the second time already better than the first.

I should have been embarrassed at how I was grinding into his face, pulling his head closer, but I wasn't. Me hands dropped, and I gripped the sheet. I held on as Cord licked and sucked me into a mind-blowing orgasm.

"Yes! Oh, God yes!" I cried out as me body shook with the most delicious feeling. Me mind left me, and I floated in the bliss. When I came down, I felt his mouth back on me clit and his fingers inside of me.

"Cord!" I nearly screamed out. I had barely recovered from me first orgasm when he was pulling another one out.

"Shite!" I cried, me body trembling euphoria raced through me body again.

I barely heard him tell me to get on all fours. Was he taking me from behind for our first time? Me head spun as I watched him lie down and flip onto his back. He reached up and pulled me hips down onto his face and licked me again.

Yes. Cord's mouth and fingers knew exactly how to take me to heaven.

"Oh God!"

My body was on fire, and I ached to release the energy building, so I rocked me hips. This one was going to be bigger than the others. *How is this even possible?* I'd had two amazing orgasms, and Cord was about to take me to another one. I wasn't sure I could survive another one.

But then he pulled away and pushed me up, making the building orgasm pause.

"Sit on my face, Maebh and ride me."

Me eyes widened in horror. *Sit on his face? What*?

"You want me to do what?" I asked, knowing that I was practically sitting on his face already. He slid up farther in the bed, taking me with him.

With a wide smile, he winked and said, "Fuck my face. Now."

Kneeling on either side of his head, me hands reached for the headboard, and I slowly moved down until I felt the warmth of his mouth again.

"Shite," I moaned out while Cord cupped me arse and squeezed.

"Cord. I don't think I can," I gasped.

He flicked his tongue, and I soon found meself rocking on his face. I could determine the speed, the pressure, where his tongue went.

"This is amazing," I whimpered.

Cord squeezed me arse as if agreeing. When I felt me buildup, I slowed down on purpose. I was being a greedy lass, but I didn't care. This felt so good.

Then his tongue went faster, and I lost control. Me hips rocked into his face as I gripped the headboard harder.

"Yes. Oh, God. Yes! I'm coming. I'm coming!"

I didn't give two shites who heard me. Me eyes rolled to the back of me head, and I swear the most powerful orgasm hit me fast and hard.

"Oh God…Cord!" I cried out as I felt me entire body go weak from me third orgasm in less than fifteen minutes.

Cord was now over me, his mouth everywhere on me while his fingers moved inside of me.

"Not again!" I cried out as he pulled me nipple into his mouth and pressed his thumb against me clit.

"Feck!" I cried out, me body trembling. Was it another orgasm? Or the same one? Christ, I didn't even know anymore, they bled one into another. All I knew was I was knackered, yet me body demanded more.

"Jesus, Maebh, you're fucking beautiful when you come."

Me head thrashed back and forth. If I had another orgasm I would die. How did he do this? Most women seemed lucky to have one, and I was on me third…or was it me fourth? Shite if I knew anymore.

Then, I felt him there.

"Are you ready?" he asked, and I opened me eyes to look at him. His ocean blue eyes sparkled.

"Condom?" I asked, my voice barely there.

"Yes."

When had he put it on? Jesus, I think I blacked out. His mouth, his hands, his body had been all over me. Shite. Why had we not had this conversation before this? I was still riding on me high and probably not thinking clearly at all when I said me next words.

"I'm on the pill."

He stilled.

"What?"

"I'm on the pill, and I want me first time with you to be without anything."

Cord's face looked pained. He shook his head. "I can't. I mean...I want to."

His gaze fell, and I knew I had ruined the moment.

Shite. I'm such an eejit.

"It's okay, don't stop. Please don't stop."

Cord lifted his eyes. "I want to protect you, Maebh. And until I can go and get tested again, I want to be safe. I care for you too much to do that to you."

Me breath stilled in me throat. He was thinking of me safety, and it nearly brought me to tears. I forced the tears back and found me voice.

"Make love to me, Cord. Please."

He smiled and pushed inside of me slowly. The feel of me opening to him was like sharp little knives piercing into me. I gasped, and Cord stopped.

"No! Don't stop," I begged, gripping his arse and pulling him deeper.

I started to speak in Irish about how amazing it felt yet at the same time how incredibly painful this was. Cord looked at me mouth and smiled.

"Agra, hope you're saying how fucking big my cock is right now because I have no fucking clue what you are rambling about."

I laughed. Cord's body stilled. He closed his eyes and moaned, almost a pained sound.

"*Fucking* yes. You're so goddamn tight, and when you laugh you squeeze my cock."

I laughed again, just because he'd said it felt good.

"*Fuck*. I'm going to come the moment I'm balls deep inside of you, Maebh."

He pushed in more, and I jerked, feeling a stabbing pain.

"Are you okay?"

I nodded as I bit back the tears. It burned like a bitch, and I knew me friends weren't lying when they said the first time hurt. It hurt like hell.

"I'm all the way in, baby."

Our eyes were locked on one another.

"The pain is slowly going away," I said.

"I'll move slowly when you tell me you're ready."

Me eyes closed, taking in the feel of him inside of me. So this was what all the fuss was about.

"I want to stay like this forever," I whispered.

He kissed me lips and then trailed soft kisses along me jaw, to me neck, and finally to me ear. Sucking in me earlobe, he blew hot breath on me, making me body tremble.

"I can arrange for this at least once a day—or more, if you want—for the rest of your life."

Tears built in me eyes. God, how I hoped he meant that.

"Cord," I gasped, me arms wrapping around his neck. "I want more."

He slowly gave me more. Pulling nearly all the way out, and pushing back in even slower. I needed more of him now that me body was adjusted to Cord's size.

"Faster," I said, wrapping me legs around him.

"Shit," Cord panted as he picked up his speed.

"Yes! Cord, yes!"

The feel of him moving inside me was almost too much to handle. I had given myself to him and a part of me was now terrified he'd break me heart. Then he looked into me eyes and all I saw was love and I knew this man would never intentionally hurt me.

Cord Parker was making love to me, and it was fecking amazing.

"Harder," I heard meself saying.

Cord closed his eyes and bit his lower lip. That one action and the change in his hip angle had me grabbing onto him.

"Oh God!" I cried out.

His eyes opened and pierced mine. "Are you coming?" he asked as I moved me hips in perfect rhythm to his.

"Yes," I whispered before his mouth crashed to mine. He kissed me like it meant everything to him.

He pulled slightly away, his forehead to mine and cried out me name.

"Maebh. I'm coming with you, baby."

And just like that, I fell even harder. Into me orgasm and in love.

CHAPTER 21

Cord

My dick twitched inside of Maebh as I forced my shaking arms to hold my body off of hers the best I could. I didn't want to pull out. If I could stay inside of her forever, I fucking would.

"Christ," I gasped. "Someone needs to bottle this feeling and sell it. They'd make a fortune."

She laughed, and her pussy tightened around me. I swear my cock was coming up again. Round two.

There was no way. I was emotionally and physically spent, and I know that with it being her first time, she needed some downtime before I ravaged her again.

"Was that good for you?" she asked, her voice sounding so unsure.

Drawing back and looking into her eyes, I replied, "That was amazing and couldn't have possibly felt any better. I can't even put my feelings into words right now. I'm fucking blown away."

She smiled, and my chest squeezed with an unfamiliar grip.

I was falling in love with this woman. When she started talking in Irish, I damn near lost it. I almost came on the spot. Her rambling and the look of pleasure and pain mixed on her face was the sexiest thing I'd ever seen. I would remember that moment for the rest of my life.

"Cord," she whispered, her finger moving lightly over my face. "Thank you for making that so beautiful."

An ache filled my chest, but it was a good ache. One that I had never experienced before, yet it filled me with so much emotion, I was unable to stop the words that tumbled from my mouth.

"I love you, Maebh."

When the words came out, I could hardly believe my own ears. But it was true. I was pretty sure I'd loved her the first moment she smiled at me. The first moment I heard her say my name.

"Cord, please don't say that because you think I need to hear those words. We've only been dating for a few days."

I pulled my brows tightly together. "Do you love me?"

Her lips pressed together, and her eyes filled with tears. "Yes."

"And I love you, so why shouldn't we say it? I knew I was falling for you, but what we just had together was absolutely unreal, and believe me when I say I'm the last person who ever thought I'd be telling a woman I loved her, let alone a woman I officially started dating a few days ago."

She giggled, and I loved how it made my heart feel.

"But I do love you, and I don't want to overthink it, or be afraid of it. I want to tell you. Hell, I want to shout it from the top of the tallest mountain. And damn anyone who says it's too soon."

Leaning my head back, I screamed, "I love you, Maebh O'Sullivan!"

She laughed and slapped her hand over my mouth. "You, eejit! Stop that."

I was still inside of her when our eyes met again, and I leaned down to kiss her.

"Are you sore?" I asked, scared to death she would say yes.

"Not right now, but I'm sure I will be."

"Let me run you a hot bath."

She grabbed onto my neck. "Will you take one with me?"

With a sexy smile, I replied, "Hell yes. I need to massage those aching muscles of yours—and get you to massage my aching muscles from that fall."

Her eyes turned dark, and I knew my sweet little Maebh was ready for round two, and I wasn't even pulled out of her yet.

Slowly taking myself out of her, I grabbed some tissues on the side of the bed and took the condom off. Tossing it in the trash in the bathroom, I started the bath water and got it to a pretty good temperature before walking back into the bedroom.

Maebh was lying on the bed looking thoroughly fucked and beautiful. Jesus, it hit me hard as hell that my heart would break into a million pieces if this woman ever left me.

"Ready?" I asked, extending my hand to her. She let the sheet fall from her, and I took in her body.

I pressed myself against her.

"I want you again, but I don't want you to be sore."

"Me pain tolerance is very high, Mr. Parker."

Laughing, I crushed my mouth to hers and kissed the hell out of her. When I withdrew, she was panting.

With a quick slap on her ass, I led her to the bath.

Maebh slipped down into the hot water and winced for a second. Shit. I wanted to punch myself for hurting her.

"You okay?" I asked, sliding in behind her and pulling her back to my front.

"Just a wee bit of a burn."

Brushing her dark hair from her neck, my lips tasted her soft skin, and she let out a contented groan that went straight to my already-hard-again cock.

"I want to stay here forever. Da can run the restaurant."

I chuckled. "We'd never see daylight again if we stayed here. I'd have you in bed every single moment of the day. Worshiping your body and trying to figure out what in the hell you were saying to me in Irish while I make love to you."

Maebh giggled, then rested her head against me while her body relaxed. My hands moved over her, finding her breasts. I massaged them as Maebh whispered my name.

Christ, there was something about the way my name came off those pretty pink lips. Like it was the first time I'd ever heard it.

"Cord, that feels…so good."

Dropping my other hand, it trailed down her stomach. Maebh pulled her legs apart and hissed, "Yes. Please."

Finding her clit, I rubbed it slow and soft.

"Oh, Cord."

Her hands landed on my thighs, and she squeezed them tight. I knew she was close, and I fucking loved how fast I could make her come.

Her moans filled the bathroom when I thought I heard a noise.

"What was that?" we both asked at once.

I stilled for a few seconds, but the silence proved it to be nothing.

My fingers went back to work as I dropped my head back against the tub and took in how her body began to build again.

She pushed her hips out and whispered, "Mmm. That feels so good."

"Whatcha doing to Maebh, Uncle Cord?"

My eyes flew open and Maebh went rigid in my arms.

"Cord, tell me I'm dreaming," Maebh whispered.

"If my niece is in this dream, we need to have a serious talk."

"Not funny, you eejit!"

Chloe laughed from the doorway. "You talk so funny! Are you Uncle Cord's girlfriend now? Why are you in the bathtub with her, Uncle Cord? Do y'all have bathing suits on?"

Looking between Chloe and Maebh, I let out a nervous chuckle.

"Of course we have our suits on!" Maebh said with a fake laugh.

Chloe gave us a look like she didn't believe us. Thank fuck I'd put the lavender bubble bath shit in.

"How come you're in the tub though?" Chloe asked.

"Well, Maebh's toe got stuck in the drain and…"

Maebh turned and looked at me like I had lost my damn mind. "My toe?"

"How come you have bubbles in there? Are you taking a bubble bath together? Are you helping her pull out her toe?"

I made a face at Maebh that said I had no fucking clue what I was doing, but that she needed to go along with me.

"And I had to slip in behind her to fit in, um…to…ahh…"

"Pull it out?" Chloe asked.

Maebh giggled while I groaned. "Something like that, pumpkin."

"Chloe?"

Paxton's voice rang out.

"Paxton!" I nearly screamed. "In here, quickly, please!"

When she came into the bathroom, she threw her hand over her mouth and lost it laughing.

"Paxton!" Maebh said, with an urgent need for her to get the other woman to stop laughing enough to help us out.

"What's going on?" she casually asked.

"Maebh, who is now Uncle Cord's girlfriend, has her toe stuck, and he was trying to help her get it out."

"Her toe is stuck?"

Maebh shrugged. "That wasn't my idea."

"Don't worry, Mommy. They have their bathing suits on. Can I see yours?" Chloe asked, pointing to Maebh.

"Sure, but I need to, um…"

"Chloe, will you run downstairs and help Grammy bring in the groceries?"

"What?" I nearly yelled out. "Mom's here?"

Paxton nodded as she ushered her daughter out the door. "We'll be right down."

"Okay!"

And like that, Chloe was gone and Paxton was handing me a towel.

"What in the fuck are you doing here? And with Mom?"

"I can't talk to you knowing you're naked. Get out and we'll talk." She headed into the bedroom and waited for us to get out of the tub. I wrapped a towel around Maebh and cupped her face with my hands.

"I'm so sorry."

She giggled. "I'm just glad they weren't here an hour ago."

My eyes closed while my shoulders sagged. "Fuck, me too."

"Love birds, you need to get your asses in swimsuits and downstairs before Chloe comes back up here."

In the bedroom, Maebh walked up to Paxton and they linked arms. Before I could say a word, they hurried out of the room and headed to the other master bedroom before I had a chance to ask why in the hell they were there.

I dried off and pulled on a pair of shorts and a T-shirt. My body was aching from the tumble down the steps and the lovemaking session, so I was pissed I'd had to cut my hot bath short. Walking up to the other bedroom door, I knocked.

"Y'all about ready?"

"Go away, Cord!" Paxton shouted.

"What? Why?"

Giggles came from the other side of the door.

"Girl talk!"

With a roll of my eyes, I leaned in closer. "Girl talk about what?"

The door opened, and I jumped back, my hand going over my heart.

"Shit! You scared me!"

Paxton lifted a brow. "If you think I'm not going to ask her about you two doing the deed, you're nuts. I've got Waylynn, Corina, and Meli on a conference call. We're about to discuss how well you...performed."

My cheeks heated, and my mouth suddenly feeling very dry. "W-what? You're kidding," I stated with a half-hearted laugh. "Right? You're not going to talk to my sisters about that. Are you?"

She shrugged and wiggled her fingers goodbye as she shut the door.

Spinning, I walked down the hall to the stairs that had nearly killed me last night.

Chloe was running around the living room singing a song to Gage.

With my fingers threaded through my hair, I silently prayed. "Please don't let anyone else be here."

When I made my way through the house, I found my mother in the kitchen standing next to an ungodly amount of food.

"Mom?"

She spun around and gave me a once over.

"Cord Parker, you scared the shit out of me. Why did you not answer your phone? I called and called and even called Maebh this morning. You left me no choice but to make the almost three-hour drive to make sure you were telling me the truth that you were all right."

My mouth hung open. "Mom, did it ever occur to you that maybe we were..."

Her brows lifted, and I snapped my mouth shut.

Shaking my head, I pointed at her. "This is all your fault."

She pointed at herself like she had no clue what I was talking about. "My fault? How is this my fault? I simply...double booked."

I tossed my hands in the air. "Double booked, my ass! You knew we would be here together and you knew something would happen between us."

Her eyes lit up. "My goodness, son, did you use protection?"

Stumbling back, I tried to find air for my now closed-up throat.

"I hope you were gentle with her. Paxton told me Maebh hadn't been deflowered yet."

Tripping over the chair, I shook my head and managed to find words. "Stop! Please…for the love of God, stop talking, Mom!"

"Dear Lord, I hope you didn't go all caveman on her like your father did me."

This time I turned and ran right into the sliding glass door. I fell on my ass and pain shot through my already aching ribs. With a shake of my head, I blinked a few times to clear my vision.

Was that…Steed? Mitchell? Tripp? Holy fuck…Dad?

"Cord! Are you okay? What is it with you falling? Did you hit your head yesterday? Are you dizzy? Do we need to go back to the doctor?"

The door opened, and Tripp stood over me, laughing his ass off. "Dude, who the hell were you trying to run from?"

My mother grabbed my chin and forcing me to look into her eyes. "Did they check to make sure you didn't hit your head?"

"I didn't hit my head!"

"Then why did you run into the glass door?" she asked, acting innocent.

"Because you said protection…and deflower…and…about your first time with…Dad!" I made a gagging sound.

"Oh hell, I don't want to know what this conversation is about," Steed said, stepping over me like I was nothing more than a barrier while he made his way over toward the sounds of his two kids.

Corina stopped in front of me. She held onto her daughter Merit. I knew by the smile on her face, I was about to catch hell. "Hey,

Cord! I knew someday a woman would knock you on you're a-s-s. Just didn't think it would happen twice in twenty-four hours."

I rolled my eyes and stood. "I thought you were on a phone call with Paxton?" I said, eyeing Corina.

"Oh, I got the *FOUR* one one, don't worry!" She put emphasis on the number four and it took me a minute to get her equating that with the number of times I'd made Maebh come. Jesus, was nothing sacred with this family? "Good job, by the way!"

I groaned. The only good thing was that my mother had long forgotten me by the time Waylynn and Jonathon walked in. She took Liberty from Jonathon's hands.

"Corina, Merit is up next!"

Tripp stopped in front of me and motioned for me to follow him outside. I did, and shut the sliding glass door behind me.

"You want to tell me how in the fuck you're all here on my weekend away?"

Tripp chuckled as he made his way down to the boat dock.

"Mom called this morning in a panic. Said she hadn't heard from you, and I said I had talked to you this morning and you were fine. She then decided we all needed to pack up and head up here."

"Why? If she arranged for Maebh and I to be here alone, why in the hell would she bring damn near the whole family?"

Tripp stopped and looked back at me. "Because, she overheard Paxton telling Amelia that Maebh was…well that she was…you know."

"No, I don't know."

Looking like he was uncomfortable as hell, he answered in a low mumble. "A virgin."

"Oh, for fuck's sake. Does the whole family know?"

He shrugged. "Pretty much. Mom freaked out and said she would have never pushed y'all together had she known and that we all had to come up here to save poor Maebh from the clutches of her manwhore son, Cord."

My eyes went round. "She said that?"

He laughed. "I made most of that last part up, but Mom was worried. She didn't want you to pressure Maebh."

"Holy fuck, what makes her think I would do that?"

Tripp stared like I had just asked the dumbest question ever. "Listen, your track record with women alone was cause for her to worry. Plus, y'all just sort of started dating and Mom felt guilty for butting in."

"Now she feels guilty. *Now*? She just fucking cock blocked me for the whole weekend, dude!"

Tripp tossed his head back and laughed.

"Tell me you're not staying here all weekend? Christ, what time did everyone get up? Did you follow each other here?"

"Like a goddamn Parker family caravan. I don't think I've seen Mom and Dad so happy though."

"Let me get this straight." I cleared my throat and scrubbed my hands down my face. "This weekend, the weekend I was supposed to spend alone, but really with Maebh, has now become a family weekend?"

He nodded. "Yep." With the pop on that p, that bastard.

My eyes closed, and I groaned. "Fucking hell."

Slapping me on the side of my arm, Tripp said, "Dude, I get it. I'd be pissed, too. If it was me, I'd pack my shit up and take Maebh back home and spend the weekend with her locked up at your place."

My gaze drifted over his shoulder to my dad. He was walking toward us, a huge smile plastered on his face. He looked happy as hell, and Tripp knew I would never leave and go back to my place. I'd have to be resourceful is all.

"Cord, I tried to talk your mother into not coming."

"He lies," Tripp whispered.

I let him pull me into a quick man hug as he slapped me on the back. "Don't worry about it, Dad."

His smile grew bigger. "This is damn amazing. All of us here. We need to hit the lake, do some fishing. Just us guys."

Tripp and I exchanged looks. I couldn't even think of the last time we'd all gone finishing together. Tripp lifted a brow. I knew the ball was in my court. I could get pissed and stomp out, or I could stay and let Maebh become a part of the family. God knows I wanted that, but I also wanted her. Again. And again, and again.

Shit.

"That would be great, Dad. Maebh caught a large mouth yesterday. Son of a bitch was huge, about ten pounds. I'll have to show you the pictures."

His face lit up. "No kidding! Then it's settled. Let's talk to the women and see when we can make this happen."

His arms landed on our shoulders, and we were soon headed back up to the house.

"We're not ruining your weekend, are we, son?"

I shook my head and felt my chest constrict. I wanted my family here, I truly did. But Maebh and I had made love for the first time this morning, and I had confessed to her that I loved her. I wanted to make sure we carved out time for just us. I also wanted to spend time with my family. I was fighting with two feelings: guilty and pissed off.

Taking in a deep breath, I blew it out and answered my father truthfully. "Not at all, Dad."

CHAPTER 22

Cord

When we walked into the kitchen, five women stared at me. All of them wore the same goofy smile.

I stopped. "What?"

Corina wiped what looked like a tear from her cheek. Harley shook her head and slapped her hand over her chest. Amelia bounced up and down like a little girl while Paxton and Waylynn smiled at me like they had just won a damn bet.

"Cord, how are you feeling?" Waylynn asked, walking a circle around me.

"This is my cue to leave," my father said, Tripp hot on his heels.

"Me, too," my brother said.

"What! Wait! Dad! Tripp!"

Tripp glanced over his shoulder and shot me a smirk.

"Fucker!" I cried out.

Waylynn made another circle around me.

"What in the fuck are you doing, Waylynn?"

"What are your intentions with our sweet Maebh?" she asked, her hands going to her hips.

"Don't most of you have kids you should be watching? Some mothers you are…" I accused, trying to step around my sister. I was blocked by her outstretched hand.

"Not me," Amelia stated.

My eyes shot over to my little sister. "Meli, help a guy out here."

She shook her head. "Answer Waylynn's question, Cord."

Threading my fingers through my hair, I felt a bead of a sweat form on my forehead.

"What do you mean, what are my intentions with *your* Maebh? She's mine, no one else's."

Amelia stepped forward. "Um, no, wrong. She was ours first. Not yours. You swooped in with your big fancy dick and stole her from us."

I nearly choked on my own tongue. "My big fancy dick? What the hell, Meli!"

She half shrugged. "Maebh might have shared a little too much information, and I will admit, I was slightly disturbed, but happy at the same time."

Feeling the need to cover my junk, I asked, "She called my dick fancy?"

"No," she said, shaking her head, "I can't tell you what she said. It would break girl code."

My curiosity piqued. "Well, hell, now I want to know."

"You can't know!" Waylynn bit out. "Now answer the goddamn question before I twist your balls up and pull them around your neck."

I stepped away from my older sister and swallowed hard. "Jesus, poor Jonathon," I whispered.

"Cord!" Paxton exclaimed.

"Fine! What do you want me to tell you? We made love, it was amazing, I've never felt this way before in my entire life. I'm scared shitless because I've never felt this way, but it's a weird kind of scared. I woke up with her in my arms, and I knew I wasn't ever going to be able to wake up again *without* her in my arms. All I can think about is making her happy and hearing that damn accent of hers. She scares me, and thrills me, and makes me want things I've never even thought I'd be wanting. I love her. I want to spend the rest of my life with her, marry her, have a couple of kids. I'm freaking out because I don't think like that! But that's…well…that's where I'm at."

I blew out a loud sigh.

All five of them stared at me with goofy grins on their faces.

"I can't believe it," Waylynn said. "Did you just say you loved her?"

"I don't care if y'all think it's too soon. It's how I feel."

With tears in my older sister's eyes, she softly said, "Cord Parker has been bit by the love bug."

Paxton smiled. "I knew the moment you first looked at her she was the one. Something about you instantly changed, Cord. Don't be scared."

"Well, I am, because I know I'm going to fuck it up."

"No, you won't," Harley said.

Corina walked up to me next. "Just be yourself, Cord. And if something scares you, tell her. Be honest with her. This is new for you and not that I don't think you can be a one-woman kind of guy, but I think you need to take things slow."

The rest of them agreed.

"Now, go upstairs and see her. We helped her move her stuff into the master you're staying in. Mom and Dad will stay in the other bedroom."

"Is she okay?" I asked, my heart beating erratically.

"Maybe a little traumatized that my daughter walked in on y'all doing…er…whatever it was you were doing, but other than that, she seems blissfully happy."

Chuckling, I shook my head and then kissed each one of them on the cheek before heading up the stairs to the second floor. The last thing I wanted to do was walk back through the main living room where everyone was waiting.

The door to the bedroom was shut. I opened it and saw Maebh sitting on the window seat, her chin resting on her knees as she stared out over the lake.

"Hey," I softly said.

She turned and smiled. "It's like a family reunion."

Rubbing the back of my neck, I sighed and shut the door. "Yeah, I'm sorry. If you want to leave…"

Her smile instantly fell.

"No, I don't mean *you* leave. If you want *us* to leave, we can."

The corners of her mouth rose. "No, I don't want to leave. I love your family and I think your mother had good intentions. The girls said she found out I was a virgin and panicked. Said she had to save me from your evil clutches."

I groaned as I sat down on the seat. Lifting my leg, I motioned for her to come to me. She did and sat with her back pressed against my chest. We looked out the window, neither one of us saying anything until Maebh broke the silence.

"Are we moving too fast? The girls were surprised we said we loved each other."

"Maybe. I don't know. I'm sure any normal guy would wait a bit before busting out those three words."

Her body shook with a light chuckle.

"But when I felt it in my heart, I wanted to tell you. I've never felt that before and why should I hold it in?"

Her body tensed in my arms.

"Talk to me, Maebh."

"What if this is just different for you? The girl you thought you didn't want, but turned out you did. The something different that you craved…and soon you'll get sick off."

Now it was my turn to tense up. I wanted her to trust me and my feelings.

"That's not going to happen."

Her head dropped back to my chest. "Cord, what if you miss being with other women? Do you really think you can stop and be with just me?"

Pushing her away, I turned so she was facing me.

"I can't even tell you the last time I slept with a woman. All I've been thinking about for months is you. I don't want anyone besides you, agra."

Tears pooled in her eyes. "Please don't hurt me, Cord. I don't think me heart could take it if you broke it."

My heart fucking felt like it was breaking in two. I never wanted to be the reason this woman cried. Ever. My hands cupped her face and I drew her mouth closer to mine.

"I feel the same way about you, baby. I've never given my heart away to anyone and you hold the power to completely destroy me if you wanted to."

Her gaze flicked across my face before landing back on my eyes.

"We've got a serious problem, though."

Pulling in my brows, I asked, "What is it?"

She chewed on her lip before saying, "I want you, and there's a whole house of Parkers."

I laughed. "Oh, I've already figured out how to handle that."

"Is that so? Care to share with me? Or better yet, care to show me?"

Shaking my head, I replied, "You'll let it slip to someone else and they'll be using our nooky place."

"Nooky place?"

Pulling her body back against mine, I said, "Yep. Our secret sex place."

Maebh laughed. "I can't wait to see where this is."

Waylynn had somehow managed to get all the women, including my mother, to go shopping in Marble Falls. It was just the guys with the kids. Our father conveniently slipped out of the house to go check on his lake buddy next door.

Sitting back with a beer in one hand and a remote in the other, Wade and I watched Jonathon, Steed, and Mitchell handle their kids. Tripp was in the corner with Chloe. Since he was married to a vet, she'd enlisted him to do surgery on her doll whose arm had been ripped off by Hemi in a tug of war between Chloe and the dog.

"Make you want one?" I asked Wade with a chuckle.

"In a way, yes. But Amelia is thinking about this movie deal and if she goes for it, I'm not sure now would be the time."

I turned to him. "Why not?"

He lifted his beer to his mouth and took a drink. "I don't want her being stressed out while pregnant. Plus, I don't think she's ready for that yet. Kids, I mean."

"Have you asked her?"

His head jerked to look at me. "Why, has she said something about wanting kids?"

I could see the hope dancing in his eyes. I lifted my hand up, "Whoa, don't go getting all daddy on me. I haven't talked to her about it and the other girls haven't said anything to me. From the look in your eyes, I'm thinking y'all need to talk about this."

Rubbing the back of his neck, he tilted it side to side, cracking it. "I know. I just want her to decide on the movie thing first before I say anything."

"Fair enough."

Wade leaned forward, his brows constricted. "Steed? What's Gage got that he's pushing up his nose?"

Steed had been showing Jonathon a trick—how to get Liberty's pants on easier—when he glanced up at his son.

"Gage? What do you got there, buddy?"

Steed's eyes nearly popped out of his head as he looked closer.

"Holy shit! Something's up his nose!" Steed cried out.

"Hell! Shit! Fuck!" Chloe yelled out, knowing her father wasn't going to get after her since her baby brother currently had something lodged in his nose.

But Tripp did. "Chloe Parker. You know better!"

Her little shoulders dropped, and she skipped over to Steed and bent down to take a look for herself.

"Daddy, let me look. I'm a mommy and I know what to do."

My gaze lifted to Steed. He shrugged. "Her baby dolls."

"It's a noodle," Chloe declared.

"Holy shit, they really are born with it," Wade whispered next to me. I attempted not to laugh as Steed stared at his daughter and then let out a somewhat scared-sounding laugh.

"A…noodle? Pumpkin, what do you mean?"

"Yep. The kind that you make 'roni and cheese with."

Steed swallowed hard. "That's up his nose? How do we get it out?"

Chloe shrugged. "Don't ask me. You're the dad."

Steed picked up Gage, panic written all over his face.

"What's going on?" Mitchell asked. He had just put Merit down for a nap.

"Gage shoved a piece of macaroni up his nose," Jonathon answered.

Mitchell looked down at Gage who was looking up at Mitchell and smiling. When my brother gagged at that noodle lodged in his nose, I nearly pissed myself laughing.

"Dude, calm down. It's a piece of pasta. Just have him blow his nose, it will come out. And Mitchell, since when does pasta make you gag?" I asked.

"Since it's stuck up a person's nose!" he replied.

Twenty minutes later, we had a crying Gage who wanted the pasta out of his nose. We were all staring at one other as we tried to come up with ideas. Gage couldn't blow his nose and only got frustrated the more we tried to get him to do it.

"You gotta do it, Daddy," Chloe said, staring up at her father. Her hands were on her hips exactly like my sister Waylynn's had been earlier today when she was grilling me about Maebh. It had to be a Parker woman thing.

"You do," I said as Tripp, Jonathon, Mitch, and Wade all nodded in agreement.

"She's going to kill me," Steed said.

"Better you than me," Chloe piped in, causing most of us to laugh. Steed was the exception.

"Wonder where she learned that?" Tripp chuckled.

"Chloe, you call Mommy from Daddy's phone."

My adorable niece held out her hand and rolled her eyes. If she had been twenty years older I could imagine her saying, *"Give it to me. Women have to do all the dirty work."*

"Hey, Mommy! Oh, it's good. Uncle Tripp did surgery on Holly, my princess doll, while Daddy showed Uncle Jonathon how to put Liberty's outfit on the right way. Uncle Mitchell rocked Merit to sleep and Uncle Cord and Uncle Wade have been drinking all the beer."

"Hey!" Wade and I said at once.

"Mmm-hmm. Yes. I know. Boys," Chloe declared. All of a sudden she seemed like she was eighteen. How in the hell did she even observe all of that?

"But, Mommy, Daddy has a problem. Gage put a mac-a-roni noddle in his nose and it won't come out. He was afraid to call and tell you."

Steed's face fell and Gage let out a little laugh. Almost like he knew his sister had just thrown their father under the bus.

Wade tried to hold his laughter in and almost succeeded. Steed glared at him and pointed. "Someday, asshole, this will be you!"

Holding up his hands in defeat, Wade forced himself to stop laughing.

Chloe handed Steed his cell phone. "Mommy wants to talk to you."

Steed shook his head and stepped away.

"For Pete's sake, man! Be a father, dude!" Tripp cried out.

Pointing to Tripp, Steed whispered, "I hope you end up with twins!"

Tripp's smile dropped. "That was just mean, dude."

Taking the phone from Chloe, Steed cleared his throat. "Hey, baby. Yeah. Okay. Hmmm, is that the only thing to do? Right. Okay. Got it. Nope, everything else is great. I love you too. Bye."

That was the fastest I'd ever seen Steed get off the phone with Paxton. He pushed the phone into his back pocket and then looked around the room before his eyes landed on me.

"Paxton said Gage needs to open his mouth, and someone has to blow into it and that will push the noodle out."

Mitchell gagged. Wade and Jonathon walked into the kitchen so fast I didn't even have time to react. That left Tripp, me, or Steed to do the deed.

"I know you're not looking at me, dude," I said.

"Cord! You know CPR! Paxton said you're the best one to do it."

Tripp looked at me and nodded.

"Yeah, no. I mean, I'll do whatever for the little guy, you need me to buy him the best birthday gift, I'm there. Need me to buy him his first car or pay for college, I'm all over that. Need me to talk to him about the birds and the bees and I'm your man…but that? No," I spoke so low to keep the little ears in the room from hearing.

Steed looked at me with pleading eyes.

"Dude! You've cleaned his butt with green poop and you can't do this?" I declared.

"How come you don't want to do it, Uncle Cord? And what would you tell him about birds and bees, about how fast they fly or how much honey they can make?" Chloe asked.

We all stared at Chloe. How was she even hearing these conversations? Parker women.

The way Steed gave me those damn puppy dog eyes had me nearly ready to break. Then Chloe looked at me, her little blue eyes questioning why I wouldn't help her baby brother get the noodle out of his nose.

"Fine. Bring him into the kitchen and sit him on the island."

Steed grinned. "Thanks, dude. I knew I could count on you. You've always been my favorite brother."

I rolled my eyes and mumbled. "Whatever."

After Steed placed Gage on the counter, I told Gage to open wide and that I was going to blow a puff of air into his mouth. Gage laughed. I guess to him, this was funny.

Chloe was practically under me as she fought with Tripp and Wade for the up-close advantage.

Mitchell gagged again, and I glared at him. Then I leaned over and went to blow when Chloe yelled, "Wait! Should we record this?"

I stared at my niece with a disbelieving expression.

"You really are your father's daughter," I said as Steed took his phone out and handed it to Chloe.

With a deep breath, I looked at Gage. Damn, he was a cute little thing. "Ready, buddy?"

He nodded.

"Open!" I leaned down and blew. What I wasn't expecting was for the noddle to fly out of Gage's nose and land on my face.

All I heard was grown men gagging. Then Chloe screaming, "Boogers!"

Gage started laughing, and I swear a long trail of booger slime from his nose flew straight to my cheek. I wiped the noodle off of my face as I let out a girlish scream. I started gagging when I felt the wetness on my cheek and hand. Mitchell ran from the room covering his mouth as he nearly threw up.

And to think, he was a cop! I tried to get myself under control. With a deep breath, I walked over toward the sink, but when Wade looked at me with a horrified expression and gagged, I nearly threw up.

Wade pointed at my face and said, "It's on...*uuuall*... your face! Dude, get it...*uuuall*...oh God...*uuuall.*"

"Stop gagging, you dick!" I shouted to Wade as I turned on the water, grabbed the dish soap, and scrubbed my face.

After scrubbing nearly all my skin off, I grabbed the dishtowel and dried my face. Turning, I noticed Steed had put Gage down on the floor, and he promptly took off after Hemi who had run in to see what all the fuss was about.

"I'm. Never. Having. Kids," Wade deadpanned. "Never. *Uuuall.*"

CHAPTER 23

maebh

The moment I walked into the house, Cord grabbed me. "Come on. We're going to our secret place."

I hadn't even dropped me bags off in our room before he was dragging me out the door.

"Cord! I need to put me bags up."

He glanced down and saw the Victoria's Secret bag. "Is that for me?"

Me face heated, and I hit him on the chest. "Let me go drop these off, then we can slip away."

Groaning, he took the bags out of me hand and rushed up the steps, taking them two at a time.

"What's his hurry?" Amelia asked.

I shrugged. "I don't know."

Cord was soon rushing down the stairs and grabbing me by the hand.

"Let's go. My truck is stuck in the garage, blocked by all the damn vehicles, so we have to take your car."

"Where are we going?" I asked again.

Cord opened the passenger side of me car and practically pushed me into it with his hand on top of me head.

"Cord!" I shouted, pushing his hand away.

He finally let me get into the car while he jogged around the front of it.

I stared at him and couldn't help but giggle.

"What is going on?"

"I've been forced to watch my brothers with their kids today, I had a noodle covered in snot hit me on the face, Wade is a motherfucker for making me nearly throw up, my cock is hard, and you walked in with fucking lingerie and the house is full of my family. I'm about to lose my shit."

Pressing me lips tightly together, I folded me hands in me lap and stayed quiet.

"I brought your lingerie, by the way."

Snapping me head to him, I gasped. "How?"

"Shoved it down my pants. I mean, there's nothing to the fucking thing."

Pulling into a hotel, Cord threw the car in park and jumped out. The valet handed him the ticket as Cord tossed him the keys.

"Are you dining with us this evening?" the kid asked.

"No, we have reservations for a room."

"We'll get your luggage and bring it to your room, sir."

Cord walked up to me and glanced back to the valet. "We don't have any."

Me cheeks heated.

"We're staying here all night?" I asked as we walked by the reservation desk. Looking confused, I asked, "Don't we need to check in?"

"No. I already did."

"When?"

"Ten minutes after the booger noodle made contact with my cheek."

Biting me cheek, I laced me fingers in his.

"This hotel is beautiful," I said, looking around for the first time. It was something I would picture me da staying in when he traveled. The marble floors and elegant vibe told me this place wasn't cheap. Cord pulled out a card and pushed it into the reader in the lift and hit the very top floor button.

"I don't need to be impressed with expensive things, Cord," I said, feeling a bit of anger pulse through me body. Me whole life I had grown up in the world of money. If given the chance to be in a single room in a hotel versus an expensive suite, I'd take the one room any day.

"Trust me, baby, I'm not trying to impress you. This was the only room they had left."

"Oh," I whispered, feeling guilty for me thoughts. I knew the Parkers had money; that was no secret. And I was sure Cord did well with his profits from the bar, but the one thing I loved about him and his family was that they didn't act like they were the richest family in the area. Unlike me grandmother. She made sure to tell everyone she was from royalty. The fact that she was English and me grandda was Irish made no difference to her. She still had royal blood pulsing through her veins, and according to her, so did I. Her dream was for me to move to England and marry someone proper. That was where Sean came into the picture while I was at uni. We had been oil and vinegar. We both knew it would never work, but me grandmother had other plans.

The *ding* of the lift pulled me from me thoughts. Cord walked a few feet and slipped the key into the door, motioning for me to walk in first.

"Are you sore?" he asked as I took in the room. It was beautiful. Floor-to-ceiling windows spanned across the entire living, dining, and small kitchen area. The view of the water and hill country stole my breath.

"Not really," I said, turning to see me bag sitting next to the sofa.

"Have you already been here?"

Cord smiled. "Yes. We can visit during the day with my family, but at night, at night I want you all to myself."

I returned his sexy grin with one of me own. "But it's not night and your ma had dinner plans."

Stalking toward me, Cord placed his finger on me chin. "We'll be back for dinner. Right now, I want my beautiful Irish cailín."

When he kissed me jaw, I gripped his arms to keep me legs steady. "Yes," I hissed. I could hear the desire in me voice, and I didn't care. Cord Parker brought something out in me that was raw. Passionate. I was his...and he was mine.

"I made love to you earlier, baby. Right now I want to fuck you."

Me heart pounded so loudly I was sure the entire top floor heard it. I warmed with the idea of Cord being inside of me. Dazed with the idea of him fucking me, no more worries about me virginity. I was a little sore, but I wanted him. All of him. I wanted to see him lose control and give me everything he wanted to give.

Before I knew what was happening, he lifted me in his arms and carried me through the massive suite. When he walked into the bedroom, I gasped. Roses of every color filled the entire room.

How in the world did he do this?

"Cord," I whispered, me voice sounding raspy from emotion. "When? How?"

He put me on the floor and cupped me face in his warm, strong hands. "When I booked the room, I asked the concierge to fill the room with roses. I told him today was a special day for us and that I needed everything to be perfect."

When he moved his mouth to mine, I let out a groan of anticipation. He kissed me like I had never been kissed before. It felt desperate, almost. Like he was trying to tell me this wasn't a dream. That we were finally together, and that he would never break me heart. Melting into his kiss and body, I prayed for the last bit of fear and doubt to melt away.

And it did. At least for now.

"Cord," I panted when he finally stopped kissing me. Our hands went to each other's clothes. It was a frantic need, each of us fumbling to remove the layer of clothing between our bodies.

When Cord had successfully stripped me bare, he took a step back and let his eyes move over me body. A part of me wanted to cover up, but his look of pure desire did something else to me. It drove me own desire even more. The heavy weight of need was pulsing between me legs. One touch, and I was sure to explode into a million pieces of bliss.

Cord dropped to his knees and I gasped when he picked up me leg and put it over his shoulder.

He licked through me hot folds, and I nearly collapsed to the floor.

I was in his arms before he would let that happen. Moving us to the bed, he set me down.

"Maebh, I need to taste that sweet pussy of yours again."

Me cheeks heated and the only thing I could do was nod. It was clear Cord liked giving me oral sex, and I wasn't about to argue. When he spread me legs, I dropped back onto the large, king-size bed and prepared for how he made me feel. The smell of roses filled me senses and brought this experience to another level. I'd never be able to smell a rose again and not think of Cord's face between me legs, licking and sucking until he nearly drove me mad.

"Cord!" I gasped, me orgasm building fast. I was sore, but not so sore I worried about him being inside me.

His fingers slipped into me and he pumped faster. A few burns pierced, and when I let out a whimper, he slowed down.

"Faster. Harder, Cord!" I demanded, needing him to give me everything.

"Fucking hell, Maebh. You're playing with your tits. You gotta warn a man when you do that."

I hadn't even realized I was pulling and squeezing on me nipples. Me hips jerked and pumped, silently begging him to give me my release.

Then his mouth was back on me clit, and I was lost to a sea of exploding stars. Light turned to dark and then back to the most brilliant light. Me body arched off the bed, and I cried out his name in one long moan.

This man was my undoing.

I felt him grabbing under me knees and pulling me barely off the edge of the bed. He lined himself up, and I had the fortitude to gasp out, "Condom?" remembering earlier when he was insistent on wearing one. I'd never been with another man before, so I wasn't worried about me, but Cord wasn't ready. And I would respect that.

"I've got one on, baby," he said, pushing his large cock into me body. I shuddered as he filled me whole.

"Oh Cord," I said when he pulled out, then pushed back in. Each time going farther inside of me.

"I'm losing control, baby."

Opening me eyes, I looked into his and took a deep breath as I let him fill me completely. His eyes looked both pained and excited.

"Then lose control," I whispered, prepared to take him. All of him.

And Cord did. He grabbed me hips and lifted me more as he pulled out and slammed back into me. The feel of his balls slapping against me arse was a huge turn on.

"Again!" I cried out.

"Fuuuuck," he groaned, doing it again. His rhythm was slow at first. I could feel him shake, and I knew he was afraid to hurt me.

"You're different, Maebh. I need you to know that."

Our eyes were locked on one another. He was pleading with me to understand his need to fuck me, hoping it didn't make me think less of him. My mind wanted to wander down a dark path. Cord fucking other women. Hard and fast. His pleasure, when he finally came inside them.

Bile moved up into my throat and I had to push the thoughts away. He stilled, almost as if he knew his words had brought the thoughts to me.

"Look at me."

Tear filled me green eyes as I gazed into his blue. "You. Are. Different. I love you and you're it for me. You're mine, and I'm yours."

I nodded.

"Say it, say I'm yours."

The lump in me throat kept me from speaking. Me mouth opened and closed. Cord pulled out of me, and I quickly shook me head, panicked that I had ruined the moment because of me stupid fears.

"Say it," he demanded. "Say that I'm yours, Maebh."

Swallowing hard, I focused on his eyes. They were filled with nothing but promises of love.

"You're mine. And I'm yours. Forever."

His eyes closed, and he let out the breath he had been holding in. "Move back onto the bed."

Me heart dropped. He wasn't going to fuck me after all. Disappointment rushed into the pit of me stomach. Cord crawled over me, kissing me up me leg and sliding his tongue back through me wetness. I gasped. He had just been inside of me. Something about that dirty act made a rush of wetness hit between me legs.

He slowly kissed up me body and to me lips. The kiss was soft and sweet. He pushed into me, not softly, yet not hard. He moved at a beautiful rhythm as he made love to me and kissed me.

His fingers trailed down me neck, between me breasts, stomach, and finally to me clit. One push of his thumb in a circular motion on me clit and I was lost again.

"That's it, baby. Fucking come on my cock while you say my name."

Me head thrashed as I did what he said. Then, he lost his control and gripped me hips. He fucked me hard and fast. It was a delicious pain that I wanted more of. Needed more of.

"Oh God!" I groaned out. "Feels. So. Good."

"Fuck, Maebh, you feel so good."

His words grunted out of him in a deep sexy voice. It fueled on me next build up. How in the hell could I be about to come again?

Cord pounded into me, bringing me hips to his with each thrust. He was hitting a spot that only he'd ever touched—that spot being pounded over and over with his cock had me toes curling.

"Don't. Stop. Right. There," I panted.

"Maebh. I can't wait. I'm going to come."

It wasn't me imagination. I felt him grow bigger inside as his balls kept up their sensual assault on me arse.

"Cord!" I screamed out at the same time he cried out me name.

Everything around me stopped and the only thing I could feel was Cord inside of me. Me body humming with my orgasm. Cord's head dropped back as he let out a long moan, spilling himself into the condom, and I couldn't help but wish he was coming into me. I wanted us to be truly connected as one. No barriers, no hiding. We'd been hiding from each other for too long and now it was our time to share everything with each other.

His body slumped, and he rested on his elbows, careful not to put too much weight onto me.

Our bodies were covered in a sheen of sweat. Chests heaving up and down as much-needed air was dragged into our lungs. Wrapping me arms around his neck, our eyes met. No words needed to be spoken. It was just the two of us in this organic, raw moment of vulnerability.

He was mine.

I was his.

Forever.

CHAPTER 24

Cord

We stayed at the hotel Friday and Saturday night, and returned to my folks' lake house on Sunday morning, at my mother's request. She felt terrible for pushing us to a hotel, even though I told her it was fine. We would all spend Sunday at the house and then home Monday morning.

"Trevor give you a call at all this weekend?" Tripp asked, casting his line out.

"Only a couple of times to say everything was okay."

My father leaned back and let out a contented sigh. Glancing over, I asked, "Dad, why are you wearing that vest?"

He glanced down to his new life jacket that the guy at the sports store had talked him into buying.

"It's a flotation device, son, that was made for fishermen. See how thin it is. Just in case something happens, and I'm thrown from the boat, it will inflate, roll me over and make sure my face is out of the water."

"You plan on falling out of the boat anytime soon?" Steed asked as the rest of us chuckled.

"You're dad's right. Safety should always come first."

We all turned to look at Jonathon, who also had the same damn vest on, looking like a fucking idiot doing the twinsie thing. "Says the kiss-ass who bought one too," I replied.

Jonathon glared at us. "I'm not a kiss-ass. I happen to believe in safety and being prepared."

Wade laughed. "So the fact that John bought one didn't factor into your purchase at all, huh?"

My father turned to Jonathon, clearly amused at where this was going. I think he loved giving his son-in-laws hell even more than we did.

"No, it didn't."

"Come on, Jonathon," my father said. "Let's call a spade a spade. You're kissing my ass."

Jonathon's mouth dropped open. "I'm not!"

"If the shoe fits, dude," Steed added.

"Why would I need to kiss his ass? I'm already married to Waylynn, and we have a baby. That makes no sense."

My father chuckled and shook his head. "Alright, boys. Let's leave Handy Smurf alone. I'd rather focus on Gutsy Smurf here."

All of us froze, especially me.

"How in the hell do you know about the Smurfs?" I asked, my face draining of blood. I was probably white as a ghost.

My father pointed to Tripp. "Your brother filled me in."

Steed and Mitchell both laughed, as did Jonathon and Wade.

"I still never got my name. Did I?" Mitchell asked.

"Dude, you're Tracker Smurf, the whole cop thing," Wade replied.

"I think I should be Brainy," Tripp said.

My eyes darted around the boat until they landed on Tripp, who was doing his best to hold back his smile.

"What's mine?" Wade asked. "Did I ever officially get one?"

Snapping my head back to him, I was about to answer when my father did. *My father*, of all people!

"Wade, I think you're Narrator Smurf. You sit back and take it all in and retell it better than the rest of us."

I swear to God, Wade's fucking chest puffed out. "Narrator Smurf, I like it."

"No, I do the names!" I called out.

My father scoffed. "Not anymore. You're tainted. You've become one of us. Honestly, I think you're better suited as Jokey Smurf instead of Gutsy Smurf."

All the men in the boat fucking pointed to me and let out a "Yes!"

I shook my head. "I do the names!" I shouted.

"Papa Smurf has spoken, dude, let it go," Jonathon said with a shit-eating grin. Being the kiss-ass that he was, he had to agree with my dad. Well, fuck that.

Walking over to him, I pulled on the yellow cord and his flotation device inflated, causing him to stumble back and go right over the side of the boat and into the water.

Raucous laughter filled the boat as I looked at Jonathon struggling in the water. When he glanced up at me and shot me the finger, I gave him a smile and returned the gesture.

"Looks like it works, Dad."

Two months had passed since that incredible weekend up at the lake house. The days were still hot, but the occasional cold front would gave us a few degrees' reprieve. Maebh and I had tried to spend as much time together as we could, but it seemed like something always came up to keep me at the bar late or her at the restaurant. Her father had returned to Ireland two weeks ago, so either I would stay at Maebh's place, or she stayed at mine. That was something I wasn't about to miss out on, regardless of our schedules. I needed her in my arms when I fell asleep and I needed to be inside her first thing every morning. It was going to kill me when she headed back to Ireland for a few days.

"It's packed in here tonight!" Trevor shouted over the live band.

Nodding, I took in the bar. "I'll take it because it'll be quiet before you know it."

Tourist season was nearly over, and soon things would calm down, but Friday and Saturday nights were still busy.

"Warning at your nine," Trevor stated.

Glancing to my left, I saw two women sitting at the bar eye fucking the hell out of me. Shit. I recognized one of them. I'd fucked her about a year ago. Walking over, I gave them both a polite smile.

"What can I do for you ladies?"

"Both of us, at the same time," the red-haired girl shouted, causing the guy next to her to glance our way. I gave him a grin and looked back at them. Groaning inwardly, I reminded myself not to use that phrase ever again when asking women what they wanted to drink.

"What would you like to drink?"

The blonde whom I had been with pouted. "Cord, don't you remember me? I'm back in town visiting my aunt, and this is my cousin, Roni. You looking for a fun time this evening?"

The fact that she was willing to have a threesome with her cousin made me want to gag. "Sorry, I'm off the market."

Her eyes widened. "What does that mean?"

Roni leaned in and shouted, "I think he's saying he has a girlfriend."

The blonde—what in the hell was her name again?—glared at her cousin. "I know what he's saying."

I let out a sigh, "So, ladies, what can I get you to drink?"

The blonde leaned forward. "Your cum when I blow you again in the back room."

And that was it. I tapped the bar, said goodbye, and walked away.

"Ross, you want to take the two down at the end?"

Ross had been with me since I opened. One of the best bartenders around. He gave me a knowing smile as he glanced over my shoulder and headed that way. Ever since I had started dating Maebh, Ross had come to my rescue a number of times. Hell, I hadn't ever realized how many women in this damn town I had fucked in the back room of this place until they all started asking for repeats. It actually made me shiver anytime I thought about it.

My phone vibrated in my back pocket. Pulling it out, I smiled when I saw her name.

Maebh: *Is it too late for pie? Can you break away?*

Looking around, I saw that Trevor, Ross, and Tammy had the bar covered. Motioning to Trevor, I held up my hand and stuck up one finger.

He laughed and shouted, "Make it two unless you want her to think you can't last long."

It was only nine and for the bar to be this busy was a good thing, but it was still early, and that meant it would be a long night. Breaking away for an hour was something I needed, or I would be crawling into Maebh's bed around three in the morning...and I really needed to see my girl.

Me: *I'll meet you over at Lilly's in five.*

Maebh: *See you there!*

I served a couple of a guys who walked up to the bar and then made my way to Tammy.

"I'm heading out for about an hour. If you need anything, call my cell."

She nodded while mixing up a drink. "Where you going?"

I looked at her, my brows pinched together. Since when did she become my keeper? I'd noticed a change in Tammy ever since Maebh and I had started dating. I was beginning to wonder if the gossip Maebh had heard from my two waitresses called for a little sit-down meeting with the manager of my bar.

Fuck. That was the last thing I wanted to do. Tammy was damn good at her job, but if she did have a thing for me, that shit needed to be aired now. She needed to know there was no chance in hell I'd ever hurt Maebh.

Ever.

"I'm meeting Maebh over at Lilly's, if you have to know."

Her face flushed, and she got what I meant.

"Sorry, have a good time," she said. "Everything is fine here."

Pushing my hand through my hair, I tried to brush off my agitation toward Tammy. Jumping over the bar, I made my way through the crowd, saying hi to friends, asking folks if they were enjoying themselves, and trying to push away the unwanted advances of strange women. I made my way to my office to grab my things.

Shit. Since when did women feel like they could grab your junk without asking? By the time I got to my office I wanted to spray my body in disinfectant. I couldn't help but laugh at myself. I'd changed the last few months and it was all due to my beautiful, dark-haired girlfriend.

Grabbing my keys and wallet from the safe, I locked my office door and went out the back. I'd have to walk down the back alley, but it was better than making my way through the sea of grabby hands.

Turning the corner, I headed up the street toward Lilly's. My chest was doing that crazy flutter it always did before I saw Maebh. I figured it would settle at some point, but it only seemed to be getting stronger. So were my feelings for her. I didn't think I could keep falling in love with her, but I was. Every touch, smile, laugh, roll of her eyes when I had to make her repeat something, made me fall even harder.

Right as I stepped up on the sidewalk, a familiar face was in front of me. My feet stopped instantly.

"Cord Parker! Oh, my God! I was just coming to the bar to say hi!"

Kylie Burks.

The only other woman I had ever had sex with more than three times, was standing in front of me. My eyes took her in. She had changed some, but she was still a beautiful woman. Not as beautiful as Maebh, but I certainly saw why I had no problems going back for more.

"Kylie, holy shit. What are you doing in Oak Springs?"

Last I'd heard, she'd married the guy she had started dating in college. Of course, I hadn't known she'd had a boyfriend back then. She'd come home over the holidays and we would hook up. I was completely unaware that she was seeing someone the last two years of college. I'd hated that she had lied to me. If there was one thing I wasn't, it was a cheater. I had pushed her away right then and there and denied her anything sexual, and she flipped out on me, only to come back the next day and say she was sorry. In her own words, sex with her boyfriend at school was dull and boring, and when she was around me she couldn't resist.

"I'm here for Missy Miller's wedding. She and Mike are finally taking the big step."

I nodded and was surprised when she threw herself into my arms and whispered against my ear, "Fuck, it's so good seeing you."

Returning the awkward hug quickly, I stepped out of her embrace and gave us some distance.

"You too. I heard you got married."

She nodded. "Yep. We live in Nashville. My husband's a record producer. Works with some big names. I actually got to meet Garth Brooks."

My hands slipped into my pockets as I nodded politely and said, "That's pretty cool."

"What about you? I heard a rumor someone finally caught your eye. Say it isn't so. The single women of Oak Springs must be devastated."

I let out a chuckle. "Not a rumor. I've been dating someone for a few months now."

Her eyes widened. "Wow. And you're only with her? I mean, *committed* just to her?"

My brow lifted. "That's usually what dating means, Kylie."

Her face flushed and she looked pained—as if the memory of that day I walked out of her bedroom hit her again. I had called her a cheater and a few other harsh words that I almost regretted.

"I'm happy for you, Cord. I'm glad you found someone who has made you want to settle down."

Rocking on my heels, I smiled. "She's amazing."

Her smile grew bigger.

My eyes drifted past Kylie when I felt her. Maebh and Amelia were walking toward us. Maebh wore a concerned look, even though I could tell she was trying to hide it. I sure as shit wasn't about to introduce her to my old fuck buddy, so I looked at Kylie, cleared my throat and said, "Listen, it was good seeing you. Tell Missy I said congratulations."

She seemed a bit surprised that I was ending our conversation so abruptly, but I didn't care. I had to get as far away from Kylie as I could before Maebh and Amelia caught up to us.

"Yeah, I will, and it was great seeing you too, Cord. Maybe next time I'm in town we can meet for dinner."

Frowning at her, she added, "With my husband and your lucky lady."

With a nod, I replied, "Yeah. Maybe."

Walking around her, I headed straight to Maebh. Amelia and I stole a quick glance and the look she gave me said Maebh had already asked who Kylie was. *Shit.* I hope Amelia told her Kylie was an old high school friend.

"Well, do I get the pleasure of two beautiful women and pie this evening?"

Amelia punched the side of my arm. "Not tonight, big brother. I was helping Maebh with some things before she has to head out of town."

My stomach felt like a hundred-pound weight settled in the bottom of it, and my smile faded.

"I hate that you're going to be so far away," I grumbled. I was positive I also wore a fucking pout, especially from the way Amelia was trying to hide her laughter.

"I'm parked right here, so I'm taking off. Try not to let your lip get stuck out, bro."

"Ha ha," I replied, kissing my sister on the forehead. "Love you, Meli."

Her eyes were soft as she said, "I love you too, Cord."

"Bye, Maebh. Let me know if you need any help at the restaurant while you're gone."

Lifting her hand and waving it, Maebh replied, "I will! Thank you for helping me with inventory!"

We watched as Amelia got in her car and drove off. Facing Maebh, I pulled her to me and planted a kiss on those soft, pink lips. "You sure you want some pie? I can think of something else we can do instead."

Her hand came to my chest where she curled her fingers into my shirt. "My place or yours?"

"How about Mitchell's old place?"

She looked at me with questioning eyes. "I have the key to Mitchell's place. He hasn't put it on the market yet to sell it. We can fornicate in there."

Maebh giggled and nodded. "Okay!"

Damn, I loved this carefree side of her. If I had it my way, I'd fuck her in every single place we stepped foot in just so I had a memory of her beautiful face as she came.

"Will Mitchell be upset?" Maebh asked, waiting for me to unlock the door.

Glancing over my shoulder, I replied, "What Mitchell doesn't know, doesn't hurt him."

CHAPTER 25

maebh

I laid in bed and stared at the ceiling. Glancing over at the clock, I sighed at the time. Three-thirty. Closing me eyes, I thought back to earlier this evening when I saw Cord with Kylie Burks. I knew I shouldn't have pressed Amelia for information, but I couldn't stop meself. Now it was all I could think about.

Walking out of Aisling, I looked across the square and saw Cord. I smiled, but it faded when I saw a woman walk up to him. They spoke for a few seconds before she threw herself into his arms.

"Amelia, who's that talking to Cord?" I asked as we crossed the street. There was a large, darling park in the middle of downtown Oak Springs, and it gave the area such a sweet country feel. It made me think of home.

"Oh…that's Kylie Burks."

I looked at her. "Who's that?"

"Ah, just someone Cord knew in high school. They were close friends."

"What does close friends mean?"

She shrugged, and I stopped walking. "Amelia, what does close friends mean? Did they date? Cord told me he's never had a girl-friend before."

With a long sigh, her eyes bounced back to Cord and this Kylie girl. "He really needs to be the one to tell you about their, um, ar-rangement."

Me stomach dropped, and I felt a lump in me throat. "Arrange-ment? Amelia, please tell me."

She looked everywhere but at me.

"Did he have sex with her?"

Amelia let out a snort. "That's putting it mildly."

I frowned, and she groaned. "They were fuck buddies all through high school and most of college. Never exclusive, by any means, but they couldn't seem to not...you know..."

Me face felt hot. "Fuck?" I asked bluntly.

She looked at the ground and kicked at something that wasn't there. "Yeah, but Maebh, that was long ago, and they were both young. I'm sure she's just here visiting someone. She doesn't live here anymore and hardly ever comes to visit."

"Her family is still here?" I asked as we started walking again.

"Yes, her parents and a brother. She lives in Nashville now. Her husband is some big time producer."

Relief washed over me. "She's married?"

It seemed to wash over Amelia, as well. She lit up like this was the ladder to get her out of the hole she had dug. "Yes! They met in college. I think her junior year. That was when Cord...well, when he ended their 'arrangement.'"

"He ended it? Why didn't she, if she was dating someone?"

Amelia shrugged. "You'll have to ask him."

With a frustrated groan, I pushed the thoughts of this girl from me mind and got out of bed. Making me way to the kitchen, I put on some water for tea and decided to call me Da.

"Half pint, what are you doing up in the middle of the night? You need your sleep."

His voice filled me heart with warmth; I couldn't wait to see him. I was flying tomorrow night to go back to Ireland for a yearly meeting with my family. I hated the idea of leaving Cord, but I also longed to go back home and see the country I loved so much.

"Couldn't sleep. How's everything going?"

"Ah, it's all grand. The lads at the distillery miss you."

More warmth filled me chest. "I miss them, too. Has any of them found a nice lady to settle down with?"

Me father's hearty laugh made me grin.

"Are you kidding? Those boys all claim to be waiting on you."

I snorted. "They'll be waiting a long time."

"Ah, that's what I told them. Said me little girl has found a man she loves. How is Cord? Still at work? Is that why you can't sleep?"

"Yeah." The sound of a key sliding into me door made me turn.

"Looks like he's home," I said.

"Ah, that's good, half pint. Now back to bed. I'll see you in a few days."

Cord stepped into the room and stopped for a moment, surprised to see me awake. Concern hit his face but melted away when I smiled.

"Tell everyone I said hi. Love you, Da."

Cord flashed me a sexy grin.

"Love you the most, Maebh."

I ended the call and set me mobile on the counter and wrapped me arms around me body. I was suddenly chilled.

"What are you still doing up?" Cord asked.

"I couldn't sleep," I replied, lifting me shoulder in a half shrug. The air in the room seemed to change. It filled with sparks of electricity; it was always that way when I was with Cord. From the first moment I laid eyes on him, he brought me body to life.

"I'm so sorry, baby. I tried to get out of there as fast as I could."

"It's okay."

Cord pulled me into his arms. "I'm going to hire another weekend manager to start closing at least one night during the weekend. I'd like for us to do normal things like go to dinner and a movie."

I snuggled into his chest. "I'd like that."

Even though I closed Aisling down nearly every night, I always took one night on the weekends off. It was important to have me own life outside of the restaurant. Me da had taught me the importance of that early on.

"Come on. Let me get out of these clothes and into a shower, then we can actually fall asleep together with you wrapped in my arms."

I leaned against the sink as I watched him undress. Hard muscles covered his body and flexed as he moved. Me mouth watered as I watched him. The simple act of Cord getting undressed was enough to cause an ache between me legs.

His eyes caught mine and a slow, sexy smile spread across his face.

"It's late, agra, but those eyes are telling me you aren't sleepy. I need to know what you want."

"I want you."

He held his hand out for me to take. When our fingers laced me breath hitched.

"You own me, baby," his words whispered while he walked me into the hot shower. The moment the water hit our bodies, we were kissing. Cord grabbed me by me thighs and pushed me against the cold tile. Hissing at the hot water, I bit his lip.

"I want to fuck you, baby, but I don't have a condom."

Me fingers laced through his wet, dark hair, and I pressed me mouth to his. I didn't care about anything but him being buried inside of me. Us being one.

"Please, Cord. I want you…all of you…and I'm tired of waiting."

Leaning his forehead to mine, he swallowed hard then lifted me and positioned his cock at me entrance. He'd gotten tested since that weekend at the lake, but we'd kept using condoms. Cord said he wanted our first time without a condom to be special, but I was tired of waiting for both of us to find the time to make it special.

"Maebh," he gasped as he pushed into me. His body trembled and he panted. "Oh, fuck. You feel so good. Shit, I'm not going to last long with you riding me bareback."

I wrapped me arms around his neck and pressed me mouth to his again. Kissing him lightly, I whispered, "Have your way with me, Cord."

His eyes turned dark, and he pulled out of me, only to push back in fast and hard. I gasped and relished it. He felt amazing. Beautiful. We felt like one as Cord moved in and out of me while he pressed me against the wall and gave me exactly what I had asked for.

"God, it feels so good. Tell me it feels this good to you, too," he panted.

"Feels…so…good," I cried out. "I'm so close."

"You're squeezing my cock like a vise, baby. I'm going to come."

Me orgasm wasn't there yet, so Cord slipped his hand between me legs and pushed on me clit, sending me spiraling into an orgasm as we both shattered at the same time.

The water sprayed down as we fought to bring our breathing back to normal. Cord had done exactly what I asked of him, and it had been absolutely amazing. The feel of him with no condom was beyond anything I could have ever dreamed.

"You know," he breathed, "I'm never going to be able to wear a condom again. Never."

With a giggle, I kissed him on the lips. "Good. I hate those stupid things."

Cord gently set me down and took me soap. He cleaned every inch of me before I did the same to him. He looked so tired and me heart hurt knowing I would be leaving him for a week.

"I'm going to miss you so much, baby." Cord looked at me, visibly as pained as my heart was feeling.

Me eyes filled with tears. It was silly; it would only be a week. Five days and I'd be back, but the thought of not seeing him nearly killed me.

"I'll miss you more."

He laughed and wrapped me in a towel before carrying me back to our bed. "Impossible."

After drying me off, he quickly dried himself before crawling into the bed next to me.

"I took tomorrow off from the bar. Tammy's going to cover so we can spend the day together and then I can take you to the airport."

Me chest fluttered at the sweet gesture. This man certainly knew how to make me swoon. When I didn't think I could love him more, he proved me wrong.

His massive arms wrapped around me, drawing me to his warm body. Exhaustion soon took over as I heard his breathing slow along with mine.

I was nearly lost in sleep when I felt a soft kiss on me shoulder and Cord whispered, "I'm going to marry you some day, my sweet Irish cailín."

I'd nearly frozen, but forced meself to keep breathing the steady, slow pace I had set. *Had he thought I was already asleep?* His declaration was so soft I would have missed it had I not been so focused on *his* breathing.

Closing me eyes, I let those words settle right to the middle of me heart. I'd never in me life been so happy.

I drifted off to sleep with a smile as big as the Texas sky.

CHAPTER 26

Cord

When my phone lit up for the third time with Tammy's name, I cursed. Glancing up, I watched as Maebh ran her hand over the horse Trevor had been saddling up for her.

Walking a few feet away, I answered it with a sharp "What?"

"Hey, I hate to bug you again, but did you authorize for Loren to have tonight off? If so, that puts us down a waitress."

I frowned. "What about Meg?"

"She has the flu."

"The flu! Fuck, it's only September."

"Got it from her kid who got it from school."

I rolled my eyes. "*School*. The place where all germs are born and thrive."

Tammy chuckled. "Seriously, though, should I let Loren go?"

Pushing my hand through my hair, I glanced back to Maebh. "Listen, Maebh needs to be at the airport by six. Let me drop her off and then I'll be in. I'll cover the bar. You can cover Meg."

"Sounds like a plan, boss."

With a deep breath, I said, "Listen, lay off the calls for the rest of the day. I need you to manage while I'm gone. I'd like to spend the rest of the day with Maebh before she leaves for Ireland."

"Hear you loud and clear."

And with that, the phone went dead. I was sure I had pissed her off. I could have been nice and not such an asshole, but she'd already pushed me to my limit of give-a-fucks for the day.

"She's a gentle giant so you won't have any problems with her," Trevor said, cinching the saddle strap. I'd never asked Maebh how much she'd been around horses. *Shit. I hope she isn't afraid.*

"I guess I should have asked how much experience you have with horses," I said.

Maebh glanced over her shoulder like I had just said the stupidest thing ever.

"Do you assume since I'm from Ireland I can't ride?"

Trevor laughed, and I felt my stomach drop. Was she pissed? I'd been witness to my Irish princess's temper over the last couple of months, and she was for sure a fireball when she wanted to be. Mostly she was laid back. Probably the most laid-back person I'd ever met. But piss her off and look the fuck out. Her temper could turn on a dime, and I never wanted to be on the receiving end of my spitfire's anger.

"I didn't assume that," I said. "Not at all."

"You should see the panicked look on your face, dude. It's fucking hilarious."

I shot Trevor a dirty look. "Fuck you."

The moment Maebh climbed up on the horse, I knew she had been around horses. She grabbed the reins and made her way over to the corral. The way she worked Spirit made both my mouth and Trevor's drop open.

"Yeah, I'm going to guess your girl knows how to handle a horse."

With a shake of my head, I laughed. "Hell, I bet she's gonna wanna race now."

Trevor laughed a bit harder. "Have fun and enjoy the beautiful weather. We don't usually get cool days like this in September."

"We will," I called back over my shoulder. Maebh came out of the corral and walked her horse up next to mine.

"Want to race?" she asked, flashing a huge smile. Trevor could be heard laughing even harder as I pressed my knees lightly into the horse, causing him to trot.

"Next time, baby. When you're not on the slowest damn horse in my father's barn."

We spent the next few hours riding all over the ranch. I stopped once to help a deer that had been caught up in one of the fences when it tried to jump. Maebh was worried the entire time the thing would kick me, but the doe was tired from fighting. Once she was set free, she ran off toward the river. Trevor and Wade had kept some feeders down there that were stocked year-round. I sent Trevor and Wade a text letting them know what I'd just found and to put a few blocks out.

"It's so beautiful here," Maebh said. "Different from home."

"I bet. Doesn't rain as much here," I said with a wink.

"So, what are you going to do while I'm gone all week?"

My body was starting to ache, and I couldn't help but wonder if it was because of the lack of sleep I'd been getting from staying at the bar late, then crawling into bed and fighting the urge to make love to Maebh. Some nights I gave in and woke her up, but most I simply held her until she woke up early and then we made love. I was only averaging three to four hours a night and it was fucking catching up to me.

"Sleep. I'm so fucking tired."

She frowned. "I'm sorry. Cord, if you want to sleep at your place by yourself, you know I don't mind."

"Fuck that. I can't sleep without you. I'm worried about you being gone. I think I need that giant-ass body pillow you sleep with."

She giggled. "Want me to spray it with me perfume?"

"Yes!" I said with a wide grin.

"You're an eejit, Cord Parker. You'll be able to sleep just fine without me."

"Will you be able to sleep fine without me?"

"No," she quickly replied, shaking her head to emphasize her words.

My cell phone rang, and I cursed. "I'm not even going to see who it is."

Maebh glanced away, lost in her thoughts for a moment.

"It might be important. Could be Trevor or Wade about the deer."

I sighed and pulled out my phone. I frowned when I saw the name. *What in the fuck could she possibly want?*

Pushing it back into my pocket, I said, "Nope. No one important."

Her smile lit up the already bright blue sky.

After heading back to the barns, we washed up the horses and headed to my folks' house. My mother had asked us to stay for lunch, and I couldn't refuse. It would only take us an hour and a half to get to San Antonio, so I wasn't worried about time. Although, I would have liked to have had Maebh once more before she left. Last night at Mitchell's old place, the shower, and then again this morning didn't feel like enough to last me a week without her.

We walked into my parents' kitchen hand-in-hand. When my mother glanced down to see our fingers laced together, she grinned like she had witnessed a Christmas fucking miracle. Maybe she had; even I was still having a hard time believing how fucking happy I was.

"How do roast beef sandwiches sound?" my mom asked us.

"Sounds good!" Maebh exclaimed.

I pulled out a bar stool for Maebh, then one for me. We sat at the large kitchen island and watched my mother move about the kitchen like a pro.

"Do you need help with anything?" Maebh asked.

"It's all under control. There are chips…I mean, *crisps*…and fruit on the island. Put some on your plate." She looked over at Maebh and smiled. I loved that my mom went out of her way to make Maebh feel like family and was even learning some of the Irish lingo.

Maebh and I both did as we were told.

After my mother had served up hot roast beef with melted cheese, I leaned back and let out a contented groan. My stomach was full and satisfied.

"Damn, woman, you sure know how to cook," I stated.

My mother shot me a smile that beamed with motherly love. When my father walked into the kitchen, his brow and shirt were covered in sweat. He took off his hat and hung it next to mine.

The back door shut again, and Steed and Trevor walked in.

"Just mind your own fucking business, Steed!" Trevor bit out.

"Watch that language in front of your mother and Maebh!" my father lashed out, glaring at Trevor.

"I'm just saying, you're playing with fire and you need to knock it off."

"What are you boys talking about?" Mom asked.

Trevor balled his fists and looked at Steed. "Don't," he warned.

Steed shook his head. "I never in my life thought I would say this about one of my own brothers, but I'm disappointed in you, Trevor."

Both Maebh and Mom gasped as I stood up.

"Take this back outside, y'all," I said. "Not in front of Mom."

"Fuck you, Cord. I'm not like the rest of you. I don't do…" he pointed to Maebh. "This shit."

Trevor's face was filled with anger, and I was positive mine matched his. I jumped toward Trevor when Maebh stood up and blocked me.

"Stop acting like eejits! What is the matter with all of you?" Trevor looked at me and then Maebh, instant regret on his face.

"I didn't mean that, Maebh. I swear, I didn't mean that."

"I know you didn't, Trevor."

He grabbed his hat before storming past Steed and out the door. Maebh turned to face me. "Maybe you should go talk to him?"

I shook my head. "I'll be right back." Leaning down, I kissed her on the cheek before making my way out the back door. Trevor was walking away from the house slowly. I jogged down the steps and made my way over to him.

"Do you want to talk about why you lashed out at Maebh back there?"

He sighed. "It wasn't at her. I'm…I'm in territory I'm not familiar with, Cord, and it's confusing. Actually I'm scared and I don't really know what to do."

"Is this about someone?"

He nodded. "I like her, and I fucked up so bad. I keep doing things to hurt her, and I don't know why." His hand pushed over his buzzed brown hair. The pained look on his face wasn't hard to recognize. "I'm so goddamned drawn to her. It's like she's got some sort of hold on me, and she won't let go."

We sat down on a bench on the other side of the yard. I imagined our mother used to sit here and watch the barn while Dad worked with the horses. The image warmed me. That was the life I wanted. A life with Maebh and babies running around. Land as far as I could see. That was my new dream.

"Do you want her to let go?" I finally asked.

He looked at me and shrugged. "Some days, yes. Some, no. I don't know what I want. I look at you and see how much you've changed because of Maebh."

"Is it that bad? That she's changed me?"

"No," he whispered, staring out over the rolling hills. "Dude, you're the happiest I've ever seen you. I mean, I always knew when you found someone, you were going to land on your ass so fucking hard it would knock you into another place, and it totally has."

Trevor looked at me, his eyes filled with sadness. "You were ready for Maebh. I don't think I'm ready."

"Trevor, I'm no expert when it comes to love, believe me. I feel something for Maebh I've never felt before and that scares me, and I know it scares her, too. I don't think love was ever made to be easy. It's something that tears at our hearts in both a good and bad way. It's something we have to take a risk on while hoping and praying it doesn't destroy us in the process. But it's not something that is meant to come along and be easy. That much I do know."

"Are you still scared?"

I swallowed hard. "Every day for one reason or the other. Will I hurt her? Will she hurt me? What if she's taken away from me? I couldn't live a day without her, and knowing that this soon into our relationship just adds to the fear. Because each time she smiles, I fall more in love. I look for ways to give more of myself to her. But she is a risk I'd take every damn time."

Trevor's head dropped, and he stared at the ground.

"I want to take the risk. I just don't know if I can."

A voice cleared from behind us. Glancing over my shoulder, I found that it was Maebh.

"Sorry, but we need to head to the airport."

Trevor and I stood. I was shocked when he pulled me into his arms and slapped my back hard. His pained voice cracked when he spoke. "Thanks, dude. I appreciate you not tearing into me when I gave you a reason to."

"You're my brother, Trevor. I'm always here for you."

He headed to Maebh, drawing her in for a hug and whispering sorry. He pushed his hands in his pockets and headed down toward the barn. His body sagged, and I couldn't shake the confused sadness in his eyes.

"I'm sorry about that," I said.

"Don't be. Your brother is hurting with something that only he can figure out. He'll find his way."

I held Maebh while we both watched my brother walk away.

CHAPTER 27

Cord

The knock on my office door had me lifting my head and calling out, "Come in."

Tammy walked in and smiled.

"Hey, what are you doing here?" I asked, leaning back and glancing at the clock. It was only nine in the morning, and she rarely came into the bar this early.

"We have the film crew coming today for the commercial, and you mentioned you weren't feeling good. I wanted to make sure the place was clean and ready to go."

I grinned. "Thanks, but I've got it all taken care of. Maebh called in a crew to come and clean the bar top to bottom. They should be here around ten."

"Maebh arranged that?"

There was no mistaking the bitterness in her voice.

"Cord, I'm your manager. Doesn't your *girlfriend* have her own place to worry about?"

My eyes widened in shock. Agitation rocked me right to the core. "What my *girlfriend* does or doesn't do with this bar is my business. You were hired to make sure the day-to-day things are taken care of. When it comes to special events, I've always handled things. If you have a problem with Maebh helping me, then I need to know about it now and this shit needs to get fixed."

Her lips moved into a forced smile. "No, no problem with it at all…boss."

I sensed some sarcasm, and I didn't like it.

She turned to the door, and I noticed what she was wearing. I hadn't paid much attention when she walked in.

What in the fuck? She had on a skirt so short her ass hung out of it. She turned back to face me, and my eyes scanned up her body to her shirt. Her tits were nearly popping out of the damn thing.

There was no fucking way my manager should be dressing like she was in a damn strip club.

"What are you wearing?"

She ran her tongue over her lips. "I have a lunch date."

I pulled my brows together. "Where? At a private strip club?"

A hurt look passed over her face before she reached up and unbuttoned a few buttons. Her shirt fell open and her tits were on full display.

"See something you like?"

My eyes jerked up to hers.

"Not one thing," I said, trying to keep my anger down. What I really wanted to do was tell her to get the fuck out of my bar, but I needed to calm down. My head had already been pounding when she walked in and now it was throbbing. The ache in my body was not because of her, but the anger that raced through it.

"I'll see you later tonight, Tammy. And make sure you're not still dressed like that. Leave now before I do something you might regret."

Hope flashed in her eyes before I added, "Like fire your ass for coming on to me in my own fucking office."

Quickly buttoning up her shirt, she reached behind her and opened my office door before rushing out. I could see the hint of rejection and embarrassment etched on her features.

When the door clicked shut, I let out a string of curse words. Maebh had been right. Tammy had just tried to make a fucking play for me.

Grabbing my phone, I hit her number.

"Hello? Cord?"

Her sweet voice filled me with something I still couldn't pinpoint. Love? Lust? Desire? A mixture of all of the above? Whatever it was, I fucking loved it.

"Hey, my beautiful Irish cailín. How are things in Ireland?"

I tried my best to say it with an accent and failed. Maebh laughed.

"Lonely without me Texas cowboy."

"Mmmm," I groaned, reaching down to adjust my growing cock. "I miss you so fucking much and it's only been a couple of days."

I coughed and reached for my water.

"Are you okay?" she asked.

"No, I think that exhaustion wore me down so much that someone from the bar got me sick. I've been feeling like shit the last few days, and it's only getting worse."

"Please go to the doctor before it gets worse. They should be able to do a flu test."

Sighing, I ran my hand over my face. "Tell me what you're doing right now."

She pulled in a deep breath. "Well, I'm currently standing on a golf course."

"A golf course?"

"Yep. It's a charity event me da goes to every year."

"Do you play golf?" I asked, my cock growing harder. For some reason, if she played I was going to reach through the phone and kiss her. I fucking loved golf and wondered how this revelation hadn't come up in conversation over the past couple of months.

"Yes, I actually played golf at me university."

My head dropped back. Jesus, this woman was like a dream. She liked to fish. Drink. Fuck. Dance. And now she hits me with another one: she can play golf.

"You're fucking amazing, do you know that? I love golf. I want to take you out to a course, not tell my brothers you can play, and watch you beat their asses. Please tell me you'll do that, baby."

Her laughter tumbled from the phone straight into my heart.

"Sure! Why not. Might be fun."

The sounds of male voices caused me to look up at one of monitors. "Speak of the devils. They're all walking into the bar right now."

"I need to go anyway. I love you, Cord. I miss you and I'm not having any fun."

Smiling, I stood, adjusted my dick in my pants and replied, "You're a liar, Maebh O'Sullivan. I hear it in your voice."

"Okay, but only about the part where I said I wasn't having any fun. Please go to the doctor, okay?"

"I will... I love you too, baby. Call me later."

Making my way out to the bar I smiled when I saw my brothers and their kids.

Fucking hell, the ache in my chest when I looked at Gage trying to make his way over to me...what in the hell was this?

That's definitely moving too fast. Shit. Slow down. Slow that thinking right the fuck down.

Gage wore a huge smile, and I wondered how in the hell he could see with the ten-gallon cowboy hat on his head.

"He's walking so good!" I exclaimed while bending down and scooping him up. I gave him a toss in the air, and he laughed.

"Mom said you weren't feeling good? Is that true?" Steed asked, concern laced over his face.

I put Gage down and nodded. "Shit, sorry, dude. I am feeling a little off. I probably shouldn't be anywhere near the kids."

Mitchell got up and walked out of the bar, his two-month-old daughter Merit tucked in her carrier.

"I'm out of here," Mitchell called out over his shoulder.

Jonathon shook his head and looked at me with an apologetic expression. "Dude, If Waylynn knows I brought Liberty around, she'd be pissed. I love you like a brother, but I fear my wife more."

Tripp clapped Steed on the back. "I'm outta here too. I'm not risking bringing anything home to Harley. She's already having a hard time with morning sickness."

Steed picked up Gage and looked my way. "Sorry, dude. Feel better."

My mouth dropped as each of them left me. Before I knew it, they were all gone. All but Wade. He looked at me and shrugged.

"No baby and no pregnant wife. I'll hang out with you, dude."

Laughing, I shook my head and motioned for the door. "Let's grab something to eat. Have you had breakfast?"

"Not yet."

As we walked out, I locked the door while Wade read a text.

"Um, if I go to breakfast with you, you can't tell Amelia."

I frowned. "Why not?"

She says Paxton told her you were getting sick. She has a signing at a bookstore in Dallas next week and said if I get her sick because I hung out with you today, no sex for a month."

"Dude, you'd risk that just to have breakfast with me?" I asked, covering my heart and batting my eyes in an exaggerated manner.

Wade nodded. "It doesn't hurt that I'm fucking starving, and you're buying."

"I'll take it. Let's go."

As the day dragged on, I felt worse. I was going to kill the person who had made me sick, but I had a feeling it was one of my poor waitresses. Three of them were all home in bed with the flu. There was no fucking way I was getting the flu. I never got sick. I had no time to get sick.

Tammy showed back up to work looking like herself later that afternoon. I had talked to Wade about the stunt she pulled, and his advice was to find another manager. I wanted to talk to her in my office. Tell her I couldn't have an employee coming on to me and that she needed to find another job.

We were already busy with people coming in for happy hour, and I couldn't imagine what the rest of the night was going to look like. I was feeling worse, and all I really wanted to do was talk to my girl and go bed.

"Cord, why don't you go on up to your place," Tammy said. "We've got it covered here. It's the middle of the week, and I think after happy hour things will slow down."

I didn't want to admit that I knew Tammy was right. Once happy hour was over I knew things would die off. I was feeling worse as the minutes ticked off the clock.

Fucking hell. I should have gone to the doctor.

CHAPTER 28

Maebh

I sat in the chair behind the large mahogany desk and pulled out my phone. I'd talked to Cord not long ago, and he had mentioned not feeling well. I needed to find out if he was feeling any better.

Hitting Cord's number, I waited for him to pick up.

A rough sounding voice filled the line. "Hello?"

My heart leapt to me throat. "Cord?"

"Maebh? Baby, what time is it there?"

He sounded bad. Really bad.

"It's nearly midnight here. Me da is having a party for his birthday. You sound terrible."

"I feel terrible. I don't even think I have the energy to go to the doctor to find out if I have the fucking flu."

Gasping, I jumped up.

"Cord, you need to have one of your brothers or sisters take you…you know your ma would take you in a heartbeat."

"It's alright. I'll go tomorrow. Right now I just want to crawl in bed and go to sleep. I feel like fucking shit."

Me heart hurt knowing he was sick, and I wasn't there.

"I'm so sorry I'm not there."

Silence.

"Cord? Cord!" I shouted.

"Y-yeah…sorry, baby. I took some medicine, and I think it's knocking me out. Baby, I need to go, my head is fucking pounding."

"Okay, I love you, Cord. I'll be home soon."

"Love you, too."

Then the line went dead. Jerking the phone away, I stared at it. He hadn't even said good-bye.

I raced out of the office and through the house. I threw the door to me bedroom open and grabbed me case. I wasn't going to stay here another minute. Cord needed me and I wanted—no, I needed— to be there for him. I sent a quick text to Amelia, letting her know I was going to leave right away. They didn't need to know I was going to take me father's private plane. I had yet to tell Cord exactly how well off me family was. I didn't want it to be a factor in anything. Not that I thought the Parker family would have liked me more, or befriended me solely because of the wealth I came from. Yet, it was still hard to trust people with that bit of information. I'd seen it change people. Sean, for one. He'd known I was from money, but when he found out how much, it became his mission to make me his wife. The money had changed him. I knew deep down in me heart it wouldn't change Cord, but I couldn't risk that yet.

After packing up me things, I set off to find me da. He was in the library with the last remaining guests. One was the Duke of Cambridge. His father and my father were good friends. This was the first time I'd met him, and I was pleasantly surprised at how nice he was. At one point in the evening, he even offered to accompany me on a walk around the garden—something that had been unnecessary, and I had to tell him why.

Me boyfriend in the States would kick his arse.

Walking up to me father, I touched his arm gently. The Duke looked at me with hungry eyes while he let his gaze sweep over me body. I gave him a polite smile and figured he had one too many shots of me da's whiskey.

"Cord is sick with the flu. I'm going to go home early. Do you think you can get the plane ready?"

He looked at his watch. "At this hour, Maebh? You want to leave now?"

"As soon as the plane can be ready. You know I wouldn't ask if it wasn't important."

He nodded and motioned to the few gentlemen left in the library. "Excuse me, I need to make a call."

They all nodded, and I couldn't help but notice the Duke's gaze drop to me chest and then quickly back up. Once upon a time, I might have been turned on by such a handsome man making his interest known, but now, the only thing I could think about was the man I loved back in Texas. The man who was sick and needed me.

I sat back in the large leather chair and wrung me hands. Me da's plane wouldn't be ready to go until six in the morning. It was midnight back in Texas so I didn't want to call and wake up Cord. Once I landed in San Antonio, I'd call Melanie to see how Cord was since it would be mid-morning by the time I landed.

Closing me eyes, I let the tiredness of me body settle in. The plane wasn't even off the runway when I was lost to sleep. Thank God for private planes with bedrooms.

Nine hours later I rushed to the car park while listening to a message from Cord. He was delirious and taking nonsense. I tried Cord's phone but it went straight to voicemail. I was thanking God I'd arranged to have Eric bring me car to the airport and leave it. It rang and went to voicemail.

"Shite!" I shouted as I jumped into me car. Before I started to drive I tried Melanie. It went straight to voicemail. I had no luck with Paxton either. Finally, Amelia answered.

"Amelia!" I shouted in a pure state of panic.

"Oh my God, Maebh, what's wrong?"

"Nothing! I'm…I'm okay. How's Cord?"

"He's pretty sick. Mom was on her way there, but Marge said she'd stay with him until Mom could swing by later."

I nodded, thankful that Cord had the best housekeeper in Oak Springs. She loved Cord like a son, and I knew she would take care of him. "Has he been to the doctor yet?"

Her silence nearly killed me. "Amelia!"

"Don't freak out, okay?"

Me heart stopped. "What do you mean don't freak out?"

"Well, he sort of got worse during the night and was too weak to go see the doctor this morning, so Dr. Peterson had to come to him. He tested positive for the flu."

Closing me eyes, I mumbled, "Shite."

"Darn it, Maebh, my agent is calling and I have to take it. It's a conference call. I'll call you back when I get off."

Before I could tell her I was back in town, the line went dead. I sent Cord a text message.

Me: *I flew back a day early. Leaving the airport and will be there in an hour and forty me GPS says. I love you.*

I waited for a moment in case he replied. Then I headed out of the car park and tried not to get a ticket driving over the speed limit to Oak Springs.

When I pulled into me parking spot at Aisling, I grabbed me phone and tried Cord again. It went straight to voicemail after one ring.

"What in the hell?" Was Cord sending me calls to voicemail? If his phone was dead, I would have thought it would go straight to voicemail, not ring and then go to voicemail.

Jumping out of me car, I rushed up to me place to change while typing out a text.

Me: *I'm home and changing. I'm going to come over. I don't have Marge's number to let her know. I'll try your mom again.*

When the phone buzzed in me hand almost immediately, I nearly screamed, then sagged in relief to see his name.

Cord: *I'll call in a bit.*

Was Cord not home? Maybe he went to the doctor. Frowning, I stared at the message, then called Melanie.

"Maebh, darling, how are you?"

"I'm in town."

"What?"

"I came back early after I talked to Cord yesterday. He sounded terrible. I sent him a message and told him I was back, and he said he would call me later."

"Oh, he's pretty out of it. I'm sure he didn't realize what he was typing, probably couldn't even focus on the words."

I remembered the last time I got the flu. I was in and out of sleep for a few days feeling like utter shite. And when I did wake up it felt like a bad dream. I was confused, and everything hurt. Me eyes, head, throat, even me brain felt like it was suffering.

"I'm going to head on over there."

"Okay, Marge should be there. Let her know I'm on my way and should be there in about an hour. I had a meeting in Uvalde today that I couldn't get out of."

"I'll let her know," I said, slipping on a pair of Converse sneakers.

Rushing out the door, I sent Cord a text when my phone was once again sent to voicemail. Why was Marge not answering it? Maybe they had it on silent, so it didn't wake Cord up.

Me: *I'm coming over now. Where is Marge?*

I nearly ran the entire block to the back entrance of Cord's apartment. I took the steps two at a time, me heart pounding in me ears. Poor Cord. He was so sick they had to have the doctors come to him.

Using the key Cord had given me, I opened the door and stepped inside only to freeze at the sight before me.

She was walking down the steps that led from Cord's bedroom. One of his T-shirts hanging off of her. Her hair a mess, like she had just had sex.

I stumbled back when she flashed me a smirk. "You're not supposed to be home until tomorrow," Kylie deadpanned.

Tears filled me eyes, and I glanced around. "Marge!" I called out while the sound of her evil laugh filled the air.

"Marge got sent home. I'm here, and *I'm* taking care of Cord. You can run along now."

Me throat went dry and tears spilled down me face. I wanted to scream for her to get out. That Cord wasn't hers. He was mine.

He's mine.

But was he? Because she was the one standing there practically naked, with only his shirt covering her. None of this made any sense. Why would Kylie be here when Melanie was on her way? Where was Marge?

"Don't be so shocked to see me here, Maebh. Did you really think a guy like Cord could stick to one woman? Don't be naïve. You were something he wanted to conquer. He did, now he's moved on to something more…familiar."

"I want to see Cord," I said, making my way to the stairs.

Kylie stepped in front of me and tilted her neck. "He's passed out cold. Seems he used all his energy letting me fuck him. He did, however, have enough stamina to give me this."

Me eyes followed to where she pointed to the hickie on her neck. I took a few steps back. Cord had never done that to me neck, but he had left marks on me upper thighs a lot of times.

"Listen, Cord and I used to be fuck buddies all through high school and college. The last time he saw me, he told me the next time I was in town to give him a call. A guy like Cord is never going to be happy with one woman. The quicker you know that, the better."

Me head spun. Fuck buddies? Sickness hit me hard in the stomach. Me fears rushed back all at once.

Spinning around, I threw open the door and ran down the steps. *How could he do this to me?*

I forced meself not to cry as I tried to sort me feelings out. Sobs raked over me body as I stumbled down the street back to me apartment. Cord had promised me he wouldn't hurt me.

He promised.

I didn't want to jump to conclusions, but a small part of me— the part that kept pushing down me fears instead of talking to Cord—reared its ugly head. It was telling me to run. Run back to the only place I felt safe.

Home.

After another round of crying, I got up and started to head to me door. My heart was telling me to run away, while me head was telling me to go back to Cord's.

I listened to me head.

CHAPTER 29

Cord

Swinging my legs over the bed, I let out a breath. *Shit.* Every fucking thing on my body ached. I got a glimpse of my phone on the table. I reached for it and saw the date.

Holy hell. I'd been out of it for at least a solid day. That's when it hit me. Maebh would be back in town today. Thank goodness Maebh arranged to have her car waiting at the airport.

Had she already been by? That was impossible. I remembered someone whispering in my ear. Frowning, I tried to think back to who it was, but soon gave up when my head started to throb.

I heard voices in the living room. My mother, Paxton, and Amelia. I also heard Marge. Sweet, life-saving Marge. She'd brought me her homemade soup earlier, and I swear it had something in it that finally broke the fucking fever.

Hitting Maebh's number, I tried to calculate what time it was in Ireland, not knowing if she was on the plane already. I stood on shaky legs and closed my eyes until the room stopped spinning. Maebh's voicemail instantly picked up.

"Baby, it's me," I said. "Sorry I've been so out of it. Call me when you get a chance. I finally feel like I'm back in the land of the living now. Love you."

My feet felt like I had iron strapped on them. I walked down the steps to where the voices were coming from. They were hushed, as if people didn't want to wake me up.

"Mom?" I called out as I rounded the corner and stopped. Marge, Paxton, Amelia, and my mother were all standing there, concern and something like anger spread over each face.

"How could you?" Amelia said, her voice so loud I would have sworn she had a bullhorn directed right at me.

"Amelia, wait until we know everything," my mother ordered. My eyes bounced to each of them and finally landed on the one who looked the most worried.

Paxton.

"Paxton, what's going on?"

Her eyes filled with disappointment, and I knew it was all directed at me...I just didn't know why.

"Maebh left."

Frowning, I asked, "What do you mean? She just left Ireland? She should be home today, right? Fuck, I don't even know what time it is. Has she already been here? I don't remember her being here."

They all looked at each other.

Paxton cleared her throat as she focused back on me. "No, Cord, Maebh is in Ireland right now. She came back early and then left again."

My head was spinning. "Wait, what? Why did she leave?"

Amelia tossed her hands in the air in frustration. "You're such a bastard. How could you do this to her?"

Now I was getting angry. I still felt like shit, Amelia was lashing out, and they were all talking in riddles.

"Will someone tell me what the fuck is going on?" I demanded.

Paxton sighed and took a few steps closer. "Maebh called Amelia and Mom two days ago. She flew home early after talking to you. She was worried about how sick you were, so she hopped on a plane to come to you."

"Must not have been that sick if he was able to fuck that whore," Amelia stated.

"Amelia! That's enough." My mother's voice was stern.

"What?" I asked. Who in the hell was Amelia talking about? I turned back to Paxton. "Why did she go back to Ireland? Is her father okay?"

Paxton looked exasperated and unsure of what to say. Amelia was beginning to lose some of her steam. She looked at me like I was a stupid bastard who wasn't following along with the story.

"Cord, she sent you a text saying she was in town and on her way over. You texted her back and said you'd call her later, which she thought was a bit strange."

Glancing down to my phone, I pulled up my text messages. I didn't have any of those texts. The only text from Maebh was her telling me she was about to call me because her father's party was boring as hell.

"The last text I have from Maebh was the night of her father's party. That was the last time I remember talking to her."

I glanced back to Paxton.

She dragged in a breath. "The only thing Maebh told me was that she walked in here, and Kylie was walking down from your room wearing nothing but your shirt. She said some things, and Maebh got upset and left. Once she got home, she realized she was jumping to conclusions and rushed back over here. When she walked back in and went up to your room, Kylie was…she was…"

My heart started pounding, I was having trouble breathing and it had nothing to do with being sick. "What! What in the fuck was she doing?"

"She was getting undressed and climbing into bed with you. Maebh left. She was beside herself and didn't know what to do, so she went back to Ireland."

Stumbling backwards, my mother grabbed me before I fell.

"What? *What*?" It was all I could say. "I wasn't with Kylie! I don't even remember her being here."

"After I talked to Maebh, I called your mother and Amelia," Paxton said. "We came right over because Marge was supposed to be with you that whole day, and Maebh had said she wasn't there. Only Kylie was."

All eyes went to my housekeeper.

Her hands covered her mouth quickly. "She told me it was okay if I ran an errand. She would make sure Cord didn't wake up and need anything. I wasn't even gone that long."

My eyes widened in horror. What in the hell did Kylie do?

"Paxton, what in the hell did Kylie tell Maebh?"

"Something about you not being able to stay away from her, that y'all were fuck buddies, and that you couldn't be tied down to one woman. That you'd gotten what you wanted from Maebh and you were bored now."

The room spun.

"Cord, let's get you to the sofa. It's becoming hard to hold you up," my mother stated.

Marge and Paxton helped my mother guide me to the sofa.

Standing straight, my mother smoothed out her blouse and took in a deep breath. "Let's get this figured out."

"I didn't fucking sleep with Kylie. I didn't even know she was here. I love Maebh. I couldn't even stand on my own to go to the goddamn toilet. How would I have had the stamina to have sex with Kylie!"

"That's enough!" my mother shouted. Turning to Marge, she asked, "Marge, tell us exactly what happened."

She wrung her hands. "Kylie came to the door and I remembered that she and Cord had been good friends growing up. Said she had run into Trevor, and he mentioned Cord was really sick. She wanted to come see him. I told her he was pretty much passed out and very much out of it. Cord had been rattling some nonsense for the last hour in his sleep. His fever was still high, and I'm pretty sure it was causing him to have nightmares, maybe even delusions."

I dropped my pounding head into my hands. All I wanted was to talk to Maebh. Tell her she had it all wrong.

"My husband called as I was talking to Kylie, and he asked me to pick up a prescription at the Oak Springs pharmacy. I told him it would have to wait until you got here, Melanie, because I couldn't leave Cord. Kylie said that she was more than happy to stay and watch him. I can promise you right now, even if the boy wanted to have sex, he was so out of it he wouldn't have been coherent enough to do it."

"Oh no," Paxton mumbled.

Amelia dropped down onto the large leather chair across from me. "That bitch," she whispered, looking at me with apologetic eyes. "I'm sorry I accused you of cheating."

"I told you I would never cheat on Maebh. She's my life. My everything. I broke things off with Kylie because she was cheating on her boyfriend *years ago*."

"I was only gone for thirty minutes, at the most," Marge said. "When I walked back in, Kylie was walking down with Cord's phone in her hands. She was flustered and acted like I had just caught her doing something. I thought it was strange. I asked her why she had Cord's phone. She said it had been going off, and she didn't want it to wake Cord up. She must have erased the calls and texts from Maebh, that evil little witch."

Sickness rolled over her face and she let a sob out. "Oh, my goodness. If I hadn't left her here, she wouldn't have been able to pull that stunt. I never thought in a million years...she must have seen Maebh texting Cord and quickly put her little plan in play."

Paxton let out a groan. "It all makes sense. Maebh said she lost it when she saw Kylie crawling into bed with Cord. She said her mind raced with everything Kylie had said, especially the part when she said they weren't expecting her to come back so early. At the time it seemed like Cord might have cheated on her. She said she ran back to her place, called the pilot and went back to Ireland."

"Wait, the pilot?" Amelia asked.

Paxton nodded. "Yeah, apparently her father has a private plane."

I stood and swayed on my feet. "I'm leaving. I need to get to Maebh."

"You're not going anywhere. Cord, you're still sick. You can simply call her," my mother declared.

Looking into my mother's gray eyes, I felt my tears building. "Mom, she thinks I cheated on her. I promised her I would never hurt her. She probably hates me right now. She was so upset she left the damn country after flying back to come take care of me!"

"You can call her and tell her everything, Cord."

"No, he can't," Paxton said. "He needs to go after her."

"Paxton's right, Mom," Amelia said. "Cord needs to go to Maebh."

My mother looked sick at the thought of me traveling overseas with the flu.

"I will not let you go until you are fever free for twenty-four hours." The back of her hand landed on my forehead.

"His fever broke in the middle of the night," Marge said. "And he's been taking the prescription the doctor wrote for him."

"Mom, I'm going to Maebh."

She sighed. "Fine, but you're not going alone."

I wanted to argue, but all of this was making me exhausted. Not only emotionally, but physically.

Glancing to Paxton, I asked, "Do you think she'll change her mind and come back to the States? I'd hate for me to fly to her only to find out she's on her way back."

"She already has plans to come back in a few days. She said she needed time to think before she came back."

"Don't call her again, okay? I don't want her to know I'm coming. She might run if she's gotten too deep into her head."

"She won't run, Cord," all four women said at once. But I knew Maebh. She'd be so pissed and hurt. She would run from me if she thought I had cheated on her. And I sure as hell wasn't about to let that happen.

As I boarded the private plane my father had chartered, I glanced back and rolled my eyes.

"I don't need a damn babysitter."

"Apparently you do, and I was voted the best person to do that," Aunt Vi stated as she strolled past me and sat in one of the large leather chairs. "And I haven't been to Ireland in a few years."

Her smile made my head hurt.

"What, no boy-toy?" I asked, sitting next to her.

Aunt Vi chuckled. "Not this trip. I promised my brother and sister-in-law I'd watch over you, and that's what I intend on doing. Now, if I happen to meet an Irish lad who wants to shag a time or two, that will be a bonus."

She winked at me, and I stared back at her, my lip slowly lifting into a snarl.

"Gross, Aunt Vi. I just got a visual, and I'm already not feeling good. Don't make it worse."

Waving me off like she couldn't be bothered, she asked, "Did you take your medicine today?"

"Yes."

"Still no fever?"

"No fever," I replied with a groan.

"Now, tell me what your game plan is to win your little Irish beauty back."

My eyes met hers. "Game plan?"

With a hard roll of her eyes, she sighed. "Christ Almighty, Cord Parker. You need a game plan. You think you're going to roll up to her front door, and she's going to jump into your arms? The girl was led to believe you messed around on her. She's hurting, she's angry, and her knee-jerk reaction will be to hit you in the balls—or, how do they say it in Ireland? Bollocks."

My hand went to my junk, and I frowned. "I was planning on telling her the truth. That's it."

Vi laughed as the flight attendant approached us.

"Mr. and Ms. Parker, we'll be leaving soon. I need you to fasten your seatbelts. If you need me after we're up in the air and before the captain has given me the okay to move around, just push this button."

The attendant reached across me, her tits brushing my arm, and pointed to a call button. Before Maebh, I'd probably be hauling her ass somewhere on the plane and fucking her. Now I pulled back and looked at her with an uninterested glare.

"Excuse me. I didn't mean to reach."

Uh-huh. Sure you didn't.

"Thank you, sweetheart, but I'm sure we'll be fine," Aunt Vi said. "Please give my nephew some water though before we take off, he's getting over the flu."

"Of course, Ms. Parker."

"I'm fine, Aunt Vi," I protested.

"You're getting over a very bad case of the flu, you're not fine. You need to rest. After we take off, you need to go and lie down.

You look like shit. I'll keep the flirty flight attendant away. The last thing you need is more women trying to come on to you."

I groaned and scrubbed my hands down my face. "I can't fucking believe Kylie would do that! Why? She's fucking married! Lives in another city, why was she screwing around with my world?"

Vi laughed like I had just asked the stupidest question ever.

"For a girl like Kylie, you were always hers."

"I was *never* hers."

"How many women have you gone back to more than twice?"

There had been plenty of women in town I'd fucked more than once. "A few."

She sighed. "Fine, more than five times?"

My heart dropped. "Only two. Kylie and Maebh."

Pointing, she said, "There you go. Even though this Kylie is married, she obviously still thinks you belong to her. Let's face it, Cord. You never were the type of guy who anyone thought would settle down before thirty-five, maybe even forty."

I frowned. "Gee, thanks, Aunt Vi."

"It's true. You were a player, you liked sex, and you had fun. There's nothing wrong with that. I like sex. I like to have sex with multiple guys at the same time. There's nothing wrong with that."

Gagging, I plugged my ears and started to sing the ABC song. It was the first thing that popped into my head. I'd sing absolutely anything to get her to stop talking, or to at least drown out her sexual fetishes.

She kicked me, making me drop my hands and look at her.

"Do you know how much you have just scarred me for life? Don't say shit like that, Aunt Vi!"

Laughing, she waved me off yet again. "All I'm saying is this girl probably found out you were in a committed relationship and that made her jealous. Now, did she work out this plan ahead of time? Hell no. She saw Maebh texting you, and she decided to try and push her away. Did she know the poor girl would rush back to

Ireland? I doubt it, but maybe she thought she could slide in and comfort you when your girlfriend all of a sudden stopped talking to you."

"That's fucked-up thinking."

She shrugged. "That's women. Not all women, but some. They like to play around and cause drama."

"Maebh isn't that way," I said softly, my heart feeling like it was breaking all over again. When I found out she had gone back to Ireland, my heart felt like part of it was in Texas and the other part had been catapulted to Cork.

"No, Maebh doesn't like drama. And that little slut knew that."

My phone beeped with a message from Amelia.

Amelia: *Found Kylie. Her husband apparently left her for another woman. Karma's a bitch, I guess. That's why she was back in town. She still has the same cell phone number in case you are interested in reaching out."*

I stared at the message before saying, "Amelia said she found out Kylie was back in town because her husband left her."

"Interesting."

Lifting my head to look at my aunt, I said, "Why is that interesting?"

"Because I'm sure the girl showed up at your place with every intent on trying to seduce you. Her husband left her, she was hurting, and her best revenge would be to sleep with the guy who had once been her fuck buddy. What's that saying? The only way to get over a man is to get under another one? You can't have a girlfriend standing in the way with a mission like that."

Anger pulsed through my body. In that moment, I hated Kylie. Hated that I had given her so much of me. Spent so much time with her. I wanted to forget every single moment I had ever been with her. Wanted to erase every second I'd been with any other woman.

"Well, she failed, and if she tries that shit again, I'll make it so she won't ever come back to Oak Springs."

A smile moved across my aunt's face as she lifted the water that the flight attendant had just handed to us.

"Thank you," I said to the flight attendant.

"Sure thing. We're about to taxi."

When the flight attendant left, I pulled out my phone and called the woman who had possibly just ruined my entire life.

"Cord, how are you feeling?"

"I want to know one thing. When you crawled into bed with me, did you touch me in any way?"

"What?"

"Don't play around me, Kylie. Amelia got the truth out of you about your husband. You played Maebh, now I want you to tell me the goddamn truth right now."

She sighed. "No. I was getting dressed when I heard her come back in. I undressed and crawled into bed with you as she walked into the room. As soon as she ran out, I got dressed because I knew Marge would be back. I'm honestly surprised she didn't run into Maebh."

"Why, Kylie?"

The line was silent for a few minutes. "I was hurt, and I needed you. I needed to forget."

"The fact that I had a girlfriend meant nothing to you?"

She laughed. "Right. Like that's ever been a concern of mine."

The plane started down the runway. "Don't ever call me again. Don't talk to me, don't look at me, don't even breathe in my fucking direction. I love Maebh and will only ever love her."

I hit End and tossed my phone on the seat next to me.

Aunt Vi lifted her bottle of water up. "To winning the love of your life back with a plan that you haven't come up with yet!"

I lifted my water to hers. We hit the two plastic bottles together, and I flashed her a smirk. "I'm a Parker, Aunt Vi. Nothing is going to stand in my way."

She winked and nodded her head. "There you are. For a few moments I thought the pussy fairies had swooped in and taken over my favorite nephew."

I chuckled and shook my head. "And here I always thought Tripp was your favorite."

Aunt Vi waved me off. "Tripp? That boy is too serious. No, my favorite as always been the rebel son. You remind me of myself, only a male version."

"Rebel son?" I asked with a hard laugh.

With a slight lift of her shoulders, Vi gave me a knowing smile. I'd been a bit of a rebel my entire life. My father had expected me to work the ranch and when I made it known I was going to college for a business major and had plans to open up my own bar, my father had nearly flipped out. I had graduated high school early, headed to the University of Texas and worked at night and weekends bartending, saving every single dime after living expenses to build up the money to buy the run-down building on Main Street.

I wasn't even out of college when I bought the building where Cord's Place now resided. My parents saw my drive and were behind me a hundred percent, even fronting the down payment for the loan to remodel the bar. If it hadn't been for them, I wouldn't own that bar. Hell, I was young and had built a successful business because they backed me. I was fucking lucky and I knew it. Although, my father reminded me often I never did finish my degree because I was too focused on owning a bar.

And now all of that focus was on Maebh.

"You'll get her back, Cord. Don't stress. Drink up that water and then lie down. Have I mentioned that you look like fucking shit? Maebh's gonna take one look at you and run for the Irish hills."

I shook my head and laughed. Aunt Vi never was one to beat around the bush. She motioned for me to drink the water.

Tilting the water back, I drank it. Staring out the window, I let my thoughts start gathering as I thought about how I was going to prove to Maebh that I was hers, only hers.

Little did I know that my aunt had already begun that process. Along with the help of my mother, Paxton, and Amelia.

CHAPTER 30

maebh

The cool wind rushed over me face as I sat on top of the paint horse. We both stood, frozen on the high cliff that overlooked the blue ocean below, reminding me of Cord's beautiful sapphire eyes.

The jagged rocks coming out of the water seemed to mimic how me chest felt. I was a mess of confused emotions that went up and down, like the waves as they pummeled the shoreline. Me heart felt empty, me soul destroyed, yet there was something I couldn't put me finger on. A nagging in me chest as I stood here, my gaze trained on the beautiful water below. Something didn't feel right. For the first time since I ran from Cord's house, I felt it. Why had I run? Why hadn't I marched past that bitch, and right to Cord, looked him in the eyes and demanded he tell me what he had done?

I knew why I had run. The sight of Kylie, the girl who Cord had been *fuck buddies* with, had shaken me core. It had brought out a fear I had buried deep inside yet pretended didn't exist. Thinking back on it now, it didn't make any sense. Cord had sounded so sick when I talked to him. Melanie and Amelia said he had been so weak he couldn't even go to the doctor. How in the world could he have had the energy or desire to have sex? I'd let her nasty words fill me head and stir up that doubt. It was her crawling into his bed that had thrown me for a loop.

I'd felt this way since I woke up from a dream. Cord was begging me to listen to him, let him explain and I wouldn't. I kept running and he kept following me. Everywhere I went, he would show up. The look of sheer panic in his eyes when I would say we were over was what woke me up, gasping for breath.

Deep down I knew I had been insecure about me relationship with Cord. He was handsome, built like a god, charming, and had a history of being a ladies' man. Women hit on him every night at the bar and for years he had acted on those advances. Was I really that naïve to think he could stop and be committed to one woman?

I closed me eyes and thought about the last time we were together. I knew with every ounce of me being Cord loved me. The way he looked at me when he made love to me was etched into me memory. More tears fell as I realized Cord would never hurt me. He had told me he loved me. He had chosen me to be with. He had been in me bed nearly every night pulling me body next to his. No other woman but me.

I had read into things and that was what Kylie was hoping for. But why had he not called? Paxton had said Cord was still sick when she called yesterday. It was then I started to doubt what had really happened. I had told her everything and assumed she would have confronted Cord by now. If Paxton could call me, Cord could, as well. Unless something had happened to him. My mind was now a mixture of even more emotions. What if things turned for the worse and Cord had gotten sicker? Surely Melanie or one of the girls would have called me. Wouldn't they? Maybe they were upset that I'd run without giving Cord a chance to tell his side of things.

Shite. Why had I acted like such a foolish child?

'Gasping at the thought that something bad might have happened, I turned the horse around and gave him a swift kick in the side. We were soon racing toward the stables.

The need to get back to America and to Cord was overwhelming. I had run away like a scared little girl and that wasn't who I was. I'd find out the truth for meself and if Cord had cheated, I'd kick his ass. If he hadn't, I'd beg for him to forgive me for not trusting him and giving him a chance to explain.

By the time I got back to the stables, I was sweating. It was cold out, but me adrenaline was off the charts and just squeezing me legs on Forest, my father's prized paint horse, had worked up a sweat. Rushing back toward the house, I heard me da's voice calling out for me.

"Maebh! Maebh! Where's the fire?"

Sliding to a halt, I rushed over. "I have to go back to him."

His eyes widened in surprise while he stood before me. He was dressed in work boots, jeans, and a T-shirt that read *Sona*, the company he had worked so hard at building and making into one of the best whiskeys in Ireland and the world.

"What are you talking about?" he finally asked.

"I have to go back to America. I need to know for sure if what I saw really was what I thought it was."

A slow curve lifted his lips and relief washed over his face. Like I was finally getting something he had gotten long before.

"What?" I asked, my brows furrowed as his slow grin grew to a wide smile.

"I think you'd be making a mistake to go to America, lass."

"Why?" I asked. Wasn't it my father who had been telling me to call Cord the last few days? To get his side of the story? Now he was telling me *not* to go.

"Before you go throwing punches at me, let's get inside for some tea."

"Da, I really need—"

He held up his hand to stop me from talking. "Give me ten minutes, Maebh O'Sullivan, before you go tearing out of here and firing up the plane again. Cool that temper and relax the desire to solve the problem this instant. Ten minutes, that's all I want."

A few minutes later I was following my da into the house, I smiled at George as he reached for me hand while I walked up the stairs of Castle Finghin, our family home. He was the butler and one of the three full-time employee's me father kept at all times.

Me heart was pounding as I followed me da through the door.

"Ten minutes, Da. That's all I'm giving you."

He chuckled and glanced over his shoulder at me. "That's all I need."

We walked through the foyer and into me father's office. He poured us each a glass of whiskey and motioned for me to sit down.

"I don't want to sit."

He lifted a brow, "Maebh O'Sullivan, sit your arse down in that chair. Trust me, for what I'm about to say you'll want to be sitting down."

CHAPTER 31

Cord

Aedin, Maebh's father, had arranged for a car to pick us up at the airport. When a Bentley Mulsanne showed up, Aunt Vi and I looked at each other in shock.

Sliding into the car, she said, "How rich is this bastard?"

I chuckled and shook my head. "I'm not sure. I know they come from money, but that's all. I've never asked Maebh, and she's never mentioned it."

"I know those Irish folk like their drinking, but damn, the whiskey business must be good here," she mused.

"Mr. Parker, Mr. O'Sullivan has asked that we make a stop to speak with him before going to CastleFinghin."

"Castle...Finghin?" I asked. I didn't pronounce it the way the driver did so I wasn't surprised when he chuckled lightly.

"Yes, the home of Mr. O'Sullivan."

Aunt Vi and I looked at each other again. "The private plane is beginning to make more sense," I whispered while she lifted her brows in amusement.

"You might want to look into Ireland for your next business venture, Cord."

I laughed and looked out the window, taking in the beautiful city. As we'd flown into Cork I'd seen all the water Maebh had mentioned. It was stunning. The farther we got out of town, the more breathtaking it was.

"Why would anyone want to leave this place for Oak Springs, Texas?" Aunt Vi scoffed. "I may never go back."

My chest tightened. It was some of the most beautiful land I'd ever seen. Maybe Maebh was missing Ireland. I knew she loved the restaurant, but I also knew Eric was capable of running it. Judging by the car we were in, I was going to safely say Maebh and her father weren't hurting for money. I'd never even bothered to ask her if they had any other businesses. When Aedin flew to Paris a month ago for business, I had assumed it had to do with Sona, his distillery. His whiskey was some of the best fucking whiskey I'd ever tasted, and I now kept it stocked at Cord's Place.

"We're approaching the front gate of the O'Sullivan family seat."

Aunt Vi hit me on the leg and leaned over. "Christ Almighty, is this family nobility, Cord?"

I shrugged. "Fuck if I know! I'm learning this all at the same time as you, Aunt Vi!"

She placed the back of her hand on my forehead. "No fever. How do you feel?"

"How in the hell do you go from nobility to checking me for a fever?"

With a grin, she winked. "Women can multitask, my dear."

I rolled my eyes.

When we stopped at a large gate, Vi and I leaned down and looked up at it. Tall bushes lined both sides of the large stone arches. Between those were two large gates with a symbol on them. Glancing to my left, a stone sign read in large, bold letters:

CASTLEFINGHIN

"Are we being punked?" Aunt Vi asked me.

My head shook slowly as I whispered, "I'm not sure."

"I thought you said we weren't going to Castle Finghin," I asked.

"Not to the house right away, sir. You're meeting Mr. O'Sullivan at his private office on the grounds."

"Did he happen to mention why?" I asked.

"No, sir."

I sighed. "I told Paxton to ask Aedin not to tell Maebh I was coming. Do you think he isn't happy about me being here?"

Waving her hand to brush away my comment, Aunt Vi said, "Nonsense. I'm sure he respects the fact that you've traveled all this way to see his daughter. Hopefully Paxton told him it was all a misunderstanding."

I rubbed my hands over my thighs. "Let's hope she did. Otherwise, the Irish mafia could be waiting to beat the living shit out of me."

The driver chuckled, which caused Vi and me to snap our heads and look at him.

"Oh, hell," I mumbled. "I'm going to die. Be sure to let Tripp know not to give Trevor control of my place and that there really is no such thing as free beer."

Aunt Vi laughed harder like I'd just said the funniest thing she'd ever heard. I knew what that was. Nervous laughter. Distract the poor bastard so he doesn't think about the pain and possible death fixin' to happen.

"Sir, I can put your mind to rest. The Irish mafia is not here to...well...beat the living shite out of you."

I let out the breath I didn't even know I had been holding.

"Thank fuck for that."

Vi slapped me on the leg. "See, you were all worried. He's probably just going to threaten you that if you ever hurt his daughter again he'll have his 'friends' take you out slowly...and piece by piece."

"Not making me feel any better, Aunt Vi."

The driveway was long and when I looked ahead, I saw a large, three-story house with what looked like two wings coming out on both sides of the white stone house. Or castle. Or whatever the hell they called it over here. It was fucking huge and made my folks' place look small. The driver turned to the right instead of taking the bridge that lead straight to the house and drove for a bit along the water.

"That's beautiful. What river is that?" Aunt Vi asked.

"That's the Blackwater River, ma'am. The salmon are amazing and fun to catch."

That caught my attention. Maebh grew up on a river, yet had never been fishing?

We pulled up to a stone two-story building and the car came to a stop.

"Are you sure you're feeling okay, Cord?" my aunt asked.

"I don't feel a hundred percent, but I'm better." It wasn't a lie. I did feel better, but I was tired as hell, even though I had slept on the plane in the private bedroom. I was glad Aunt Vi kept the flight attendant at bay after she had come in once and asked if I needed anything. I got the distinct feeling she'd meant something sexual.

We stepped out of the car, and I walked around to stand next to Aunt Vi.

"I believe he only wants to see you, sir."

Swallowing hard, I looked at my aunt and said, "If I don't make it out alive, tell Maebh I love her very much."

With a roll of her eyes, Aunt Vi pushed me toward the building. "For Christ's sake, boy, get your ass in there so you can get this over with and finally see Maebh."

I took in a deep breath and blew it out as I walked up the large stone steps. This was his private office. Shit, Maebh had certainly kept a lot about her life in Ireland from me. I didn't care; none of it mattered, but I sure as shit wasn't expecting this.

I glanced over my shoulder at my aunt for moral support and all I got was her waving me on. I caught her looking to her right, and she let a huge smile play across her face. I wanted to step back and see who she was smiling at. Was it Maebh?

My heart started pounding, but I kept moving forward. Once I was inside, an older woman approached me. She wore a long black skirt, black high heels, and a white blouse that was tucked neatly into her skirt.

"Mr. Parker?" she asked politely. That was a good sign. Surely Aedin wouldn't kill me with witnesses around.

Clearing my throat, I replied, "Yes. Cord Parker."

"I'm Jess, one of Mr. O'Sullivan's assistants."

One of them? Shit. Who is this guy?

"It's nice to meet you," I replied with a tight smile.

She nodded and then handed me a bottle of water. "Your mother has asked that you keep hydrated since you're still getting over the flu."

Staring down at the water, I couldn't believe my mother's powers reached across the goddamn Atlantic Ocean.

"Um, okay. Thank you," I replied while taking the water from her. She waited for me to actually open it and take a drink. When I did, she smiled with satisfaction.

"Follow me, sir."

I glanced out one of the large windows and saw Aunt Vi was talking to someone. A man. We walked by so quickly though that I couldn't tell who it was, but it sure as hell looked like Aedin.

I started to sweat. He was going to have me roughed up first. Have one of his *guys* teach me a lesson.

My hand raked through my hair, and I let out a groan.

"What was that, sir?" Jess asked.

"Um, nothing."

She opened the door to a large room that housed a table on one side, probably for meetings and such, and on the opposite side a stunning desk that sat in front of floor-to-ceiling windows.

"It will only be a few moments, Mr. Parker. Make yourself at home. In the corner is a bar if you'd like something stronger than water."

I nodded while looking around. Behind the meeting desk, book-shelves covered the entire span of the wall. The shelves reminded me of the ones in Aisling.

"Thank you," I said, making my way farther into the room. The door clicked behind me.

Blowing out a sigh, I made my way over to the bar. I hadn't eaten anything except the apple and two bananas Aunt Vi had practically pushed down my throat. I walked behind the bar to see what the stash was, and my eyes widened in disbelief.

"Holy fucking shit."

My eyes scanned the booze. Johnnie Walker Blue Label, Bunnahabhain Limited Edition, Macallan Sherrywood forty-year-old single malt scotch, which I knew was about a fourteen-thousand-dollar bottle. Dalmore, Glenfarcias…and shit. He even had Glenfiddich. One of the best damn Scotch Whiskys around.

I shook my head and opened the water, taking a long drink from it. I moved back around the bar and over to the small sitting area. There were two chairs that flanked a large sofa. I sat down and dropped my head in my hands after I placed the water on the table.

My head was fucking pounding, my entire body aching from this damn flu. I was honest-to-God surprised my fever had broken. I felt like crap. I rubbed my fingertips on my temples and groaned. Maybe it was just the idea of meeting with Maebh's father.

"Fucking flu," I said as I moved my hands and scrubbed my face before closing my eyes and dropping my head against the sofa. I knew if I wasn't careful, I'd fall asleep. I let my body relax some and the most beautiful green eyes popped into my mind.

I smiled and whispered, "Maebh." I slowly felt myself slipping into sleep before someone cleared their throat.

A shiver ran down my back, and I knew she was in the room.

"You look like shite."

My stomach dropped at the sound of her voice and me smile grew bigger. "I feel like it, too."

Lifting my head, I saw the most beautiful woman on Earth standing with her hands crossed over her chest. The woman I loved more than my own life. The woman I planned on winning back. The woman I planned on making love to by the end of the day if it killed me. That woman was dressed in a white lace outfit that instantly had my cock going stiff. Under the lace was a bra that looked like a damn sports bra and white shorts that looked like nothing more than the boy short panties she loved.

"Maebh," I whispered as I stood. Closing my eyes, I tried to get the room to stop spinning.

"Are you okay?" she asked, my entire body to shuddering at her touch.

"I am now," I breathed out, staring in her beautiful emerald eyes.

Her mouth twitched with a smile.

"Wait, am I dreaming?"

Now she did smile. A full-blown, knock-me-off-my-damn-feet kind of smile. "No, why?"

"Well, for one thing, you're standing here with me. You're not yelling and accusing me of cheating. Your dad's not in here threatening to have the Irish mafia kick my ass. Something's wrong."

Maebh doubled over laughing and moved next to me, prompting me to sit down on the sofa. The back of her hand came to my forehead the moment I sat. She shook her head and let out a breath.

"What are you doing flying across the ocean when you're sick, you eejit?"

"The moment I heard what bullshit Kylie pulled, I needed to get to you. You needed to hear it from me that nothing happened with her. I swear on my family's life, nothing happened."

"So you jumped on a private plane and flew here?" she asked.

I nodded. "My mother wouldn't let me leave unless I was fever free." I pouted and Maebh shook her head, trying to hide the grin.

"Smart woman," Maebh whispered, reaching for my water and handing it to me. "You don't have a fever, but you certainly don't look like you feel well."

I leaned my head back and closed my eyes. "I don't. I feel like shit." Lifting my head again, our eyes met. "Maebh, I need you to know that *nothing* happened between me and Kylie. I would never hurt you, I promised you I would never—"

Her fingers pushed against my lips. She moved quickly and positioned herself with her legs straddling me and her body over my hardening cock.

"I already know nothing happened, and I'm sorry I ran."

My brows pulled together in confusion and I stared at her. What did she mean she already knew? Why the hell did she leave and come to Ireland then?

Confused, I spoke the only word that would come out of my mouth. "Huh?"

Maebh let out a soft sigh and kissed me on the forehead before locking her gaze with mine. "I'm sorry I let her pull at those small doubts in me mind. She pushed the right buttons and caused me to turn and tuck tail. What I should have done was march past her little arse and straight up to you. If I had paid attention the second time I came over, I would have found you passed out from a fever and known she was bluffing. I think I knew deep down at the time she was lying, but it took me stubborn Irish arse time to realize it. I was going to leave to head back to America earlier today when me da stopped me. Melanie had already called him and told him you were on your way here. And to tell me nothing happened between you and Kylie, and that Kylie had played a cruel joke on me and even erased me text messages." Her brow lifted as she added, "She is a piece of work, that one."

"She'll never bother us again. I want you to know I talked to her before we left, I needed to make sure she didn't do anything to me while I was passed out."

Her breath caught in her throat.

"And?"

"She told me she had been getting dressed when you came back. She got the idea to crawl into the bed with me because she heard you coming up the stairs."

Maebh's eyes filled with anger.

"I told her to never look my way. She'll never be a problem again, I promise you."

"Okay, but I need you to know something. I'm not the type of woman who runs away from a problem, Cord. But seeing her standing in your place with nothing but your shirt on, and the things she said… It messed with me head a bit, I won't lie. I don't want to be jealous, but I am a wee bit."

I cupped her face with my hands. "You're the only woman I want. The only one I want to spend the rest of my life with. I want to build a house together and fill it with babies and puppies."

Maebh giggled. "Babies?" she asked, her eyes lighting up like Christmas morning. "How many babies are we talking about?"

"As many as you want. I love you, and I will always love you and *only* you. You're it for me, Maebh. I can't imagine living this life without you. I may have been scared when we first started dating, but I'm not anymore. I can't promise you I won't fuck up because this is still so new to me. All I know is that you make me feel alive and I've never loved anyone like I love you Please tell me you're coming back home with me."

Her teeth sank into her lip, and it felt like my entire world stopped in that moment as I waited for her to speak. I didn't breathe, my heart didn't beat, everything was at a stand-still.

"This will always be home, Cord. But now I have two homes. Here *and* Oak Springs."

Relief rushed over my body and I took in a breath.

"I learned something the last few days though."

"What's that?" I asked, my thumb gliding over her soft cheek.

"Ireland is a part of me. I need her spirit to fill me soul. I want to come back often. Me da is going to be staying here, with the distillery. They need him, and I know that. But I want to visit more often."

I nodded. "I think we can do that. Especially if he sends that private plane of his."

Maebh giggled.

"Speaking of, Jesus H. Christ, Maebh. What in the fuck is all of this? You live in a castle? Darlin' you've got some explaining to do."

She rolled her eyes. "It's not a castle like the Blarney Castle. Me family on Da's side does have a bit of Irish nobility though. Not that it means much today. Me Da's grandmother though, she is of British nobility. Lady Darby Grady is her given name. She is a very wealthy woman and *very* English. And me great-grandmother as well. They are both decedents of King Henry the eighth."

"Wow. I'll have to keep that bit of information in mind when we have fights cuz ol' Henry didn't fare too well at the end." I rubbed my neck, and she playfully hit me on the chest, her body now fully seated on me. My cock was pushing up into her pussy and not only was my head spinning from being sick, but also because she was sitting on me.

"No, seriously, that's pretty cool."

She shrugged after a few seconds. "I don't think much of it and neither did my parents. Me father built the distillery on his own and made it what it is today without the help of his ma or grandmother. She of course thinks we are Irish fools who don't respect her English ways."

"Is she right?"

Maebh simply winked and leaned down to kiss me. "We'll talk about me family later. For right now, I want to kiss those lips. I hope you're not still contagious."

"I'm not, and if I am, I'll take care of you when you get sick."

Wrapping her arms around my neck, she leaned closer. My hand slipped behind her neck and brought her mouth to mine in a hard, needy kiss.

The emotion we both poured into the kiss was evident. Each of us saying how sorry we were, and how nothing like this would ever come between us again. It was fucking amazing what could be said with the silence of one kiss.

Maebh pulled back first, her forehead rested on mine while she breathed deeply.

"Promise me something, agra."

"Anything," she panted.

"You'll talk to me next time. If anything scares you, or you think something is happening, talk to me before you leave."

She drew her head back and pierced my eyes with hers. "I'll never leave you again, I swear. And I also promise you I'll never run again. If we have problems, we'll talk to each other first."

I closed my eyes and whispered, "Thank you," before catching her gaze again. "I don't think I could take you leaving me again. I couldn't breathe while you were gone."

"Neither could I," she confessed. "And, Cord, I don't want you to think I'm avoiding talking about me family. I think by now you've guessed I come from money, but it doesn't mean anything to me. It's not who I am or what defines me."

It was my turn to press my fingers to her lips. "Maebh, I don't care if you come from money or not. None of that changes who you are in here."

Taking her hand, I pressed it to my chest.

"Money doesn't mean anything to me either. All I want is for the two of us to be happy and pop out a couple of kids who are going to talk so fucked-up between your Irish accent and my southern drawl that we won't know what in the hell they are saying."

She laughed and slid her hands through my hair.

"I love you so much."

"And I love you, my beautiful Irish cailín."

CHAPTER 32

Cord

"Kiss me again," I whispered against her lips.

"Cord, me da and your aunt are waiting outside. We have to go."

"No, we don't have to go. We can stay here and…" Glancing around, I realized we were in her father's office. "Yeah, we better get out of here."

She climbed off of me. I slowly stood, letting the dizziness settle before reaching for my girl's hand and walking back out.

When we emerged from the building, Aunt Vi was talking to Aedin. I'd never seen her smiling like that at a man before.

"Oh, hell."

"What's wrong?" Maebh asked.

"Aunt Vi is smitten with your father."

Maebh glanced to them. "You think?"

Nodding, I wrapped my arm around her waist and guided her closer. Neither her dad or Aunt Vi even noticed we had walked up. We stood there and stared before glancing at each other. Maebh chewed slightly on her lip while trying not to smile. I couldn't help but wonder how she felt about her father moving on with someone else. I knew he'd loved his wife more than anything, but even Maebh had been worried he was beginning to get lonely.

I cleared my throat and that got Aunt Vi and Aedin's attention. Looking our way, their faces brightened.

"I take it things are all good?" Vi asked, glancing down to my arm around Maebh.

"Yes. They're perfect!" Maebh declared.

"I hope you don't have to rush back to the states. I'd love to fish some in the river, Cord, when you're feeling better," Aedin said.

"Yes, I'd love that." I made a mental note to ask Maebh why she had never fished before when she lived on this fucking amazing river. I'd be out there every damn day.

"I think we should head to the house. Cord isn't feeling so great, and I think he needs to lie down." Maebh said.

Aedin motioned for us to get into the car. The drive up to the main house wasn't that long. The car pulled around the circular drive and up to the massive house.

"Tell me about this place, Aedin," Aunt Vi said.

I could see the pride in his face when we all stepped out of the car.

"Castle Finghin has been in my family since the early eighteen-hundreds. My family has occupied it since, with the exception of when me da married me ma. They moved to England for a bit before me da couldn't take it and moved back. The house sits on a large amount of land."

"How many acres?" I asked.

"Three hundred, though at one time, most of the small town we drove through once belonged to me family."

"Wow," I said, as Aunt Vi made her way up the giant stone steps.

"It's four-story, forty-five-thousand square feet with ten suites and ten additional bedrooms. There is also a twenty-seat-cinema, a library, a spa with an indoor pool, and two wine cellars."

"I'll sleep in one of those cellars tonight," Aunt Vi stated.

We all laughed as the door opened and an older man stepped out and greeted us.

"George, this is me boyfriend, Cord Parker. And his aunt, Vi Parker."

George gave us both a small bow. "Your room is ready, ma'am. I'll personally show you to it."

Aunt Vi smiled and replied, "Thank you so much."

"Once you rest, we'll take a trip into town, and I'll show you around," Aedin stated.

A scenic tour was going to have to wait. My head was killing me, and I needed to spend time with Maebh.

"We'll see how Cord feels in a bit. Let's get you settled in, shall we?" Maebh said, looking back over her shoulder at the guy who had been our driver. "Dalton, you can leave Cord's bag there. We can get it."

"Yes, Ms. O'Sullivan."

It was strange having people waiting on us, and I was positive Maebh knew I felt that way. Aunt Vi didn't mind it, but I wasn't about to let some guy carry my small bag up the steps. Fuck no.

"Let's go," Maebh said, quickly taking my hand as I reached for my bag and we walked through the door.

My mouth dropped at the sight before me. The foyer was fucking beautiful. I looked straight up and saw a stained glass dome ceiling. A massive chandelier hung down and stopped at the second level. The iron work on the stair railing had the most beautiful details I'd ever seen.

"There's a jeb door at the top that leads to a forty-acre rose garden on top of the house," Aedin said, causing Aunt Vi to gasp.

"A rose garden?" she asked, her eyes lifting all the way up.

"Yes, ten thousand rose bushes."

"I have to see it, this instant."

Aedin's face lit up. "Do you like roses, Vi?"

"Do I like roses? Do cows shit in pastures?"

Maebh covered her mouth to hide her giggle while I let out a groan. Aedin laughed his damn ass off. Clearly he liked Aunt Vi's crude sense of humor.

"Come on, I'll take you up there. You can get settled after we take a stroll."

Aunt Vi started up the steps and then stopped, glancing over her shoulder. "Maebh, you've got babysitting duty now. I'm off the clock."

Lifting her hand and saluting my aunt, Maebh replied, "Got it. I'll take the job seriously."

Aunt Vi lifted a brow and smirked. "I'm sure you will, dear."

And like that, my aunt had gone off with the master of the castle. This was going to be interesting.

"Come on, let's go," I said.

We headed up the stairs to the top floor. Of course, her room would be on the top fucking floor. All of a sudden I felt weak and wanted to lie down, especially after climbing all the stairs.

"You okay?" Maebh asked, giving me a concerned stare.

"Tired."

"We're almost there," she said as she walked down a hallway that I swore was the length of a damn football field.

"You grew up in this house?" I asked.

"Yep."

"Too bad you didn't have any siblings. You could have some kick-ass hide and seek games in this house."

She walked backwards and took my hands in hers. "I guess that means our kids will have to have all the fun with that."

My heart skipped a beat. The old Cord would be freaking the fuck out if a woman mentioned kids. But Maebh mentioning it only made me want it that much more. "I think I'm going to have fun practicing this whole making babies thing."

Her cheeks turned pink, and my chest tightened. I loved this beautiful Irish fireball with my whole heart.

"Me, too."

We finally got to the end of the long hall and stopped outside a large curved door. "Me room," she whispered.

"Are you going to let me in or are we going to stand out here and give each other fuck-me eyes?"

Maebh rolled her eyes and twisted the brass handle. When we walked into the room my legs nearly buckled out from under me—and it had nothing to do with recovering from the flu.

"Holy. Shit."

The first thing I saw was a king size mahogany bed. Above the headboard was a large blue tapestry that came around the front of the bed and barely flanked it, making it look like privacy curtains. At the end of the bed was an antique chest. On either side were matching mahogany nightstands with an antique lamp on each one. My eyes moved over the room. The walls were painted sage green with the most intricate woodwork framing the doors and windows, along with the molding at the top of the walls. Antique furniture filled the room. A small dresser sat under a painting of a beautiful little girl.

Once I saw those green eyes, I knew it was my Maebh. She was precious. Dark curls framed her little face, and she wore the same smile she had now. I was captivated even by her younger self. A large window sat in the middle of the room flanked by two slightly smaller windows. The view of the countryside left me breathless. The Black River could be seen through each window.

"This desk used to belong to me great-grandfather. He wrote books. Did I ever tell you that?" she asked, running her finger along the oak desk.

"No, you didn't. What did he write?"

Glancing over her shoulder, her teeth sank into her lip. "Naughty stories for me great-grandmother."

I lifted my brows. "Really?"

She leaned against the desk. "But he also wrote mysteries. He was very popular here in Ireland. Even today his books are still best-sellers."

Another explanation for the fucking mansion I was standing in.

"I'm named after his sister."

A slow smile spread over my face. I did love her name.

She took the bag from my hand and dropped it to the floor. I leaned against another desk on the opposite side of the bed.

"Let's lie down so you can rest."

"Best idea ever," I said, reaching behind me and pulling my shirt over my head. I watched as Maebh stared like it was the first time she'd ever laid eyes on my bare chest. I fucking loved the way she looked at me with hungry eyes. I never wanted that look to fade.

I pulled her to me, "Stop looking at me like that, baby, or I'll be forced to fuck you and I'm questioning my physical abilities right now. I may not be able to finish what I start."

With a chuckle, Maebh placed her hands on the side of my face. "I bet we can think of something to do that won't have you exerting too much energy."

She quickly had my belt unbuckled and my pants undone. She was pulling them off my legs once I had toed off my boots.

"Commando?" she mused, looking up at me through those eyelashes.

When she licked her lips, I moaned and felt my cock growing harder by the second. She placed a soft kiss on the side of my cock and slowly stood. Taking my hands in hers, she walked toward the bed. Drawing the blankets down, she motioned for me to crawl into the bed. I did so while she took off her sexy, white lace outfit, leaving her thong and bra on.

"Why are you not naked?" I asked when she slipped in next to me.

"I want you, but I also want you to sleep. I need something between us right now."

The low rumble in the back of my throat made her smile.

"Fucking hell, Maebh. If you're that horny, baby, I can make you come."

Shaking her head, she snuggled next to me. "No, I want to lie here with you. Please rest, Cord."

My arm went around her, pulling her closer to me. It didn't take me long to start to relax. The sound of her breathing quickly drew me toward a much-needed sleep.

And sleep I did.

CHAPTER 33

maebh

"How are you feeling?" I asked Cord for the fourth time since we left the house.

"Better than I have in the last two weeks."

He squeezed my hand, then lifted the back of it to his lips.

"I'm totally leaning over and kissing the stone," Vi stated with a huge smile.

"Um, you should probably know, the local kids have been known to piss on the stone," me da said.

Vi's smile instantly faded. "What the hell? Those little Irish bastards!"

We all laughed, and I settled into Cord's side. He had slept that first day for almost twelve hours. When he finally woke up, we spent the next four hours rotating from me bed to the shower, back to me bed. Sex with Cord was always good, but the last few days it had been amazing. Each time he came inside me, I fell even more in love with him. Me heart felt like it could explode I loved this man so much.

"What else would you like to see while you're here in Ireland?" I asked.

Vi lifted her eyes in thought, and I felt Cord's hand squeeze me hip. I knew exactly what he wanted to do, and it involved locking ourselves in me room all day.

"Honestly, I think I'd like to fish for some salmon," Cord said with a smile.

Me father's eyes lit up, and I couldn't help but notice how he looked at Vi. They had an obvious connection. Was me da falling for Vi?

Me chest squeezed at the thought. A mix of emotions overcame me all at once. Happiness for him, that he had opened his heart again, and sadness knowing he was thinking of another woman like he thought of me ma.

"Are you okay?" Cord asked, his mouth pressed against me head.

"Yes," I whispered. Vi and me da were lost in a conversation when Cord pulled back.

"Are you sure?"

Me eyes filled with tears, and I fought to keep them back as I softly answered him. "I'm happy, so very happy, but it seems like maybe another door is closing and I'm not sure how I feel about that."

"He'll always love your mom."

I nodded. "I know."

"He deserves to find happiness. This may just be a temporary thing. They obviously enjoy one another's company."

We looked back over to them as they laughed at something Vi had said.

"Yes, they do. And she makes him laugh. I don't think I've heard me father laugh this much in a long time."

The car came to a stop, and Cord stiffened at my side when Dalton, my father's driver, announced our arrival at Blarney Castle.

"You excited to see it?" I asked as I looked back at Cord. He was pale and looked like he was about to be sick. He nodded quickly and turned away from me.

Shite. Maybe he's getting sick again. He jumped out of the car and jogged around to get me door before Dalton could.

"After the castle tour, I've arranged for a lunch for the four of us," Cord said, making me look up at him in surprise.

"Really?" I asked.

He was avoiding me eyes, and I swore he was sweating. Reaching up, I felt for a fever. Nothing. He felt normal.

"How in the world did you manage that?" I asked with a chuckle.

This time he did look at me and winked. "I have my own connections, Ms. O'Sullivan."

Me brows lifted. "I guess so, Mr. Parker."

The tour was entertaining, especially with Vi and Cord there. I wasn't sure why Cord had such a hard time understanding everyone, but he had to have things repeated at least three times before Vi would tell him what was said. And I thought all this time it was just me he couldn't understand.

"So where is this lunch?" I asked as we strolled through the gardens. Vi and me da were walking a good way ahead of us.

"We're getting closer, I believe. I hear the waterfall."

Smiling, I peeked up to Cord. "The Bog Garden?"

He winked and that was it, I had to know his secret.

"Tell me!" I said, tickling his side and causing him to jump away from me.

"Woman! Learn to be surprised, will you?"

"Cord, tell me. It kills me not knowing."

With a chuckle, he replied, "I see that."

I sighed. "Please? I'll do whatever you want if you tell me."

He stopped walking and faced me, making me breath hitch in me lungs. Lifting his hand, he brushed a piece of hair behind me ear.

He leaned down and bushed his lips over mine before he whispered, "Close your eyes, agra."

Squeezing them shut, I felt his hands on me shoulders as he turned me around.

His hot breath caused me entire body to shake with a desire only he would ever bring out in me.

"There isn't anything I wouldn't do for you, Maebh. I'm going to show you each and every day how much I love you. There has never been a single doubt in my mind that you and I don't belong together."

Even with me eyes closed, I felt tears slip free as I whispered his name.

"Cord."

"Every morning when I see the pink sky spread across the Texas hill country, I'm going to thank God for you. Every night when I look up at the stars I'm going to thank God for giving us another day together, and I'll pray for a million more."

A sob slipped from me mouth as I covered it with me hand.

"Our life is only just beginning, my beautiful Irish cailin. Open your eyes, baby."

When I did, I saw a beautiful blanket set up on the lawn in front of us. A basket was at one end and a champagne bucket sat to the right.

"Oh, Cord," I whispered as he placed his hand on me lower back and guided us over to the blanket.

"Maebh?"

His voice made me turn. I gasped when I saw him down on one knee. He held open a blue jewelry box that contained the most beautiful diamond ring I'd ever seen.

"I'd travel to the ends of this Earth to make you happy and to see every single one of your dreams come true. Agra, will you…"

Cord's eyes filled with tears as he looked up at me. When his voice cracked, I instantly dropped to me knees. Cupping his face with me hands, I stared into his blue eyes.

Me thumbs wiped his tears away as I let mine fall freely down me face.

"Marry me and become my wife. I can't live without you, Maebh O'Sullivan. You mean the absolute world to me."

With a shaking chin and a tear-soaked face, I replied, "I've always been yours, Cord. Nothing would make me happier than to be your wife."

He pulled me to his body, our mouths crashing together in the most passionate kiss I'd ever experienced in me entire life. Me stomach did endless somersaults, and I'd never felt me heart so full.

I wanted him to lay me down on this blanket and make love to me, but I had a feeling me da and Vi were somewhere watching this all play out.

Cord drew back and leaned his forehead against mine.

"Can you feel that?" he softly asked as he placed me hand over his chest. "Can you feel my love for you?"

Another sob slipped from me mouth as I nodded, "Yes. I feel it."

Taking the vintage-looking ring out of the box, Cord slipped it over me finger and then kissed the back of me hand softly.

The way it sparkled in the sun was breathtaking. The large oval diamond was surrounded by smaller, round, brilliant-cut diamonds with the platinum band covered in diamonds, as well. It was stunning.

"This ring belonged to my mother's mom," Cord said. "When she passed away, my mother wore it every day until one day I told her if I ever asked a woman to marry me, I wanted to do it with this ring."

With a soft chuckle, he shook his head and kept talking. "She took it off right there and told me to keep it in a safe place until the time came to give it to the woman I loved. I honestly never thought I would use the ring and even asked Tripp if he wanted it. He declined because he had bought a ring for Harley years ago. I think he knew deep in his heart they would get the chance to marry someday. Anyway, my mother gave the ring to Aunt Vi to bring to Ireland and when she told me she had it, I knew this was the right time and the absolute perfect place to ask you to marry me."

I smiled, loving this story.

"This makes it all the more special," I said, leaning in and kissing him.

When we broke apart, Cord motioned for me to look to me right. I laughed when I saw Vi and me da standing there. I could have sworn I saw tears glistening in me da's eyes.

Vi held up her phone and yelled, "I got it all on video for the rest of the family!"

We both laughed tears of joy, and I gasped when I saw me da reach for Vi's hand as they strolled back toward the castle.

Cord squeezed me hand, drawing me attention back to him. "You okay?"

I nodded. "Yes. I've never been better."

Inhaling deeply, I pushed away the unsure feelings about me father's life moving on from me mother and glanced at the champagne. Cord pulled the bottle out and poured us each a glass.

"I have food in here, too, if you're hungry."

"Famished!" I said, dramatically placing the back of me hand over me forehead.

An hour later we sat on the blanket together, me tucked between Cord's legs as we watched birds and listened to the sounds of nature. Every now and then a couple would walk by and smile, or a family would rush past, kids yelling, delighted to be out in the unseasonably warm weather.

"What are you thinking about?" Cord asked. His fingers moved lazily up me arm, making it tingle with each pass.

"I was thinking I want to get married in Ireland." Looking up at him, I waited for his reaction.

"That's a great idea."

Me cheeks burned with how hard I was smiling at his reply. "Are you serious? You'd get married here? In Ireland?"

"Yes, of course I would. You'll have to do all the talking with everyone since I can't seem to fucking understand a damn word being said. But I know of this fabulous castle that could serve as the wedding venue, and I hear the price is too good to pass up."

Laughing, I lifted me hand and placed it on the side of his face. "Deal!"

He leaned over and kissed me gently on the lips. As much as I loved our little picnic, the throbbing between me legs was begging to be taken care of.

"Take me back to Castle Finghin and make love to me, my fiancé."

Wiggling his eyebrows, Cord replied, "Your wish is my command, baby."

CHAPTER 34

Cord

Dropping my head back, I looked up at the beautiful blue Texas sky. The cool October breeze was giving us a reprieve as we worked on the fence across the south pasture.

"How's Harley feeling?" Wade asked Tripp.

"Good. She's finally gotten over the morning sickness and her belly is starting to show a bit."

There was no denying the happiness on my older brother's face.

"Gonna find out what it is?" I asked before driving the post hole diggers back into the ground. Sweat was pouring off of me so I stopped, took off my cowboy hat and wiped it away with my sleeve.

Tripp nodded. "I think so. Harley really wants to know so she can plan the baby's room."

Trevor slammed the truck door and started cursing as we looked his way.

"What's going on with him?" Mitchell asked.

Steed sighed as he dropped the shovel. "Who knows. He hasn't been this way since last spring. Always fucking moody, miserable as hell, and won't admit to anyone, especially himself, that he fell for a certain little brunette."

"Scarlett?" Tripp asked.

"Yep," Wade answered. "I've never seen him like this. It's like he's drawn to her, but won't admit it. I called him out on it this morning when we saw her at Lilly's. She walked in and Trevor had been flirting with some chick he knew from high school. I could see the hurt on Scarlett's face when she saw him."

"What did you say to him that has him so pissed off?" Mitchell asked.

"I told him he either needed to let her go or be with only her. I could see by the look on her face that she has feelings for him. I'm not a hundred percent sure what's going on with them, but I do know Trevor's gone over to Scarlett's place many times."

"Maybe it's just casual for her, as well," Steed said.

Rubbing the back of his neck, Wade replied, "I don't think so, man. She looked hurt. When Trevor saw her, she spun on her heels and walked right out of Lilly's. He went after her, and she gave him a pretty big push away, yelled something, and got into her car. He looked pretty messed up after that."

"That's when you decided to say something to him? After that happened?" I asked.

Wade frowned. "Not smart on my part, but I hate seeing him like this. I know he cares about her."

Steed picked up the jack hammer and moved it into the hole I'd just cleaned out. Before he turned it on, he said, "Well, no matter what we say to him, he has to make the decision for himself. He either wants to be with Scarlett or he doesn't. He's going to come to realize she won't wait forever for him to get his shit together."

I stared at my younger brother, knowing something about how he felt. When I started to have feelings for Maebh, it freaked me out, but I couldn't imagine my life without her. The only difference between me and Trevor was that I stopped running to other women, and he hadn't.

"Maybe that's what he needs," I said, feeling all their eyes on me.

"What do you mean?" Tripp asked.

Turning away from Trevor, I said, "He needs to lose her, to see what he has right in front of him."

Maebh and I sat in the doctor's office and waited. My leg jumped up and down as I looked at the different posters hanging on the walls. My eyes wandered over to the model fallopian tubes on the counter and then back to the stirrups.

"This room freaks me the fuck out," I stated.

Maebh looked up from the magazine she was reading. "Why?" She wore a smirk on her face.

"There's posters of vaginas on the wall. One with a fucking baby coming out of it." I shivered. "Look, over there…fake fallopian tubes! Why in the fuck do you need fake fallopian tubes?"

Her gaze swung to where I was pointing, and she shrugged. "I don't know, but I'm sure they're there for a reason."

I rolled my eyes. "And there is lube on the counter. Lube, Maebh! And you are wearing a paper fucking coat that I swear you can read the Lord's Prayer through. What the hell kind of place is this?"

"Would you stop it? I told you to stay in the waiting room. You were the one who had to see what this was all about."

Standing, I walked up to the stirrups. "And these. You're not putting your feet in these, are you? Cause I'm going to have to punch the living fuck out of this doctor if you do."

Maebh covered her mouth and laughed before dropping her hands and saying, "Cord, maybe you should go out to the waiting room."

"Hell no. Mitchell and Tripp talk about coming back here with Harley and Corina all the time. I want to be here for you."

"Be here for me? I think I've got it. I'm not pregnant, they are. I'm sure it's very different when you're pregnant and when you're coming in for an exam."

Shit. I hadn't thought about it that way. Maybe I should head to the waiting room. Before I had a chance to make a decision, a light tap on the door had us both looking that way.

I jumped back, and Maebh set the magazine down on the table.

"Come in!" my future wife said in a cheerful voice, as if she was inviting someone into her home for dinner and a movie.

The door opened and a guy not much older than Tripp walked in. A good-looking guy.

Hell fucking no.

"Maebh O'Sullivan?" he asked with a stupid-ass smile on his face.

Prick.

"That's me!" Maebh said, holding up her hand with one finger pointed to herself. I looked over at her and snarled. She gave me a half shrug and mouthed *what*, looking all innocent.

"I'm Dr. Buten."

I laughed. "Ah, dude, I hate to break it to you, but Dr. Buten delivered me, and I'm pretty damn sure you aren't that much older than me."

He turned to see me and reached his hand out for mine while he chuckled. "Dr. Jon Buten, Junior. That's my father you're referring to. Jon Buten, Senior."

I gripped his hand hard as we shook.

"And you are?" he asked, pulling his hand out and shaking it while he flashed me a smirk.

Pussy.

No, wait, definitely the wrong word to use to describe this guy. He looks at pussies all day long, so I'm gonna have to stick with prick.

"Her *fiancé*. Cord Parker."

His smile grew bigger. "Tripp, Steed, and Mitchell Parker's brother?"

I nodded. "That's me."

Dr. Buten took a seat and motioned for me to do the same. "I delivered Paxton and Corina's baby, and I'm Harley's doctor, as well. Actually, I see both of your sisters, too."

My body quivered, and I made a gagging sound. "Dude, knowing you're looking at all my sisters *and* sister-in-laws, *plus* my future wife, is sort of freaking me out."

"Cord!" Maebh gasped.

Dr. Buten laughed and turned to Maebh. "So, it's Maebh? Correct?"

"Yes, May with a v," Maebh replied.

"Welcome. We're glad to have you as a patient. I hear you're getting married." He glanced my way and smiled.

"Yes," Maebh and I answered together. Her answer was polite; mine stated that she was mine, so this motherfucker better not get any ideas with that lube sitting there.

"Are we thinking kids right away, or waiting?"

Maebh and I looked at each other, and I let her speak. I'd do whatever my Irish cailin wanted.

"I think we're going to wait a wee bit. I'd like to spend some time with me lad, before it's late night feedings and no sleeping for days."

Dr. Buten nodded. "I think that's smart. I know a lot of couples want to move into parenthood quickly, but my wife and I think along the same lines as y'all. We like to travel some so we're holding off a few years before we take that journey. I really like my fishing trips too much right now."

Fuck me. This guy is rubbing off on me a little. Of course, it didn't hurt he mentioned a wife…and fishing.

"So, we're here for an exam and a new prescription for birth control. Your last doctor was in Ireland, correct?"

Maebh nodded and peeked my way. She lifted her brow and motioned for the door, as if giving me one last chance to bolt.

Dr. Buten waited for me to decide whether I was staying or going. When I didn't move, he nodded.

"Let's go ahead and lean back then, shall we?"

Maebh scooted to the end of the table and propped her feet into the stirrups as Dr. Buten got a little too up close and personal with my girl.

"Whoa, hold up," I said, standing and glaring at the good ol' doctor. "What do you think you're doing?"

Dr. Buten looked amused. "I'm about to examine my patient."

I went to tell him there was no fucking way he was touching her, when Maebh reached over and grabbed my wrist, jerking me back to her side.

"Maybe you should wait outside." The smile she wore on her face was not a friendly one, but more of an *I told you not to stay in here* smile. My Irish-tempered lass was just under the surface and this was my one warning.

My mouth dropped open. "While he's in here touching you?"

"Examining," Dr. Buten corrected me.

I glared at him, and he smiled. Again.

Bastard.

"Cord, he's not touching me. Stop behaving this way or you'll never be allowed to come back with me again. Even when I'm pregnant."

Going to protest, the good doctor cleared his throat and shook his head slightly, as if telling me to stand there and keep my mouth shut or I'd regret it. I decided to follow his silent advice.

Sometime during all of this the nurse came into the room. She gave me a soft smile and got to work helping the doc *examine* my girl.

Maebh and Dr. Buten carried on a normal conversation about the goddamn weather in Texas, comparing it to Ireland. The weather of all things! He successfully ignored the death rays I was trying to shoot his way while he worked. When he stood, everything he said started to sound like he was talking into a can. I couldn't focus on the words, I was watching him too closely. He moved to Maebh's breast while continuing to talk about his wife taking up knitting classes, and Maebh mentioned she was interested in knitting, as well. When the nurse chimed in about preferring Bunco games I knew I was in an alternate universe. I'd fallen into the fucking Twilight Zone where a situation like this was completely fucking normal.

What in the fuck is happening?

"I'll get the information about where she's taking the classes for you," he said while ripping off his gloves and tossing them in the trash. "Everything looks good. Be sure to continue with your monthly breast self-exams. My nurse will call you with the test results, no matter the results."

Dr. Buten started to wash his hands, looked at me, and chuckled. I'd never wanted to hit a man so much in my life.

"I bet this is the last time you ever stay in the room, isn't it?" he said with a snort laugh.

"You have no idea how badly I want to punch you right now."

"Cord Parker!" Maebh said, smacking my arm.

The doc laughed before shaking his head. "Trust me, I know exactly how bad you want to punch me. You're not the first man who has decided to stay in the room…and then regretted it."

The nurse helped Maebh sit up as she shot me a dirty look. Then she focused on the doctor. "Thank you, Dr. Buten. Next year he won't be present."

He nodded and said, "Unless we're in here before then."

He winked and Maebh blushed. It took me a few seconds to catch the meaning.

Babies.

"You can get dressed now, Maebh. Our office will call you in the next few days."

Maebh nodded and thanked the nurse and the good doc again as they left the room and shut it behind them. I fell into the chair and buried my hands in my face while letting out a long, frustrated moan.

"Holy fuck. That was intense. Why did I think it was a good idea to stay?"

"I told you," Maebh said as she got dressed. "You didn't want to listen to me when I said what was going to happen."

"He touched your tits!"

She rolled her eyes. "This is why they don't want the guys back here. Are you happy now?"

My stomach rolled. "No! I feel like I'm going to throw up because I now know what in the hell happens back here." I covered my mouth and gagged when the memory of Dr. Buten saying he was my sister's doctor hit me like a brick wall.

"Holy fucking hell. He's touched every tit in my family except for my mom's and Aunt Vi's. I need out of here. Now!"

Pushing past Maebh, I rushed out of the room and down the hall. Dr. Buten stepped in front of me, reaching his hand out, forcing me to stop.

"Congratulations again on the engagement, Cord. I can't wait to hear all about the wedding."

I glared as I walked around him and headed out to the safety of the waiting room.

Maebh was right behind me, the sounds of her laughter not lost on me.

"Me purse!" Maebh said as she turned to go back to the room. The door opened, and Scarlett came walking out, nearly crashing right into Maebh. The shocked look on Scarlett's face made her take a few steps back.

"Ms. O'Sullivan, you left your purse," the nurse called out.

"Thank you," Maebh said as she took the purse and then smiled at Scarlett.

"Scarlett, how are you?" Maebh said as she hugged Scarlett. I wasn't even sure when the two of them had even met.

Scarlett's eyes looked past Maebh, and when they landed on me, her face turned white as a ghost.

"Scarlett?"

Jerking her eyes back to Maebh, she forced a smile. "I'm…fine. You?"

"I'm great. We're just leaving. If you are too, we'd love to have you join us for lunch," she said, glancing over my shoulder. "Cord, wouldn't it be lovely to have Scarlett join us?"

I nodded and smiled. "Yes, of course. How are you, Scarlett?"

"I'm doing well, thank you. I, um…"

Before Scarlett could argue, Maebh had her arm wrapped around Scarlett's and was walking her out the door toward the elevator.

My phone rang and when I pulled it out, I saw it was Connor, the new manager I'd hired to replace Tammy. When I came back from Ireland, I finally let Tammy go. It was hard letting a good employee go, but the last few months Tammy had slipped, and I knew why the day she flashed me her tits in my office. The only thing on her mind was fucking me, and there was no way that was happening. Ever.

"This is Cord."

"Hey, boss, I hate to bother you, but we have a surprise inspection from the health department."

I rolled my eyes. "Great, I'll be right there."

Hitting End, I turned to Maebh. "I'm sorry, ladies. Looks like the health inspector decided to pay a little visit. I can't do lunch."

"Oh no! Was this a planned visit?" Scarlett asked.

"No, it wasn't. Y'all can still do lunch, if you don't mind Maebh driving back into town with you, Scarlett."

She smiled and replied, "Not at all."

"Is that okay with you, baby?" I asked.

"Of course, this gives me and Scarlett more time to get to know each other."

Kissing Maebh softly on the lips, I said, "I love you, and I'll see you in a few hours. Have fun, okay?"

"I will, and I love you, too."

Waving to Scarlett, I said, "See ya around, Scarlett!"

Her hand lifted. "See ya, Cord."

As I walked to my truck, I glanced back to see Maebh and Scarlett already deep in conversation. I was glad to see Maebh getting to know Scarlett. Even though she was friends with the girls, I had a feeling she and Scarlett would get along well, especially since they were closer in age. Plus, maybe Maebh could find out some information on what in the hell was going on with Scarlett and Trevor. The sadness in Scarlett's eyes was hard to miss...and seemed to mirror my brother's.

With a deep sigh, I pulled out of the parking lot and headed toward the bar, my mind racing about how I could make Trevor see what he was missing out on.

CHAPTER 35

Maebh

"A wedding in Ireland? How romantic!" Scarlett gushed as we got out of her car and walked toward Aisling. We'd parked around the corner of the restaurant in a small public car park since it was lunch time and parking along the square and directly on Main Street would be insane. As we rounded the corner, Scarlett came to a halt and stared across the square toward Lilly's Café.

Following her gaze, I watched as Trevor stood outside the café, talking to a girl with blonde hair. The girl laughed when Trevor leaned in and whispered something in her ear, and even twirled a piece of her hair. There were a group of people standing around them, a few guys and two other girls.

Me gaze went back to Scarlett's, and I couldn't help but notice her eyes welling up with tears. I jerked me head back to Trevor. He placed his hand on the blonde girl's back and led her over to the car. All three girls got in and when the blonde tried to pull Trevor into the car with him, he laughed and backed away.

Scarlett was frozen in place. Even when I touched her arm to get her to move, she didn't. She watched the whole scene play out, nothing but hurt and despair etched on her face while her chest heaved.

The car drove off and one of the guys slapped Trevor on the back, saying something that made them all laugh. Trevor turned and looked our way, almost as if he could feel the intense stare coming from Scarlett. His smile faded when he saw her. This seemed more a battle of wills than two people in love, but what did I know?

"Scarlett, let's go into the restaurant. Come on," I said, pulling on her arm, trying to break her stare. When her tears fell, I moved to stand between Scarlett and Trevor. I liked Trevor a lot, but right now I was pissed at him, and I didn't want him to see that he had made Scarlett cry. Not for his sake, but for hers.

"Do not let him see you cry."

My stern voice broke her intense stare. She let her eyes drop to mine. Another tear fell and I spun her around and guided her toward the door to the Aisling.

Once we were inside, I looked around. There were a number of people here for lunch, and I knew Scarlett was about to have a meltdown. I'd seen that look before on me own face after the whole Kylie thing. I smiled at the patrons and kept me hand on Scarlett's wrist, practically pulling her through the restaurant as I welcomed people and told them to enjoy their lunch.

When we entered the kitchen, Eric looked up at us and smiled, but then lost his smile when his eyes landed on Scarlett. "What's wrong?" he asked, concern in his voice.

"Nothing. Can you send two lunch specials into me office?"

He nodded and replied, "Or course, right away."

Once we'd walked into the office, I let Scarlett go. She walked over to me sofa and sat down, her face buried in her hands, sobs making her body jerk as she let go of her emotions.

Rushing to her, I placed me hands on her knees. "Sweet, dear Scarlett, don't cry. He's not worth one tear if the eejit doesn't know what he has right in front of him."

She shook her head and cried harder. "I'm…so…stupid, Maebh."

Her hand dropped to her lap, and she looked at me, chestnut brown eyes puffy and bloodshot from her tears.

"Why do you say that?" I asked, pushing a piece of her long, dark hair from her cheek where it was stuck from the wetness of her crying.

"I thought maybe he cared about me. He told me I meant more to him than the other girls, and I stupidly believed him. He's never going to give up his way of life, and I'm only a midnight call when he has nothing better for the evening."

"That's not true. He does care about you. I think he's confused and terrified."

She scoffed and rolled her eyes.

"Scarlett, have you told him how you feel?"

Her eyes filled with tears again. Her teeth dug into her lip and she nodded. "Y-yes."

"And?"

When her chin trembled, me heart broke.

"He told me he isn't the type of guy to settle down. That's not him. At least he said it wasn't him right now."

I squared me shoulders. "Then you have your answer. I know you like him but don't let him treat you this way. You won't sit around and wait for him to sow his wild oats. It's time to move on."

Her hand came up to her mouth, and she attempted to hold back her sobs. When she had some control over her motions, she pressed her lips tightly before she dropped a bombshell.

"But I'm pregnant…with Trevor's baby."

Me mouth fell open, and I tried to say something, but the shock made me fall back on me arse.

Her face was once again buried in her hands, and she cried harder than she had when she first came in here. Scrambling to me feet, I sat next to her and held her tightly. Me hands ran over her soft hair as I gently rocked her.

"*Shh*, it's going to be okay. You're going to be okay."

The soft knock on the door had me calling out, "Eric?"

"Yeah, it's me."

"Come in."

Eric walked in with a tray full of food. He stopped and stared, his eyes immediately going to the crying woman in me arms.

"Maebh, there's someone here to see you."

I shook me head and motioned for him to set the food on the desk. "Thank you, Eric, will you set the food over there? Please tell anyone looking for me that I'm no longer here."

"Yes, of course."

"But if it's Cord, let him know I'm in here with Scarlett."

"Cord only?"

I gave him a questioning look before replying, "Cord only. Everyone else, I'm not here."

"Of course. Do you need me to do anything?"

Giving him a polite smile, I replied, "No. Thank you, though."

Scarlett must have been exhausted because it didn't take her long to cry herself to sleep. She was lying on me sofa when I slowly got up and made me way to me desk. Reaching for the phone, I sent Cord a text.

Me: *We have a problem.*

He replied within seconds.

Cord: *What? Are you okay?*

Me: *Yes, but Cord, Scarlett's pregnant. With Trevor's baby.*

I waited for the reply and jumped when me phone rang. Quickly stepping out, I rushed into Eric's office so no one would hear us. Unfortunately, Eric was in there, but it was too late to rush up to me house.

"What do you mean?" Cord asked without even saying hello. "Are you sure?"

"Yes, that's why she was at the doctor's office today. To confirm it. And before you ask, she's sure it's Trevor's. She hasn't slept with anyone other than him."

"Fuck," Cord said.

"The worst part? She saw Trevor flirting with a girl outside of Lilly's earlier. She cried, Cord. She cried right there and that bastard brother of yours saw it and didn't even bother to come check on her."

"Uh, that's not true," Eric said.

Spinning around, I stared. "Hold on, Cord. What do you mean, that's not true?" I said to Eric.

"He did come in and asked where you and Scarlett had gone. You told me not to let anyone disturb you, so I told him you both must have slipped out the back door."

I turned from Eric and frowned. "Did you hear that?" I asked.

"Yeah, I heard. Shit. Has she told anyone?"

Me heart ached for Scarlett. "I don't think so. She pretty much cried herself to sleep after she spoke to me for only a few minutes."

"What do we do?" Cord asked. I could hear the uncertainty in his voice, and I wanted more than anything to take that away. To tell him everything would be okay, but it wouldn't. Trevor wasn't admitting his feelings for Scarlett, and I feared the first thing he would think was that she was trapping him with a baby.

"We wait to see what Scarlett wants to do," I said. "This is her baby and her life."

"But it's my brother."

I sighed. "I know. But we can't interfere, Cord. She admitted her feelings for him right to his face, and he told her he wasn't going to settle down."

"Fuck. If she tells him she's pregnant, he might think she did it on purpose."

"It takes two to tango" I added.

"Right, you're absolutely right. Are you going to tell her you told me?" Cord asked.

"Yes, I'm not going to lie to her. She is going to need someone to be there, and I plan on being that person, no matter what your brother decides to do."

"He'll do the right thing. If he doesn't, my mother will kick his ass."

I smiled slightly. I had a terrible feeling Cord was wrong. I didn't want to think that way, but I saw the way Trevor was flirting with that other girl. He had no intentions of being faithful or committed to Scarlett.

"I better go before she wakes up."

"Tonight is dinner with my folks. I'll be by in an hour or so to pick you up. Do you think Scarlett will be okay?"

"Yes, she's a strong girl. She may not think so right now, but she'll be fine. I'll be ready as well."

"I love you." His voice sounded sad and I knew his heart was just as heavy as mine.

"I love you, too."

When the call ended, I turned to Eric. He held up his hands. "I won't say a word to anyone. I will say I'd like to kick that little bastard's arse. She's a lovely girl and doesn't deserve to be treated that way."

Me hands went to me hips. "And how do you know Scarlett?"

He grinned. "She works at the courthouse. I met her while trying to get the permits for this beast of a restaurant."

"Oh," I replied with a smile. "Well, you stay away. The girl is pregnant with another man's child, and I saw the way you looked at her when we walked through the kitchen."

Eric held up his hands. "What kind of a monster do you think I am?"

Narrowing me eye, I pointed to him. "The kind that wants to swoop in and save the damsel in distress. Don't. They'll be able to work it out."

Eric's pinched brows said he didn't think I was right.

"Stay away!" I warned once more before walking out the door. By the time I had made it back to me office, Scarlett was up and eating half of the sandwich Eric had made for us.

"Hey, how are you feeling?" I asked.

"Fine. I'm sorry I broke down like that. I haven't told anyone about the baby, and I think seeing him flirting and going about his normal life after confirming what I already knew just broke the dam that I had built up."

Wringing me hands together, I looked at her. "I told Cord."

The sandwich froze at her mouth before she stared at me. "Why would you do that? Maebh! He's going to tell Trevor, and I'm not ready for that."

I took her hand in mine. "He won't. He promised me he wouldn't."

Her eyes closed. "I don't know what to do. I'm so scared, and I feel all alone."

"Don't be, I'm here for you. *We're* here for you. There are so many people who love you and care for you, Scarlett. What about your parents?"

She shrugged. "I'm sure they'll be disappointed. My father will be upset, my mother will probably be over the moon. She's clueless when it comes to Trevor's bad boy reputation. She'll have a silly notion we're going to live happily ever after." Her voice cracked.

"When the time comes, and you're ready to tell Trevor, I'm here for you."

The way her face softened made me chest squeeze. "Thank you, Maebh. I don't have a lot of friends in town. Most of my friends didn't live in Oak Springs since I went to a boarding school in a different city."

"I'm your friend now. And so is Cord."

A tear slipped from her eye, and I quickly wiped it away.

"Thank you, Maebh. Thank you so much."

Smiling, I pulled her to me for a hug.

"It's all going to be okay, I promise."

For the first time in me life, I was making a promise I knew was most likely going to be broken.

CHAPTER 36

maebh

Cord kicked me, causing me to pull me death stare off Trevor. I'd been staring at him since he showed up late for dinner. He sat down and smiled at everyone. When he got to me, I gave him the evil eye, making that pretty boy smile drop instantly.

"Stop looking at my brother like you want to punch him in the face," Cord whispered.

"But I do want to punch him in the face," I insisted.

"So, Maebh, Cord, any more thought on the date of the wedding?"

Melanie's question made both of us look at the other end of the table.

"How are we going to get Patches to Ireland?" Chloe asked, concern on her face.

Me mouth dropped. I'd heard the stories from Amelia about Patches the goat and weddings. I'd been around enough family dinners to know that Patches was a part of this family in Chloe's eyes, and because of that, he needed to take part in almost every family event. Especially weddings.

"We can't bring Patches, Chloe," Cord said, trying to let her down easy. "They don't allow you to bring animals to other countries."

"Oh," Chloe said, her eyes filled with sadness.

"But we have goats in Ireland," I quickly added. Everyone at the table turned and looked at me with shock and wonder. Waylynn mouthed '*why*' as Paxton slapped her hand to her forehead.

"Er, um, ah, come to think of it," I said, trying to think quickly. "I don't think goats are allowed to be in weddings in Ireland."

Amelia gave me a thumbs up. "Fast on the feet there."

"Why not?" Chloe asked.

"Yeah, why not?" Corina asked, giving me a smirk. She was enjoying this a little too much. Here I thought she was the sweet one.

Clearing me throat, I answered. "Well, they tend to eat the flowers."

"We'll get the goat a basket just for him to eat so he won't munch on the wedding flowers!" Chloe said.

"They'll eat all the grass, and where we're getting married, the grass is…"

Chloe looked at me with those big blue eyes, waiting to hear what I was going to come up.

"It's, um, sacred."

All eyes were on me now. Waylynn actually handed Liberty to Jonathon and placed her chin on her hand and mused, "This ought to be good."

I could feel Cord's eyes on me as well. "Sacred?" he asked, a slight chuckle in his voice.

"Yep. It was planted by a king…long ago. He made a…vow that no one would ever be able to destroy the grass and…he put a curse on it for those who tried to eat it!"

Waylynn's eyes lifted, and I was really wishing she wasn't sitting directly across from me. Amelia covered her mouth, attempting not to laugh.

"A curse?" Chloe asked, her eyes wide with excitement. "What kind of curse?"

"Yeah, what kind of curse, Maebh?" Waylynn and Amelia asked together.

I rolled me eyes at both of them. Damn Parker sisters.

"What kind of curse?" I repeated, stalling for time. One glance down at Melanie told me I was on my own with this one. Not even she was helping me out.

"Well, the curse was that if anyone were to put an animal on the grass, that animal would disappear for all time."

Chloe gasped and covered her mouth with her hands. "Disappear!"

Cord leaned down and whispered, "Jesus, Maebh, don't scare the shit out of my niece. Just tell her goats aren't allowed on the property where we're getting married."

I scrunched up me face. "That would have been easier," I whispered.

"Wait, no. I'm getting that confused with another sacred grass. No, this grass they just don't allow goats on. They'll eat it, and they want it to stay pretty, so no goats allowed."

Chloe dropped back in her chair and let out a very dramatic sigh. "Thank goodness. But we can't risk getting the grasses mixed up and inviting goats and then have them disappear…the wedding people would be so scared if that happened."

"Exactly, Chloe. You understand why that would be a bad idea." I had to agree to ensure that this conversation was officially over with.

Waylynn reached for her water and pointed over at me. "Amelia, I don't think you have to worry about this one being your competition in the book world."

Amelia laughed, and I tossed me napkin at Waylynn. "Ha ha."

After dinner, I helped Melanie clean up the dishes, telling the other girls to enjoy their kids and family time. Cord was also in the kitchen, helping me and Melanie.

"So, what's on your minds, kids?"

"What?" Cord asked, looking at his mother like he had no idea what she was talking about.

"Something is on both of your minds. I can see it written all over your faces."

I shared a glance with Cord and then turned to his mother. "Wedding stuff. We've picked a date."

Melanie stopped washing a pan and turned to us. A huge smile covered her face. "You did! When?"

"June twentieth."

"Summer in Ireland! Oh my goodness, this is going to be amazing!"

Cord wrapped his arms around me and pulled me back to his chest. "We thought that would give everyone time to book flights. You don't have to book a hotel, there's plenty of room at Maebh's father's place."

Melanie clapped her hands in excitement. "I thought you were looking at early May?"

"Well, we figured the weather would be better in June."

Our original date had been May sixth. But with Scarlett's due date being mid-May, we pushed it to June. No one had to know why but Cord and meself.

"This is so exciting," Melanie said.

"What's exciting?" Trevor asked, stepping into the kitchen.

Me body tensed in Cord's arms, and I know Melanie caught it because her smile faded just a little.

"That we've picked our wedding date," Cord said, kissing the top of me head.

Trevor gave us a genuine smile. "You did? When?"

"June twentieth," I said, giving him me best grin. Faking it as best as I could. Melanie was watching me now, and I had to wonder if she had seen me giving Trevor evil looks during dinner.

Trevor walked over to us, and Cord dropped his arms from around me. Pulling me into a hug, Trevor said, "Congratulations, I'm so happy for y'all."

Then he hugged Cord and slapped him on the back.

"Looks like you're the last one, dude," Cord said.

Trevor forced a smile but didn't say anything. Had Scarlett told him about the baby? He was too calm and collected. There was no way she'd told him.

"Speaking of, have you seen Scarlett lately?" I asked. Cord stiffened next to me, and Melanie turned to look at Trevor.

"I ran into her yesterday. She looked beautiful," Melanie stated.

Trevor grabbed a beer out of the refrigerator. He eyed me carefully as he answered his mother, never taking his eyes off of me. "She always looks beautiful."

The urge to roll me own eyes was strong.

"I don't know why you don't date her, Trevor. She's such a lovely girl," Melanie stated.

He took a drink and looked out the window. "I like my life as it is, Ma."

She huffed.

I let out a lighthearted laugh. "If Cord could settle down, there's hope for you, Trevor."

Cord squeezed me hip, a signal from him to not go there.

Trevor faced me again and laughed. "So, tell me something, Maebh. What have I done to piss you off?"

Melanie turned her attention on me, and I felt me face heat.

"What do you mean?" I asked, leaning back into Cord. I'd opened this can of worms, and I was hoping he'd gather them all up and put them back in and lock the lid. Why did I poke Trevor in front of his mother?

"You were shooting me death rays across the table all through dinner."

I turned to Melanie and smiled. The last thing I wanted to do with his mother standing right here was get into it with Trevor. I needed to be careful.

With a carefree shrug, I replied, "I wasn't meaning to. Sorry."

He didn't believe me, that much was clear. "I saw you and Scarlett today outside Aisling. I stopped in, but Eric, I believe that was his name, said you were both gone."

Me eye twitched. "We saw you too. Actually watched you from a distance for a wee bit. Scarlett was having a bad day and needed to talk to someone. She was upset. Someone made her cry."

Trevor swallowed hard, and Cord leaned down and whispered, "I know you're mad, but don't go there. Not here, not now."

Melanie gasped. "Who? Who would make that sweet girl cry?"

Cord walked around me. "Do y'all mind if I steal my future bride? We're supposed to call her dad in Ireland, and I don't want it to get too late."

Melanie looked at the clock. "Isn't it late there already?"

Without saying a word, Cord ushered me out of the kitchen, but not before Trevor and I shared one more charged glance.

Trevor followed me and Cord out of the kitchen and through the house to the den. He spoke the moment we walked into the room and shut the door. "It wasn't what it looked like."

Spinning around, I pushed him on the chest as hard as I could. Trevor stumbled back, and Cord got between us.

"Maebh, don't do this."

Pointing around Cord, I glared at Trevor. "It *was* what it looked like, Trevor. You're fecking around with her heart, and it's not fair. She cares about you and all you care about is shagging anything that walks on two legs, only reaching out to her when you don't have something better at night."

"*Maebh*," Cord pleaded with me.

Trevor's eyes turned dark. "You don't know what the fuck you're talking about."

Cord turned to his brother, his fist balled. "Don't talk to her like that, Trevor."

Trevor's cold eyes jerked to his brother, and he pushed his hand over his head. "Maybe she should mind her own business then."

Anger raced through me veins, and I pushed Cord out of the way, getting right into Trevor's space.

"It's me business when she sits in me office and cries herself to sleep because you keep breaking her heart, you arse! You're an eejit for not seeing what is right in front of your damn eyes. You're going to lose her, Trevor. That is, if you haven't already."

Trevor's eyes filled with regret, and for a moment I swore they filled with tears.

"She was crying?" he asked, his voice the weakest I'd ever heard.

I folded me arms over me chest. "You have no idea what it does to her to see you go off with other women. Make a fecking decision, Trevor, before you destroy her."

"I can't let her go."

Cord pushed his fingers though his hair. "Damn it, Trevor. What do you mean you can't let her go?"

Trevor started pacing. "I told myself the first time we slept together it was only that one time. Then we ran into each other a week later, and we ended up back at her place and we slept together...again. Then she ended up getting sick and she called me over to her house. We didn't sleep together that night, but I fucking stayed and took care of her, holding her in my arms and I *liked* it. I liked it too much. Something about that night changed everything. Holding her like that. It messed with my head."

Cord sighed. "And that's a bad thing, Trevor, to feel something for a woman?"

"Yes! It is. I'm not the type of guy who wants to be tied down to one woman. I'm not. I like sex. I like women. Fuck, I'm only twenty-five and just starting my life. I'm not looking for a relationship."

"Then why do you keep going back to her?" Cord asked.

"I don't know. She's got some weird hold over me."

His hand sliced over his buzzed head again, and the pained expression on his face almost made me feel sorry for him. "She's constantly on my mind and the only way I can get her out is if I'm with other women."

"That's fucking stupid, man," Cord snapped. "That's called having feelings for someone. Wanting to be with that person."

Trevor shrugged. "I can't."

"You can't…or you won't?" I asked.

His gaze dropped to the floor. The look on Cord's face told me he was about to drop the news on Trevor. Stepping up to him, I placed my hand on his chest and shook me head.

With me voice low, I said, "It's not yours to tell."

Lacing his fingers with mine, Cord pulled me to the door but stopped before opening it.

"Do you know how mom has always said that true love only comes once in a lifetime?"

Trevor's eyes met Cord's.

"You've got it right in front of your fucking face, but you're too goddamn scared to see it. I feel sorry for you, Trevor. You don't even know what you have, dude. And if you aren't careful, you'll never get the chance to find out."

Trevor let out a gruff laugh. "That's where you're wrong. I know exactly what I have, Cord. And I'm happy with my life."

Me heart dropped and me chest ached for Scarlett and for Trevor. And for their unborn baby.

With a shake of his head, Cord let out an exasperated breath before he spoke again. "You keep telling yourself that, bro. Let me know how it works out for you."

CHAPTER 37

Cord

Maebh leaned her body back into mine and traced a pattern on my thigh as she stared up at the stars. We'd made love earlier, and she'd asked me to sit out on the rooftop patio with her. We'd been sitting in silence for the last few minutes, each of us lost in thought.

"I can't imagine me life without you in it," she whispered.

My arm wrapped tighter around her. "I feel the same, baby."

"We're going to mess up."

"Yes, we are."

She tilted her head back and gazed up at me with those beautiful green eyes of hers.

"When we do, we'll work it out."

Bending over, I kissed her nose. "Yes, we will."

"Because what we share is the most amazing thing I've ever experienced, and I never want to lose it."

I let go of her body and turned her to face me. She straddled me, like it was the most natural thing in the world, her arms resting on my shoulders, her fingers playing with my hair.

"Want to do something daring?" she asked with a sexy-as-sin smile.

"Depends. Does it involve my cock in your pussy? Or your mouth on my dick? Or my mouth in between your thighs?"

Her cheeks turned pink. "That mouth of yours, Cord Parker."

"You like it. Admit it."

The corner of her mouth rose slightly. "I do like it."

Squeezing her ass, I said, "Tell me about this game."

"Okay, so this game does involve sex."

"I like it already. How do we play?"

She twirled my hair more, and it was relaxing as fuck. "Well, it's not really a game."

I faked a pout and she giggled. "Then what is it?"

"It's more like an adventure of sorts."

I lifted my brow. "Keep going."

"I want to have sex out here on the roof. Right now."

Fuuuck…" I groaned out. "Maebh, I don't want anyone to see us."

She smiled. "It's late and me back will be the only thing facing out."

"And your ass."

Chewing on the side of her mouth, she looked sexy as fuck.

"No one is seeing my girl's ass."

She giggled, then pressed into me. "Come on, Cord. Let's be daring. Remember that day on your boat at the lake?"

My cock grew painfully harder. "Fine. Stand up and strip out of your clothes."

Maebh stood and moved to the side of the lounge chair. I stood on the other side and nearly ripped my damn sweats off. Reaching for my shirt, I pulled it over my head and tossed it onto my pants. Maebh undressed in record time. My eyes scanned over the other rooftops across the square. No one lived between Maebh and me, and both of us owned the corner of each block. We stood there naked on the rooftop in the dark with nothing but the moonlight and stars casting a soft glow.

I sat down on the chair again and motioned for her to crawl on me.

"Did you see anything?" she asked, her cheeks turning a slight pink.

"No, but if someone is watching, they're fixin' to get a show."

She giggled and buried her face into my neck, her sweet, wet pussy pressing against my cock.

"I'm going to come the moment you slide down on me, darlin'. You've been warned."

With a pout, she replied, "Let's hope not."

My hands went to her hips where I guided her right over my throbbing cock. We both moaned when she started to move down me.

"Take all of me, baby. Fuck yes," I hissed.

"Cord," she panted. "I want to scream or moan, but what if someone hears me?"

"That makes it even hotter, baby. I won't stop you if you start." She gave me this sexy-ass smirk that almost had me coming right then and there.

I pinned her hips, not letting her move. "Let me just feel myself inside you, agra." My eyes closed, and I took in how warm her body was.

"Please," she whimpered, circling her hips to get friction.

Moving my hands to her ass, I pulled her toward me.

"God, yes," Maebh hissed out, her head dropping back while she let out a soft moan. Leaning forward, I took a nipple into my mouth and rolled my tongue over it, flicking it a few times before sucking on it hard.

"Cord!" she cried out as she placed her feet onto the ground so she had better control of her up and down movement. Pressing her hands on my chest, she pushed me so I was lying back in the chair.

"Oh, Cord, you are so damn deep this way. I swear you haven't been this deep before."

"Oh, I have, but damn, you are hitting all the right places. That's it, baby. Look at me when you fuck me. I want to see you when you come on my cock."

Her eyes snapped open and our gaze met. "Cord!" she softly moaned, her orgasm hitting her and making her squeeze around me. Her body trembled, and I fucking loved seeing her come undone. I wasn't going to last much longer.

"Baby," I whispered, gripping the back of her hips and pumping into her hard and fast.

Her body looked to be building up again. Her eyes glassed over, and she reached up and grabbed her tits, giving them a squeeze while she moaned out my name. That right there was my undoing. I came so fucking hard my body spasmed and I gasped her name.

She collapsed onto my chest, both of us breathing like we'd run a marathon. Sex with this woman was unlike anything I'd ever experienced. There was something about fucking out in public that made this time more exciting. I'd come so damn hard I saw stars.

"Cord, that…was…incredible."

My arms wrapped around her and I held her to me. Both of us were covered in a slight sheen of sweat. Even with the cooler temperatures, our passion was overwhelming.

"Yeah, it was."

"I like sex out in public in the middle of the night with the low probability of someone seeing us."

I laughed.

We laid like that for a few more minutes, neither one of us attempting to move or even get dressed. When Maebh finally pushed up off my chest, she gave me that sweet smile I'd fallen in love with so many months ago.

"Shower?"

With a nod, I lifted her off of me and reached for my shirt. After cleaning myself off, I folded it and handed it to Maebh. I carried her into the house and straight to her shower. Afterward, we made our way to the bed and collapsed onto it. Two more amazing rounds of lovemaking left me exhausted.

Maebh curled into my side, her head resting on my chest as her finger moved around my stomach and back up to my chest, then back down again. I'd never been so completely relaxed in my entire life.

"Do you know the most perfect thing on this Earth?" I asked, sliding my own fingers over her arm.

She tilted her head and looked up at me like she was trying to figure out what I would say.

"What?"

"This love. You, me, our life together. I don't think I could ask God for anything else and feel this happy."

Her smile made my chest squeeze, and my stomach drop.

"Maybe a baby someday," she said.

My face broke into a wide grin as I looked into the eyes of the woman I loved more than the air around me.

Lacing my fingers in hers, I leaned in for a kiss. "Yes, a baby for sure, maybe sooner rather than later. I hear there's something in the Irish water, so who knows what we'll bring back with us after the wedding."

Keep reading for a sneak preview of *Reckless Love*,
the 7th and final book in the Cowboys & Angels series.

Reckless Love Sneak Peek

Trevor

"Why don't you let me give you a ride home? You're pretty trashed," Wade yelled at me.

"Fuck no! It's Brad's fucking bachelor party. I'm not leaving until I see him get fucked by the stripper...and I'm not trashed."

Wade rolled his eyes. "Dude, he's not fucking a stripper a few days before his wedding."

"Why not?" I asked as I eyed the blonde. Those seemed to be the type I was going for lately. They had to be blonde, or I couldn't fuck them. As a matter of fact, I was finding myself having a hard time fucking any woman lately. I hadn't been with anyone in weeks. Hell...maybe even in a few months.

"I'd fuck her," I deadpanned.

The stripper looked my way and grinned before she walked toward me. She had wrapped up her little dance and was talking to Brad. She sat right on my lap, her glorious tits all in my face.

"Want to go home with me, baby?" I asked, my mouth against her ear, my hand on her thong-covered ass. She leaned back and winked as she pushed into me. Too bad my dick wasn't really in the mood.

"Hell yeah. I'm getting lucky tonight," I said, standing and reaching for her hand.

Wade pulled me to a stop and shook his head. "Damn, Trevor. Are you sure you want to do this?"

"Why wouldn't I?"

He shrugged and then leaned in closer. "Scarlett?"

I tossed my head back and laughed—even though her name felt like a knife in my chest. I'd tried calling her earlier when I was still sober, I wanted to stop by and talk, but sent me to voicemail. Like she did every time I called her. She'd been avoiding me ever since that day she saw me talking to Traci Stephens, Sierra's best friend, and the maid of honor in a good friend's wedding.

We'd all met that day to talk about the destination wedding Brad and Sierra were having. I hadn't met Traci before and she was flirting with me something fierce. I gave her some harmless flirting back, with no intentions of sleeping with her, and Scarlett had seen it all go down. I knew what it looked like. I also knew I was a motherfucker for the way I had treated Scarlett a month before that. It was the last time we'd slept together, and the only time I'd ever been reckless while having sex.

I vowed to myself I wasn't going to sleep with her again, but I saw her out running near her house. Watching her sprint up the sidewalk, do a few stretches, and make her way into her house did something to me. There was no way I could stop the attraction I had toward Scarlett. I'd tried to push her away, but she always pulled me back to her. Parking in front of her house, I got out and made my way up the porch. All I wanted to do was talk to her. She'd been so upset with me the night after she admitted her feelings, and I basically told her there could never be anything between us.

I hadn't been able to sleep the whole night. All I saw was the hurt in her eyes when I told her I could never settle down. That I wasn't a one-woman kind of guy. She nodded and walked to her front door.

"It's over, Trevor. I'm not doing this anymore. I need you to leave and not come back."

Scarlett's words haunted my thoughts the whole night, keeping me from sleeping.

Stepping up to her door, I knocked. When Scarlett answered, I pulled her into my arms and kissed the living fuck out of her. She didn't return my kiss right away, but soon we were in her house, clothes being ripped off on the way to her bedroom. We hadn't fucked that day. We made love. I went slow, and it had never felt so fucking good in my entire life. It was too late before I realized why it felt so damn amazing. We'd gotten so caught up in each other we made love without a condom.

When I realized what I'd done, I freaked and jumped out of the bed. I never even looked back at her after I got dressed and rushed out of her house.

I shook the memory from my head and slapped Wade on the back. "Dude, Scarlett is done with me, and I'm done with her."

"You're done with her?" he asked, anger filling his eyes. "Was she a used piece of furniture or something?"

Anger hit my chest and nearly knocked me on my ass. "You know what? Fuck you, dude. You don't know anything."

Wade's hands slipped into his pocket as he looked at the girl to my side. "I know if you leave here with her, you're going to regret it."

Forcing myself to smile, I lied. "Yeah, I don't think so."

As the blonde and I walked toward my truck, Wade's words hit me again. *"You're going to regret it."*

The stripper was all over me. Her hand landed on my deflated cock that wasn't the least bit interested in her as she pushed me against the truck and licked my neck.

"I can't wait to have your strong arms holding me up while you pound into me," she said against my lips.

What in the hell am I doing?

I didn't want this. No, I did want it. I wanted to fuck her brains out; I wanted to fuck someone's memory out of my own head, but a part of me wanted to push her away. I was so fucking confused, but once I came to my senses, I knew what I needed to do.

I needed this woman away from me right now.

Pulling my mouth away from her, I went to push her away, but before I had the chance, I saw her out of the corner of my eye.

Scarlett.

I pushed the stripper and shouted, "Enough." When I turned to look at Scarlett, she was walking away. A guy was walking with her, his hand on her lower back, guiding her away from me. He whispered something to her as they kept moving.

"Scarlett? Scarlett! Wait!" I shouted as I made my way toward her. "Please, wait! I wasn't going to do anything with her."

The guilt hit me right in the gut because I had let this woman touch and kiss all over me not two seconds ago.

When the guy glanced over his shoulder, I stopped in my tracks.

Eric. The guy from Maebh's restaurant. He shot me a dirty look and ushered Scarlett into her car and climbed into the driver's seat. My eyes darted over to her, and she was crying. My legs felt like they were going to give out when I saw exactly how hard she was crying.

"Scarlett!" I screamed, causing her to look up at me and then say something to the bastard in the driver's seat. He pulled out and did a U-turn on Main. I stood there and watched her car until I could no longer see the red taillights anymore.

Dragging my hands over my face I let out a frustrated groan. "What did I do? What the fuck did I just do?"

Look for *Reckless Love*
(The seventh and final book in the Cowboys and Angels series)
to be out January 2019

PLAYLIST

Contains Spoilers

Camilia Cabello – "Never Be the Same"

Shania Twain – "No One Needs to Know"

Blake Shelton – "Why Me?"
Maebh telling Cord she's a virgin.

Demi Lovato – "Hitchhiker"
Cord and Maebh dancing in kitchen at lake house.

Justin Timberlake – "Filthy"

Justin Bieber – "The Feeling"

Chris Young – "Woke Up Like This"

Miranda Lambert – "Tinman"
Maebh thinking Cord cheated.

Keith Urban – "All For You"
When Cord goes to Ireland after Maebh.

Brooks Jefferson – "To Make You Feel My Love"

Foreigner – "Waiting For a Girl Like You"

Foreigner – "Hot Blooded"

Boston – "More Than a Feeling"

Shania Twain – "Swinging with My Eyes Closed"

Full playlist on Spotify – username Kelly Elliott

THANK YOU

Kristin, Laura, and Tanya – Thank you for always dropping what you're doing to read for me!

Cori, AmyRose, Elaine, and Julie – Thank you for all your hard work and helping me put out the best book possible. Y'all are the best!

Charlene Crawshaw – I couldn't have written this book without your help. Thank you for Maebh's name, for the help with the Irish dialogue, and for just being a sweet friend! It's appreciated more than you know!

To my readers – thank you for your support. This series has been so much fun to write and we've got one more Parker to go! I hope you're just as excited to get Trevor's story as I am to give it to you! Thank you for all of your support!

Darrin and Lauren – I love y'all to the moon and back.